NICOLE MARIE

THE LEAD STORY

First edition

ISBN (paperback): 979-8-9950683-1-0
ISBN (hardcover): 979-8-9950683-0-3

This book was professionally typeset on Reedsy.
Find out more at reedsy.com

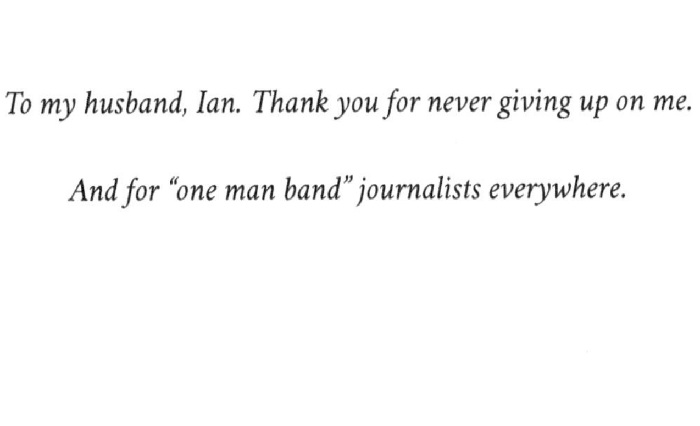

To my husband, Ian. Thank you for never giving up on me.

And for "one man band" journalists everywhere.

Contents

1	PROLOGUE	1
2	THE COLD OPEN	20
3	THE BEAT REPORTER	28
4	THE NEWSROOM	37
5	THE INTERVIEW	45
6	THE WIDE SHOT	52
7	THE DOUBLE SHIFT	60
8	THE RUNDOWN	70
9	THE LOWER THIRD	79
10	THE (WO)MAN ON STREET	86
11	THE LIVE SHOT	94
12	THE STAND UP	104
13	THE RECORD	114
14	THE WRITER	121
15	THE SOUNDBITE	130
16	THE PHOTOGRAPHER	142
17	THE TELEPROMPTER	152
18	THE KICKER	163
19	THE TEASE	176
20	THE "A" BLOCK	188
21	THE "B" BLOCK	201
22	THE "C" BLOCK	213
23	THE FOLLOW UP	226
24	THE CONTRACT	233

25 THE JURY TRIAL   246
26 THE STANDBY   254
27 THE ONE (WO)MAN BAND   261
28 THE B-ROLL VIDEO   268
29 THE DEADLINE   277
30 THE "D" BLOCK   281
31 THE FIELD   295
32 THE STATION   306
33 THE VOICE OVER   312
34 THE SWEEPS PIECE   320
35 THE CUTAWAY   328
36 THE SIGN OFF   334
37 THE FAST FORWARD   342
38 THE FEATURE STORY   348
39 THE WRAP   355
40 EPILOGUE   364
About the Author   380

One

PROLOGUE

DECEMBER | NEW YORK CITY, NEW YORK
TWO YEARS EARLIER

"I can't believe I'm standing in front of you all tonight accepting this award," I whisper into my bright purple hairbrush. Its rubber handle is clenched in the grasp of my left hand, and I look down to notice strands of curly brown hair tangled throughout its bristles. *I should probably clean this thing.*

I stare back at my reflection in the mirror, positioning my fictitious microphone back into place below my chin. My black pajamas are a sparkly ball gown. The messy bun on top of my head is an elegant topknot. My fuzzy pink slippers are a pair of rose gold pumps. Last night's mascara smudge is a smoldering smoky eye. My apartment is an auditorium. My vanity is a podium. The horns and sirens reverberating through my window pane are just hoots and hollers from audience members.

I clear my throat and continue reading. "I have been dreaming of accepting this award for Best Morning Show Host for years."

The messy words are written in a new journal I just bought before moving to the city. The cover is a basic outline of the New York City skyline, which stretches across to the binding and even around the back. It lies on its spine in the middle of my vanity to allow the navy blue, handwritten words to face the ceiling.

The heading on this page is titled "Acceptance Speech." Who am I accepting this ultra-specific award from? I have no idea. But I find my next line and keep reading on.

"If you had told me — back when I was just a little intern fetching coffee at The Sunrise Show in New York City — that I would someday be the show's morning anchor, I would have never believed you. That's why this award proves so many things: full circle moments are possible, you can achieve anything you set your mind to, and following your dreams *does* pay off in the end." I grab a chilly bottle of dry shampoo and lift it into the air, pushing it toward the crowd. "This goes out to all of you at home."

I technically have an audience of *two*. That's if you count myself *and* the man in the two-by-four-inch picture frame smiling back at me. The wooden brown fixture, fraying on its edges, rests on my mirror. Its mount broke off years ago. The man holds a college diploma in his hands, and his long dark hair is slicked back into a low ponytail. *I wonder what he would have thought of this imaginary performance.*

"Noelle!" Eliza whispers through the crack in my door. Her

soft knock on the door knocks me right back into reality. Her voice is the classical music kicking me off the fancy stage.

"Coming," I whisper back. I'm startled, but not surprised. *I should have started getting ready fifteen minutes ago.*

My imaginary gown hits the floor before I hike up my real-life black work pants. They have tiny white polka dots on them, and their stretchy waistband has become my new favorite thing in the world. The city has taught me to prioritize *comfort* over *fashion*, and while I would still technically call these stretchy pants *fashionable*, I know I'm wearing them today solely for *comfort*.

"Last day, last day, last day," Eliza chants softly through the crack, mindful of the women in their REM cycles with whom we share paper-thin walls.

Even though it's 6:00 in the morning, and many of the residents of Westerfield Apartments have already left for their corporate jobs, a majority of them are probably still sleeping in their 90-square-foot rooms. In the city that never sleeps, it's always a good idea to *whisper* around here, no matter what time of day it is.

I maneuver around my shoebox of a room — which only holds a twin bed, a loud radiator, and a broken dresser — and change my clothes at world-record speed. I pull a white sweater over my head to match the polka dots on my pants. Once I am fully clothed, I unlatch the chain lock on my door to reveal a tall Eliza Swickley wearing a deep green dress that I haven't seen her wear before. It contrasts with her long, straight blonde hair.

"Wow." I motion for her to come inside. "That's a great *last day of your internship* outfit."

"Zara." Eliza twirls into my room before taking a seat on my bed. "I'm going to miss that place. More than you, probably."

"That's what online shopping is for." I rip my brush through my brown curls before pinning them back in a low chignon. "Or we could start saving money for once."

"My bank account is parched," Eliza says. She crosses one leg over another and looks up at the ceiling fan dramatically. "It's practically *begging* me to get out of here."

I first met Eliza Swickley on the first day of our internship orientation. We both moved to New York for our dream internships at The Sunrise Show for the semester without knowing a single soul. Even though we grew up on opposite ends of the country — me in Ohio and her in Florida — our hometowns were so small that we had similar reactions to living in one of the world's biggest cities. It wasn't until we were halfway into our lunchtime Caesar salads that we realized we both lived at Westerfield Apartments, just one floor apart from one another.

"I'm in room 433," I had told her in the cafeteria of our office building.

Mid-bite into a crouton, she looked at me wide-eyed. "I'm 533."

Since then, we have gone to work together every single morning this entire semester—splitting the cost of Ubers when it was either *too* cold to walk or *too* early to ride the subway. Today will be our last departure to our dream workplace. In a city of nearly nine million strangers, *at least we've had each other this whole time.*

I slide my winter coat around my arms. "Can you believe when we first got here in September, it felt like summer?"

"I always thought I loved the tree," Eliza says, putting on her coat. "But the tourists make me hate it. At least we'll be out of here before Christmas."

"Now it's full-blown tourist season." I tie a bright red scarf around my neck.

"They're the worst," Eliza says, acting like we've lived here our entire lives.

I laugh. "Since when did *we* become *non*-tourists?"

I take a quick peek out my window and see tiny snowflakes falling, descending from the tops of giant skyscrapers to the surface of crowded streets. My room overlooks a row of buildings. The Byzantine Catholic Church shares a wall with a liquor store called Sip City Wine and Spirits, which in turn shares a wall with a religious community center, which then shares a wall with an Italian restaurant called Rocky's. Worship, wine, worship, sauce. *This street should be called Hallelujah and Heartburn.*

"Let's go," I say. "We're going to be late."

Eliza shrugs. "What are they gonna do, fire us?"

We walk down the humid hallway to reach the elevator. *HomeGoods* style pictures and portraits of New York City line the walkways to get there. Westerfield Apartments is known for having the slowest elevators in America, and it looks like a line has already formed. We stand behind a handful of silent people, all looking down at their phones.

Eliza adjusts the New Yorker bag on her shoulder. "When do you leave?"

"Tomorrow afternoon," I whisper. "What about you?"

Eliza sighs. "Flight is tomorrow morning out of La-Guardia."

When the elevator doors open, a young woman flies out of it with the same urgency as a bat flying out of a cave. She holds a stack of small, business-card-sized rectangles and wears a wide grin. She hands the papers to everyone *entering* the elevator as she *exits*, happy to be met with the early-morning rush of residents. She looks a little *too* cheerful for this hour. *It's too early for this.*

"New club at Westerfield Apartments," she says. "Everybody, take some info."

She hands Eliza and me each a copy, and we take it against our will. I hold it in my hands and stare down at the words. The header, which looks like it was designed on an outdated version of Microsoft Publisher, reads: *Book Writing Club. Westerfield Apartments. Tuesdays from 5:30 to 6:30 in the dining hall. Come write a book with us!*

Eliza scoffs once she is done scanning the page. "Yeah, I don't think I'm going to be participating in this." She folds the paper and tucks it into her bag. "How do these people have so much energy to do all these extra projects?"

I adjust my purse on my shoulder. "Adrenaline?"

Maybe if I had *just* gotten here and *just* started my internship, I'd try something like this. But not on my *last* day. I'm not in the mood to ever try anything new, ever again, for that matter. I've had enough of the *new* within the last four months. I'm sad to leave the city, but I crave ease. I crave small. I crave quiet. I fold the paper in fourths and tuck it into the pocket of my polka-dot pants.

I follow Eliza onto the elevator, which is getting more crowded by the second. We squish ourselves into the back left corner of the metal box, anticipating another slow-moving ride down to the lobby.

"At least I won't have to worry about getting stuck in here ever again," I whisper to Eliza.

"But you never actually *got* stuck," Eliza reassures.

"But every single time I'm in here, I feel like I'm going to be." I pretend to beat my head against the elevator wall before closing my eyes. "I'm going to miss this. I'm going to miss you. I'm going to miss this internship. I don't know how to feel right now."

"I'm not sad." Eliza nonchalantly pulls out her front-facing phone camera and fixes her lipstick. "We'll both be working here again someday. In a much *higher* capacity."

"Until other people are getting *us* coffee," I add, eyes still closed.

Eliza presses the back of her hand to her forehead. "I can't possibly deliver one more latte."

The elevator doors open, and our shoes are greeted with the cranberry carpeting of the Westerfield Apartments lobby. A geometric-patterned rug is spread out under a set of vintage leather chairs. Old-fashioned brass chandeliers reflect light from the ceiling onto us. It's a room that hasn't been updated since the 1950s, and it's perfect.

As we walk towards the front door, I turn to face Eliza. "Let's go get coffee for the last time."

* * *

While I could never include "professional script printer" or "avid coffee fetcher" on my resume under The Sunrise Show internship bullet point someday, that's exactly what I've been doing these past four months. But we all need to start somewhere, right?

The walk into The Sunrise Show studio *never* gets old. The room is massive, the lights are bright, and the floor is sparkly. News reporters, floor directors, and camera operators constantly rush around, trying to avoid tripping over cables and equipment. It's loud and chaotic, and everybody is much more important than me.

"Let's go, people," one of the floor directors shouts.

I watch from the sidelines as Hilda Harrison takes a seat at her highly-coveted over sized glass desk. She shuffles through a pile of scripts as her hair and makeup people touch her up before the show begins in a few short minutes. Her blonde, blown-out hair reaches the tops of her shoulders, and her eyelids shimmer in a rose gold sparkle. Go time.

I walk up to her desk, placing the cold brew americano with a double shot of espresso on the Sunrise Show coaster like I'd done every morning for the past sixteen weeks. But this is the last time I'd ever do it. I never thought I'd be sentimental about getting coffee for someone.

Hilda flashes me a wink. "Thanks so much, honey. Last day?" *I am still just as starstruck as I was on day one.*

"Last day," I repeat. "I can't believe it."

Hilda raises her americano up to my line of sight. "Thanks for all of these."

When someone asks me what I want to be when I grow up, I say: Hilda Harrison. Hilda worked her way up the corporate news ladder just like everybody else in the news industry. She started at a tiny television station in South Dakota (market 171), moved up to a slightly bigger station in Texas (market 89), worked at a dream news station in Las Vegas (market 40), climbed to a big channel in Boston (market 10), and eventually made it to New York (market 1). *She made it.* Five cities, five markets, five moves. She made it to the top, and she couldn't go any higher.

I want to follow the exact path she took so I can get the

same results she did. I want her job someday. I need to follow her journey so I can reach the same destination.

The Sunrise Show theme song starts blaring through the studio just as I make it back to my desired *intern standing spot*. Eliza looks at me sentimentally from across the room. This is the last time we'll ever hear this song live again. Until we are working here for real someday, of course.

A floor director chants to Hilda before pointing his finger at the little red light on top of the teleprompter. "Five, four, three, two—"

"Good morning. Thanks for starting your day off with us here on The Sunrise Show. We're so happy you're here with us."

Eliza looks at me with a frown, pretending to draw the path of a tear traveling from her eye down to her cheek. I dig my fingers into the corners of my mouth and lift them up into a smile.

"A spike of crime in Midtown Manhattan has been reported by law enforcement officials in recent weeks," Hilda announces into the camera. "We have a correspondent live at the scene to share how city leaders are fighting the problem, and what the Mayor says needs to be done to prohibit crime from impacting tourism and economic development." She stares into the camera for a few seconds before that little red light goes out.

I used to watch The Sunrise Show with my mom in the mornings before school. Hilda's voice was always on in the background while my mom tamed the ends of my curly hair, healing it from looking like it had just been slept on. The show was part of our morning routine.

But it wasn't until I went on a 24-hour day trip to New York

City in middle school with my class that I realized just how spectacular a production the show actually was. Watching it in person left me awestruck. We got a picture with Hilda. I remember thinking, "That is what I wanted." *She is who I wanted to be.*

Hilda gets to share stories on live television to millions of people every day. People *know* who she is, and they trust her because of it. She gets to interview A-list celebrities starring in the most popular movies of our time. She travels all over the world to cover the biggest stories in history, from emerging wars to the annual Olympics. She's gone live from Rome, Vienna, Tokyo, Delhi, Sao Paulo, Beijing, Cape Town—you name it, she's covered a story there. Her job seems like the coolest one possible to me, and ever since that first glorious New York City day, there is nothing else I want more for my future self.

"Keep dreaming," Hilda had told me before walking away to take another picture with the tourists beside me. I don't think she realized that I'd continue to spend the next decade dreaming about having *her* job.

"Girls!" Hilda whispers, waving Eliza and me over in her direction.

We approach her desk like the altar in a Catholic Church, slowly and with caution. Once I reach the vicinity, I catch a whiff of her coconut-scented hairspray. She's wearing red-framed glasses that match her red turtleneck sweater.

"So tell me," Hilda asks us, taking a sip of her americano. She places her hand under her chin and props her elbow on the desk, leaning in as if she were gossiping with friends. *I can never believe that somebody as important as her would want to talk to us.* "Where are you girls off to now?"

My eyes widen. "I got a job at my hometown TV station. Reporter. I graduate in the spring," I answer nervously, untangling my foot from a microphone wire below me. "It's in Joyfield, Ohio. WJDN News. It's only market 150."

"I started at a smaller market than that, so you're already ahead of me," Hilda reassures. She turns her attention to Eliza. "What about you?"

Eliza tucks a blonde piece of hair behind her ear. "I got a reporting job in Junction, Florida. WJRF News. It's market 142, also just a map dot."

The hair and makeup ladies are now back, fluffing and powdering Hilda. "You girls are on the right track. Start small, get experience, make mistakes, and move up. Climb the news market ladder. There's no other way to do it. Wouldn't it be nice if you could just start at a place like this? It took me twenty freaking years to get here."

Windows line the studio's perimeter, creating a portal to the outside world. Tourists and taxis move rapidly past a backdrop of holiday decorations. Colorful lights snake around telephone poles and street lamps, creating a bokeh effect of multicolored blurry circles behind Hilda's head in the camera frame. The snow picked up from this morning when I first looked out my apartment window— it was now falling in clumps that resemble cotton balls. They glisten on their descent to the ground, like a scene from a holiday movie.

The floor director gives his cue again. "We're back in five—"

Eliza and I rush back to our unofficial intern spots on the studio floor, playing a game of mental hopscotch among the wires and cords on the ground to get there. I watch as Hilda's face transitions back to a serious one, looking back up at the little red light on the teleprompter. She starts reading the next story, which is juxtaposingly about puppies. That's the thing about morning news. One minute it's serious, the next minute it's lighthearted. *As lighthearted as a story about puppies can get.*

"We have to go," Eliza mouths to me, pointing at her watch. We have to go back to The Sunrise Show corporate offices to say our goodbyes and return our badges. We start walking on eggshells towards the exit door as Hilda continues reading off the teleprompter.

I look back over my shoulder towards the glass anchor desk. *One last glance.* The people. The sparkly floors. That massive desk. The background of New York City. I take a deep breath and soak it in before my eyes. I made it to the place I have wanted to be since I was a little girl. *I made it here, and I will make it back here again someday.*

Even though she is still reading a news story, Hilda shoots us a thumbs-up out of the frame of the camera. Tears begin to form a puddle in my lower eyelids, blurring the view of the studio. The door shuts quietly behind us. The entire experience is over in an instant.

"I can't believe it's over," I whisper to Eliza once we get into the hallway. I can see a crowd of fans bundled up in jackets outside the window.

"We'll be back." I can tell that Eliza isn't phased by the end of this era. She has a knowing confidence. "We'll be back."

* * *

I stand on the sidewalk outside of Westerfield Apartments with my suitcases as I watch my parents arrive in their oversized, navy blue Suburban. Once my dad pulls over and parks along the street — nearly dodging a yellow taxi and a bicyclist — he turns on his four-way signal so my mom can run out of the car and hug me.

I can't believe that my small-town parents drove in the middle of New York City just for me. The Lincoln Tunnels would throw me over the edge. *I don't think I have the nerve to do that for anyone.*

Once my mom gets to me, she wraps me up in an embrace and makes an *I'm squeezing something* sound. "We've missed you so much," she says, swaying me side to side.

"I missed you, too," I say. My eyes dampen. "Time to go back to real life."

My dad waves at us through the window as my mom lets me go. She looks me in the eyes. "Let's get you out of here."

I look up at the snow falling from the sky. It lands on our heads and shoulders like dandruff. I look at my suitcases and shrug. "I'm ready."

I get my long, dark hair from my mom. Known to the rest of the world as Kelly Fenwick, my mother is a labor and delivery nurse in our local hospital back home. People always say we look like twins. The edges of her smile are lined with small wrinkles, and there are strands of gray hair shooting out from her side part. It makes me sad to see my mother aging, but since she is still so beautiful, it makes me look forward to what I'll look like someday. My genetics are filled with hope.

My dad rushes over, grabs my luggage, and shoves it into the back of the Suburban. "Hey, kiddo," my dad says, giving me a short hug on the way. I could tell that the hustle and bustle of 34th Street makes him nervous. "Is this everything?"

I look up towards the apartment. "I think so. Unless I forgot something."

My dad, Dominic Fenwick, works in finance at a local accounting firm. That's his *real job*, but he's also a photography stringer on the side — more professionally known as a *freelance photojournalist*, as he likes to call it — capturing photos of high school sports and regional community events for our local newspaper. He's loud and boisterous with a contagious personality that makes him a presence everywhere he goes, whether it's in Joyfield or beyond. He has dark hair like my mom and me, but he's going much grayer. Salt and pepper, if you will, that no amount of *Just For Men* products can touch.

I hit the jackpot in the parents department. Overbearing? Sure. Overprotective? Yes. Did I have to fight them to let me move to the city for this internship? Definitely. But I know that they love me more than anything in the world. *They tell me every day.*

"I missed you, honey," my mom whispers as she slides into the passenger seat. I take my usual back seat behind the driver's side. We have been sitting in this car arrangement ever since I was in a car seat. "I'm happy we're taking you home."

My dad continues shoving my luggage into the trunk. "All done," he announces after trying to fit the last one in like a puzzle piece. He makes his way into the driver's seat and sets the GPS on his phone to Joyfield, Ohio. "Eight hours and 27 minutes. Off we go."

"I can't believe I let you live here," my mom says, looking up at the skyscrapers out of her sunroof. We pull out of our parking spot and accelerate. "What was I thinking?"

After driving for about 20 seconds, my dad slams on his brakes when a nearby driver tries to cut in front of him. "Eyyy, ohhh, forget about it," my dad screams, sending my mom and me into hysterics. He raises a hand in the air to act like a real New Yorker. "I'm drivin' heaahhh."

As we drive through Times Square, I rest my chin on my hand and look out the window. The electronic billboards blink through flashy advertisements ranging from clothing stores to Broadway musicals. A mother and daughter walk down the sidewalk, holding up foot traffic as they gaze up at the New Year's Eve ball. A businessman wearing a red scarf prances down the sidewalk, dodging tourists while talking on the phone. An old couple bundled up in winter coats share a slice of pizza. A handful of teenage girls hold shopping bags. The Macy's holiday window display blasts an upbeat oldies version of *There's No Place Like Home For The Holidays*, and for whatever reason, my eyes become wet.

My mom has basically been turned around, talking to me our entire drive so far, so she noticed right away. "Are you crying?"

It's like crying in Disney World. It's one of the happiest holiday songs in the world, and it's making me insanely depressed. The irony almost makes me want to laugh. The nostalgia for the place I'm leaving, combined with the nostalgia for the home I am returning to, makes me feel like I am stuck in emotional purgatory.

"I just really missed you guys," I admit. The tears start to fall. It was true. I loved my time in New York City. I'm so happy I got to live out my dream. "I just don't know how to feel."

"Feel happy that you're getting out of this hellhole," my dad jokes, his eyes meeting mine in the rear-view mirror.

"We can come back every single Christmas forever if you want to," my mom reassures.

My dad slams on the brakes just as an Uber tries to jut out in front of him. "But maybe we won't drive next time. I heard the buses here are pretty cheap."

We eventually reach the Lincoln Tunnel. It looks like a mile-long line of cars is stopped ahead of us. "I never understood this tunnel," my mom says. "It's a set of metal tubes slicing through the Hudson River. How is that even physically and logistically possible?"

"It has to do with air pressure," I explain. "Something about the reinforcement of the concrete. I only know because they did a story about it on The Sunrise Show last month. It was a little feature story."

"You're a lot smarter now than when we first dropped you off here," my dad says. "Thank goodness. I was getting worried."

My mom hits him in the arm. "She's always been smart," she says, sticking up for me. "Let's just say…you're a little more *worldly* now. With college and all."

I am set to graduate from college in June. That means I only have six more months of freedom, if you can call it that.

I go to *Joyfield University* in my hometown, live with my parents, and commute to my classes. Because of that, I never felt like I had a true college experience. That's one of the secret reasons getting an internship away — for at least one semester — was so important to me. I wanted a taste of college life, and I feel like I had it. (Thank goodness for the *online* classes my college offers, or else I wouldn't have been able to do this.) *At least this internship counted for three credits, too.*

Once we pass through the light at the end of the Lincoln Tunnel, the New York City skyline is in full view ahead of us. My forehead is pressed up against the glass as we pass it. *It looks so small from here.*

The needle on top of the One World Trade Center pierces through a puff of gray clouds. The windows of the Empire State Building reflect against the tiny bit of sun still left in the sky. I know Westerfield Apartments is somewhere in that cluster. I'm staring into the city where the first dream of mine ever came true, and I can't help but beam at the thought of it.

As the city moves further out of view, I feel the strongest wave of relief. I exhale a quiet sigh. There is no elephant sitting on my chest. There is no heavy pulse rushing through my veins. There is no tension in my shoulders. I made it, I did the damn thing, and now I'm going home. *Check.* I completed what I had set out to do, and I could not be happier about it. For the first time in my life, I'm at peace. While I hope to be back there again…*at least I know I was there at all.*

The skyline eventually vanishes from my passenger window, giving way to rows of New Jersey apartment buildings. And then shopping complexes. And then houses. And then nothing but trees. Snow and ice rest on their branches. Due to the scenery, I'm starting to feel like I'm inching closer and closer towards home.

"I haven't driven a car in four months," I say to my parents.

My dad turns his head as far as he can towards me without taking his eyes off the road. "Want me to pull over?"

"No," I laugh. I shut my eyes and rest my head against the window. I feel like I can truly relax. "I think I might take a nap."

My mom asks her next question with caution. "Have you heard from Josh at all?"

Josh. The name that I had just gotten out of my mind these past few months. My eyes open wide. "No, why?"

I started dating Josh at the end of my freshman year of college, and after celebrating with me when I found out I got The Sunrise Show internship, he dumped me right before I moved. I should refer to it as 'taking a break,' as *he* called it. He made a lot of claims about 'long distance ruining relationships' and 'taking some time to focus on ourselves for a while.' But when he posted a selfie with another girl on Snapchat over Halloween weekend, I knew we were beyond done with each other. It wasn't that he wanted time away from me before getting back together. *He just didn't want to be with me at all.*

"Just wondered," my mom says. "Just chill back there. Take your nap." She turns around to look at me, and her soft eyes make me feel right at home. "I'm going to get carsick if I keep turning around, but I just want to look at you. My little girl."

"Relax to the sound of this." My dad skips to the next song in his queue. *Take Me Home, Country Roads* by John Denver starts to play.

"Is this the West Virginia song?"

"Yes," my dad announces, humming along.

"Are you taking us to West Virginia? We live in Ohio."

My dad points out the long road in front of him. "See these country roads? They are taking us home."

We are actually on the New Jersey Turnpike, but it does look like a country road compared to the streets of Manhattan.

I listen to my parents as they sing the rest of the song. My eyes remain closed, my chest still light and airy. I am *home*, even though I'm not actually *home* yet. It feels good to be out of the largest city in the United States and on my way to my small hometown.

But in true Eliza spirit, I know I'll be back in New York City someday. I don't know when or how, but it's a feeling deep inside my soul. I know that I'm destined for big things. Bigger than Joyfield, Ohio. Not because it has anything to do with me, but because I know that life's too short *not* to be destined for big things. Everyone should be.

I love my parents, but I don't want to live a simple life. I want to live a *big* life. I got out of Joyfield once, so I can do it again. I know I'll get back to The Sunrise Show again someday. But instead of getting Hilda coffee...*I'll be drinking it with her.*

THE COLD OPEN

"For continuing coverage of this story, stay with us here on WJDN News. Reporting live in Joyfield, I'm Noelle Fenwick," I announce into my wobbly camera. I stare into the center of the lens, waiting to hear those magic words from my producer: *you're clear.*

The snow is lifting, but my hands are still stuck to my handheld microphone like a child's tongue sticks to a telephone pole. Since I am now presenting live television reports *outdoors* in the snow for a living — and my daily tasks go beyond getting coffee in warm break rooms — the winter season isn't as romanticized as it once was during my New York City internship days. But the snow always takes me back there.

"You're clear." The voice of Myra Cole, our WJDN news producer and my self-proclaimed work bestie, finally rescues me. I hear her deep voice through my flimsy earpiece.

"Good, it's freaking freezing out here," I say once I know I'm off the air. I rub my hands together, trying to generate some warmth. I reach towards the camera to start disconnecting the wires and cables. The sooner I break this stuff down and get it into my car, the sooner I can go home.

Two years ago, I was returning home from New York City. I was looking ahead to six months of capstone projects, college graduations, and career preparations. But today I'm in Joyfield, already nearing the end of my contract at WJDN News. I'm now looking ahead to six months of soul searching, job interviewing, and self reflecting.

I have until June to tell my boss if I will renew my contract at WJDN — possibly staying for another two years here — or leave for good. I could *finally* make the first leap up the broadcasting ladder to a *new* station in a *new* town. One step closer to my dreams. One step closer to being Hilda Harrison. I'd have to start applying to jobs. *Am I ready for it?*

I can hear Myra laugh in my ear. "It's pretty warm in the control room right now," she sings. "And that's saying something, because you know I always have a blanket lying across me in here."

"I'm going to unplug you now," I say into the lens, pretending to remove my earpiece. Even though I can't see Myra, she can see me on her giant control room monitor.

Myra is from Virginia Beach. Since that is market 44, which is usually a reporter's second or third job, she has to start someplace smaller and work her way back up. That's the same for everyone else working at WJDN. It's just a stepping stone, a rung on the ladder, and a section of the resume to eventually land something bigger and better.

"Wait!" Myra screams just before I hang up.

My cold hand is just about to disconnect my camera from my tripod. "Yes?" I respond impatiently, staring back into the lens.

"Are you going to The Highball tonight? Happy hour? The new girl is coming."

"I don't know." I kick a rock beneath my feet and let out a sigh. "I'm planning on lying with a heated blanket in bed watching Sex and the City."

"Come on," Myra says with a sigh. "I'm going if you want to go."

I bite the fingertips of my gloves and use my teeth to take them off my cracked hands. My frigid fingers are still frozen, so I hold them up to my mouth and blow warm air onto them. This thaws them just enough to let me toggle all my camera switches off and organize everything neatly inside my bag.

"I'll let you know," I say.

Camera bag over my shoulder and tripod under my arm, I finally begin the trek towards my news car. I take caution with each step down the courthouse stairs, avoiding patches of snow and ice.

I've spent the last two work weeks inside the courthouse's granite and marble-filled rooms covering a criminal trial. Trials aren't my favorite things to cover as a reporter, but at least the court schedule gives me some consistent hours for once. Starts at eight, ends at four. One-hour lunch break. *I could get used to these hours.*

I make it to my news car, now covered with a thin layer of snow. I use my free arm to open up my trunk, and as I swing my bag inside, my heart starts to vibrate. I turn to see a white truck swinging around the corner, barreling in my direction. The bass of the truck's sound system grows louder as it moves closer. It eventually feels like I'm sitting next to the speakers at a rock concert.

I throw my tripod haphazardly on top of the camera bag and slam the trunk door shut, hopping up onto the sidewalk. As the truck inches closer to me, the driver picks up speed, passing his front tire through a slushy, dirty puddle. It shoots cold liquid filled with shards of ice directly into my eyeballs.

"Fake news!" The driver screams out the window. The truck becomes smaller and smaller as it speeds off into the distance. The vibration in my chest eases, but the anger in my forehead intensifies.

I stand for a few seconds with my mouth agape from the shock of it all. I can't comprehend what just happened to me. Sure, I'd been flipped off and yelled at a few times for no reason besides working for the local news. But I had never been almost intentionally hit by a car. *This seems like a new low.*

I brush the dirty water from my coat and stare into my reflection in the car window. *I'm soaked.* Anger builds up inside of me like a tea kettle getting hot enough to start whistling on the stove top.

"I went to college for four years and majored in how to be fake," I say to nobody.

"Are you okay?" A deep voice asks from behind me.

I turn around to see a well-dressed man walking down the steps of the courthouse towards my car. He looks a few years older than me, but I can tell he's still within my age range.

His dark gray overcoat covers up a professional-looking

white shirt and black tie. He has thick, curly brown hair — which can go unruly and wild at any moment — but it's purposefully tamed with a strong comb and an equally strong hair product. He is clean-shaven, and even though I haven't seen him smile yet, I can tell he has the right face shape to result in some form of dimple formation. The long, narrow kind that look like 'smile lines.' He is extremely cute, and I can't help but stare.

"I've been better," I tell him as he reaches my news car.

"Did you get their license plate by chance?" He holds a hand over his eyes to shield them from the golden hour sun, looking down the road in the direction of the vehicle's exit route.

I wipe dirty water from under my eyes and flick it onto the ground. "I couldn't see anything with the water in my eyes," I tease.

He looks back at me, and when his eyes meet mine, I feel a chill rush through me that isn't a result of the cold weather. He's about a whole foot taller than me, and he's even more handsome when he's this close up. I can tell he wants to continue the conversation, but he doesn't know what to say that doesn't pertain to the truck fiasco.

"I'm Levi." He sticks a hand out to shake mine. "Levi Winters. I'm a prosecuting attorney. I've been working on this trial."

I try to hide my blushing cheeks as I watch him grin. *Dimples.* He has the line dimples. I knew he would. I notice that I feel extremely at ease. Usually, when I'm in the presence of a handsome man, I don't say anything other than things I painfully regret later out of embarrassment. But I feel a strange sense of calm right now.

"Noelle Fenwick," I say as I shake his hand, noticing a warmth forming between our palms. "How have I not seen you in there?"

"I've seen you." He flashes a small smile by accident. *It's a great smile.* "I've been sitting in the back of the courtroom. I just got out of law school, so I've been observing. Job shadowing, I guess. But I like to say I'm *working* on the trial. Makes me sound like I'm actually doing something, you know?"

"You're just reframing what you do. That's just a good lawyer skill." I catch one of my brown curls flying in the wind and tuck it behind my ear. I motion my head towards the courthouse. "So if you've seen me in there for two weeks, can I ask you a question?"

"Yeah?"

"Do I always have *resting bitch face* like I've been told?"

Levi shoves his hands in his pockets. "I've only been staring at the back of your head, so I don't really know. I just know that you're the news girl."

"Oh, so you're literally in the back of the courtroom."

"Last row."

"You should sit in the front," I reassure him. "Where the important people sit. Then people will think you're important. Well, you are important—"

"I like to just observe," he says. "There's no pressure back there. I can sit with my notebook and stare at the back of your head, apparently."

I smooth the back of my hair. "I'm going to be self-conscious tomorrow," I admit.

Levi looks inside my news car towards the passenger seat. His expression shifts from curiosity to confusion when he realizes no one is sitting in it. "Where's your cameraman?"

I raise my hand. "Here. Camera *woman*, to be exact."

Levi tucks a hand in his overcoat pocket and tilts his head. "Who's standing behind the camera when you're standing in front of it?"

"Nobody." I motion towards the trunk of my car. "I stand *behind* the camera to set everything up ahead of time, and then stand in *front* of it when it's time for my live shot."

Levi folds his arms across his chest, causing the threading of his overcoat to tighten around his biceps. "Isn't that a little dangerous?"

"It can be," I shrug. "Especially when you're alone at night. But it's the nature of the job. It's what we signed up for, you know?"

His eyes widen as he shakes his head. "I wouldn't have guessed. But you have someone do your makeup and stuff, right? I mean, that's a given."

"Nope." I scrunch some water out of my hair. "All me."

"But it looks so—"

"What?"

"It looks good." His smile shows his teeth this time, a display that looks like it was the result of equal parts braces and whitening. "Professional. I don't mean that to sound weird; it's just the first time I'm seeing the front of you. I just—"

I laugh it off. "It's fine."

I feel a little ping inside my chest, but I try to ignore it. I can't tell if this is some form of a *tease* — like he's trying to test the waters to see how I'll react — or if he genuinely misspoke a line of flirtation. I notice that his lips look like perfect little clouds, and I've *never* noticed a man's lips before in my entire life. I didn't even know men could *have* nice lips.

Levi motions towards the parking lot. "Hey, I should get—"

"Me too," I say.

I watch as he grabs a business card out of his pocket and hands it to me. "If you ever need anything, like an interview, since I'm supposed to do them someday, you know."

"Got it." I slide it into the pocket of my coat. "I definitely will be needing you at some point. I cover all the trials here."

"Anytime," Levi says. His eyes appear worried or something. Like he doesn't want to leave, but he knows that he has to. "Nice to meet you, Noelle."

"You too." I notice that I'm trying to avoid making direct eye contact. *Why am I so awkward?*

I get in my car, and before plugging my phone into the charger, I stare out at the snowy road in front of me. I sit in silence, letting the artificial heated air hit my cheeks. *Levi Winters.* I squint at nothing. I just envision his face and recount every sentence he said to me.

Levi doesn't look or seem serious enough to be a lawyer. He looks like a nice guy. Friendly. *Fun.* I imagine he's the type of guy who would be fun to go to parties with. I feel like I've known him for a long time. I can't get his face out of my mind, and I haven't felt this kind of excitement about meeting anyone since Josh back in college.

I pull out of my parking spot along the side of the road and head off into the sunset. Golden hour tints the snowy streets of Joyfield in an orange hue. In light of recent events, I decide to meet Myra at The Highball. *I need a drink.*

Three

THE BEAT REPORTER

I hate walking into The Highball. The entrance is the focal point of the bar, so every time the door opens, all necks turn to identify the newest patron.

The bell jingles as I open the door, which doesn't help my anxiety in this situation. I can feel my shoulders tense as everybody's eyeballs stare at me when I walk in.

"Hey, it's the weather girl!" a drunken man yells.

"She's a news reporter," Myra corrects. I can't see her yet, but I can hear her voice. While I'm one to let comments go, she never backs down from a minor verbal altercation.

Once Myra finds me, she grabs my hand and leads me to our unofficially sponsored WJDN table. Her black, curly hair bounces with each step, and her beautiful dark skin glistens under the bar lighting.

She turns around and gives me a knowing look. "Glad you could make it," she says.

I dodge off a few glances from the bar goers. "Me too, I guess," I say.

The Highball is Joyfield's oldest bar— so old that my parents even came here back in college. It's always dark, sticky, and grimy. The wooden floorboards are lifting, and the stained wallpaper is peeling. Even though there are non-smoking signs on the walls, you can always smell traces of cigarettes in here. It's the perfect dive bar home of the world's best mozzarella sticks.

"What happened to you?"

The question comes from Nate Kerrigan, our assignment editor. He's sitting at the head of the table with a half-full glass of Miller Lite. I notice that his unruly red, puffy curls are actually styled into place tonight. I have never seen them like *that* before. He's wearing a nice but casual button-down. He pushes a tequila sunrise in my direction.

"Nice to see you too," I say, taking my usual seat beside him. I scan him up and down. "What's the occasion?"

Nate's green eyes widen. He subtly tilts his head towards who, I assume, is *the new girl.* She sits with a nervous look, clutching what appears to be a vodka cranberry.

He looks down at his shirt and then back up at me. "What are you talking about?"

Nate and I are both graduates of *Joyfield Area High School.* If you had told me back then — that the annoying kid who used to blow spit wads at the back of my head in social studies class would someday *work* with me in a professional capacity — I would have never believed you. But here we are. We're now the only Joyfield *natives* at WJDN, swimming in a sea of transient news professionals who are all from out of state. It is because of our hometown knowledge that we can help them all pronounce the names of nearby towns and the last names of criminals.

I turn my attention to the new girl. "Nice to meet you," I say, sticking out a hand for her to shake.

When she shakes my hand back, I notice her hot pink acrylic nails. "It's so nice to meet you, Noelle. I've heard so much about you." Her fingers are damp from the condensation of her glass. "I'm Paige Martinez. New reporter, obviously. I start tomorrow. I just moved here last week, and I'm super nervous—"

"You'll be fine," I say calmly.

"We get through it together," Myra adds. She is holding an orange cocktail in a fancy glass. "We'll go easy on you."

I nod in agreement. "Plus, I'll be the one training you. I mean, I'm the only other reporter here, so you're stuck with me."

Nate leans in. "Yeah, Noelle is a real bitch. You're gonna hate her."

"I don't think that's the case," Paige says with a laugh. She hits Nate in the arm, and I'm afraid it's going to send him into oblivion.

The new girl, Paige, is a kind of obvious beauty. Her long, blonde hair twists into loose curls. Her eyelash extensions resemble caterpillars. Her naturally olive skin would take me months in a tanning bed to achieve. While my first impression of Paige is that she's extremely sweet, she also gives off the "I'm only in journalism, so I can be on TV" vibe. *I guess we'll find out tomorrow.*

"Can I just say," Paige says, leaning in towards me. "I stalked your Instagram. I can't believe you interned at The Sunrise Show."

I chomp on a vodka-infused ice cube. "I like a girl who does her research," I joke.

There's something about local newsroom coworkers that you can't find anywhere else. Nate and Myra have seen me when I *started* a shift at 3:00 in the morning, and when I *finished* a shift at 3:00 in the morning. They've seen me in good moods and bad moods, awake and asleep, healthy and sick. There's no hiding your true feelings in the newsroom. Nobody puts on a professional face for anybody. Our job is so demanding that we don't have any extra energy to worry about what people think of us. *We are who we are.* We take it all as it comes. Because of that, Nate and Myra probably know me better than my own family.

I start my unofficial interview. "Where are you from, Paige?"

She lets out a sigh. "San Francisco. Market 10. Which is why I'm starting here."

"That's really far," Myra says. "That's like, the farthest place you could be from, ever."

"No, it's not," Nate corrects. "She could have said she was from, I don't know, Madagascar."

Myra leans in. "Who moves to Joyfield from *Madagascar?*"

Nate shoots his hands out at his sides. "I'm just saying, there are farther places in the world than *California.*"

"That's not the point," Myra yells. "I'm just saying that San Francisco is far away. It's on the opposite coast."

"We don't live on a coast. This is Ohio," Nate says.

Myra shuffles her chair so that she is only facing Paige. She points to Nate without looking at him. "Rule number one: ignore this man. At all costs."

The bell above the door jingles, and we all unintentionally

turn our attention to the entrance. A group of professionally dressed men walks in. Lots of khaki pants, overcoats, shirts, and ties. I find myself thinking of Levi. *Why am I subconsciously hoping that one of these well-dressed men is him?* I find myself scanning. Not him. Not him. Not him. And then suddenly...*him.*

My heart starts pounding as I watch his eyes find our table, but I'm surprised when he recognizes Nate first. Levi raises an arm into the air and shouts, "Hey, man!"

"Hey!" Nate shouts back to him.

I turn to Nate so quickly that I could have induced vertigo. "You know him?" I whisper frantically.

"Yeah. Levi," he responds in an obvious tone. He finishes his Miller Lite and sets the empty glass on the table. "You don't remember him? Cantner."

Levi went to Cantner? Our rival high school? I continue interrogating Nate, not caring that Myra and Paige are listening. I need to get to the bottom of this. "How do I not know who he is? Did I ever meet him before? What grade—"

"Maybe because you didn't pay attention to sports," Nate teases. "He was like four years older than us. We played each other in football. But you wouldn't know, since you never actually watched any of the games."

He got me there.

"What else do you know about him?" I ask Nate, my eyes narrowing in on him. "You're like the local attorney *beat reporter*—"

But Nate doesn't get a chance to report any additional details. After Levi gets a beer from the bartender, he starts walking over to our table.

I position my body towards the back wall as if I'm *hiding,* even though I'm in plain sight. I feel him moving closer. *Why can't I just turn around?* I act like he's some kind of three-headed monster headed my way. Well, he is the most handsome man I've ever seen in my life, so maybe that's kind of the same thing in my mind.

"He's really cute," Paige whispers.

Myra leans in. "Can you get him to set me up with that guy back—"

"Long time no see, man," Levi shouts to Nate once he is just about a foot away from our table. He shakes his hand, causing him to lean in closer to me.

"How's it going?" Nate asks. He bumps my arm with his elbow. "Heard you met my friend Noelle here."

Blood immediately rushes to my cheeks. I want to send a spitball between Nate's eyes, but instead, I turn around and look up at Levi. No more hiding. "Hi again," I say.

"Uh, Noelle, hey." The recognition immediately hits his face. "I thought I recognized the back of your head."

"Yeah," I say. "I'm not stalking you, I promise."

Couldn't I have come up with something better? Anything better?

Levi turns his gaze to Myra and Paige. "I'm Levi. Nate and I used to play football against each other back in the day."

"I'm assuming you always won?" Myra teases.

Levi runs a hand through his hair and smirks. "You assumed correctly."

"I don't know about that." Nate brushes the conversations away with his arm. "So what brings you back to town?"

"Just graduated from law school. I was away for three years. I've been shadowing the trial you guys have been covering this week." He motions towards me with the tilt of his head.

"Which is where I met Noelle. Just today, actually."

Myra smirks. "She's our favorite reporter."

I fold my arms over my chest. "I'm the only reporter."

Levi takes a sip of his beer and directs his attention to the rest of the group. "I've been staring at the back of her head for two weeks, so it was nice to put a name to the face. Or head, I should say."

"I have a new source," I say. "He'll have to do an interview with us at some point."

More khaki-wearing professional men walk into the bar, so Levi leans towards them. "I should probably get going," he says. "Have a good night. Nice to see you again, Noelle."

"Bye." I act nonchalant.

Once Levi starts walking away, Paige leans towards me. "Are *all* the men in Joyfield that hot?"

Nate leans back in his chair, resting his head in his hands. "Must be something in the water here. We get that a lot."

Paige takes a sip of her vodka cranberry and winces from the taste. She rests the back of her palm under her chin and her elbow on the table before leaning in dramatically. "So, what are *your* love life situations?"

I decide to take one for the team and answer her question first. "Single," I blurt out. "My college boyfriend dumped me right before I left for New York City. I haven't dated since."

Paige squints her eyes in disbelief. "You haven't dated since *college?*"

"Nope." I shake my head. "Nate, you're up next."

Nate sighs. "I just downloaded Tinder again. Maybe it will work the 67th time." He looks at Myra to take the attention away from himself. "Myra has the juiciest love life of all."

She rolls her eyes. "No, I don't. No, I would *not* like to talk about it."

"She has a mystery man back home in Virginia Beach," Nate answers for her. "She won't let us meet him."

"His name is Ethan," Myra says with a glare. She finishes the rest of her cocktail with one final swig. "What about you, new girl?"

"Similar situation to Noelle," Paige answers honestly. "Just got dumped before moving here. Why are guys so scared of long distance?"

"I'd say it's a pretty short distance between you and me right now," Nate tells her.

"We are not hitting on the new girl," I reprimand. "We don't want to scare her away."

Paige giggles. "How often do you guys come here?" She uses a napkin to wipe away the condensation ring on the table in front of her.

"Usually a couple times a week," Myra says. "Depends on our shifts."

"You come here on weeknights? Or nights when you have to work the next day?"

"Pretty much," Myra explains. "Since we all work a combination of weeknights and weekends, every night is *technically* a weekend for someone. You know how *it's five o'clock somewhere?* It's always a weekend for somebody."

I raise my glass. "I'd like to make a toast to Paige. Welcome to Joyfield. Where we drink alcohol on weeknights, even when you have to work in the morning."

Nate touches his empty beer glass to my drink. "Cheers to the new girl."

Our glasses clink together, and I chug the remainder of my drink to get it over with.

I turn around to observe Levi's table. He's smiling and laughing, and I notice just how perfect his side profile is. *How have I never heard of this guy before?*

When he makes eye contact with me for a split second, I panic and turn back around. I wince in imaginary emotional pain.

"I think he likes you," Paige says.

She caught me. "Is he still staring?"

Myra laughs. "Just at the back of your head."

Four

THE NEWSROOM

I swing open the rusty metal door that leads to the WJDN newsroom and step onto the stained, deep blue carpeting that has lined the floor since the 1950s. My eyes are blinded by the illuminated sign on the back wall displaying the call letters W-J-D-N in a flashy yellow ink.

The newsroom is a giant loft with no separations or dividers within its pale-yellow-painted walls. Just rows upon rows of cubicles, most of which are not filled with human beings. Layoffs, hiring freezes, and just a lack of new people joining the industry— the usual stuff that comes with working for a corporation in today's day and age.

I walk past the WJDN assignment desk, where Nate spends at least fifty hours a week. The police scanners are blaring extra loudly on this particular Monday morning: static, squelches, beeps. *All units responding. Attempted robbery. Suspect description is male, blonde hair, red jacket. Firefighters are arriving at the scene. Altered mental status. Copy. 10-4. Request backup. Over.* Dispatcher voices overlap one another, and I can't tell which tragedy is happening in what part of town.

"Good morning," I sing to Nate with a fake cheerfulness.

"*I'm* about to have an altered mental status." Nate runs a hand through his hair. "There's a fire somewhere. There's a robbery somewhere else. I'm trying to figure out *where.* I just got here."

"Happy Monday to you, too." I'm surprised that Paige still isn't here. "The new girl starts today, right?"

"She should be here." He is clearly still frustrated by the lack of information from the dispatcher. "I thought she started today."

That's when a blonde mess of hair rolls into the newsroom like a beautiful tornado. Paige holds a cheetah tote bag in one hand and a frappuccino in the other. It's drenched in whipped cream and caramel.

"I'm here, I'm here, I'm here." Paige runs over to my desk in her nude high heels, stomping with a type of urgency that appears to be for show purposes only. "Traffic was just *crazy* this morning."

There's never any traffic in Joyfield except on the day of the annual Halloween parade, but I play along for the sake of keeping the peace. "It happens," I say. *It's one thing to show up late, but it's another thing to show up late with a coffee in your hands.*

I pull up a tattered swivel chair beside me, and with a huff, Paige takes a seat in it. She places her coffee on my desk and her tote bag on the filing cabinet. "Nice place you got here," she says, scanning my desk.

My desk is…*fine.* I don't like a lot of clutter, so it's just home to a few 'officey' things: a stapler, scissors, tape, paper clips, the usual. But I do have a picture of Eliza and me in front of the Rockefeller Center Christmas tree next to my speaker. Our arms are in the air, and we are looking at each other smiling. It makes me sentimental every time I look at it. I find myself staring at it when I'm having writer's block. *Or just a general lack of motivation.*

Next to that photo is the little two-by-four-inch frame, which holds the smile of the man with the diploma and ponytail. I stare at his straight, frizz-free locks from time to time, wishing I inherited his silky hair in addition to his hair color. *But no.* Brown frizz it is for me. The frame leans up against my speaker, vibrating when an audio setting is just a little too loud.

The police scanners ramp up again, creating a melody of beeps, whirs, and hums. The voices of dispatchers infiltrate the constant static in the background. *Unit 30, proceed to Seventh Avenue for a possible disturbance. 10-4. Do you copy?*

"Dammit," Nate screams at nobody. He pounds his fists on the desk.

Once Paige drapes her long, tan coat behind her chair, she picks up her coffee. "Do they do that all day?" She uses her straw as a spoon to shovel caramelly whipped cream into her mouth.

"Does what do what all day?"

"Those beeping noises," Paige explains with a mouth full. She pops the plastic lid off her drink to get better access to the whipped cream. "Is it always like *that* in here?"

"You'll drown it out after a while." That was a lie. *You actually just get really good at working through the distraction of it.* "But you can't drown it out too much, because that's how we hear what breaking news is going on. Fires, robberies, shootings."

Paige smacks her mauve-painted lips together. "How do you know who is saying what?"

"That's his job," Myra yells from her desk on the other side of the newsroom, pointing to Nate.

"Yes, that's what the assignment editor does." I shrug my shoulders. "But everybody in here is sort of *half* listening. One of us picks up a detail that the other doesn't. Then we collectively piece it together like a puzzle."

I watch Paige as she looks around the newsroom. I remember my first day at WJDN. I was so naive. You don't know what you don't know. And if I knew *then* what I know *now*, I probably would have bolted on day one.

Paige tucks a blonde curl behind her ear. "How do your days normally go?"

I open up my email and see that I have fifteen new messages. "Have you ever watched The Great British Bake Off?"

Paige tilts her head in skepticism about where this conversation is headed. "Yes?"

"It's *nothing* like that," I say.

"Okay."

I swivel my chair around to face her. "Have you ever watched Hell's Kitchen?"

"Like the show with Gordon Ramsey? It was on the Food Network?"

"Yes," I say. "Picture that show."

Paige squints her eyes. "Okay?"

"The chefs have a challenge to complete each episode. They put thirty minutes up on the clock. Gordon Ramsay counts down: five, four, three, two, one, *go*. They sprint to their little kitchens. They have to preheat, cook, chop, bake, and make something that not only tastes good, but also looks pretty. All before the clock strikes zero. The pressure intensifies. The music builds. The hearts pound. When time runs out, hopefully their meal is *complete*. The first chef's meal is super yummy, but tastes like shit. The second chef's meal tastes amazing, but looks like shit. The third chef's meal both looks and tastes great, but they didn't get it done in time, so it doesn't even matter. Are you following?"

"Kind of." Paige sucks up the last of her coffee.

"That's our job," I say. "We have a story to complete every day before showtime. Five hours are on the clock. Bill Calloway counts down: five, four, three, two, one, *go*. We drive to our stories. We drive, film, write, interview, edit, and make something that is not only well written but interesting to watch. The clock ticks. The anxiety builds. The stress hits. You might have a literary work of art, but the videos are shaky. You might have produced a cinematic masterpiece, but it sounds like it was written by a fourth grader. If you're lucky, your story both looks and sounds good, but if you don't get it on TV in time, it doesn't even matter."

Paige folds her arms. "Is this a bad time to say that I *prefer* watching The Great British Bake Off?"

"Too late."

Paige sighs. "Should I be...*scared*?"

"They don't call us Multimedia Journalists for nothing. MMJ for short. That's our official job title nowadays, by the way. Being *just* a *reporter* has gone out the window."

"Let's go, ladies and gentlemen."

The deep voice comes from the mouth of a grumpy Bill

Calloway, who emerges from his office and motions towards the morning meeting desk on the other side of the newsroom. The gray hair tousled on top of his head lies in curly little clumps, and he's wearing one of his infamous sweater vests. Bill has been the boss of WJDN since he was in his thirties, and I assume that he's now at least seventy-five.

Paige leans in and lowers her voice to a whisper. "Is that—"

"Yes," I answer. "That's him."

"He interviewed me over the phone," she says. "I didn't expect—"

"Yeah," I say.

Paige and I trudge over to the morning meeting desk, where we take seats between Myra and Nate. We exchange telepathic looks that communicate *we shouldn't have drunk so much last night*. Our shoulders slump like we're sitting in a high school math class.

Bill adjusts the glasses on the bridge of his nose. "We have a new addition to the WJDN team," he says without breaking eye contact with his laptop. "Everybody, this is Paige Martinez."

"Hi Paige," we say in unison as if we're welcoming her to an Alcoholics Anonymous meeting. *He has no idea that we already know her pretty well.*

"This is our daily morning meeting," Bill says to Paige, folding his hands on the desk. "This is where we figure out who is writing what stories for the day. I expect you to come here with *two* story pitches every morning."

Paige swallows out of pure anxiety.

"Noelle, you're up." Bill shifts his focus to me. "What do you have for us today?"

I open up my New York City skyline notebook from college.

Up until I started my job at WJDN, it only had one entry: my random *Acceptance Speech* on the first page. It's still there, and I still read it from time to time. But now, the following fifty pages of this notebook are filled with *story ideas.* From human interest and features to muck racking and investigations. These pages are an extension of my mind. *Many of which never make it past my gatekeeper of a boss.*

I flip to my most recent page, which I've bookmarked. "Okay. First idea— the Joyfield Community Soup Kitchen just received a $250,000 grant from the county to renovate its entire facility. They should now be able to feed three times as many people. The executive director already told me he's available for an interview, and he even has a single mother willing to talk—"

"Soft." Bill sits back in his chair and folds his arms. "Too soft for today. Second?"

Trying to hide the annoyed expression on my face, I flip to the next page and continue my pitch. "Second, there's a new coffee shop that just opened up in downtown Joyfield. It's called *Brew For You.* They employ people with special needs and disabilities, and I think it's a phenomenal mission—"

Bill looks at Nate, completely ignoring me. "Hey, didn't we hear something on the scanner this morning about a fire?"

"Yeah," Nate answers. "About an hour away."

Bill leans towards Paige. "See, *that's* the type of story you should be pitching. Noelle's are what you call— back pocket stories. Stories for a rainy day. Ones that you have simmering on the back burner for when there's nothing else going on. Those fluff pieces should *never* be your first choice. Off you go. See you later."

On the way back over to my desk, I can feel heat rushing

to my face. My heart starts to pound. But instead of saying anything to Bill, I whisper to Paige. "Oh, I forgot to tell you one more thing."

"Yeah?"

"If it bleeds, it leads," I say.

"What?"

I turn around to face her once we reach my desk. "Bill only likes stories involving blood and mass destruction of any kind. Murders, shootings, robberies— all of those things. But I know that *my* stories are the ones that people want to see. The ones that people need to see. So, I keep trying. And you should, too."

Paige's eyes widen. "That's concerning."

I slide my coat over my shoulders. "Oh, and one *more* thing."

Paige does the same. "Yeah?"

I fling my hair over my shoulder and look her in the eye with a soft, knowing look. "Welcome to Hell's Kitchen."

Five

THE INTERVIEW

"Here we are," I say, plopping my camera bag down on the damp sidewalk.

Paige drops my tripod a little too hard onto the ground. "I need to hit the gym." She rolls her shoulder back in a circle three times. "That thing is heavy."

"You'll be jacked in a few weeks." I flex an arm muscle at her, even though my puffy jacket prohibits the sight of any sort of bicep. "Trust me."

Paige is wearing a pair of my old rain boots — that I made her retrieve from the back of my news car — once I saw that her nude high heels would not tolerate the slushy snow. That's her first news reporter lesson of the day. One day, you're sent to interview a state senator wearing snow boots. The next day, you're sent to a pig farm wearing high heels. You just never know. *That's why I keep shoes of all kinds in the trunk.*

I take a breath and look around to assess the scene. Paige stands next to me and does the same. The dead-looking home is at the end of a dead-looking street. Firefighters are still moving inside the house with hoses and flashlights, and smoke is still pouring out of the top corner of the roof. The smell of char and ash hits my nostrils like a Sharpie marker.

"How many of these have you covered in your life?" Paige asks, looking up at the gray smoke infiltrating the already gray sky.

I tilt my head. "About 800," I tease.

"How long have you worked here?"

"It's coming up on two years." I crouch down and unzip the bag containing my camera. "Six more months to decide what I'm going to do."

"What are your options?" Paige asks.

The top flap of my camera bag opens fully. "I can stay here longer. Or I can move up to a bigger station."

Paige remains standing, looking down at me. "Where would you go?"

"I really don't know," I say, pulling my camera out of the bag. I assume a standing position and get a little dizzy once I'm eye level with Paige. "Stood up too fast."

Paige points at the bag. "So you get your squats in here, too?"

"Arm workouts, squats, your ten-thousand steps per day... this job is great exercise."

Paige attempts to set up my tripod, and after two failed attempts, I do it for her. She observes. "Thanks," she says, embarrassed.

"Anytime."

"Where do you want to end up? Like, retire someday?"

The word *retire* feels so far away that it sounds foreign. "Retire?" I hesitate for a second. "New York City. The Sunrise Show. That's the end goal."

This is the first time — in my adult life, at least — that I ever said this out loud. It's easy to tell someone your future dreams while you're still *in* college. The pressure is off because it's so far away. But telling someone your future dreams while you're actually out there working *towards* them is different. It's so much more real…like it's not just a dream anymore, it's a *plan*. A plan that I'm now in the middle of.

Paige observes as I connect my camera to the tripod. "How long until you think you could make it back there?"

"Many years." I exhale sharply. "I'd need to work at probably *three* news stations after this one. Three stepping stone stations. But I don't know what those are yet: what markets, what cities, all that stuff. And even after that, it's still *nearly* impossible."

Paige kicks a snowy piece of mud across the sidewalk and onto the road. "The time will pass anyway, right? Might as well spend it working towards what you want to do."

Good advice from the new girl.

I'm in the middle of showing Paige how to format the memory cards when her attention becomes focused elsewhere.

"Is that the guy we saw at the bar last night?" She nods in the direction of the home's smoky front door.

"What guy?" I feel my chest tighten at the thought of Levi. *That has to be who she is talking about.* "That guy is a prosecuting attorney. Only firefighters, and occasionally police officers, come to these types of scenes."

Paige insists. "I'm telling you. That's him."

I look up from my camera's blurry viewfinder, and what

appears to be an exhausted Levi Winters comes into focus. He steps out onto the home's dilapidated front porch and uses the back of his hand to wipe ash away from his forehead. My mental prayers, saying, "Don't look this way," do not work—his eyes lock on mine immediately, sending his arm up in a wave.

"Actually, you're right," I say, waving back. I quickly look back at my camera, trying to distract myself by adjusting its audio levels.

"I think he's coming over here." *Paige seems much more interested in the hot attorney than in learning to operate a camera.*

With each step Levi takes towards us, my heart thumps harder and harder. He's wearing a winter coat and dark jeans, and his hair is mildly disheveled. I think about him outside of the courthouse. I think about him at The Highball. I think about how this is going to be my *third* encounter with him, and how, due to proximity, there's probably going to be *many* more. Once he makes it close enough to see his smile and hear his voice, I feel butterflies swarming around in my midsection.

"Long time no see," he yells, hands cupped around his mouth.

"I didn't know you moonlighted as a firefighter," I say.

"Arson." He shoots a thumb over his shoulder. "We think someone did this on purpose. I'm going to be prosecuting the case."

"Is this on the record?" For work purposes only, I make eye contact with him.

Levi shoots me a grin, walking closer to us. "Just between you and me. And—"

"Paige," she reintroduces.

Levi squints his eyes, appearing to look guilty for not remembering. "Paige. I'm sorry. I'm terrible with names. But I do remember that this is Noelle."

I know that he's just trying to make a statement, but once I hear him say my name, it sends a shock right down through me. I try to hide a smile, but I can feel it appearing on my face anyway. I let it happen. *What's the worst thing a smile can do?*

"So what *can* you tell us, Attorney Levi? How about an interview?" I motion the WJDN microphone in his direction.

"I'll have to do one of these eventually." Levi anxiously runs a hand through his hair. "I guess this is what I signed up for."

"Paige will do the interview," I say. I'm thankful to use *her* as a scapegoat to take the attention off of *me*. "First interview for both of you. Sounds like a learning experience. Deal?"

"Deal," Paige says confidently.

"Deal," Levi repeats nervously.

I hand Paige the WJDN microphone, and she holds it in the direction of Levi's vocal projection. I watch as both of them become nervous. I figure that it's time to give *both* of them my pre-interview pep talk. I step out from behind the camera and face both of them.

"Here's the good news. This *isn't* live. You could accidentally say *shit,* and it wouldn't matter. This can all be edited. Just take a deep breath. No pressure, okay?"

"Okay," they say in unison.

"Anddddd…*action.*" I clap my hands in front of the camera lens, pretending to be a movie director with a clapperboard. I take my position behind the camera and make sure Levi is in perfect composition for the shot. *He's even cute through the lens.*

Paige clears her throat. "Okay, first question. Can you say and spell your first and last name, and give me your title, so we have it correct for the graphic?"

"Levi Winters, prosecuting attorney. L-e-v-i W-i-n-t-e-r-s."

Paige swoops a blonde chunk of hair off her shoulder. "What can you tell us about this investigation? What do we know so far?"

"Yeah." Levi stares down at his shoes for a moment. He looks back up at Paige when he seems to be ready. "The fire broke out around 8:00 this morning. We're at...I think... 311 Walnut Avenue in Joyfield. The house had major fire damage in the upstairs back bedroom, where we believe this fire started. One person was sent to the hospital for smoke inhalation, but should be fine, from what I'm told." He scratches his forehead. "What am I forgetting?"

"Can you say anything about the arson thing?" Paige whispers.

"Good job," I tell her from the sidelines.

Levi laughs at our commentary. "Hang on, I have to be serious," he says, clearing his throat. "Noelle, if there appear to be any signs of me smiling, can you edit that out?"

"Nope." I clap in front of the camera for effect. "Andddd... .action again."

Levi goes back to seriousness. "We do believe that one individual started this fire intentionally. But that's all we can say at this point, pending an official investigation."

"A soundbite is a soundbite," I say. "See, you're both professionals."

"You both make it easy," Levi says, appearing to be relieved.

Paige lowers the WJDN microphone away from his face.

"Thanks for being my first interview," she says. "Besides college, I guess."

"Anytime." Levi motions towards the house. "I'd better get going. I'll see you both soon, maybe at The Highball."

"Thanks," I say without emotion.

Levi turns and walks towards the smoking home, crouching under a line of caution tape to get to the other side. He pulls a small digital camera out of his pocket and continues taking photos of the interior.

Paige leans into me. "I think he likes youuuu," she sings.

"He does not," I reject. "He's an acquaintance."

"I think you like himmmm," she sings again.

I roll my eyes while trying to restrain a smirk. "You're fired."

Six

THE WIDE SHOT

I pull into the driveway of my pale blue, cape cod style childhood home and put the car in park. The structure looks so peaceful with my mom's Christmas wreath on the front door, the snow blanketing our front lawn, and the little battery-operated candles glistening in each window.

I grab my purse, wallet, lunchbox, oversized water bottle, and phone while choreographing practical maneuvers to fit them all into my arms. Once I'm standing outside of the car, looking like I need a shopping cart to carry it all, I kick my driver's side door shut with my foot.

I begin my waltz to the front door of the Fenwick Headquarters. It's a performance that resembles Rachael Ray on her old cooking show— carrying all her ingredients from the fridge to the countertop in one trip. But instead of juggling milk cartons, dried spices, glass bowls, and fresh vegetables, I'm squeezing my daily necessities close to my chest.

I make it into the mud room and set my bags down. I see my parents both sitting in their respective living room recliners.

"I'm home," I yell to them.

"Hi, honey," my mom says, glancing over at me. "I liked your outfit today on TV. That color looks really good with your hair."

"Thanks," I say, walking further into the kitchen. I can smell the concoction of cinnamon sticks and orange slices that my mom boils on the stove for aroma purposes only.

The kitchen is decorated in my mom's favorite 2000s Tuscan Italian theme. Stereotypical chubby Italian chefs with thick, black mustaches stretch across the room— from the figurines on the countertops to the designs on the place mats. The decor looks like it's straight out of a magazine.

"Hey, my buddy wants you to do a story for him," my dad says, looking up from his newspaper. "Something about his sister's cousin's son's baby?"

"Give him my number," I say flatly. I'll add it to my notebook. But whatever the story is about, I know Bill will just consider it to be a *story for a rainy day.*

The walls of the downstairs of my house are plastered white. The countertops are beige. A bouquet of red fake flowers sits in the middle of the dining room table. As I look around, I still can't find the one thing missing from the Fenwick household.

I squint my eyes in confusion. "Where's—"

"Here I am!"

A dark-haired girl pops out from behind the kitchen table, jazz hands waving high towards the ceiling. She wears a giant grin on her face. Even though she's only about five feet tall, her presence takes up the whole room. She has the same dark hair as I do, but hers is pin-straight (with no frizz). This girl is my little sister. The heart and soul of my life. My mini me with Down Syndrome.

"Delilahhhhhhh!"

"Noelleeeeeeeee!"

She runs over to me and gives me a tight squeeze, and we sway from side to side. I can smell her fruity shampoo, which matches her fruity perfume. She's wearing a green sweater, baggy jeans, and white fuzzy socks. In her arms, I feel like I'm home inside of my *actual* home.

"Hey there, Delilah," I sing.

Delilah sings directly into my eardrums. "What's it like in New York City?"

We've been singing these lyrics to each other ever since the song came out, but it has brought on an entirely different meaning since I went to New York City for my internship. While I loved every minute of living there, it was nothing compared to the joy Delilah brings me when I come home from work. The thought of leaving her for New York City again someday — more *permanently* than before — makes me want to break down and sob my eyes out.

"How was your day today?" I ask, motioning her into the den. It's a tiny, separate living room off the kitchen. *We always need some privacy for our conversations away from my parents.*

"I have tea," Delilah says. She folds her arms across her chest as if she were physically withholding the information from me.

"That she is soooo excited to tell you about," my mom shouts from the other room.

"Mommmm," Delilah groans.

My eyes widen. "What's the tea?"

We take our usual seats on the couch together. The cushions, perfect for napping, are covered in a blue-and-white plaid pattern. There are coffee and pasta sauce stains on the armrests, but we rest our arms on them anyway. I give Delilah my full attention.

She bobs up and down with excitement. "I got the job."

I drop my jaw. "You got the job?"

"Mmmhmm." She rests her hands under her chin in a dramatic fashion. "The manager called me today."

"Congratulations!" I grab her shoulders as a feeling of gratefulness fills my chest. "I am so excited for you. I can't wait to come there and get coffee!"

"We are so excited for our little DD over here," my dad shouts from the other room. "The Fenwick girls both have big girl jobs."

Delilah rolls her eyes. "I got a present for you."

"Yeah?"

She runs to grab a plastic bag that she hid behind the TV. I can't help but smile at her joy. When she comes back and hands it to me, I open it to reveal a bright green *Brew For You* t-shirt. I run my hand over the soft cotton material.

"Did you steal from your employer *already*?" I joke.

Delilah smiles. "I had to get my uniform there today, so I bought this for you."

My mind flashes to Bill rejecting the story I pitched about this place earlier today. Seeing the excitement on Delilah's face creates an ache deep within my chest. I can't believe someone wouldn't *want* to do a story on a place like this. Yes, I secretly wanted to interview Delilah. I knew she'd get the job. But I don't understand how anybody could turn this story down.

"Thank you," I say, holding the shirt up to my body. "It will fit perfectly."

"I will learn how to make an americano," Delilah says.

I have made my coffee drink of choice an *americano* ever since I got millions of them for Hilda Harrison at The Sunrise Show. I always wondered whether my family and friends secretly wondered why I had changed to such a strong, bitter taste after ordering the sugariest drinks on the menu for so many years. Would I prefer a caramel macchiato? Of course I would. I don't even actually *like* americanos. I just drink them as a tribute to Hilda Harrison.

"I'd love an americano," I half lie. "I really would."

I walk up the thirteen beige-carpeted steps leading to my childhood bedroom. These were the steps I used to sprint up, but now I slowly trudge.

I become face-to-face with my purple, plastic doorbell that hangs in the shape of a princess crown on the outside of my door. The words *Noelle's Room* written in purple puffy paint at the bottom of it had started to peel off over the years, so it now displays something that resembles … *Elle's Room*. It's me. *I am Elle now, apparently.*

I quietly shut the door behind me, resting my back against it to take a deep breath. I close my eyes to cut out the visual stimulation that the day has brought me. I make it to my final dwelling place. *I was home.*

I sit at my childhood desk — covered in sparkly paint and sharpie marker remnants — that holds the mirror I get ready at every morning. There are hearts written in red lipstick on the corners of my mirror, and even some sparkly gems that I must have gotten in an arts and crafts kit. Maybe *someday* I will have an adult-looking get-ready area. But with my current salary, that day is *not* in the near future.

I organize my work bag, throwing away my old gum wrappers and putting my lipsticks back in their intended pouches. I come across my notebook, and slide my fingers up and down its New York City skyline. I take a shallow breath. *I miss it there.* This notebook lived there, and so did I. It feels like a million years ago.

I open to the first page and see my *Acceptance Speech.* I think about the dozens of mornings I spent in New York reciting these words. Performing them. Acting them out. In my pajamas with my hair in a messy bun, staring into the mirror like I was staring out into a crowd of thousands of people. The navy blue ink still shines. While I still don't know exactly what I was supposed to be accepting, I appreciate the manifestation of each sentence.

"I can't believe I'm standing in front of you all tonight accepting this award," I whisper to myself.

It all comes back to me. I envision my shoebox-sized apartment. I picture my view of the old Catholic Church and Sip City Wine and Spirits. I hear the horns and sirens that kept me awake at night. I think about Eliza, and how we were just two girls from two random small towns who happened to be trying out their dreams at the same time together. I want it all back again. *Someday.* I want some version of my past to become another version of my future.

I continue reading in a whisper. "If you had told me — back when I was just a little intern fetching coffee at The Sunrise Show in New York City — that I would someday be the show's morning anchor, I would have never believed you. That's why this award proves so many things: full circle moments are possible, you can achieve anything you set your mind to, and following your dreams *does* pay off in the end."

I decide that if I really want these words to come true, I need to *see* them more often— more often than when I'm just flipping from page to page filled with *dead* story ideas. I crease the page and start to tear it out from top to bottom, slowly to avoid ripping the thin paper. It comes out as a single solid piece.

I open the junk drawer in my desk and find some old tape. I tear off a piece and tape the *Acceptance Speech* to my mirror. I take a step back and stare at it, putting my hands on my hips to assess the placement. Looks good. Constant reminder. *Where it needs to be.*

I read the last line to myself in the mirror, grabbing a bottle of hairspray and lifting it up towards the ceiling. I think of The Sunrise Show. I think of Hilda Harrison. I think of Westerfield Apartments. "This goes out to all of you at home!"

I continue reading the rest of my mysterious *Acceptance Speech* to myself.

> *I've dreamed of this moment since I was a little girl in Joyfield, Ohio. I never knew what I wanted to be when I grew up, but I always knew I wanted to be a writer. When I landed on journalism in college, I knew that it was for me. Not so that my face could be on television, but so that I could share important stories with the masses. For every person I interview, they are trusting me to share their story with the world. I am the person who holds their hand, guiding them as they take that step up onto the platform to share their voice. I am simply their catalyst. I am the vessel through which these people can connect with you, the*

viewers at home. This is my life's work. Highlighting the good. Holding those in power accountable. Trying to help people who need the spotlight shone on them. Supporting free speech and the importance of the First Amendment. Transparency. Trust. Truth. I am so grateful for this award and for knowing that I am, in fact, striving to do this each and every day. Thank you again for this award.

I don't know when. I don't know how. I don't know what the steps look like to get there. But I will make it back to The Sunrise Show someday. *I will be reading this speech somewhere, someday, somehow.*

Seven

THE DOUBLE SHIFT

"I have an idea," I whisper to Paige. "Follow me."

We are in the WJDN News dungeon — a.k.a. *the garage* — organizing our camera equipment and charging our batteries. There are half a dozen cubbies in here filled with all of our stuff. The noon newscast is broadcasting live in the room next door.

Paige follows me through massive wooden doors that lead into the studio. We walk on eggshells as we enter the huge room, wincing with every step. We pass the giant Hollywood mirror with those flashy light bulbs and the rickety table — home to curling irons, eye shadow palettes, and crinkled suit jackets — and catch sight of the live broadcast.

"Are you sure we're allowed in here?" Paige whispers.

"No," I answer honestly. "Look in there."

The floor is a deep, sparkly navy color. The letters W-J-D-N are illuminated on the back wall behind the anchor desk in yellow, similar to those in the newsroom. It's no comparison to The Sunrise Show, but there's nothing like the feeling of a news studio, no matter how big or small it is.

"Stay with WJDN News as we follow this investigation," Ed announces into the camera. The overhead lights reflect off his overly-sprayed hair.

Ed Sterling is a household name in Joyfield. It seems like he's worked here for 80 years, even though he's probably only 45. I remember watching him on TV when I was little, and even asking for his autograph when I saw him at a restaurant. *Everybody knows his name.* His black hair is slicked back on the sides of his head, and while it's not visible on camera, you can definitely see traces of foundation on his face in person.

"We're going to turn it over to Chief Meteorologist Ruby May for a check of our weather forecast." Ed turns to camera three. "What can we expect for the rest of the day?"

Ruby walks in front of the green screen, her strawberry blonde curls bouncing with each step she takes. She's wearing a black dress with dark purple flowers, and a pair of heels that make her four inches taller than she really is.

"Good news, we can expect more sunshine today." Ruby stretches her arms out towards the green screen. "Another cold front is movin' through the southern part of the region later this week, so that means there's a high chance it will snow again soon."

"Is she reading off of anything?" Paige whispers to me.

"Nope," I say. "She ad-libs. Pretty impressive, right?"

I explain to Paige *why* Ruby is pointing at a green-painted wall. I tell her that our producers put the weather graphics in behind the scenes, so Ruby is really pointing at *nothing* in real life. I never understood how meteorologists do it. For the number of people who call me a *weather girl* out in public on a daily basis, I could never actually be a *weather girl*. It's a job that takes a lot of skills that I don't have.

During my explanation to Paige, the show goes to a commercial. The monitor starts broadcasting an advertisement about how you can buy the newest viral, ultra-absorbent cleaning towel. Ed leaves to get up for an apparent bathroom break without even saying hello. He just shoots a little hand wave in our direction before whistling away.

Ed was never intentionally friendly. With new reporters coming and going out of WJDN every *two* years — like a revolving door that never stops swinging — he probably figures that meeting anybody new would just be a waste of time. He's probably worked with thousands of reporters in his tenure. Deep down, I don't blame him. *We'll all be leaving from here soon enough.*

"Hey, y'all." Ruby's heels click against the sparkly floor as she runs over to us. "Is this the new girl?"

"This is her." I motion towards Paige. "Meet Paige Martinez, new girl."

"Love your accent," Paige tells her immediately.

"I figured you'd be able to tell that I'm not from here," Ruby says. "Moved here from Nashville, Tennessee, a few years ago for my first meteorologist job."

"Ruby gets up insanely early," I explain to Paige, looking at the old-fashioned clock on the wall. "What time again?"

"I start at 5:00." Ruby presses her eyebrows together, mentally recounting her daily timeline. "I get up around 3:00 to drive into work. Then I have to do my hair and makeup. I don't just wake up like this."

"You must drink a lot of coffee. Or energy drinks," Paige

says.

"I love me a caffeinated beverage. And an alcoholic one too." Ruby looks at the clock. "Speaking of, I'll be at The Highball later if y'all wanna come join me."

"I could do that," I say.

Paige looks at me. "Me too."

"Great," Ruby says. "I gotta get behind the desk. Talk to y'all later."

Paige and I start tiptoeing back to our cubbies. The difference between the glamour of the studio and the scariness of the garage is alarming. It's like moving from Hawkins to the Upside Down within a matter of seconds.

"I don't know how she has all that energy," Paige whispers.

I shake my head. "You have no idea."

* * *

Once we get to The Highball, Paige and I walk into the entrance together. We are still in our news reporter dresses and full-fledged makeup, causing some heads to turn and look at us. I always wonder if people here think to themselves, *how do I know those girls?*

"Do people ever recognize you?" Paige asks, squeezing her way past the bar.

"Sometimes," I say, squeezing between two barstools. "But usually, if they know me, it's only because they know my parents. Or my sister. Or someone in my family."

"Hey, Fenwick!" A man waves.

I wave back. "See?"

We find seats at the bar, and I hand Paige a greasy menu. "They have the best pizza here," I say, immediately flipping to the *carbohydrate* section.

"I could go for some pizza," Paige says, fixing a fake eyelash with her pointer finger.

I open the drink menu. "But what I would *really* like is a Cosmopolitan."

"Did somebody say Cosmopolitan?" The voice comes from under the bar, and while I know exactly who the voice belongs to, I know that Paige is in for a surprise.

A disheveled Ruby May pops up to a standing position. Her strawberry blonde curls are now tied up in a messy bun, and she is wearing a Highball t-shirt. A damp towel rests in the grasp of her right hand.

"Wait, what?" Paige looks at us with speculation.

"Made a mess of vodka on the floor, spillin' a shot. Floor is all sticky now, just cleanin' it up." She wipes a bead of sweat from her forehead with the back of her hand.

"You work...*here too*?" Paige looks at me, and then at Ruby, and then at me again.

"Didn't you tell her?" Ruby wedges a stack of napkins between the salt and pepper shakers in front of us.

"I wanted her to find out for herself." I point at Paige. "She'll take a Cosmo too."

Paige ignores the fact that I had ordered a drink for her and sticks out a hand at her side in uncertainty. "When you said you'd see us at The Highball tonight, I thought you meant you were meeting us here as a *customer*."

Ruby rests a hand on her hip. "Most people are just as surprised as you are."

"Not only is Ruby May WJDN's chief meteorologist, but she's also The Highball's chief bartender," I say in a fake announcer voice. "She delivers the weather forecast from

5:00 to 1:00 during the day, and delivers Cosmos from 3:00 to 11:00 at night."

Paige's eyebrows are still furrowed. "How do you get enough sleep?"

"Sleep doesn't pay the bills." Ruby fills two tall glasses with ice. "WJDN pays my student loans. The Highball pays my rent."

I've found that working a second job is common in the news industry, and if I didn't live at home with my parents, I would be doing the same. There are always journalists on online forums and Facebook groups asking questions like, "Best part-time jobs for busy news reporters" or "How to make passive income while working a full-time job." It's a necessity. But it's also a necessity not to tell your *news boss* that you're doing it.

"So, what other secrets are you guys not telling me?" Paige rests her chin in her hand, visibly craving more insider information.

Ruby measures out two shots of vodka and tips them into our glasses. "I make more money in tips *here*…than I make hourly at the news station."

"If you want to change your hair color, you have to ask management," I chime in.

"Luckily, I always plan on being a fake blonde," Paige says.

Ruby tilts her head in thought, while also tipping some ice into our glasses. "Your personal days don't roll over to the next year. You have to use 'em, or you lose 'em."

"I made that mistake last year," I admit. "Nobody tells you that because they just want you to *work* those days. That's why *we're* telling *you*."

Ruby slides my Cosmo across the sticky bar and into my

hands. "If you quit before your contract ends, you have to pay the company, like, thousands of dollars," she says. "It's a scare tactic to keep you here on your worst days, even when you want to quit."

I take a sip. *Strong.* "They say safety first, but they don't mean it. They'll send you somewhere where a shooter is still on the loose. Always stick up for yourself," I say.

Ruby holds a glass towards the light, checking for any smudge marks. "Request your vacation at least *one* month in advance, or it won't get approved," she adds. "Also, you can't take more than one week at a time."

I bite the inside of my cheek, trying to rack my brain for secrets to tell Paige. *Things that I wish someone had told me.* "Oh, I know." I swivel my bar stool towards her. "Lots of unintentional…*or maybe intentional*…sexism in this business. Ed Sterling could complain about something, and it would be seen as *constructive.* I could complain about the *same* exact thing, and I would just be known as a *bitch.*"

Ruby starts to fill a glass with beer on tap, making sure she achieves just the right amount of foam. "Always ask around to see what your male counterparts are making," she says, finishing up her perfect pour. "We had a guy reporter here a while back who was making *ten thousand* more than us. For no good reason, well, other than the fact that he was a *man.*"

"Oh, another thing." I take a long sip of my pink colored drink. "If you get a creepy message from some creepy dude on social media, immediately block them. Don't even entertain it for one message."

Ruby laughs. "And if the message says *one attachment,* spare yourself the nightmares and just *don't* open it. Trust me, you don't want to see what it is."

"Speaking of social media," I add, tapping my chin in thought. "You can write an award-winning story, produce hard-hitting investigative journalism, and deliver a picture-perfect script...and you'll *still* have some internet bully message you about how *ugly* your outfit was that day."

"Love when that happens," Ruby says. "One time, I was broadcasting for an hour straight when a winter storm was comin' in. All I got in my inbox was an old woman telling me that I needed to lose weight."

"You? Lose weight?" Paige asks, shaking her head in disbelief.

"Oh, believe me, I've heard worse." Ruby folds her arms across her chest. "People are always nitpicking in the comments."

"We don't get overtime," I blurt out, as soon as I've thought of another piece of insider information. "One time, Bill just told me to *work faster.*"

"This place is *my* overtime," Ruby says.

"You guys are making me want to chug this," Paige says, pointing to her drink. "Should I quit now or later? Well, apparently now I can't quit, or I'd have to....*pay them?*"

I laugh, but I start to feel bad subconsciously. I don't want to *scare* Paige away from the job that we all truly love so much. I just feel like it's my duty as a *veteran* reporter to educate the incoming newbies on what they can expect. What they have to watch out for. What they can get taken *advantage* of.

"We don't mean to be talking about this negative stuff in front of you," I clarify. "We're just transparent. We want you to be as informed as possible."

"We still love our jobs," Ruby assures, wiping the counter with a dirty rag. "It's just important to know...what they don't *want* you to know."

Ruby leaves our little area to wait on the other patrons at the bar. She shoves a loose curl into her messy bun and slings a towel over her shoulder, hungry for her next tip. Paige and I sip on our drinks, taking in the subtle cigarette smell. Even though the place is now non-smoking, it still lingers in the walls, *and I don't think it will ever truly leave.*

"Can we talk about money?" Paige whispers to me.

"Of course." I smile deviously. "I'll tell you everything I know."

Paige sets her drink back down on the sticky bar. "Bill wouldn't negotiate my salary any higher than $28,000. Is that normal?"

"Mine was $27,000. You beat me."

Paige frowns. "What do other people at WJDN make? Do you know?"

I crunch on an ice cube that I grabbed from the surface of my drink. "Myra and Nate probably make about $25,000. It's not fair, but if you're not on camera, you make less."

"That isn't fair," Paige says. "What about Ed Sterling?"

"Since he's the main anchor and has worked here forever… I'd say he probably makes close to $80,000."

"What?" Paige slaps her hands on her thighs. "How fair is that?"

"It's not," I admit. "But the idea is that he worked his way up the ranks. He started out as we all did. Even though back in the day, he had a camera person. It was much easier for *him* than it is for *us* today. But still, it's about seniority."

Paige stares down at the wooden bar, taking it all in. She motions towards Ruby, who is now pouring a beer out of the tap. "How much do you think she makes?"

"Probably $35,000?" I whisper. "She had to get extra education to become a meteorologist, so she has a lot more student loans than I ever did."

"Ugh, student loans," Paige groans. "I'm still in my grace period. I don't have to start paying them back yet, and I'm taking advantage of it for as long as possible."

I sip the last tablespoon of alcohol out of my glass. "I had a journalism professor who once told me that being a journalist means you're *poor* and everyone *hates* you." I raise my glass. "Welcome to the club."

Eight

THE RUNDOWN

"I'll have one americano," I tell Delilah. "With cream and sugar."

Delilah is working behind the counter at *Brew For You*, wearing a bright green apron and a matching visor. This job *had* to have been made for her, since *green* just so happens to be her favorite color in the world. Her work attire now matches her bedspread, room decor, clothes, and phone case.

"Coming right up," she says, grabbing a cup.

I look around the large loft, taking in the coffee shop vibes. The green employee uniforms contrast against the dark wooden floors and beige colored walls, decorated with paintings and patterns of coffee beans. Another employee is restocking the baked goods display, which is filled with various flavors of cinnamon rolls and scones, as well as seasonal, holiday-inspired Christmas cookies. *Hell, I want to work here, too.*

I watch as Delilah makes my fancy coffee. She then walks back to the counter and hands it to me. "Here you go," she says proudly.

"Thanks, sis." I know I'm going to burn my tongue, but I take a sip anyway. "It's soooo good." *Dammit*. I did burn my tongue. I guess I'll do anything for Delilah.

"When are you going to do a story on us?"

The question comes from a large man with muscles popping out of his *Brew For You* shirt. He's taking a coupon out of the cash register when he flashes me a cheesy grin. His arms are covered in tattoos, and he looks too scary and bulky to be working at a place like *this*.

"I'd love to," I say honestly. "I tried already. Just have to get my boss on board—"

"Your boss wouldn't want to do a story on *this* place?" He lifts his palms towards the ceiling, moving them around to showcase the interior.

"My boss only likes stories about *bad* things," I joke. "If it bleeds, it leads. So, if someone gets *murdered* here, expect a story first thing."

The man shoots a hand out at me with a laugh. "Mike Mason. They call me Manager Mike. Nice to meet you. At least you'll be a returning customer here, at least."

I look at Delilah. "I guess I have to be." I cupped my warm americano in my hands. "This one right here is my little sister."

"DD is your little sis?" Manager Mike motions to her. "She's one of our favorites."

"Ours too." I look up at the exposed bulb light fixtures hanging from the ceiling, giving off a modern industrial vibe. "I always wanted something like this design for my future kitchen. I love this place."

"Did it all for him." Mike motions to a scrawny, dark-haired boy piping icing onto cinnamon rolls in the back kitchen area.

"Are you talking about me again?" The boy says from a distance, not even bothering to turn around.

"No," Mike teases. He raises his eyebrows. "You're the inspiration for this place, how could I *not* be talking about you again?"

The boy seems to be about Delilah's age. He has dark hair, just like Mike, and thick-rimmed black glasses that frame his brown eyes. When he walks over to join our conversation, I can see Delilah start to blush.

"This is my son, Anthony." Mike squeezes his shoulders with his strong hands. "Now we work together all the time."

"I've had enough of you already," Anthony says with a dramatic eye roll.

Delilah lets out a loud giggle that she doesn't even try to hide. *I can't help but laugh at the interaction.*

"Hellooooo," three voices sing in unison from the entrance of *Brew For You.*

It's Myra, Ruby, and Paige— all sleepy and hungry and uncaffeinated before their shifts at work. *I may or may not have bribed them with free drinks to meet me here this morning.*

"Noelle, it's your friends," Delilah says, beaming at them from behind the cash register.

"*Our* friends," I correct her. "They're your friends, too."

Myra gets a mocha latte and an oatmeal cookie. Ruby requests a hot tea and an everything bagel. Paige orders an iced caramel latte with whipped cream and a chocolate chip scone. Out of the goodness of my heart, and the fact that I *want* them to support my sister, I pay for all of them.

Delilah makes all of their drinks, and Anthony fetches all of their baked goods. *I love watching them work together behind the counter.*

The four of us sit down at a rectangular wooden table near the window, where we have a great view of the tiny snowflakes falling to the ground. (We also have a great view of Delilah, who is already counting out her jar of tip money.)

"It's like a romantic movie," Ruby says, staring out the window.

"In that case, I'm ready for a hot man to come in here and sweep me away," Paige says. She takes a bite of her whipped cream using her green straw. "Any day now."

"Not sure if you'll find that here." I take a sip of my americano, taking in the warm vibes of Hilda Harrison's signature drink. "Anyone going home for Christmas?"

"I wish," Myra scoffs, taking a bite of her cookie.

"I'll be in front of the WJDN green screen on December 25th," Ruby adds.

"Same," Paige says. "I mean, not at the green screen. But I'll be working somewhere."

I smile at them deviously. "I'll be working, but I'm already technically *home...*"

"Not fair," Myra says with her eyebrows squinted together. "Really not fair."

"I know, I know," I defend. I slide the sleeves of my sweater over my palms. "When's the next time you're all planning on going home?"

"January," Myra says. "I'm going home to Virginia Beach just for a long weekend. Using my floating holidays from working Thanksgiving, Christmas, and New Year's Day."

"My birthday is in February," Ruby says as she raises her

hand. "I'm going home for a few days. Gonna go bar hoppin' on Music Row in Nashville with my college friends."

"Bar hoppin' on Music Row," Paige repeats with a southern twang. She giggles and puts a hand up to her mouth. "I'm sorry. I just really like your accent."

"I don't take offense," Ruby says with an intentionally *exaggerated* southern accent.

Paige takes a bite of her scone. "Bill actually let me have a few days off in March. I'm flying home to San Francisco for my high school friend's wedding."

Myra's eyes widen at the announcement. "How did the new girl get time off so fast? Does PTO not, like, accrue anymore?"

"I just asked, and he said yes." Paige shrugs. She crumples up the edge of the green place mat closest to her. "I was just as surprised as you are."

"Maybe he's learning that he has to start being *nicer* to his employees in order to keep them," Myra says.

"So, little Miss Noelle." Ruby rests her chin in her hand. "When's this contract up? Are you gonna be leavin' us soon?"

"I still have six months," I say, sticking out a hand. "Don't pressure me."

I look over at Delilah, who is pouring coffee into a travel mug. It feels like a sin to discuss this topic in *her* presence. Leaving her *again*? I know Delilah is fine without me. She has her own life, her own friends, her own job. She doesn't *purposefully* make me feel guilty for having dreams and plans. I just put it all on myself.

I love Delilah, and I don't want to know a world without her. But if I want to get to New York City again — this time to play the long game — I have to get a move on. I have to start figuring some things out. Sure, I could stay at WJDN for a few more years. *But is that only putting off the inevitable?*

"You should figure out what your stepping stone stations are if you want to make it back to New York," Paige says, folding her arms and sitting back in her chair. "We can help you."

"How long would that take?" Ruby asks. "To get back there?"

I rest my hand under my chin. "Let's see. I'm currently at market 150, and New York City is the number *one* market in the country. So, at that rate, I have 900 more years."

"Virginia Beach is market 44," Myra chimes in. "It's a huge jump, but it's a second job for a lot of reporters. My friend from college just got hired there after working somewhere else, similar to Joyfield, before that."

Ruby takes a sip of her tea. "Nashville is 26. Could be your next stop after that one."

"The San Francisco Bay Area is market 10." Paige takes a bite of whipped cream. "There was a reporter at the station I grew up watching who made it to New York after working in the Bay Area for just a few years. So, it's a possible jump from there."

"I don't know," I say.

"I got it." Ruby grabs a pen out of her purse, slides the nearest bright green paper place mat directly in front of her, and starts drawing.

"What are you doing?" Myra asks, observing from a distance.

"Creating a masterpiece," Ruby shoots back.

I watch as Ruby writes the names of their hometowns from left to right on the placemat — Virginia Beach, Nashville, and

San Francisco — with a line connecting them.

"She's drawing a map," Paige observes. "Like Dora. God, I loved Dora."

"Here you are." Once her sketch is completed, Ruby turns the placemat around to face me. She taps the drawing with her finger, staring me dead in the eyes. "Our *hometowns* can be your stepping stone stations."

"I like it," Myra approves.

"One, two, three," Ruby says, pointing to each city with the tip of her pen. "It's the perfect plan. A road map from the *small town* to the *big city*. These are the stops in between."

"Interesting," I noncommittally play along.

"You could come with *us* on our trips to go back home," Myra says. "You can see if you actually *like* these places. If you actually *want* them to be your stepping stones."

I shake my head. "I couldn't intrude on you guys—"

"Mine would be your first stop, even though the beach sucks in January," Myra says. "But regardless, Virginia Beach in January…*check*."

"My birthday weekend is gonna be so fun," Ruby says. "I would love it if you came down. Nashville in February… *check*."

"You can be my wedding date!" Paige gasps in excitement, striking me in the arm. "You know, since I don't have a plus one anymore. San Francisco in March…*check*."

"How much time *off* do you guys think I have?" I stare at the map drawn on the placemat. "Actually, how much *money* do you guys think I have?"

"Bitch, you live at home with your parents," Myra says, rolling her eyes dramatically. "You're basically rich."

Paige turns the map to face her. "This is actually starting

to look more like *Eat Pray Love* than Dora the Explorer."

"But instead of Italy, India, and Bali— it's Virginia, Tennessee, and California," Myra jokes. "Glamorous."

"I could use some of my sick days. I haven't used one since this summer." I lean in and take a closer look at the map. "But this is *a lot* of days to be sick."

Myra starts counting on her fingers. "Migraines. Period cramps. Vomiting. Flu. You can always say you have the *shits*. That one always works like a charm."

Paige narrows her eyes. "What do we *call* this plan?"

Ruby tilts her head up at the ceiling in thought. "How about...*Noelle's Soul Search?*"

"Too mushy," Paige says, tapping her chin. "How about... *Noelle's News Journey?*"

"Eh," Myra says, taking a sip of her drink. "From a producer standpoint, this kind of is just like a rundown. Like, a rundown of a show."

I tap my foot. "How about *The Rundown?*"

"I love it," Ruby says. She turns on a fake TV announcer voice. "Tune in to watch *The Rundown* and see where Noelle Fenwick goes next."

Paige lifts up the map and brings it closer to her face. "It's like each of these stops, these cities, are just *blocks* in the rundown," she says. "Like the A Block, B Block, C Block—"

"Look at the girl fresh out of college, knowing her broadcast journalism terms," Myra teases. "So, you did learn something!"

"I like the news symbolism," I confirm. "Let's go with that."

Their hometowns do look like three pretty good, reasonable rungs on the news market ladder to help me reach the top. Plus, with the girls, I have connections with all three of them. If I'm going to have to spend the next few years of my life bouncing from station to station anyway, it would help if I were at least *familiar* with them first.

I look up at Myra, Ruby, and Paige and raise my empty coffee cup. "*The Rundown*, here I come."

Nine

THE LOWER THIRD

"You guys have to hear this," Myra says from her computer.

"I'm good," Nate shouts back. "No need."

"Listen," she commands. "I'm reading this article online from somewhere in Oklahoma. A state senator verbally attacked a reporter during a press conference. He didn't address her question — which was something about his alleged involvement in a bribery scandal — and instead just called her *inadequate* and *ugly*. How messed up is that?"

"Seriously?" Paige swivels her chair around to face her. "Is that even allowed?"

"That's what politicians do when they want to take attention *away* from the issue at hand," I explain. "They do it intentionally. It's a tactic."

Paige tilts her head. "It's a way for them to *avoid* the topic?"

"Changes the headline," Myra adds. "Now the story is about what the state senator *called* the reporter. The bribery allegations are out the window for today's news cycle."

"That's not fair," Paige says, shaking her head. "Isn't the free press about holding those in power accountable?"

"Exactly," I say with a sigh. "Things are taking a turn for the worse."

"Getting the public to believe the news is *biased* or *untrue* is also a tactic," Nate adds from the assignment desk. "But it goes against what we believe in as a country. The First Amendment supports free press and free speech. Making viewers *doubt* that is scary and dangerous, in my opinion."

"And there's nothing in it for *us* to be biased or untrue," I explain. "We couldn't be, even if we tried. We'd get sued. News organizations would get sued. *Everyone* would get sued. So, that argument is invalid. We're just here to ask questions and report the facts."

"And if you don't like the facts, *too bad*." Myra stands up in solidarity. "Just because you don't like something, doesn't mean it's fraud. Don't shoot the messenger."

"We're just the messenger." I point to my chest. "That's why people get mad at *us*."

While staring at my WJDN computer monitor, I begin to hear the strumming of guitar strings coming from the stairwell. This is a telltale sign that David is working. The melody grows louder and louder, until it's inches away from the back of my head. I turn around and see the wooden guitar across his body. *It's the most David thing I've ever seen.*

Today, he sings the lyrics to *Have You Ever Seen The Rain* in his soft, raspy voice. Midway through the first verse, he stops and peeks into Bill's office to make sure he isn't in there. I'm assuming that he isn't, because David continues strumming and singing all over the newsroom. I watch as he walks from desk to desk like a rock star walking across a stage.

I'm looking at a timeline of unedited video clips on my desktop for a two-minute package I'm working on. I'm in a rush to export the sequence before the show, but when he passes by my desk, I give him a high five like the *groupie* I am. Since Paige's permanent desk is now right next to mine, she follows suit, high-fiving David as if they're friends, even though this is their very first interaction.

David gives off seventies-rock energy: cool, relaxed, and just a *little* bit stoned. Being in his presence is like being in the eye of a hurricane: a calming spirit in the midst of the newsroom's chaos and mayhem swirling around us at all times. I wish I had his calm demeanor. He never gets worked up. On his final strum, Paige and I applaud.

"You're really good," Paige says. "Who are you?"

"Nice to meet you, new girl," David says. He pulls up a tattered swivel chair from the empty desk behind me and sits beside us. "I'm David Fenwick."

Paige looks to me with confusion. "Fenwick?"

"He's my uncle," I explain. "My dad's brother. And no, he did *not* get me a job here."

Nate overhears my statement from the assignment desk. "Bullshit," he coughs dramatically into a closed fist.

I dismiss his accusation with a laugh. "David is our master control operator," I explain. "Presses a bunch of buttons. I don't really understand what he does every day."

"*Nobody* knows what David does every day," Nate teases.

I motion towards his guitar. "But he's really a guitarist. That's who he really is. A rock star just *posing* as a master control operator."

David twirls his class ring around his pointer finger and

motions towards Paige. "You don't really want to hear the story, do you?"

Paige nods her head. "Anything to *not* do work right now. Go on."

David crosses one leg over the other. "After high school, I moved to New York City to play guitar. It was in a rock band called *Taste*. Parents weren't really happy about it, and my mom almost disowned me for going. But it was my dream. I toured the world for about *two* years, then came back home. Got a real job, and decades later, here I am."

"I don't know why you left that life," I say. "Sounds like *the* life."

"Same kind of thing as your dad," David says. "My brother, Dominic. He wanted to become a professional photographer and work for National Geographic. Was gonna travel all over the world and run his photos in the magazine. But he decided that wasn't the life he wanted after all, I guess. Now he works in finance here in town and does photography on the side. The Fenwick boys are like boomerangs, I guess. We always come back."

Paige folds her arms. "So every Fenwick lives in Joyfield?"

I watch as David's eyes glance at the tiny wooden picture frame — encapsulating the man holding the diploma with the long ponytail — on my dusty desk. It's still leaning up against my speaker, right where I had first put it when I got my job at WJDN.

"Not all of us," David says. He motions to the photo with his pointer finger. "Noelle ever tell you about that guy sitting on her desk?"

Paige leans over and looks at the picture frame, eyebrows knitted together. "I always wondered who that guy was. He's cute."

"That was my…*other* uncle," I say, looking back at the brown eyes in the picture. "My dad is Dominic. You just met David. This guy was Daniel. They were the Fenwick *triplets*."

"You're a triplet?" Paige asks him.

"Technically, yes." David runs a hand through his hair. "But now I'm just a twin."

"You'll always be triplets," I reassure. "Even if the third one isn't exactly…*here*."

Paige nods in understanding. "Dominic, David, and Daniel. The three D's."

"That was the name of *our* childhood band." David looks up towards the ceiling as if there's a projector shining up there, playing out all of his favorite memories. "We had a garage band together in middle school. We called ourselves the *3Ds*. I was on guitar, Dominic was on drums, and Daniel was our singer— he was the only one in the family with a *voice*."

I tie my hair into a low ponytail with a rubber band I find on my desk. "I would pay money to see footage of that. Especially my dad on drums."

"We had to persuade him to take the role," David admits. "He just wanted to call himself our publicist and take photos the whole time."

Paige hesitates before speaking. "What happened to Daniel?"

David hesitates, then sighs. "Car accident. He was hit by a drunk driver right before his college graduation." He points to his photo in the tiny wooden frame on my desk. "That was his last real picture. Got it just a few weeks before he died."

"What did he want to be?" Paige asks.

"He wanted to be an actor." David smiles to himself, looking down at the ground. "He was graduating with a degree in theater. Which was always funny to us, because he was a jock in high school. Real manly, big muscles, deep voice. But it was his passion, and his decision shocked us all at first. He was going to move to New York City after graduating. Had big Broadway plans. Eventually wanted to star in movies."

Paige turns to me. "You could have had a *famous* uncle?"

"Hey, *I* could have been the famous uncle," David jokes. "To be honest, out of the three of us, it was always Daniel. Your father and I gave up. We came back to town. We got normal jobs. But that was *never* going to be the case for Daniel. He was the one who was going to make it. He was going to make it *big* on the big screen."

I stare at my uncle in the tiny wooden picture frame, holding his diploma. There is so much hope in his eyes. It's like he was staring into his future when he was staring into the lens of the camera.

"I never actually met him, by the way," I add. "He died the year before I was born."

"Then why do you keep his picture there?" Paige asks. "Wait, that sounded super insensitive. What I actually meant was—"

"It's fine," I laugh. I look at the picture. "He's just kind of my reminder that life's too short, you know? He's my inspiration to go after my dreams. I always admired that he was planning on chasing after his."

I can't sing or act to save my life. I never could. But I can write. I can speak. Becoming a network broadcast journalist always seemed like the biggest goal that I could achieve with those two qualities. I know that Daniel would want that for me. If he were still alive today, I'm sure he'd tell me to go for it.

Since *he* couldn't achieve *his* dream, I subconsciously use his life as an inspiration to achieve mine. It's something I've discovered in recent years while trying to figure out my *why* for pursuing this crazy career. Thinking about Daniel's story reminds me that life is short, and it could all be taken away from you at any moment. I think he's part of the reason *why* I'm going for a career as big as I am. *It was always because of him.*

"What's going on here? I see a lot of sitting. A lot of sitting."

Bill Calloway suddenly appears in the newsroom — wearing his usual *Chandler Bing* wannabe sweater vest — walking at a brisk pace towards his office.

"Here we go," David mumbles under his breath, getting out of his seat to go back to the master control operator booth downstairs, where he *should* be.

Bill reaches his office within a few short seconds. "Noelle, story change. Ask folks how they feel about repaving 322. The road will be closed for two full months. Hurry out there, now."

I try to hide the annoyance in my voice. "Do we have a statement from officials? Who will we get interviews from?"

"No," Bill answers through the wall, answering only the first part of my question. "Door knocking. Take Paige."

"Door knocking?" Paige asks me quietly with a puzzled look on her face.

I remind myself to be as cheerful as possible around a new employee. "It will be fun," I lie. "Just follow me."

"Good luck, girls," David shouts over his shoulder.

Ten

THE (WO)MAN ON STREET

"Ready?" I ask.

"I'm a little nervous." Paige slides her hands up and down her thighs. She sits with the seat warmer on *high* in the passenger seat.

"You should be," I tease.

Once we arrive at the closest neighborhood to Route 322, I put our news car in park. We survey the area in front of us through our front windshield. The street has about 20 homes, varying in color and design but similar in size and height. Each house is an arm's width away from the next.

I unbuckle my seat belt. "All we're going to do is knock on doors. If someone wants to do an interview, great. If they don't, great. No pressure. Well, there is pressure, because we *want* an interview. We *need* one, actually. But if it doesn't happen, what are you gonna do?"

"Isn't it a little scary?" Paige unbuckles her seat belt and steps out onto the pavement.

"Most definitely," I say, slamming the driver's side door shut.

"Do you do this a lot?"

"No," I say. "Because sometimes I tell Bill that nobody wanted to do any interviews. I *lie* and pretend like I tried to knock on doors when I really didn't."

"Good insider knowledge."

Paige and I move to the sidewalk. The air is cold, and while the snow has stopped falling from the sky for the first time in days, there are still traces of it on the road. We start walking towards the first row of houses, careful with each step to avoid ice.

Paige motions to the news car. "Wait, aren't we forgetting the camera?"

"We don't need that right now," I whisper. "Walking up to someone with the camera looks too intimidating. They're more likely to say no. We'll come back and get it if we have someone who says yes."

"Got it."

The definition of door knocking in the news is the same as its title: knocking on doors. It's also called M.O.S. — meaning *man on the street* — when you try to get interviews from *people* on the street. It's to see how random people feel about random topics. It's usually a last resort when you desperately need an interview for a story. In this day and age, especially for a young reporter, I don't know how it's still allowed. But if Paige is going to have to do it eventually, I'm glad she's learning *how* from me.

I brandish my bright purple mase container at Paige. "Always strap yourself with one of these. I always keep mine in my coat pocket during the winter. Do you have any?"

"No," Paige says. "I had one in college—"

"I'll buy one for you," I say. "Think of it as a new reporter gift. Just remind me."

"Thanks," Paige says, looking guilty. She flashes her long, pink acrylic nails at me. "I do have these, though. I could, like, scratch them."

I admire the sharpness of their stiletto shape. "That works," I laugh.

An old man is sitting on his porch, smoking a cigarette. The house is pale yellow, and the roof shingles have started to fall onto his yard. Most of them are buried in snow.

I gesture in the cigarette man's direction. "Let's try that guy first."

We walk up to the home, careful to stay on the sidewalk. The man appears to be about 70 years old, with gray hair and glasses. He shoots us a threatening but confused look when he sees us walking up to him.

"Hi, sir," I say when we're still a couple of feet away. I am met with silence. "We're reporters with WJDN news. Are you familiar with the station?"

The man takes a drag of his cigarette. "Used to have a buddy of mine who worked there back in the day. Morning editor. I always used to watch it in the evenings, but now I don't like the stuff people are sayin' on there anymore. I don't watch it now."

I decide to change the subject in a positive direction. "We're looking for people to tell us how they feel about the Route 322 closure," I explain. "Since this is the neighborhood closest to it, I wondered—"

"I ain't talkin' to no news people." The cigarette man stands up and walks back inside his home. The door slams in our faces.

"And that's usually how it goes," I tell Paige. "And we didn't even have to knock on a door. Let's try this one."

We walk over to the green house right next door. Kids are crafting a snowman in the yard. We wave to them as we walk towards the porch, stepping up onto it and knocking on the door.

Moments later, a young woman answers, opening her door no further than an inch. I can see that she has brown hair, and that's about all. "Can I help you?"

"We're with WJDN—"

"Get the hell out of here. And stay away from my children." Once again, the door is slammed in our faces.

"And there you have it," I say. "Third time's a charm. Let's try one more."

We walk to a friendly-looking beige-sided house across the street. There appears to be no sign of life on the inside. I figure we can knock on that door, add one more house to our mental door-knocking count, and, in the words of that last lady, *get the hell out of here.*

Once we get there, I knock. Nothing. Paige knocks. Nothing. We turn around and start walking back to our news car, making it to the sidewalk. But when we hear the creaking of a door opening, we turn around to see a middle-aged man holding a gun in his hand.

"We were just leaving," I say calmly.

"Get your fake news asses off of my porch," he says.

His gun is pointed at the ground, his demeanor is nonchalant, and the look on his face is nonexistent. If somebody were to be standing in front of me with a gun, I would want it to look just like this. There is no harsh threatening, loud yelling, or quick motions. Just a slowness that screams: *just leave, and nobody gets hurt.*

Nothing comes to my mind except for the word: run. So, that's what we do. We spring back to our car. I hear the slam of the man's door behind us. We escape. *My purple mase is no match for a freaking gun.*

We make it back to the car and rush to get inside. I immediately lock the doors, put the car in drive, and start speeding away. Our breaths are heavy and loud. We are quiet for a few moments, soaking in what just happened to us. We make it to the highway.

"That was…kind of awesome," Paige finally says.

I look over at her in disbelief. "That was so totally *not* awesome!"

We are quiet for another moment, but then Paige smiles. "But…it was *kind of* awesome."

We both burst into laughter. "Get your fake news asses off of my porch," I mock, transforming my hand into the shape of a gun and holding it up into the air.

"Get off my lawn!" Paige tries to hide her laughter with her hand.

"I think he said porch—"

"And this fake news business," Paige says. "What do these people think we do all day? Figure out ways to make up lies?"

"I think that's *honestly* what they think," I laugh. "Can you imagine?"

"That sounds like a fun job."

Paige and I go back and forth, mocking the cigarette man, the mean mother, and the gun guy. "That's why you have to put your own safety first," I explain. "Bill just wants his ten-second soundbites from random people. He doesn't know what it *actually* looks like to get those soundbites."

Paige fixes a tangled eyelash in the passenger side mirror. "I'm really glad I have you to tell me all of these things," she says. "I mean, obviously, you *have* to train me. But like, all of the stuff they don't tell you. I appreciate you telling me."

"Just remember. Management would rather get the story than have you be safe," I explain. "They won't protect you. It's up to you to protect yourself."

I look down and see that my cell phone is ringing. It's an incoming call from Bill Calloway. "Shit," I say. I answer the phone through the dashboard screen of my car. "Hello?"

"Murder!" Bill screams.

"Murder?" I ask.

"Murder?" Paige whispers.

"Route 42. Highway. Coroner. Joyfield Running Trail. Go!"

We always make fun of Bill for communicating the logistics and limited information of incoming breaking news with randomized, unhelpful terms. He's known for hollering various nouns with no further explanation, like — *Fire! Murder! Accident! Ambulance! Police! Arrest!* — all in a frantic voice with his hands in the air. You have to give it to him. Bill Calloway loves his job. He loves the news, and he definitely creates a sense of urgency by spiraling everybody into a panic.

"So, no more repaving story today?" I ask.

"Scrap it," Bill says with a huff. "Come drop Paige off at the station. Some rule about no overtime for new hires. Then go back out there. I want 5:00 *and* 11:00 live shots."

"Okay," I agree, mentally accepting my fate. "I'll have her back soon."

"Hurry!" The phone hangs up.

As I drive Paige through the slushy streets of Joyfield, we discuss more of the *dos* and *don'ts* of being a young female news reporter in today's day and age. Once we reach the snowy parking lot of WJDN, I unlock my doors to let her outside. Her heels clomp onto the pavement as she steps out of the news car. The snow picks up just in time for *her* to go *home*, and just in time for *me* to go *outdoors*.

"Hope I didn't scare you off today," I shout out the window. Paige laughs. "Just a little."

After driving along Route 42 for a few minutes, I reduce my speed once banners of yellow caution tape come closer into view. I start to make out the silhouettes of police cars, ambulances, and fire trucks. Red and blue flashing lights illuminate the canopy of snowy trees above. I've slowed down to about ten miles per hour, and since it's just a long stretch of pavement ahead of me, I'm not really sure where to go from here.

There's no pull-off area. Just one lane heading north and one lane heading south. Two solid yellow lines separating between them. I know that the running trail is around here somewhere, but I don't even know how you'd get to it from here. I need to park somewhere around here. I decide to make *my own* pull-off area.

I find a patch of snowy grass on the side of the road and decide *this* will be my news car's temporary home for the night. I won't be able to find anything closer. It looks to be a few feet wide before it descends into a cliff.

I pull off the brim of the road, bouncing up and down with my news car, and settle into my makeshift parking spot. I put my car in park and take a deep breath. I made it...*technically*.

I'm parallel to the highway, and my driver's side door is just about five inches away from it. Dangerous? Probably. Do I have any other options? No.

I get out of the car and stand on a tiny patch of dirty snow. I stretch my arms up into the air, looking up into the quickly dimming sky. It's about to get dark within the next hour or so, I predict. I am about a quarter mile from the caution tape, and looking around, this is really the *closest* I could get to the action.

I can see first responders traipsing through the woods, wearing heavy coats and boots. Beams of light from their flashlights move across the trees and brush like mini spotlights. Ambulances and firetrucks continue to have their lights flashing. Law enforcement officials hold notebooks and cameras as they talk among themselves, trying to piece together what happened. I observe and take it all in. *This will be a long night.*

Eleven

THE LIVE SHOT

The numbers 10:45 appear on my car's electronic display, signaling that it's time to get this 11:00 live shot over with and go home.

I step out onto a patch of dirt, shutting the car door behind me. I look up into the Joyfield sky. The only light source comes straight from outer space itself: the moon and the stars. It's peaceful, in a way. Other than the fact that I am outside, on the side of a highway, alone. I know I can get attacked by an animal, or a human, for that matter. But at least it's so dark that nobody even knows I'm here. I walk around to the trunk and start unloading my tripod, camera, and microphone onto the snowy ground.

I assemble it all close to the driver's side door. It's a little trick I've picked up over the years— if I ever have to make a quick escape during a live shot, I can just hop in my car and drive away faster than if I were, say, the whole way across the street from my car. So, inches from the driver's side door and steering wheel, I find myself again. *Safety first.*

I get out my LED light and stand, plug in the batteries, and toggle the switch to on. Nothing. *That's weird.* I toggle it off and on again. *Still nothing.* I take out the batteries, blow on them for whatever reason, make sure they're going in the right way, and try to turn them on again. Nothing. *Dammit.* No light?

There is no possible way I can be on television, in this particular instance, without an additional light source. The moon and the stars just won't do. The shot wouldn't be anything other than pitch blackness. They have to cancel my live shot. There's no way around it. Ed Sterling would have to read my script for me. I pick up my phone and call Bill.

"Hello?" Bill sounds confused on the other line. I imagine him at home and in bed, but when you're the boss, you're the boss at all hours of the day.

"Hey, sorry to bother you," I say, embarrassed that I have to call him at this hour. I look up at the stars. "I'm getting ready for my live shot, but my light, or batteries, or whatever…is not working. To sum it up, I don't have any light. I was wondering if Ed could just read my script."

Bill pauses for a moment before speaking. "You didn't charge your batteries?"

"Yes, I charged them," I say with a breathy exhale. "I don't know what the problem is, but something isn't working." *I want to say that it's probably because this equipment is from the eighties.*

"You still have to be the one to read your story," Bill says. "It shows that we have a reporter with boots on the ground there."

"But you can't see me," I explain. I grab my LED light as if it would magically start working.

"Streetlight?"

"There aren't any—"

"Can't you just turn your car lights on?"

I look at my news car. "You mean, like my headlights?"

Bill's voice sounds tense. "Position your car headlights on you. That will light it up."

I stand in front of the car and notice that the headlights would only come up to my stomach, if that. In no way will they illuminate my face. I can barely see where I'm walking, let alone assess anything in front of me.

"I don't think they're tall enough—"

"You have no other option." Those are Bill's last words before he hangs up the phone.

I'm left with a phone up to my ear with nobody on the other line. My top and bottom teeth grind up against each other as I lower the phone back into my pocket. *Fine.* If he wants the shot to look like this, then that is what he'll get.

I grab all of my camera equipment from beside the driver's side door — sad to leave my safe haven escape route (even if it's only by a few inches) — and move it all in front of my car's headlights. This is a first. *I look like I'm trying to run myself over.*

I shove my earpiece into my left ear and connect the wire to my phone. I dial into the control room. It's a few seconds before Myra can see me on her giant screen back at the station. I'm relieved when I hear the sound of her voice.

"Testing, one, two— jeez, Noelle. What kind of a shot is that?"

I laugh out of anger while toggling my microphone's switch to on. "My lights stopped working, so this was Bill's genius idea."

"Couldn't we just have had Ed—"

"Read my script? I tried." I kick a rock across the street. "So, if this is what he wants, this is what he gets."

Myra pauses for a moment. "Those headlights are lighting up *your* headlights…just perfectly."

"Doesn't it frame my boobs and belly in the most flattering way?" I stick out my chest and pretend to model. "Can you even see my face?"

"We're just seeing what our old male viewers want to see," Myra jokes. "You have about five minutes, by the way."

I look past my camera and into my car's windshield. Before college, I always assumed there would be a cameraman behind my camera, not a news car that would ultimately serve as my light source. Not only that, but *nobody* on the other side. I didn't realize how many times news reporters are out there alone. Spending their days alone. Meanwhile, the public thinks we have people doing our hair and makeup.

As I wait for Myra's final countdown, I hear a faint, soft crunching of leaves behind me. It's far off into the distance, but the sound is prominent enough to raise my shoulders to my ears. *Maybe it's just a deer. Maybe even a cute little bunny.* I dismiss the thought. I convince myself that it's nothing. It has to be an animal. *I am in the woods, after all.* But as the crunching grows closer, the more uneasy I become.

"Three minutes," Myra says.

I turn around, but I can't see anything through the blackness. I start to grow tense. More crunching. My chest tightens. I realize that it can't be an animal, because the movement sounds like it's the result of *walking...*from two human legs. My heart pounds. *I'm almost done. Just ignore it. I'll be out of here soon.*

"Hey," a voice whispers from behind me.

"Holy shit!" I yell breathlessly. A shock wave pulses through me. This is a person. A *human* person. A man.

"It's okay, it's okay," the voice says in a panic. "It's Levi. It's Levi. You're okay."

Levi? I clutch my heart with one hand and grab my knee with the other. "What did you do that for?" I'm out of breath like I had just run a marathon.

"I was over on the scene, and I saw the WJDN news car, and—"

"You decided to scare the shit out of me?"

"I guess so, yeah."

As he moves closer to me, I watch as he transforms from a dark silhouette to a real person. The car headlights cast a beam on his body. He's wearing a tan overcoat, which is professional considering the time of day and the scene. His hair is messy, and there's a trace of dirt on his forehead. Something about his presence makes me feel relieved. Relieved that there's another person in the vicinity, but also relieved that it's *him.*

I still try to catch my breath. "I thought you were a deer. Then I thought you were a human. Well, you are a human, but like a bad human. I—"

"I'm sorry for scaring you," Levi says. He motions to the woods. "I was taking pictures of the scene because I'm prosecuting this case. First official case, by the way. I saw a news car over here, so I wanted to make sure you were safe, in case it was you—"

"Two minutes," Myra says through my earpiece. "Is that—"

"Yes," I tell Myra.

"What?" Levi asks.

I point a finger at my camera. "I'm talking to Myra."

Levi squints his eyes. "Is Myra the name of your...*camera?*"

"She talks to me through this," I explain, pointing to my ear. "She's back in the control room at WJDN. She can see me on her monitor, and now you, too, apparently."

"I'll get out of the way—"

"You can stand right there." I point to the passenger side of the news car. "Be careful not to block my only light."

Levi walks to the passenger side door and plants his feet firmly into the ground. "Good?"

"Perfect," I say. "I have about one minute by now, probably."

Levi looks intently at me and folds his arms. "Why does your car—"

I look down at my body. "Have its headlights shining on my torso? Don't ask."

We stand in silence for a few moments...for longer than what feels comfortable...as I wait for Myra's cues. I look up at the sky. Levi shuffles a pile of leaves around with his foot. I never thought we'd be in each other's presence for this long...*silent*. But here we are.

"Thirty seconds," Myra says.

"Thirty seconds," I repeat back to Levi.

"Thirty seconds to action," Levi says.

I laugh. I can't tell if the butterflies in my stomach are from pre-show jitters or from the handsome man staring back at me. *Or from the fact that I was just scared half to death a few minutes ago.* I'm guessing that it's all of the above.

"Stop looking at me." I dramatically turn my head away

from him, holding up a hand to shield the side of my face. I hide a laugh. "I feel awkward with you staring at me."

Levi shoots out his hands at his sides. "What the hell else am I supposed to look at right now?" His line dimples form as a result of his grin.

"Ten seconds," Myra says.

"Ten seconds," I repeat to Levi.

"Is it too late to ask me to do a live interview?" Levi says.

"Damn, I should have thought of that," I whisper.

I wipe the last piece of smile off my face just in time for the WJDN News fanfare introduction. I hold a finger up to Levi to signal: it's time. I stare into the camera lens, even though I can feel a pair of eyes glued on me. *Maybe he's just staring at my headlights.*

"Noelle Fenwick is live at the scene now," Ed Sterling announces. "Noelle, can you tell us more about what happened there tonight?"

"Go," Myra follows.

"Good evening, Ed. I'm standing along Route 42 in Joyfield, where law enforcement officials say an alleged murder took place this evening. As you can see here behind me—"

As I read the rest of my script aloud, I realize that I'm not actually thinking about the *words* I'm saying. I'm thinking about the *cute guy* staring at me. I feel embarrassed. Like I'm reading a paragraph of a textbook out loud in middle school, knowing that my crush is listening. My lips are moving, but my mind is on what's in front of me. I can't think about the story. I can only think about my *audience of one.*

"The victim's identity has still not been released to the public, pending notification of their next-of-kin. We will keep you updated on this breaking story as it develops. Noelle

Fenwick, WJDN News." I stare into the lens of the camera for a few seconds.

"You're clear," Myra says. "Have fun with the hot attorney."

I smile knowingly into the camera at Myra without saying anything out loud to *confirm* this new nickname. I like it. *The hot attorney.* That's exactly who Levi is, after all. He is an attorney, and he definitely is hot. I disconnect my earpiece.

Levi claps slowly and dramatically. "Bravo."

I laugh and roll my eyes. "Applause?"

He runs a hand through his hair. "I never saw the real thing. Like in person."

I take my camera off its tripod. "You didn't need to stand here and watch me."

Levi looks up at the dark sky, tree branches obstructing its beautiful view. "Somebody should be with you."

"My thoughts exactly." I crouch down and condense my five-foot tripod back down to one foot. "Especially when your light breaks, and your boss just tells you to use your car headlights."

He points to the WJDN news emblem on the car's hood. "That's what was going on here? I thought you were just trying something new. A creative lighting moment, maybe."

"A creative lighting moment does not include me shining a car headlight on my boobs." I cringe at the fact that I just said *boobs* in front of the hot attorney.

He then noticeably looks, well, *at my boobs.* "I think that could be—"

"What?" I prompt him to finish his sentence. "Tell me what that could be."

"Nothing," he laughs, looking towards the ground. "I'll take it back."

I stand back up from my crouching position and get a little dizzy. I can't tell if it's from the low blood pressure of standing too quickly or from Levi's continuous presence. The darkness outlines his body, showing just how tall and thin he is, yet how muscular.

"You can seriously start heading back," I say. "I'm fine here."

"I'm not leaving until you leave," he says, leaning his back against the news car.

"You really don't—"

Levi shakes his head in disapproval. "I am not leaving here until you leave."

"Fine." He watches as I carry my equipment towards the back of the car.

Levi opens the trunk for me. "That's a lot of stuff," he says.

"It's not the best quality." I plop everything into the trunk and slam it shut. "They don't invest in the good stuff."

Levi and I are now facing each other, about one foot apart. He is staring intently into my eyes, not pressured to look away. "They invested in you, didn't they?"

"Very funny." I feel an electric shock pulse through my midsection, but choose to ignore it. "Why were you out here taking pictures so late at night?"

"The guys were here late at the scene." He runs a hand through his hair, still not backing away from me. "I just got carried away, I guess. Since this is my first case. I was just getting ready to leave, I swear. I just wondered about the news car. Figured it was you."

I move a piece of hair away from my face and tuck it behind my ear. "I *am* the only reporter in Joyfield, pretty much."

I notice the outline of Levi's jaw. His eyes are soft and kind, and knowing that they're staring back into mine makes my stomach feel uneasy. He's tall, appearing to tower over me. I like that he's a little older. Not by much, anyway. I like being in his presence, and I'm happy that he's here right now. The worst part about this moment is that I know it has to end soon.

"Can't believe they let you out here like this." Levi motions towards the woods.

"Yeah." I look up at the sky. I notice the little dipper among the various formations of the stars. "Thanks for staying here. I really appreciate it."

"Anytime, seriously." He moves back towards the accident scene. "You can call me any time. For an interview or to protect you in situations like this, I suppose."

I open my driver's side door before getting inside. I try to hide a smile that makes its way to my cheeks anyway. "I'll keep that in mind."

Twelve

THE STAND UP

"How much longer does happy hour last?"

Ruby checks her imaginary watch. "Five minutes ago?"

"Damn," Nate says.

Ruby taps her pen on her notepad. "But I think I can make an exception for y'all."

It's karaoke night at The Highball. While Paige, Myra, Nate, and I sit around a table — in selfish anticipation of alcoholic beverages and cheap appetizers — Ruby is slinging drinks and taking orders. Having *her* wait on *us* all the time makes me feel guilty. But in addition to needing the money, I know Ruby really likes being a bartender. She's a social butterfly, and that makes me feel a *little* better about it.

We shout our orders to Ruby over the loud voice of an older woman singing her unique rendition of Shania Twain's *Man, I Feel Like A Woman.* She's on the tiny stage near the bar's entrance, holding a bulky microphone as a disco ball shines flashes of light on her.

"Cosmopolitan and a hot pretzel, please," I say.

"Margarita and chips and salsa," Myra adds.

"Miller Lite draft and jalapeno poppers," Nate says.

"Vodka cranberry and mozzarella sticks," Paige chimes in.

"Comin' right up." Ruby shoves her notepad into the front of her apron. Her strawberry blonde bun bounces with each step she takes back to the bar.

The four of us applaud when the Shania Twain wannabe's performance ends, and watch as she passes the microphone to her friend to perform Pat Benatar's *Love Is A Battlefield*.

"So, Noelle, how was your night with the hot attorney?" Myra smirks.

I cringe at the thought of her bringing this up to Nate and Paige. I don't want them to think our relationship is something that it's not. There is no relationship. We're just work acquaintances. Nothing happened, anyway. We just *happened* to run into each other during my live shot— and Myra just *happened* to have seen it unfold *live*.

Paige leans in towards me. "You spent the night with that guy?"

"No." I shake my head. "I did not spend a night with—"

"Sounds to me like you spent the night with him." Nate takes off his sweatshirt and slings it around the back of his chair. "I'm actually just starting stuff. I don't even know who you're talking about."

Myra rests her elbows on the sticky table. "Last night, when Noelle was doing her live shot, the hot attorney walked up behind her."

"Yeah, and he scared the shit out of me," I interrupt.

Myra leans in. "Turns out, it *was* the hot attorney. The one she met at the criminal trial."

"Yeah, Levi from high school," Nate says with an obvious expression.

Paige shakes her head in perplexity. "Wait, can somebody explain to me what happened?"

I roll my eyes. "When I was doing the story on that murder, Levi was at the scene taking pictures. He's prosecuting the case. He saw a news car and came over. He didn't even know it was me. He stayed for my live shot, and we talked. That's all. Literally nothing happened."

Paige is quiet for a moment before inching closer to me. "You like him," she says.

I laugh and shake my head. "I do not like him!"

"Then why are you smiling? Myra asks.

I scoff. "Because whenever somebody asks you *why* you're smiling, but you're not *really* smiling, you automatically *end up* smiling, even when you're guilty of *nothing*."

Paige folds her arms. "I mean, he definitely likes *you*. That's obvious."

"You think he likes her, too?" Myra asks.

"Enough!" I slam my hands on the table. "Our paths cross from time to time. That's it."

Ruby bun bounces back over to us, carrying our drinks and appetizers on a black circular tray. She lowers it to our table without spilling anything.

"Here you go," Ruby says, placing everything in front of us.

My mouth waters when I see my salty, hot pretzel. "Thank you, Ruby."

"Of course." She places the empty black tray under her arm. "Y'all need anything else?"

"Just for you to sit down with us," Myra says, dipping a chip into her salsa.

Ruby sighs. "You know I would. But I got a *second* job here to do."

"I"ll save a popper for you," Nate teases. He pops one into his mouth. "If there's any left."

"I get them all for free." Ruby motions back towards the bar. "Holler if you need me."

The woman's rendition of *Love Is A Battlefield* ends, and the jukebox transitions to generic background music. Nobody is next in line for the microphone.

"Guys, let's go now." I shove an edge of my hot pretzel into my mouth. "Let's get it over with. We have to."

"But I just got my chips," Myra says.

"What are we doing?" Paige asks as she stretches out a mozzarella stick.

"Come with me."

The stage is a raised platform — that a regular four-top table sits on any other night of the week — but on karaoke nights is transformed into a glamorous stage. Myra and Paige follow me to it, shoving our way through a sea of drinkers: from the regulars sitting on barstools to our left to the underage college kids sitting at tables to our right. We bring our drinks as props.

We step up onto its old wooden planks, and the karaoke-operator-guy hands us three microphones. The song *Nine to Five* by Dolly Parton starts playing.

I tilt my head in confusion. "We didn't pick a song—"

"Coming!" Ruby slings a damp washcloth over her shoulder, runs over to join the three of us on stage, and grabs another microphone from the karaoke guy. "I picked it."

The stage is not big enough for two people, let alone

four. We start bumping hips and singing along to the lyrics displayed on a small monitor on the ground in front of us. At the chorus, we start waving our hands in the air, hilariously unchoreographed from side to side to the beat of the music. I laugh hysterically. *Everybody is staring at us.*

The bell above the entrance to The Highball jingles. A few guys walk inside, single file, to fit through the narrow entrance door. Mid song lyric, my heart jolts. *This looks like the group Levi was in here with last time.* I follow each one of the men with my eyes. Not him, not him, not him. Then, at last, at the end of the line, it's no other than *the hot attorney.*

When his eyes rise up to spot me on stage, he immediately waves. I'm mortified. But I'm performing. This is kind of fun, albeit embarrassing. I'm not going to *not* sing and dance. So I continue my country rendition.

Levi watches while he stands in line at the bar for a drink. His hair is messy, and his eyes look tired, but he looks extremely handsome. I assume he just got off a long shift at work. I like knowing he's here. I like knowing that we're both here *together* at the same time.

I look extra good tonight, too. I actually washed my hair for the first time in a week *and* straightened it. It makes my hair look longer than it actually is. I'm wearing my black lace blouse and tight jeans— my stereotypical *going-out* outfit. It gives me an unusual confidence and power that I typically do not exhibit. But on this particular night, when I know that Levi Winters is watching me perform on a stage, I feel *double* the liquid courage I normally do.

Myra and I link our right arms together, taking sips of our drinks through the physical tangle. Paige mimics Ruby's spontaneously invented line dance, and I laugh at them. Paige and I sing into each other's microphones. Ruby and Myra twirl each other around like ballerinas. When the song ends, applause erupts through the air. We bow.

Ruby begrudgingly returns to the bar, and the rest of us walk back to our unassigned WJDN table. Our drinks are now empty. I glance at Levi as I pass by him, faintly mouthing the word *hi*, but not giving him any more attention. But without my invitation, he follows us back to our table anyway. He even goes one step further as to sit down next to us. *I can't get away from this man.*

"How's everyone?" Levi asks once he takes a seat between Myra and me. He's across the table from Nate. "Is this the only place you guys go?"

"I can't get these girls to go anywhere else," Nate says. I cringe at the fact that he calls us *girls*....as if we're *his girls*. We are as platonic a friend group as it could get, even though I'm sure Nate would date any one of us.

"That was some performance." Levi tilts his head in the direction of the karaoke stage. While the comment is aimed at all three of us, he makes direct eye contact with me.

"We try," I say. "It's a tradition at this point."

"I liked it," Levi says. His hazel eyes pierce into mine, sending a shock down through my midsection. "I won't hold you up. Nice to see you guys."

Levi walks back to his friends across the bar. He has the build of a swimmer: broad shoulders and a small waist. While I find him insanely attractive, I can't get over his free spirit and funny personality. It's something that I wouldn't have expected from someone in his profession, even though he's the only attorney I know. He just doesn't match the stereotype I have in my head— argumentative, stubborn, mean. Levi is none of those things. In fact, he is the polar opposite. *I want him to stay at our table.* But I watch as he walks away, and push the intense feeling deep down into my gut.

"You want to date the Cantner football player." Nate points his pointer finger and middle finger towards his eyeballs. "I can see it with my own two eyes."

"He's no longer the football player," Myra corrects. "He's the hot attorney now. Grow up."

As we resume eating our cold appetizers and sipping on *another* round of drinks, I begin my weekly journalistic interrogation: asking everybody else about *their* personal lives. It's true, I do enjoy asking other people questions. I love getting to know people deeper. But sometimes, I think it's a subconscious tactic so that they don't focus on me.

I ask Myra about Ethan. She tells me that they've been dating long-distance. I ask Nate about his dating apps. He tells me that he matched with someone new just this morning. I ask Paige about the boy who dumped her. She tells me that the distance has helped her to get over the breakup.

"Are you turning off your *reporter mode* now?" Nate asks. "I'm sick of the questions."

"That's enough questioning you all for today," I say. "More to come next week."

Myra slings her purse over her shoulder. "See you guys tomorrow. Not looking forward to this wake-up call."

"Early morning shift?" I ask.

"Same," Nate says. He puts his sweatshirt back on his scrawny body. "Even worse, since I have to work it with this one."

Myra scowls at him in rebuttal. "Goodnight, guys. Have

another drink for me."

Paige and I are the only ones remaining at the WJDN table. Ruby is still behind the bar, cleaning a spill with a rag. Levi is still over at his table with a beer in his hand. Most of his friends are gone. A majority of the barstools are now empty. Things are slowing down, and I can't stop yawning. I know that it's time for me to go home.

"Can I give you a ride home?" I ask Paige. "I need to sleep. I can't keep my eyes open."

"Ruby and I live a minute apart from each other," Paige says. She crosses one leg over the other. "She can take me home. Told me she would earlier today."

"Sounds good. I'll see you tomorrow."

I wave goodbye to Ruby as I walk past the bar. Levi is sitting with his back towards me, so I sneak quickly behind him. I rush through the door without him seeing me. *Mission accomplished.* I'm too tired to entertain possible feelings with the hot attorney right now. The Irish goodbye is the only goodbye I can handle tonight.

The cold winter air hits my face as I start walking towards the parking lot. It's not snowing anymore, but the wind feels like it's going to immediately crack my skin open.

With each snowy step I take, I think about Levi. It would be *dangerous* to start something with a work acquaintance, right? What if we dated, then broke up, and I had to continue interviewing him? There's no getting around interviews, either. No matter how much I don't like someone, if the story calls for it, you have to interview them. We wouldn't be able to separate ourselves. *Not as long as I'm still a reporter at WJDN and he's still the hot attorney in town.*

But it's not just about that. I could also be *leaving* Joyfield in a few months for a new job in *who knows what* city. Do I really want to see if there's anything between us — which could take six months to even figure out — and then I'd be leaving right whenever we'd fall in love? It's just bad timing. Bad timing and bad placement. *Workplace. Romance. Long distance.* Lots of words that don't add up.

I grab my freezing cold door handle and look back in the direction of The Highball before getting into my car. The neon beer signs in the windows pierce through the dark night sky. I think about all the memories this place holds for not just me, but everybody in Joyfield. All of the times I've spent inside of those four walls with past and present WJDN employees who have turned into my best friends. It's one of my happiest places with some of my happiest memories.

All my sentimental feelings are replaced by curiosity when I notice two silhouettes on the side of the building, near the dumpsters. *Maybe they're employees taking out the trash.* But these people aren't really moving. They appear to be talking. They're pretty far away, but as far as my eyes can see, the two people look like they're against the side of the building...*kissing.*

I take a few steps closer. *I need to see who these people are.* The more intently I look at them, the better my eyes adjust to the darkness. I hide behind a telephone pole and observe from a distance. I recognize that sweatshirt. I recognize that purse. It's a drunken Myra Cole and a drunken Nate Kerrigan.

Myra is pressed up against the wall. Nate is leaning against her, resting his arm above her on the concrete wall. Myra's lips are on his mouth. Nate has his hand tangled up in her hair. Myra's hand is up his jacket. Nate is reaching up under the back of her shirt. Myra Cole and Nate Kerrigan. *I wouldn't have guessed this if you paid me a million dollars.*

I tiptoe back to my car and get inside. I don't want them to see me, and I really don't want them to know that I saw them. I stare at my steering wheel for a few seconds. I feel like I can't even move. My heart is pounding, and I need more information. I want to run over there with my arms flailing in the air and say: *I got ya!* But instead, I drive away.

Have they been secretly dating, or just hooking up? Is Myra cheating on her long-distance boyfriend? How long has this been going on? Are they going to tell me about this? Were they even planning on telling me about this? *Next week's interrogation is about to be a lot worse.*

Or...I'll just keep this under wraps until one of them spills the beans themselves.

Thirteen

THE RECORD

"You're clear," Myra tells me.

"Good." I unplug my microphone from my camera. "How's it going?"

I just got done presenting a live report on the demolition of five blighted buildings in Joyfield. The snow-covered construction war zone behind me has been my backdrop for the last few hours. The population of our area has decreased from about 60,000 in the 1950s to about 20,000 today. That decline has resulted in hundreds of buildings in the Joyfield area being reclassified as, well, *abandoned*. Once bustling stores, banks, and restaurants are now neglected, deserted, and empty structures. Thousands of square feet of uninhabited space. It's a shame, really. People are moving out of Joyfield in search of better opportunities. *But in six months, I could become one of them.*

"Oh, you know," Myra says through my earpiece. She seems

completely herself. No traces of secrets or guilt in her voice. "It was a late night and an early morning."

"Long day for you." I know that Myra can see me on her giant computer monitor, so I throw my microphone in my camera bag to distract myself.

"I can't believe I'm still here," Myra says. "Bill said he'd let me out early but—"

"Did you have fun at The Highball last night?" I cringe *immediately* after I ask the question. So quickly. *Suspiciously quickly.* I clear my throat. "Sorry, did you say something?"

"It was okay," she says. "I had the worst heartburn from that salsa last night. They must use some secret ingredient. I haven't stopped taking antacids since I got here."

I can think of another type of heartburn she experienced last night.

"Nate usually eats most of them," I say, trying to bring him into the conversation.

Silence.

I decide to try again. "Speaking of Nate, he was looking at you kind of funny last night. Do you think he likes you?"

"I don't care who Nate likes," Myra says. "He's freaking annoying."

I succumb to the fact that I'm not getting anywhere with Myra today. "Bye. Have a good rest of your shift."

"I'll try."

My tripod clicks as I disconnect my camera. I arrange everything into my bag like a jigsaw puzzle — camera, batteries, memory cards, wires, microphone — and heave it all into the trunk of my news car. I run into the driver's seat as quickly as I can without slipping on the ice.

I'm shoving my cold fingers into the warm vents when I

notice I'm getting an incoming call. A call from someone I haven't heard the voice of in what seems like forever.

I put the car in drive. "Is this who I think it is?"

"Hiiiii," her high voice says on the other line. "How are you?"

My brain is immediately transported back to winter two years ago, almost to the day. The americano runs. The mid-afternoon Zara shopping trips. The late-night Taco Bell runs. The Sunrise Show. New York City. It's Eliza Swickley, and I could not be more thrilled to hear her voice.

"Oh, you know." I jerk my steering wheel to avoid hitting a patch of ice. "Currently driving through the snow. But you wouldn't understand."

"Guess where I am?" Eliza asks.

"Where?"

"The beach." Wind whips in the background of her call. "I'm off today."

"That's nice," I joke. "It's like negative twenty degrees up here."

"Can you hear that?"

"What?"

"Waves crashing," Eliza says. "I don't think I ever want to leave Florida. Screw climbing the corporate ladder. The only thing I want to climb is through sand."

I look out over the streets of Joyfield. The sun is setting, casting a beautiful orange glow over the distant mountains. "My climb might start pretty soon."

"Six months, right?" Eliza asks.

"What would happen if we just applied for reporter jobs in New York City right now? Do you think they'd just crumple up our resumes and laugh?" I ask.

"Don't even mention the words *New York City* to me," Eliza says. "When I hear the name of that city, it's like a punch in the gut. I miss it so much."

"I get that feeling too," I admit. "Best four months of my life. No doubt."

"How's work going for you?" Eliza asks.

"It's going," I sigh. "It's not the pitching, filming, interviewing, writing, and editing that's getting to me. It's doing it all in, like, a four-hour time frame."

"Dude, same." An ocean wave crashes against the sand in the background.

"I have to remind myself that Hilda Harrison started this way, too." I picture her sitting behind that beautiful glass anchor desk, fluorescent lights beaming in her face, with Christmas lights all blurry and colorful in the background. *It was perfection.*

"But did she?" Eliza asks. "All of the reporters had *cameramen* back in the day. Think about all the extra help they had. They weren't doing the job of five people."

"True." I turn down the street that leads to our local grocery store and post office. Their roofs are dusted with a powdered-sugar coating of snow. "If Hilda were trying to climb the ranks *today*, do you think she would have put up with it?"

"I'm not sure," Eliza says. "They had their own problems. No Google Maps, no cell phones, no digital....*anything*. I can't imagine what it was like to be a reporter back then. But still. Hilda was probably never out there *alone* like us."

"I don't know which is worse," I say. "No electronic maps or putting your life in danger."

"Speaking of that," Eliza says, laughing. "A guy ran after me on the sidewalk the other day. I just finished my live shot, and it was dark outside. I made it to my car and locked the doors just in time. It was like a literal horror movie."

"Last year, some guy came into the background of my live shot and started yelling profanities at me. I finished reading my script and just pretended like he wasn't there," I say. "Then, when it was over, I just grabbed my stuff and ran into my car. Ignored him."

Eliza groans. "My coworker was live the other day to cover a shooting with the shooter *still on the loose.* Running through the neighborhood that she was reporting in."

"One of these days, something is going to happen." I see my childhood home in the distance. The golden hour light looks so gorgeous against its pale blue siding. "It's a safety hazard. We could be attacked."

"I just think of New York when I'm in those situations," Eliza says. "It's the only thing that keeps me going. Knowing that it won't be this way forever, hopefully."

"Do you remember how early we had to leave to get there in the mornings?"

A gust of beach wind whistles on the other end of the line. "Sometimes, I'll wake up in the middle of the night to pee, and I think about how if I were still living in New York, I'd have to get up and start putting makeup on. But I just breathe a sigh of relief and go back to bed. I don't know how we did it."

"I'm so lucky that I work the day shift now," I say. "I was only a morning person for those four months, and that's just because I worked at The Sunrise Show."

"Do you remember what it was like to sleep through the night at Westerfield Apartments?" Eliza laughs. "Sirens and horns. One time, I woke up to people screaming outside. It was so loud. I don't know how we got any sleep."

"I don't think we *got* any sleep." I picture my little shoe box of a room. "Do you remember our late-night Taco Bell runs?"

"I still can't believe their Taco Bells had *alcohol*," Eliza says. "I ate so many quesadillas and packs of cinnamon twists."

"For me, it was the Oreo cake." As I pull into the driveway, more New York City memories come rushing to the forefront of my mind. "Remember when we went to get that psychic reading in that sketchy apartment?"

"I was told that I was an old soul," Eliza says. "I thought I was so unique. But then she said that *you* were an old soul, too. I didn't feel as special anymore. She must have told everybody the same things."

I put my car in park and stare at my closed garage doors. "Do you remember when we got on TV for like, two seconds, because we were in the background of that one interview?"

Eliza giggles. "I found the segment online the next day, so I took a screenshot of us in the background. I printed it out, put it in an old frame, and hung it in my room. It's like my little motivation to get back there someday."

I find a loose ponytail and throw my hair up into a messy bun. "Remember when the New York City marathon was happening the next day, but we didn't know, and we went to Little Italy to get pasta. The waitress asked us if we were *carb loading* for the big day. We were like, no, we're just *carb loading* in general."

Eliza laughs before she lets out a long sigh. "I miss it," she admits.

"So do I." I can see my mom through the upstairs window, folding laundry. "Want to plan a trip? A reunion trip? I think we're in desperate need of one."

"Yes, immediately," Eliza says. "When do you want to go?"

"Sometime in the spring?" I ask.

"We could go in May," Eliza says. "For our birthdays."

I forgot we both have May birthdays.

"That sounds great," I confirm. "It's as if I have unlimited amounts of money and time off. But hey, life is too short, right?"

"Right." Eliza sighs, and I think I can hear an ocean wave crash in the background. "New York City round *two*."

"I can't wait." I grab my purse, water bottle, lunch box, and about 800 other things from the passenger seat to bring inside. "I wish it were tomorrow."

"Me too," Eliza says. "Because I have a secret to tell you when we get there."

"Seriously?" I groan. "You have to tell me in person?"

"I have to show you," Eliza says. "I can only *show* it to you in person."

Fourteen

THE WRITER

Delilah is still awake when I get home, but my parents are sleeping. I can tell because my parents aren't on their respective recliners, and the lights are off in the living room. Like me, Delilah loves her alone time. I'm thankful that my parents let her have it.

I turn the corner to see a sleepy Delilah on the couch in the den, eating mint chocolate chip ice cream. The soft sound of Carrie Bradshaw narrating her upcoming Sex and the City article is playing on TV.

"Hey there, Delilah." I throw my coat on the arm of the couch and take a seat beside her. "Excuse me, are we doing this *without me* now?"

"I need to see if Carrie is going to break up with Aiden," Delilah defends.

"I think you know what happens," I say.

We've watched the show at least *eight* times through by

now. I think our obsession with the show *today* stems from my mom's obsession with watching the show *without us* at the turn of the millennium.

"I have some tea for you," I say.

"Tea?" Delilah says, with a mouthful of ice cream. She pauses the show. "Piping hot?"

"Piping hot," I reassure. I fold my right leg underneath myself and lean in towards her. "Do you remember Nate and Myra from my birthday party last year?" I pull out my phone and show her a picture of them.

"Yeah?" The blue light from my phone screen beams onto Delilah's face.

"Get ready for this." I lower my voice to a dramatic whisper. "They kissed."

Delilah gasps dramatically. "That's some piping hot tea," she confirms, placing her hands over her mouth. "When?"

"Just a little bit ago," I say. "I caught them when I was leaving The Highball. Can you believe it? You have to promise me you won't tell anyone."

"Promise Thomas," Delilah says, zipping up her lips and throwing away the key.

I rest my hands behind my head and close my eyes for the first time all day. "How's *Brew For You* going? Anthony seems nice."

"Stop." Delilah hides a smile by going in for another spoonful of ice cream. "He's Manager Mike's son. We cannot and will not date."

"That doesn't matter," I say. "Manager Mike would be happy. He loves you."

Delilah glances at the paused TV screen. She points the remote at it. "Can we—"

"Why are you changing the subject?"

"Stopppp." She sets her empty ice cream bowl on the end table beside her.

I kick my feet up next to her. "Fine."

The episode of Sex and the City ends, and Delilah clicks *next episode* to continue her binge. I missed these nights while I was away in the city where Carrie Bradshaw lives. Our FaceTime dates in the evenings weren't the same. There's nothing like this.

"Hey DD?" I look over to see the TV lights illuminating her face in the darkness.

"Yeah?" She doesn't even make eye contact with me. She just keeps staring at Aiden.

I roll my head back and look up at the ceiling. "I'm going to be taking some trips after the New Year. But I'm not, like, *leaving leaving.* I'm just going to be doing some little weekend vacations with my work friends."

"Why, because you hate me?" Delilah shoots the words at me with severe sarcasm.

"Very funny. I'm just going to see the hometowns of my work friends. Myra, Ruby, and Paige. I won't be gone for very *long* each time. Just little trips here and there."

"Fine," she scoffs. "But I have a life, you know. I can make my own plans."

I look over to her. "I love you."

"Love you too." She glances at me briefly before gluing her eyes back onto Carrie Bradshaw, who is holding a Cosmopolitan in one hand and a cigarette in the other.

I quietly walk up into my childhood bedroom, slinking past my parents' bedroom door to avoid waking them. I pick out a pair of fresh pajamas, which is my usual matching shirt-

and-sweatpants set from high school, and carry them into the bathroom with me.

My nightly makeup removal process is the bane of my existence. I dip a cotton ball into micellar water and wipe it over my left eyelid, then my right. I douse another one to wipe my nose, cheeks, and lips. With the amount of makeup I wear as a reporter on a daily basis — and the number of reapplications I make throughout the day — I need the number of cotton balls to remove my makeup that would fill an entire overnight extra-strength period pad.

I wash my face and dry it with my mom's sage green towel, stealing a dollop of her moisturizer. I look at myself in the mirror, noticing the traces of mascara that still remain under my eyes. *I look like a raccoon.* But I'm so exhausted. I'll spare another cotton ball and just blend it in with tomorrow's makeup.

The shower is hot and relaxing. The steam seems to melt into my muscles, erasing the tension in my shoulders. I decide not to wash my hair, even though I probably should, so I shield my bun away from the stream of water. I close my eyes and take a deep breath, letting the warmth run all over me. I see my mom's shampoo. My dad's bar of soap. Delilah's fruity conditioner. I take in the mixture of scents. The scents of home.

Once I change into my *alma mater* pajamas and get under the sheets, I stare up at my ceiling fan through the darkness. This is the same white ceiling I've been staring at for my entire life. I remember trying to find characters and images within its plaster swirls like a child looking for animals among the clouds. *How many more nights will I be staring up at this ceiling?*

The very *real* possibility of moving out within the next few months hits me. It feels like simmering water reaching the point of a boil instantly. It could be just six short months before I'm packing up and moving to another apartment— where I'll lie in a bed staring up at a *different* ceiling.

But then again, I could be here for a couple more *years*. It could be hundreds and hundreds of *days* before I ever see a moving box in my childhood bedroom. But either way, it will happen someday. It's just a matter of...*when?*

I tilt my head and look at the photo of Delilah and me on my nightstand. We're in Times Square, holding our arms up over our heads. My mom and dad stood on the other end of the camera, smiling at *our* smiles through the lens. They all came to visit me while I was living in New York City for a long weekend. We went to see Broadway musicals, The Rockettes, and the Rockefeller Center Christmas tree. That trip with the four of us was a dream. *A dream come true.*

Delilah absolutely loved *visiting* New York, but she was *heartbroken* when I originally moved there. She didn't want me to go. I promised her a nightly FaceTime— which we did every single night for those four months. We sang *Hey There Delilah,* and most times, we'd end up with tears in our eyes. We missed each other so much. I reminded her that it was just temporary. That I would be home soon. And just as I had promised her, I came back. But if I moved there for real someday, *I wouldn't be coming back.*

No matter how Delilah feels about it, I know that New York City is where I belong. It's where my dream job is. It's where my dreams are. It's the only way I can fulfill my love of writing— the love I've had since I first learned the alphabet. Writing news stories. Telling stories that matter. Uplifting shadowed voices. This is the path. This is the way.

I roll over on my side and think about my desire to write. I always liked writing research papers in middle school, fake newspaper articles making fun of my family members, and poems in my childhood diaries. There's something about the organization of words that settles my commonly overcrowded mind.

When I was in eighth grade, our old-fashioned, conservative English teacher, Ms. Rover — notorious for sending girls home early for wearing tank tops and short shorts — gave us an assignment on what we wanted to be when we grew up. It was a research paper followed by a PowerPoint presentation. *As if we had the life experiences we needed at that time to make such an informed decision.*

We went around the classroom to announce our future professions to the class. One girl said: *Doctor.* Quiet oohs and aahs followed her declaration. One boy said: *Lawyer.* A proud look formed on his face when Ms. Rover gave him an approving head nod. Another girl said: *Physical Therapist.* The students beamed at her with confidence. Nurse, dentist, accountant. Stable, normal, expected. Good pay, good hours, good choices.

"Your turn, Noelle," Ms. Rover said to me.

"Writer. I want to be a writer."

To my surprise, my announcement was followed by subtle giggles and weird looks from my classmates.

"What kind of writer?" Ms. Rover played along.

"I don't know yet," I admitted. "But I like to write. So, I want to be a writer."

The future doctor and physical therapist girls scoffed. The class giggled. No message of approval ever came from Ms. Rover's cherry-painted lips.

"Okay, moving on," she said instead, moving on to another student who claimed that he wanted to be a scientist.

I felt ashamed. Embarrassed. I wanted that look of approval, too. That look of: *wow, she's cool for wanting to be that.* I was never expecting anything other than a career endorsement from my peers and teacher. What was I thinking about saying that? What even is a writer, anyway? What jobs even constituted having the title of writer? And above all else, why did I choose to say it out loud? I wanted to take it back.

After class that day, the future doctor and physical therapist came up to me. This encounter revealed to me that they were the mean girls.

"You're stupid for wanting to be a writer," the doctor said.

The physical therapist chimed in. "You know you're not going to make any money, right? Don't you want to make money?"

Money. I never thought about the money until that moment. My parents always told me to do something someday that I was passionate about. Something that I felt I could make a difference doing. Something that I was good at and actually liked. I never thought about the money aspect of it. I just assumed that if I had a job, I would also be making money. That's what a job is for, right?

I skipped lunch to go to the library that day. I sat on a swivel chair in front of one of the outdated, chunky computers. They were considered outdated even back then. I typed "writing jobs" into the search engine. There's got to be something out there. A list of potential dream jobs appeared before my eyes. *I can still see it now.*

SCREENWRITER: Someone who writes scripts for movies

and television shows. Starting salary: $20,000.

JOURNALIST: A person who writes for newspapers, magazines, or news broadcasts. Starting salary: $20,000.

GRANT WRITER: Someone who writes grant proposals to secure funding for organizations and projects. Starting salary: $15,000.

No wonder they were laughing at me. At the time, I didn't know what a good starting salary was, but I knew those salaries didn't seem particularly high. I sat back in my library chair and gave it some thought. I thought about the mean girls and wanted to defend myself. There had to be some positives to going into a writing career.

Screenwriters who, over time, create successful television shows and movies end up becoming millionaires. Journalists who work for the network news level rake in the big bucks. Maybe even grant writers could make six figures, depending on the organization they work for.

It seemed that all careers in writing made you start by scraping the bottom of the salary bucket, but as you rose to the top, you could be more *financially* successful than any doctor or physical therapist would ever be. If I kept working hard enough, I could become richer than the mean girls someday. And based on their judgment, *they would never see it coming.*

It was that day that I formally decided to become a writer. Not just to prove the doctor and physical therapist wrong, but to prove myself *right*. I knew that whatever type of writer I chose to be, I would work my way up to the top. I'd make it big. *That* was the path that I ended up choosing for myself. I didn't know how, I didn't know when, and I didn't know why— but I would become a writer and share fascinating, important stories with the masses.

And now, I am faced with my next steps to do just that.

Fifteen

THE SOUNDBITE

The fleece blanket — that is usually draped over the back of my chair — is pulled tight over my shoulders as I stare at the editing software on my computer monitor. The temperature has to be in the negatives today, and the chill has infiltrated the newsroom. I can see little puffs of snow falling down out the window like cotton balls. I take a sip of my warm, shitty break room coffee (swirled with a nearly-expired Italian Creme flavored creamer that I stole from the fridge). I pretend to be in a coffee shop as the sweetness hits my lips.

The newsroom phone starts to ring.

"WJDN newsroom," Nate answers flatly. The caller speaks on the other line before he responds. "Oh, hey. Yeah, she's right here."

I turn my head to see Nate holding the phone out in my direction. Nobody ever calls the station for reporters *personally*, let alone for *me*.

"Who is it?" I whisper.

"Your lover." Nate motions the corded landline phone toward me again, with force and impatience. "Just come get it."

I'm working on a story about a severe power outage that hit the town next to ours. The wind knocked over dozens of power lines, leaving hundreds of people without electricity and water. After desperately trying to find an interview — yes, I door-knocked against my will — a little old lady agreed to share her story. *I think she just felt bad for me.*

I strip the fuzzy blanket off my chilly shoulders and walk the few feet over to Nate's assignment desk. My favorite pair of blue light glasses is still resting on the bridge of my nose.

I hold the phone up to my ear. "Hello, this is Noelle."

"Hey!" The deep voice on the other end sounds urgent at first, then tempers itself with the soft clear of a throat. "Hey. It's Levi."

I feel like I'm living in the 1950s. A gentleman caller contacting my workplace on our old-fashioned, spiral-corded landline phone to ask me on a date. I mean, I don't know why else he would be calling the news station. *What century am I living in?*

I try to sound cool and calm. "Oh, hey. How are you doing?"

Myra's dark eyes peer above her computer screen and squint at me. I roll my eyes back at her in a nonverbal effort to jokingly say: *Mind your own business.*

"They released the identity of the person who was killed the other night," Levi says. "I have all of the information. I was wondering if you wanted to do an interview?"

"Oh, for sure." I feel an electric bolt of lightning strike down through the center of my body. I don't know what I'm more excited about— the fact that I could be breaking a major news story, or the fact that I could be seeing Levi again. "When?"

"Today?"

Today. I clear my throat. "Yeah, I can meet you right now, if you have time?"

"That's great," Levi confirms. "Can we meet at the site?"

"Yeah," I say. "See you in a bit."

I hang up the phone and run over to my desk, grabbing my coat and keys.

"Where are you going?" Myra shouts.

I glance over sarcastically at Nate. "To go meet my *lover,*" I whisper.

Bill walks into the newsroom and eyes the purse over my shoulder. "Where the hell do you think you're going?"

I sigh. "Got an interview about the murder. Attorney with more information." *I wish I had made it out of here without running into his sweater vest.*

Bill rubs his palms together like an evil villain in a cartoon. "Find out how the person was killed. With a gun? With a knife? Was there blood everywhere—"

"Yeah, I got it." I turn and head towards the door. "I got it."

* * *

Driving along Route 42, I start to feel bubbles in my stomach. Light and airy, floating from side to side like one of those old desktop screensavers. I'm about to see Levi. I picture his soft lips. The thought of him makes me…*giddy.* Like a girl in elementary school having a crush on a boy for the first time. But I remind myself that I am not going on a date. I am going to interview this man. For a *murder*, I might add.

I find my makeshift parking spot on the side of the road and pull into it. The ground is more snow-covered than it was the last time I was here — when I substituted my car lights for studio lights — in the pitch black. I'm glad that now I'm here in the daytime. I put my news car in park. Now I just have to sit back, relax, and wait for Levi. *Bubbles.*

I check my teeth in the rear-view mirror to make sure there's nothing in them. But there can't be. All I've eaten today is coffee. *Coffee breath.* I reach into my purse and pull out a stick of minty gum. I start chewing, releasing the minty sweetness into my mouth. *That's better.* I take another look in the mirror and notice that my cold lips look…*winterized.* I slide my hand back into the same pocket where I retrieved my minty gum and pull out a light pink lip gloss. I apply it to my top lip, then my bottom, and then rub them together. Perfect. Gum and gloss. *What more could you need for confidence?*

I'm checking my pout in the mirror when the presence of a tall man looms in my window.

"Shit," I say, grabbing my chest. I roll my window down. "Do you love to scare me…here? In this specific location?"

"I'm sorry." His hazel eyes reflects against the sunlight. He points down the road. "Why are you parked all the way up here?"

I look around at our surroundings. Road, trees, snow. "I don't know where else to go."

"It's just down the hill a little," Levi says. "Not too far."

I follow Levi around to the back of my news car. Our feet are covered in about three inches of snow— the kind too fluffy to make a snowman with, but too heavy to actually enjoy shoveling. While the flurries have stopped, the frigid temperature remains. *At least I won't be sweating off my makeup today.*

I open the trunk, and we're faced with my oversized camera bag and lengthy tripod case. Both are embarrassingly dirty, with a great deal of wear and tear— thanks to the dozens of other reporters who used this equipment before me. *It's communal.*

"Thanks for volunteering to do this." I sling my camera bag over my shoulder.

Levi motions to my tripod case. "I can at least get that one," he says.

I ignore his request and grab it with my free arm. "I don't usually have help, remember?"

"You do today." Levi takes *both* off me— holding the camera bag with his left shoulder and the tripod case under his right arm. "I got it."

"You can't carry *all* of my stuff," I say, shutting the trunk shut.

"Yes, I can." In an act of rebellion, Levi starts walking down the hill ahead of me. "These aren't even heavy. Maybe you're just weak."

"I am not weak." I follow behind him, carefully stepping inside each one of his footsteps, thankful that he's clearing a path for me down this snowy hill. "I'm just small."

"Small is code for weak," Levi shouts over his shoulder. He's wearing the long overcoat that he wore on the first day I met him outside of the courthouse.

I can see that we're almost to the walking trail, but the trees and brush are getting more congested the further down we go. It's a terrain that you'd have to drive a quad down, and here we are walking down it. Even though I've lived in Joyfield my entire life, I've never walked or run on this trail before.

Probably because my neighborhood is the only place you'd ever need to do either of those things. It's quaint, peaceful, and spacious. *And with this murder, I'm glad I haven't had to be here.*

I wave a tree branch out of my face. "Are you sure you're not taking me down here to murder *me*?"

"I was. But you just made it weird, so maybe another day." He turns around and looks at me, my equipment draped all over him. "You good?"

"Yeah."

I can't help but laugh at the sight of him. The hot attorney is carrying all of my stuff. I wish I could take a picture of this to show Myra. I decide to take a mental picture instead.

Levi smiles, line dimples hugging his mouth. "Why are you laughing?"

"Nothing." I can't stop giggling. I don't even try to hide it. "Keep walking."

We make it to the head of the trail. A huge rectangle of caution tape surrounds the perimeter of a patch of dirt, which I eerily assume is the patch of dirt where the murder occurred. There is a pavilion and park bench on the other side of it, so that's where we head next.

"This is creepy," I tell Levi. I look up at the wooden beams of the pavilion. "Scary."

He sets my bags on the picnic table. "Sad. Terrible, actually."

I pull my tripod out of its case and extend its legs. "Where do you want to sit?"

"I have to sit for this?" Levi looks around and points to the end of the picnic bench. "Over there? So you can see the caution tape in the background?"

"Perfect." I pull my camera out of its bag and start attaching it to the tripod head. "It's like you read my mind."

Once Levi assumes his position — and I finish formatting the memory cards and adjusting the camera settings — the energy between us shifts. I begin preparing for the questions I'll ask throughout the interview. Levi is staring down at the wooden splinters on the table, mentally rehearsing what he's going to say for each response. There's silence. The mood darkens. It's time to do what we came here for— talk about the person who was murdered here on this trail behind us.

I zoom the camera in on Levi's eyes, focusing my lens on them. It's the first time I've seen his eyes this closely. I linger on them a little longer than I need to— noting the specks of gold among the deep green. The camera is a good excuse to stare at him without actually staring *at* him. When I catch his eyes staring back into the camera lens, I snap back into reality.

"How much of me will you be able to see?" Levi brushes off the front of his jacket.

I put my hands under my boobs and move them up past my face in one swift motion. "From here up," I answer. "Pretty close up, but not too close up."

"From my headlights up. Got it." He acts serious when he says the words, not even cracking a smile.

"Let's not relive that night," I say. I hand Levi the small, clip-on microphone and plug the other end into my camera. The long, thin cord stretches between us.

He points to his shirt collar. "Just clip it here?"

I make a motion signaling that he needs to string the wire under his shirt. "It hides the cord," I explain. "Looks more professional. Is that okay?"

"Sure." Levi begins to snake the cord up under his shirt. The fabric bunches up at the bottom, revealing a slice of abdomen. "Sorry," he says, correcting it.

"You're good," I say, focusing my attention on a snow-covered tree in the distance.

"How's this?" He clips the microphone to his collar from the inside. "Hidden cord."

"Perfect." I clear my throat. "Ready?"

Levi crosses his arms across his chest. "Ready as I'll ever be."

I press record. "Let's just start with what happened here. Can you tell us what you know at this point?"

Levi adjusts himself on the uncomfortable wooden bench. "The murder that took place here the other night was unfathomable." He motions to the caution tape behind him. "The preliminary stages of our investigation are now complete, so we want to share this young woman's story so that it doesn't happen to anyone else."

I raise my eyebrows. "Young *woman?*"

Levi exhales. "We just received word from the coroner this morning that the victim killed in this homicide case was a young woman. She has been identified as Kaylee Wood, just 22 years old. Her family said she was in town visiting a friend at *Joyfield University* for the weekend, and innocently decided to go for a run here on this trail."

I shake my head. "That's so…scary," I manage, not knowing what else to say that would match the gravity of the situation.

"From the witness description and security cameras, law enforcement identified the alleged suspect as Brandon Smith, 32 years old. He was taken into police custody this morning when he was apprehended."

"Did they know each other?"

"No." Levi picks his hand up and sets it back down on the table in disbelief. "We asked the family. At this time, investigators do not believe that the individuals knew each other."

I tucked a loose curl behind my ear that was flying around in the cool breeze. "Do you know how it happened?"

"There was a witness," Levi explains. "An older man walking his dog. He wasn't super close to the scene, but he saw enough from a distance to tell investigators what he saw. This Smith guy allegedly grabbed Kaylee's ponytail and tried to pull her toward him. Kaylee fought back. They engaged in a physical altercation. She put up a really good fight."

I shake my head. "Did the old guy try to help at all?"

"He called the cops. Shit, professionally I should say *police*— can you cut that part out?"

"You're fine. Keep going."

Levi clears his throat. "He called the police, but by the time they arrived, it was too late. Smith allegedly fought her to the ground, beating her when she resisted."

I look at the caution tape waving in the breeze. "What happens next?"

"I'll be prosecuting the case," Levi says. "I want justice for Kaylee. We *all* need justice for Kaylee. She was a young woman who had a full life ahead of her. She was just going out for an innocent evening run. Women shouldn't have to be *scared* of doing that. It's not fair."

I can see Levi's face turning to stone. I can see the wheels turning in his mind. I watch his mouth move into a straight line. His eyes are fixated on the wooden table in front of him. I can tell that he has forgotten about me, the camera, the interview— he's now just thinking about Kaylee and *his* specific role in bringing her killer to justice. I find myself drawn to his seriousness, gazing at his eyes that aren't staring back into mine.

I speak gently. "Any final thoughts?"

Levi looks up at me. "I just don't want this to happen to anyone else."

My mind flashes to Paige. Then Eliza. Then me. Then *all* of the young, female reporters out there. There must be tens of thousands of us. What happened to Kaylee could happen to any one of us….at *any* given moment.

I had already almost been purposefully run over by a truck. I had a gun pulled on me. I can't even pinpoint the hundreds of times that I've felt unsafe working for WJDN. There have been dozens of dangerous situations — that Bill has willingly and knowingly placed us in — that could have been avoided. Suddenly, I'm internally fuming. But I substitute my anger with another question.

"Any words of wisdom or advice for other young women out there?"

Levi shuffles in his seat. "We don't want women to feel afraid— we want all of the young women in our community to feel *safe*. That's why we are going to fight this case with every ounce of our being," Levi says. "Just know that our team is doing everything we can to make sure this reality doesn't continue here in Joyfield."

As the interview ends and I start packing up my equipment, I can't help but think about Kaylee Wood. I can't help but think about how a young woman can't go for a simple run in the evening without fear of getting attacked. I feel sad that this is the type of world we live in, and I feel angry that reporters get placed in hazardous conditions every day.

Something needs to change. I need to change something. *Joyfield does not need another Kaylee Wood.*

The walk back towards my news car doesn't have the same energetic feel as the walk down did. The spirit of Kaylee Wood lingers in the air above us. Levi insists on carrying both of my equipment bags up the hill, and he gives me no choice but to let him. We walk in silence for a few moments— the only sound from our feet traipsing through the snow. Small flurries of snow start to fall onto us.

"This might be a weird time to ask," Levi says as we approach my news car. "But could I get your number?"

I clench my jaw. "Sure—"

"Like for interview purposes," Levi specifies. He looks calm and cool, as if he does this *all* the time.

I look at his side profile. "You mean you don't want to have to call the news station *every* time you want to talk to me?"

"Preferably not," Levi says. "I don't want Nate intercepting my calls to you."

I open up the trunk of my news car. "I did put your number in my phone. Back when you gave me your business card."

"I'm offended." Levi shoves my equipment in the trunk and slams the door shut. "Why haven't you ever texted me?"

"I haven't needed to." I feel warm blood rush to my cheeks. "I mean—"

"Wow, that was harsh." Levi hands me his phone. "Put your number in here. That way I have yours, too. You know, for breaking news tips."

"No middlemen." I type my number in his phone and save my name as *Noelle Fenwick WJDN.* "Be careful what you wish for. It's dangerous to give your number to a reporter. We'll blow up your phone when we need an interview."

Levi smiles, line dimples and all. "I won't mind."

Sixteen

THE PHOTOGRAPHER

Early shifts. Late shifts. Weekend shifts. Overtime shifts. Another norm for local television news reporters: the holiday shift. That's what I'm scheduled to work today— reporting on Christmas. *There's no place like WJDN for the holidays.*

"Noelle," Delilah whispers in my ear. She gently shakes my arm, which is resting under my comforter. "It's time to go downstairs."

I force my eyes open, take one look at her excited face, and shut my eyes again. I notice my scalp is hurting from sleeping in a messy bun last night. No matter how precious Delilah looks on Christmas morning, I can't bring myself to wake up at a moment's notice. Not for anything. But for her, I'll at least try my best.

"What time is it?" I stretch my arms towards the wall behind my head.

Delilah taps my phone screen as if I should know the

answer. "5:30," she says. "Hurry up."

While 5:30 is early, it's not as early as Delilah has woken me up in past years. She usually comes into my room sometime *before* 5:00. This is a new record for her.

"Okay." I mentally count backwards from five before forcing myself to swing my legs over the edge of my bed and sit upright.

"Yay!" Delilah silently squeals, fists clenched. "Meet me downstairs."

Delilah and I are wearing the same thing: matching pajamas with red-and-white candy-cane stripes on the front. My mom makes us annually *twin*. Last year, we had Elf night-gowns with Will Ferrell's face on them. The year before that, we had thin robes with blue snowflakes trailing down the sides. Do I feel childish waking up in my childhood bedroom on Christmas morning in my mid-twenties, wearing exactly what my baby sister is wearing? Surprisingly, no. I think it's sweet. I just play along.

Delilah stopped believing in Santa when she was five, citing an uneasy feeling about a stranger coming into her house while she was sleeping. But this year, she still hopes that he'll bring her a vintage Polaroid camera. Yes, I think this has something to do with my dad. He has been dropping subliminal messages to instill his love of photography in her, and, given the number one gift on her wish list this year, I think his subconscious attacks are working.

I follow Delilah, who looks like an energetic candy cane, down our beige carpeted stairs. We turn the corner, and the Christmas tree looks more magical than ever. The twinkling lights, the sparkly red tinsel, and the personalized ornaments. Dozens of gifts lay under the tree, as if they were personally waiting for us to arrive. My mom and dad are in their respective recliners — and by the tired looks on their faces — I can assume Delilah woke them just before she came into my room.

"Good morning," my mom whispers. "Time to see what Santa brought."

"What *you* brought," Delilah corrects.

"It's the most wonderful time of the year," my dad announces joyfully from his recliner. "I can start singing it if you'd like."

"No," Delilah says, waving me off. "That's okay."

We assume our annual positions seated on the shiny, hardwood floors in front of the glistening tree. I'm on the left, and Delilah is on the right, just like it's been every year prior. She's almost done unwrapping her first present — a pair of bright green fuzzy slippers — by the time I even grab my first package. I place a small, sparkly-wrapped box in my lap.

I look across the living room floor at my parents. They're smiling back at us, and their joy makes me want to cry. My eyes actually sting just a little bit. We're technically adults now, and my parents are just as happy to see us unwrapping gifts today as they were when we were in the *single digit* ages.

I open the box to reveal a thin, silver necklace with the tiniest New York City skyline at the center. "I love this," I say, immediately fastening it around my neck. I place my hand over the cold metal as it lies on my chest. "Thank you so much."

"Thank you, Jesus!" Delilah interrupts. She holds a vintage Polaroid camera box above her head. "This is exactly what I wanted!"

Delilah stands up and walks over to my parents, hugging each of them. This is when it hits me— I don't know how many more Christmas mornings like this one I'll have left. How many more years will Delilah wake me up? How many more years will my parents be staring back at me? How many more years until I'm waking up alone...*in some random apartment?* I don't know when the clock will run out, so I want to savor each moment. This could be the last morning like this...*ever.*

"Your father might have had something to do with this," my mom tells her.

My dad exhales sharply. "It's just a Polaroid 600 Super Color instant film camera with built-in flash, automatic shutter, and retro stripes. No big deal."

"We have presents for you guys, too," Delilah says.

For my parents, we created little coffee-themed gift baskets with merchandise from *Brew For You*. We filled the branded, bright green mugs with packs of ground coffee, sugar, and creamer. Delilah is proud because this was *her* idea, but I encouraged her when I found out about her 10% employee discount. We watch as my parents perform their annual *oohs and ahhs* as they pull out every last item.

"I love this so much," my mom says, pretending to drink invisible liquid out of the coffee mug. "I'm going to drink out of this every morning."

"They must be paying you the big bucks down there," my dad adds, examining the coffee mug up close with my mom's botanical print readers. "Thank you, girls."

Delilah and I finish unwrapping our gifts and go to lie under the tree's base. It's a weird tradition my mom introduced us to when we were little— probably to keep us entertained while she got ready for family to come over. We use my mom's plaid tree skirt as a pillow under our heads, lie on the cold floor, and stare up through a sea of branches, ornaments, and lights. Specks of dust fall into our eyes, but with just a few quick blinks, we're back to looking up at the yellow-hued lights.

I sigh. "I have to go soon." I find a constellation of five lights that form an unintentional star shape above me.

"Where are you going?" Delilah asks, turning her head over to look at me. A small branch scratches her in the eye upon the movement. "Ouch."

"Watch out," I say, laughing. "I have to work today."

"Christmas?" Delilah asks. *I could have sworn I told her.*

"Come and help me pick out an outfit," I say, trying to make some sort of positive come out of the conversation. "Let's go."

Delilah follows me up the stairs, new Polaroid camera in hand, talking a mile a minute about the difference between their classic and modern series. I'm used to her talking nonstop. It's one of the things I like most about her. I never have to fill up a silence or think about what to say next. *She already has it covered.*

When she takes a seat on my bed, she puts the camera up to her eye. She stares at me through it, nervous to take her first picture and waste her first sheet of film on me.

I pull open my closet doors and start swiping through my collection of blouses, dresses, and pants. I've had many of these items since my college internship days, and looking through them now, I think my wardrobe is in desperate need of a refresh. *Too bad the closest Zara to Joyfield is literally in New York City.*

I present Delilah with a red sweater, holding it up against my chest. "What do you think? Red for Christmas?"

"Boring," Delilah says. She snaps her first picture, and the flash blinds me.

"Hey," I say, shielding my eyes with the back of my hand. "What a waste of film."

"I had to." Delilah giggles when she sees the frame roll out of its exit slot, then pulls it out once it reaches the end.

I put the red sweater back and continue swiping through the rack. "I should have known. You probably want me to wear green."

"Yes, green. Find it." Delilah shakes the film back and forth, turning on my lamp to speed up the image's development. "Almost done."

I pull out a deep green dress and hold it out towards her. "Is this good enough for you?"

"Perfect," she says, her attention on the film. "Noelle, come quick! It's done!"

I walk over to my bed and sit down next to her. She holds the developed frame in her hands, displaying me, mid-sentence, holding up that red sweater.

"Look at your face!" Delilah slaps her knee and laughs hysterically before trying to mimic it herself. "You look like this—"

"So rude," I joke, grabbing the picture from her and staring at it myself. "I think I look beautiful. And that sweater did look good."

"Beautifully...*horrendous*," Delilah says. She can't stop giggling. "Let's take a selfie this time. Make a nicer face this time."

"Well, I will, because I'll be *prepared* this time." I put my candy cane arm around her and press my face next to hers. "Give me a countdown at least."

Delilah stretches out her arm and turns the camera around to face us. "Three, two, one—" She smiles widely and tilts her head, throwing her other arm around me at the last second.

I squint. "That was…bright." The powerful flash of light feels like it's going to stain my corneas forever.

"Come on, come on," she chants to the exit slot, as if her words will make the picture come out faster. "Almost ready."

I notice the Polaroid camera reflected in her eyes. "I think you might have a new calling," I tell her. "You can charge a lot for photography."

Ignoring my advice, Delilah pulls the picture out of the slot and starts to shake it into existence. This one develops faster, slowly revealing a tired-looking me and an excited-looking Delilah within the frame. She hands it over to me for closer inspection.

"Can I keep it forever?" I hold it against my chest.

"It can be a Christmas present for you." She points to the picture of us from New York City that I keep on my nightstand. "Keep it right…*there*."

"I like it." As usual, I do what Delilah asks me to do. I tuck the film in the bottom left corner of the frame, and smile at our Christmas morning faces staring back at us. "Good?"

"Do you promise you'll keep it forever?" Delilah asks, admiring her work.

"Promise Thomas."

"You can see it every night before you go to bed." She slinks off my bed and starts walking towards the door. "I'm going to take more pictures now. Bye—"

"Wait!" I stand up and slide my Delilah-approved green

dress over my shoulders, smoothing out the wrinkles with my hands. "How's this?"

"Good," Delilah responds, uninterested. She's already halfway out the door.

I put my hands on my hips and look at myself in the mirror. "I just can't stand in front of the green screen at all today. Or else I'll be a floating head."

I think about getting a quick nap in before work, but I'd rather start to drink my morning coffee instead. It's the most blissful part of my morning routine, so much so that I think about drinking it in the morning when I'm lying in bed at night. Plus, once I'm up for the day, I'm up. I might as well stay awake.

After I get a shower and put on makeup — adding some extra silver sparkles in the corner of my eyes for some added holiday glamour — I pull my unruly curls into a messy bun and try to make it look professional. I add a bright red coat to my ensemble, knowing this is the only day I can pull off an outfit that's primarily red and green.

When I walk down the stairs, my dad is reading a day-old newspaper with my mom's readers still on. He's admiring his latest string of photographs that he submitted of the Joyfield Christmas parade. My mom is watching The Holiday on TV while painting her fingernails with a new nail polish my dad got her. Delilah is still experimenting with her Polaroid camera, eyeball millimeters away from the viewfinder. I take a mental snapshot of my view to embed it in my memory forever. *All of the people I love, in one place, together.*

"Bye, guys," I tell my family collectively, trying to hide the disappointment in my voice that I have to work on Christmas Day. "Delilah, take lots of pictures. I want that film gone by the end of the day."

"Don't encourage that," my dad teases. "You have to savor each picture, Delilah. Really think about what you want to take before you take it. It's limited. They don't go on forever."

My goodbyes are interrupted by a call coming in on my phone. It's Bill Calloway. *On Christmas?* I answer, fully aware that my entire family is listening.

"Hello?"

"Noelle," he says in a panic with no holiday greeting. "You have to anchor tonight."

"I'm…what?" I notice my mom and dad looking concerned.

Bill huffs on the other end of the line. "I forgot that I gave Ed Sterling off today. He's all the way in Colorado visiting his family."

My heart starts to pound. "But I've never—"

"Today is the perfect day to learn!" Bill tries to fake a happy tone. "Myra is producing today. She can walk you through it. Good luck." He hangs up the phone.

I put my phone back in my pocket, staring out at my sea of family members in disbelief. I don't even know what to tell them.

"What is it, sweetie?" My mom asks.

"I'm…*anchoring*."

"The news?" My dad asks, as if there could possibly be another answer. "That's great!"

"Honey, you're going to be a star. A Joyfield star." My mom gets up to hug me, and when she does, we sway back and forth. "You'll be great."

Delilah points her camera up to the TV. "I'll photograph it," she says. "*Captured*."

My eyes are wide, and I feel like I can't stare at anything

but the white plastered wall behind the Christmas tree. I can feel my heart thumping. I've started to overheat to the point where I feel like I need to ditch my red coat entirely today. This might be the beginning stages of a panic attack, but I can't tell yet.

"It's the *first* for *Noelle*! Get it— the First Noel?" My dad laughs, but I don't find it funny.

"I guess I have no choice," I say nervously. "Ed Sterling isn't even in town."

Anchoring? Does Bill seriously think I can just anchor an evening broadcast with no prior experience...or even practice? I can't tell if I'm nervous, excited, or both. This is my first shot at becoming Hilda Harrison. It's a Christmas miracle. *But it's definitely a first for Noelle.*

Seventeen

THE TELEPROMPTER

I was a dancer from the time I was three years old until I graduated from college. It was one of the biggest parts of my life — from dance competitions, recitals, and practices filling up every ounce of free time — until I stopped just a few years ago. I sometimes forget that dance was once the *biggest* part of me. My mind has been elsewhere these days.

I've always been obsessed with the cute costumes and pop music that come with jazz and tap choreography, but lyrical and contemporary are my personal favorites. Each dance tells a story through the lyrics, music, and movement *without* spoken words.

During my junior year of high school, we performed a lyrical number in which half the class portrayed homeless people. The other half dressed as business people walking past them on the streets. It was a symbolic juxtaposition between *greed* and *need*. The dance brought tears to the eyes of countless audience members, as I was told afterward. That was the exact moment I fell in love not just with writing, but with *storytelling.*

That's what I loved about being up on that stage. Three uninterrupted minutes of...*pure attention.* Not attention on me, but attention on the *story.* The audience soaked in its meaning through our choreography. The dance could make them feel something. It could make them more *aware* of something. It could make them feel inspired. I loved the platform that I had, and it's similar to the one that I have now as a reporter. And soon...the one I'll have as a first-time anchor.

I stomp up the WJDN stairwell leading into the newsroom. My boots are slick with dirty, watery snow— something that only people in the north could truly understand. The moisture creates a squeaking sound with each step, reminding me of my anxiety for the day ahead. But I don't know if it's actually anxiety...or *excitement.*

I try to convince myself that because it's Christmas, I need to be filled with joy. It comes with the territory. But the joy is *not* coming naturally. I'm a ball of nerves thinking about anchoring. My insides feel like they're twisting into noodles.

I swing open the door to the newsroom and spot Myra sitting at her desk. "Merry Christmas!" *I'm going to fake it until I make it.* "Isn't this a glorious morning?"

Myra rolls her eyes without even looking at me. "The best," she says.

The police scanner's digital noises — ranging from beeps to rings to static and scratches — swirl around Nate's head, who sits at the assignment desk with the same level of excitement as a mortician. His eyes are heavy as he listens to the mechanical voices of dispatchers: *Do you copy? Request backup. All units responding. 10-4. Over.*

"The scanner doesn't know that it's Christmas?" I ask him, setting my bags on the filing cabinet beside my desk. I begin to feel butterflies in my stomach.

"What are you so happy about?" Nate asks.

"I'm faking it until I make it," I respond. But there *is* something that I am a little happy about. *I'm going to be a star today.*

"That's what we're doing today? Okay. I guess I'll play along," Myra says.

"You can't even *pretend* to be happy," Nate tells her.

Myra scoffs. "It's almost the new year. How about…new year, new me?"

"I'd *love* a new version of you," Nate says. "Someone who is actually nice to me."

Myra and Nate don't know — that *I know* — that this playful newsroom banter is really just a mask over their secret relationship (or whatever it is). While I've tried to bring it up multiple times to both of them individually, they've given me *nothing* to work with. *Their secret is still safe with me, I guess.*

"Did you both hear the news?" I swivel around in my chair to face them.

Without even looking up, they both shake their heads *no* and continue working. They consume so much news on a daily basis that they couldn't care *less* about whatever *my* news could possibly be.

"You're looking at the new Ed Sterling." I stand up and slide my hands down my dress, finishing my dramatic choreography with a little twirl.

"You're *Ed* today?" Myra asks, shooting me a scowl.

"They must have been down bad," Nate chimes in.

"Don't be so excited, guys." I sit down and start checking my emails. I continue explaining over my shoulder, ignoring the loud scanner noises. "Bill let Ed go to Colorado for the holidays, and he forgot about it. He called me in a panic, saying that I'm doing it."

"Nice of him to tell me. I have to change all of my scripts from *Ed* to *Noelle* now." Myra repeatedly hits the backspace tab on her keyboard. "Okay, producer rant over. I'm excited for you."

Nate sits back in his chair and looks up at the ceiling, resting his hands under his head. "Ed Fenwick. Or would it be Noelle Sterling?"

"We aren't getting married," I say, kicking my boots up onto the filing cabinet. "I'm just replacing him. For one night and one night only."

I begin editing scripts on my computer, adding dashes where I want to remember to read more slowly and adding pronunciations where I'm afraid I'll flub up tricky last names. It's my first taste of becoming a *real-life* Hilda Harrison. My heart is pounding in my chest so hard that I'm afraid Myra and Nate can hear it.

* * *

I walk into the WJDN news studio and hear my snow boots squeaking against the sparkly floor. There are about a hundred lights on the ceiling — fastened in with black cords and wires angled in all different directions — but they are all off. The darkness of the usually well-lit studio creates a sense of unexpected calm. The lights aren't on, so there's no need to panic…*yet.*

I'm holding a stack of scripts in my arms— my backup contingency plan in case the teleprompter goes out (which I've heard has happened a time or two). I take a look at the set in front of me. While it's not The Sunrise Show level of astonishing, a set is a set. All live television studios always give off the same sort of magical feeling, no matter where you are in the world. And even though I'm just a little underpaid reporter in minuscule Joyfield, Ohio, *I'm feeling it now.*

I walk up onto the anchor desk platform, set my scripts on the glass, and take a seat in the tattered, swivel anchor chair. Within the amount of time it takes to flip a switch, ten bright spotlights blast directly into my eyeballs, causing me to squint my eyes and hold a hand up to my forehead. My pupils slowly adjust. I wonder if the perfect timing is from a motion sensor detecting my *motion*, but when I see Myra sitting in the control room, I know it was her doing.

"Hellooooo," she says into the earpiece that I am just now molding into my ear canal. "Doing okay out there?"

Through a glass window near the large, wooden studio doors, I can see her sitting in her usual control room seat, with a blanket sitting on her lap and about fifty computer monitors sitting in front of her. She looks comfortable and confident, two things that I am currently *not.*

"Testing one two, testing one two," I respond dramatically, angling my vocal projection into a microphone that I'm now stringing up my dress. I clip it onto my collar. "Can you hear me okay?"

"You sound *just* like Ed Sterling," Myra says. "Your appearance is uncanny, too."

I've been in this studio hundreds of times, but sitting at

the infamous *anchor desk* is a new high. The teleprompter in front of me cues up my name. I take a mental snapshot of my view, filing it away in the imaginative scrapbook of my life. The lights shine on my face and warm my cheeks, just like those stage lights when I danced back in the day. Same feeling, different space. *Performance time.*

"Ed, is that you?"

An energetic Ruby May walks in front of the green screen, the sound of her high heels clicking and clacking along the way. Her strawberry blonde waves are in a high bun, and she's wearing a deep red dress. The little sparkly Santa hats dangling from her ears communicate that she is ready, if not excited, to work on Christmas.

"I aged backwards." I prop my hands underneath my chin and tilt my head at her. "Don't I make a cute Ed Sterling?"

"The cutest." Ruby snakes the wire of her microphone up under her dress, clipping it onto her collar. "How are you feeling, girlfriend?"

"I can't tell if I want to throw up or pass out." I check my teeth using my phone's front-facing camera. "Hopefully I don't do both."

"You'll be fine," Ruby says. "I'm right here with you. Don't you worry 'bout a thing."

Myra waves at both of us through the glass, and I can see her press a button on her switchboard. "Can you both hear me?"

"Loud and clear," Ruby says.

Myra pantomimes a dance move that looks like *raising the roof.* "Five minutes. Good?"

"Oh, you know," I say. "Just a nervous wreck as per usual."

"You're just reading off of a teleprompter," Myra comforts.

"You're usually out in the middle of nowhere, fighting with creepy dudes and bad weather. Now, you're just reading words off a screen. You made it. You deserve this."

"Thanks for the pep talk." I shuffle through my scripts for no reason other than to fidget with something.

Ruby stands in front of the green screen *TV ready*, one leg crossed in front of the other, and her hands clasped. "If you need to *vomit*, just shoot me a look. I can take up more time with the weather." She drops her voice to a whisper. "Hell, I could do weather for the entire duration of the show if you need."

Before I know it, the fanfare introduction is blasting in my ear. *The show is beginning.* I can see the WJDN graphics dancing across a tiny monitor behind the teleprompter. I know that *my face* will be on that tiny monitor next, and the thought of it sends a bolt of heat through my chest. My ears are on fire. *A couple more seconds.*

Ruby shoots me a knowing look from the green screen. Myra dances excitedly through the glass. My heart thumps in my ears like a bass drum. *Boom. Boom. Boom.* I feel like my microphone will pick up the sound.

The little red light appears above the teleprompter. *It's go time.*

"Good evening and welcome to WJDN News. Merry Christmas to those who celebrate. I'm Noelle Fenwick. Ed Sterling has the night off." I can see myself on the monitor out of the corner of my eye. *I don't know how I feel about that.* "We seem to be having a white Christmas, so we're going to turn it over to Chief Meteorologist Ruby May for a check on our holiday forecast. What can you tell us, Ruby?"

The camera switches to Ruby at the green screen, and I feel

relieved. I sit back in my anchor chair, taking a deep breath from the belly. I made it through, like, a half dozen sentences, and I still have an hour to go.

Ruby is doing the weather for the next 90 seconds, so it's the perfect (and only) 90 seconds to check my phone. I have four texts.

Mom: "You're doing great, sweetie!" (Santa Claus and Christmas tree emojis.)

Dad: "Good job." (Thumbs up emoji.)

Delilah: "The green looks good with your hair." (Three green heart emojis.)

Levi: 1 Attachment.

An attachment? From Levi? I open it to reveal a picture of *me*...on an old-fashioned television screen with the message: "Family is watching TV at my grandma's house for Christmas dinner. Nice surprise to see you." (Smiley face emoji.)

Seeing my picture on his grandma's TV screen...*makes me cringe.* Remembering that the possibly flirty text came from Levi *makes me giddy.* Levi is watching me, and probably will be for the remainder of this broadcast. *As if I wasn't nervous enough.* I feel like I'm dancing on stage, knowing that my high school crush is in the audience.

"Ten seconds," Myra says, snapping me back into reality. I slide my phone under my right thigh faster than the speed of lightening and look back up at the teleprompter.

"Thanks, Ruby. Moving on to a local investigation, where law enforcement officials are reporting an alleged robbery at a grocery store in Joyfield. WJDN was on the scene of the reported crime earlier today, where police officers told us that the incident is still under investigation."

I continue to mindlessly read the rest of my scripts. Word

after word, sentence after sentence. The white, capital letters sliding up the black background of the teleprompter make my eyes glitch if I go too long without blinking. My throat is starting to get dry from all of the talking I'm doing, but the swarming butterflies and heart palpitations are beginning to fade. I feel myself kind of just…fading. *Going on autopilot.*

After the fifth story, staring into the camera's lens, I start to feel myself getting…*bored.* Like I'm a talking bobble head paying more attention to my raspy voice and facial expressions than to the stories I'm reading. I shuffle my scripts, fold my hands, lean back in my chair, repeat. Sit up in my chair, tuck my hair behind my ear, look into a different camera, repeat. I feel like a robot. A talking, *stiff* robot. Can this show be…I hate to say it…*over already?*

My brain continues going in and out of focus, planting itself elsewhere. I think about the Christmas morning Delilah and I spent together. I think about Kaylee Wood and how I'm going to do her story justice. I think about going on *The Rundown* after the new year to find my next stepping stone stations. I think about what I'm going to eat when this is all over. *Domino's? Some kind of pizza. Something with sauce…*

"We'll be right back after the commercial break," I say through my daze of thinking about carbohydrates. A commercial airs to advertise a window replacement service.

"What do you think?" Ruby asks. She's scrolling on Instagram on her phone, sitting at the weather center. "Having fun yet?"

"Talking to you during the commercial breaks is the most fun thing about this entire show," I say. I swivel around in my chair, swaying side to side like a child. "And seeing Myra work really hard through the window."

"I heard that," Myra says into our earpieces. "Three minutes until we're back."

"So, this is it?" I watch as a person demonstrates how to use the latest and greatest vacuum in the next commercial.

"Pretty much," Ruby says. She flashes her phone at me. "Did you see this meme—"

While Ruby's southern voice infiltrates my brain, I start to secretly daydream. I realize something: I didn't actually *write* today. I edited some scripts, sure. But I didn't actually *write* any of these stories myself. I'm just reading stories aloud that *other* people have written for me. If being a reporter is all about writing, I'm finding that being an anchor is all about…*reading*.

I didn't want to get into the news industry to read. I wanted to get into it to *write*. To interview people. To share insights. To highlight problems. To hold accountability. To tell stories. To amplify voices. Sure, I'm sharing all of those things with the masses — literally on this broadcast right now — but I'm just a *figurehead*. I didn't come up with any of this stuff. *I didn't write any of this stuff.* And I'm finding that simply reading it aloud is very, very boring.

What did I *think* anchoring would be like? Sure, this is Hilda Harrison's job. She does what I'm doing right now all the time— reading off the teleprompter, fixing her hair, clasping her hands, repeat. But she does *more* than that, too. She travels to see every corner of the world. She interviews international leaders. She's at presidential inaugurations. She even covers freaking *Paris Fashion Week*. That's what happens when you're at the *network* news level. They do all the big stuff. But at the *local* news level, I guess I'm just stuck reading off a teleprompter.

I thought I'd be more excited to try anchoring. I thought I'd be bouncing up and down with excitement. I thought I'd do it and immediately fall in love with the craft. I thought I'd do it...*and immediately become some clone of Hilda Harrison.*

But what if I *only* want to become Hilda Harrison when she's experiencing a career-defining moment? What if I'm *only* chasing after the high points: interviewing celebrities, traveling internationally, and attending premieres? Do I still want her life when it's just an average Wednesday? *Or do I only want to be her when she's on top of the world?*

Maybe I've coveted the main anchor position at The Sunrise Show for the wrong reasons. Maybe I've been paying attention to the wrong bullet points within the job description of an anchor. Maybe I *wouldn't* be happy working in network news on your average Wednesday. Maybe my dreams aren't what I thought they were. *Maybe I'm just destined to be a small-scale news reporter at WJDN forever.*

Eighteen

THE KICKER

New Year's Eve has always been so sentimental to me.

I always spend the last day of each year flipping through my calendar, sitting with the entries scratched into each little box. Working doubles at WJDN. Karaoke nights at The Highball. *Brew For You* visits with Delilah. Shopping trips with my mom. Winter photography shoots with my dad. *Meeting Levi.* I never have a blank square, and that's the way I like it.

When I flip past December, I think about what next year will bring. I'll be determining what the next chapters of my life look like. I'll be checking out Virginia Beach, Nashville, and San Francisco. I'll be planning out — if and when — I'll be living in each of these cities. I'll figure out whether I'll be moving out of my childhood home forever or staying at WJDN for two more years. I'll know if my crush on Levi will turn into something more, or fizzle out into oblivion. I'll spend my birthday with Eliza in New York City.

Next year's calendar will consist of 365 blank squares, each filled with 365 possibilities. Next year at this time, I will know exactly how they read. But at this particular moment, I do not.

These are the thoughts running through my mind as I slip my silver, sparkly blouse over my shoulders and pull my dark, shiny jeans up my legs. I pull my waves into a loose, messy bun with some pieces hanging down in the front. It's time for Nate's annual New Year's Eve party, and with all of these unknowns running through my brain, this is the best place I could be going to clear it all out.

I worked the late shift tonight — covering a story for the 11 o'clock news about how local emergency services are preparing for a huge snowstorm projected to hit the area tomorrow afternoon — so I will be going to his party late, of course. But I *had* to change first before I went home. I couldn't celebrate my favorite holiday wearing a WJDN News fleece jacket. My only goal is to make it there before midnight, and I'm happy that I'm arriving with about fifteen minutes to spare.

I enter into Nate's apartment through a door frame fluttered with silver streamers. An immediate waft of sour kraut and hot dog smell hits my nose, giving me the same feeling as walking into a high school cafeteria. Humid. Greasy. *Gross.* But even though it might be the worst-smelling holiday, it's still my favorite.

"Come in here," Nate waves to me from the kitchen before disappearing back into it.

"Coming!" I kick off my shoes — thankful that I'm wearing socks — and place them neatly along the dark wooden wall. I traipse through Nate's living room, moving through the path of balloons and decorations like I'm venturing through a jungle.

Nate moved into his own apartment in Joyfield after graduating from college and returned home to work at WJDN. Between the dirty wooden walls and stained beige carpeting, you can tell Nate calls this place home. I could never understand how he could afford it all— rent, student loans, car payment, bills. It seems like a hefty price to pay for the sole purpose of not having to live with your parents (even though they live right down the street). He told me that he wanted his *own* space now that he's an official adult.

When I turn the corner into the kitchen, I find a party of people gathered around a tub of jungle juice. I don't know most of them— they must be Nate's college friends. They look to be about my age. Living in a town as small as Joyfield, I'm always surprised when I don't know every person in a given room. But I feel right at home when I spot Myra.

She's in the middle of dumping her red solo cup directly into the murky jungle juice, filling it up to the brim. The edge of her gold lace shirt almost touches the surface of the liquid, and I can see that her eyes are glassy. Tiny tendrils of hair cover her eyes, and she wipes them away from her line of sight with the back of her sticky hand.

"Sanitary," I say to Nate, motioning to what she is doing. "You couldn't have splurged on some ladles for this occasion?"

Nate shoots his arms out at his sides. "What does this look like, a palace?"

"Noelle," Myra screams, standing upright once she sees me. Some of her mystery concoction spills onto the floor. Myra is *not* the hugging type, but she surprisingly squeezes me in an embrace. "I'm so glad you're here."

"Hi, Myra," I say in a childlike voice, laughing into her ear. "You feeling okay?"

"I feel great," Myra says, slurring her words. She motions to the countertop behind her. "Grab a cup. They're right over there."

I obey her drunken request, grabbing a clean cup and dumping it into the jungle juice mixture against my will. "What's even here? Just pure heartburn?" I only fill it up about halfway, and the scent of strong rubbing alcohol hits my nose.

"This year, we're calling it the WJDN special," Nate explains. "Vodka, rum, tequila, cranberry juice, and I think even some White Claws were thrown in there. Think of it as a Long Island iced tea on steroids."

I take a sip of the hangover-inducing mixture and wince. "This is just what I needed."

I notice Paige and Ruby chomping on tortilla chips on the other side of the kitchen. They shoot me a simultaneous *thumbs-up* of approval once they observe the drink in my hand. That's my sign to walk over in their direction, moving away from Myra and Nate's increasingly drunken conversations.

I snake through a sea of sweaty people in Nate's overheated kitchen, the sparkles of my blouse catching on the wooden island separating the crowd. It's dimly lit — due to an outdated light fixture hanging overhead — which sets the tone for a party vibe. Balloons filled with confetti are taped to the ceiling. I give Nate credit. *At least he decorated the place for the occasion.*

Ruby clinks her cup to mine. "We were afraid you weren't coming!" She leans in closer to me and drops her voice to a whisper. "Your hot attorney is here."

"Yeah," Paige confirms before I can get a word in, nudging my shoulder. "We were so excited for you to get here and see him."

Paige and Ruby are both wearing variations of ripped blue jeans and dressy black blouses, the stereotypical party outfit for women in their twenties these days. It appears they called each other ahead of time just to plan what they were wearing, but I know they didn't. *Their* outfit is usually *my* party outfit, too. But since I love New Year's Eve, I swapped my usual look for sparkles.

"He is not *my* hot attorney," I say with an eye roll, but my insides start to tingle. "Okay, maybe he *is* my hot attorney."

Ruby squeals and hits Paige in the arm. "See, I knew she'd admit it."

Paige giggles. "You should kiss him tonight. At midnight. It's the perfect excuse."

I can't help but laugh at the request. "Guys, come on. We work together."

"You do not work *together*," Ruby corrects. "You see him sometimes *through* work. Those are two totally different things."

Paige crosses her arms. "Give us one good reason why you can't date him."

"Fine. I'll give you *multiple* reasons."

I *have* thought about this before. A lot more than I would have liked to admit, actually. Levi checks all of the perfect boyfriend boxes: sweet, handsome, kind, cute, friendly...*sexy*. All of these things combined with the way he makes me feel when I'm around him? It seems like it would all work out perfectly. But there is too much at risk.

I tap my pointer finger. "Reason one. As I mentioned, we work together…*sometimes*. If things didn't work out, things would just be weird. I'd still have to interview him, and that would be so awkward for both of us."

"Way to think positively," Ruby laughs.

I tap another finger. "Reason two. I might be moving in six months. It could be the start of my lifelong trek to New York City. I don't want to start something now if we'd never be in the same town again."

"True," Paige says. She turns to face me, smirking. "Then he could just be a fling."

"I don't want a fling," I laugh. "Because that's what flings turn into. Either potentially awkward future interactions or potentially long-distance boyfriends. I don't want either."

"Those are both shitty reasons," Ruby says. "What other excuses do you have?"

"I don't know," I say, biting my lower lip. "Wouldn't it be like a conflict of interest? Could we both get in trouble at work for dating each other? I feel like both of our bosses would *not* approve."

"It's not like you're the host of Good Morning America and he's the Mayor of New York City," Paige rejects. "This is Joyfield. The stakes are low. It doesn't even matter—"

"Hey."

We hear his voice before we see him, and it sends a shock through my chest.

I turn around to spot a handsome Levi Winters standing behind me. A black t-shirt stretches over his chest underneath a button-down flannel jacket. The sleeves are rolled up, exposing his muscular forearms in the most perfect way. I've never seen him look this casual before, and I like it. He cracks open a bottle of beer with the opener on his key chain.

"You ladies look lovely this evening."

"Thanks," Paige giggles, as if *she's* the one with the crush. "Especially Noelle."

I roll my eyes and can't help but laugh. "Thanks, Paige. Appreciate it."

Ruby does a better job of avoiding awkwardness. "We're gonna get some more jungle juice." She points toward the tub across the kitchen. "You two have fun."

I don't think they could have made the interaction any more obvious. I watch as their matching ensembles leave the area, and all at once, Levi and I are alone. Well, not technically. There are about a dozen other people still in the dimly lit kitchen. But we are alone at this particular countertop space.

"I think they were drunk," I whisper to Levi. "Hi, by the way."

"I'll say." His mouth curls up into a grin. His hair is loose and free, controlled only by his hand as he moves his curls into place. "You *do* look lovely tonight, by the way."

I avoid his compliment in the most mature way possible: by not addressing it and by not making eye contact. "So, is this your first *Nate* New Year's Eve party?"

"Yes," Levi confirms. "But I did go to a few parties in his parents' basement back in high school. He always knew how to throw a banger."

"I can imagine," I say. *The professional hot attorney just said banger.*

Levi runs a hand through his hair. "Listen, Noelle—"

"Guys, come on!" Nate screams from the living room. "Thirty seconds!"

I follow Levi into the living room. Thousands of people

bundled up in winter coats are being broadcast live from Times Square. Seeing a glimpse of New York City, even if it's just through a screen, fills my chest with happiness. It all flashes like a montage through my mind— Eliza and I running through those streets at 3:00 in the morning after late-night Taco Bell runs, working at The Sunrise Show even if all I was doing for four months was getting coffee, and that wonderful weekend when my parents and Delilah came there to visit me. I think about how different my life is *now* compared to how it was *then,* and how in some weird way, I've grown to love both versions of my life equally.

Paige and Ruby are near the window, Myra and Nate are by the couch, and Levi is right next to...*me.* We're watching the crowd on TV roar: *Ten! Nine! Eight!*

I now have less than ten seconds to make a decision. *Will we kiss?* We can't kiss. I have a million reasons why we can't, and I even spoke them into existence just a few minutes ago. But my chest tightens as the number gets lower. Everyone in the living room mirrors the shouting: *Three! Two! One!*

"Can I kiss you?" Levi whispers to me.

"Okay." I agree without thinking. I say it without logic. I say it without reason.

The clock strikes midnight. Everybody in the room screams, "Happy New Year!" The confetti poppers Nate bought start launching off. *It's time.*

Levi gently sweeps my hair off my right shoulder, and it falls behind my back. He rests his hand on my cheek, and I look into his hazel eyes. Our faces are about two inches apart, and he smiles— the most subtle, knowing smile. An electric shock shoots down the center of my body like a lightning bolt as he presses his lips to mine. *One, two, three, four...*

His lips feel exactly how they look. Soft. Plush. Gentle. And all at once, Levi is kissing me. This is *more* than a New Year's Eve kiss. This is a...*real kiss*. It's romantic and passionate, but not too much. *It's more than I had ever secretly envisioned in my head.*

Levi pulls his lips away from mine, his hand still softly grazing my cheek. He's staring into my eyes, and I feel like everything else in the living room is a blur. I'm not focused on anything else, and for the first time in my life, I don't even care if someone is watching. I am completely and intensely focused on Levi's face right in front of me.

"Was that okay?" He asks, inches from me.

I clear my throat, too stunned to speak. "That was...*yeah*. That was okay."

"Good." Levi laughs. "I'm gonna go grab another drink, do you want—"

"No," I rush. I hope my cheeks aren't as red as they feel. "Thanks, though."

Levi walks back into the kitchen, and I feel like I'm in a trance. I don't even know what to focus my attention on. Should I grab my phone? Should I start talking to somebody? It's like my mind left my body and is somewhere else in the universe. *Levi and I kissed.*

Ruby and Paige rush over to me. With perfect comedic timing, in their perfectly similar outfits, they begin their interrogation.

"Guess your rules went out the window now?" Ruby teases.

"How was it?" Paige whispers.

I'm too stunned to do anything besides blink. "It was... great."

"I want to hear all about it, but we have to tell you something first," Ruby whispers.

She makes me follow her into the corner of the living room with Paige, and I'm careful not to step in the wet patches of beer spills on the carpeting. I feel like I'm at an elementary school sleepover, where my two best friends are taking me to some secret corner of a classroom to tell me some intense fourth-grade gossip.

"This is big. Huge news. You won't believe it," Paige says.

"Okay, I'm ready for it."

Ruby leans in, moving a strawberry blonde wave away from her face. "Myra and Nate kissed. Like, when the ball dropped. We saw it with our own eyes."

Paige balls her hands into fists in excitement. "Can you believe this?" She whisper-screams. You can tell that she is *living* for this.

I want to act surprised, but I'm not. I want to tell them that I saw Myra and Nate making out at The Highball the other night. I want to tell them about everything I saw. But if I tell them *now*, they'd be mad at me for not telling them *then*. Plus, I want to keep their secret. It's not my secret to tell. I decide to be a good friend to Myra — and a bad friend to Ruby and Paige — by pretending to act surprised.

"No way," I say, dramatically opening my mouth. "Do they know you caught them?"

"They're so drunk that the answer to that is *no*," Paige says. "Two dramatic kisses in one night. This is just, like, so exciting, you know?"

"I wouldn't call mine dramatic." I look at Ruby and Paige, narrowing my eyes at them. "Wait, who did you two kiss?"

Ruby and Paige look at each other, and then back at me.

"You guys didn't—"

"It was either each other or Nate's gross college friends," Ruby says.

"Yeah," Paige confirms. "I couldn't even pick out *one* that I wanted to kiss."

I laugh. "Glad everybody got a New Year's kiss tonight."

Once I decide to take a break from the gossip, I slink through the kitchen and onto Nate's back porch, craving the feeling of the cold winter air on my cheeks. I need a few seconds alone for the first time all night, and it's so hot in this house that I need some air. I shut the sliding glass door behind me, and the frigid cold temperature of the wind feels good. But once my eyes adjust to the darkness, I notice that someone else is also standing out here. It's Levi...and it's *too late* to turn around.

"Sorry, I didn't see anyone out here—"

"It's okay." Levi turns his head over his shoulder. The only light out here is coming straight from the moon, and it's streaming onto his face. "Come over."

I walk over and stand next to him, balancing my forearms on the wooden porch railing to mirror his. Our upper arms are pressed together, thankfully separated by the fabric of our shirts. I don't think I can handle any skin-to-skin contact right now.

We stand in silence for a couple of seconds, faces angled up at the stars. It feels nice to be right next to him, without the pressure of looking directly at him.

Levi breaks the silence first. "I was trying to ask you something earlier."

"You did ask me. If you could kiss me," I tease.

I can see Levi's giant smile and dimples light up under the stars as he laughs. "I did ask you that," he says. "But I wanted to ask you something else *before* that."

A swarm of butterflies flies into my stomach, swirling around as if they're trapped there forever. "Ask away," I say, still looking up at the stars and not into his eyes.

Levi looks at me. "I was wondering if I could take you out sometime."

I smirk, knowing that I *have* to look at him to answer this question. And I do. His face looks so romantic in the moonlight, and even though he's not as close to me as he was during our kiss, he's just close enough. He gives off a level of comfort that makes me want to cuddle up right against him.

"Okay," I say.

All of my excuses and reasons for why the answer to this question should be 'no' fly right out the window. We can figure that stuff out later. We can talk through the logistics later. We can address the negatives later. But right now, I know there's only *one* response I can possibly give him.

"I'd like that."

After some flirtatious small talk — and more strangers coming out on the balcony to get some air — I slink back through the kitchen in an attempt to find Paige and Ruby. I can't think of two people who would be more *thrilled* to hear about the question that Levi just asked me, and I can't wait to tell them.

They're not in the kitchen. They're not in the living room. There aren't too many other places where they could be. I turn the *wrong* corner and find a drunken Nate and Myra drunkenly kissing on the stairs.

"Shit," I say, shielding my eyes.

"Noelle," Myra slurs. "We were just—"

Nate lifts his arm in my direction. "What are you—"

"It's okay," I say, walking away. I finish my sentence from the living room, shouting back to them in avoidance of their eye contact. "You guys…just…umm…yeah."

I run into the kitchen. My heart is pounding. But something inside of me lights up. *The secret is out.*

Nineteen

THE TEASE

Once we arrive at *Mama Bella* — the most popular, fancy Italian restaurant in Joyfield — the host takes us to our reserved seat near the bar. Levi made the reservations. (He also brought me flowers when he picked me up.)

We sit down across from each other, awkwardly removing our coats. The cushions on the booth are bright red with white stuffing protruding from the sides. The decor on the walls reminds me of the *cute, chubby chef* theme in my mom's kitchen, drenched in reds and greens to symbolize the Italian flag. *Maybe this is where she got it from?*

My goal for tonight is to be flirty and simple. No pressure. Nonchalant. I don't want to get too deep, because this *can't* get too deep. This isn't going to go anywhere, because it *can't*. I'm going to be moving hundreds of miles away, and even if it won't be *this* year, it will be *some* year. Because of that, I'm going to keep it light. I'm going to keep it flirtatious. I'm going to keep it *fun.*

"Can I tell you something?" I ask, opening up my menu.

"Already?" Levi leans forward. "Go ahead."

I lean in and drop my voice to a whisper. "We secretly call you the *hot attorney.*"

He laughs, his line dimples cupping the sides of his lips. "Who is...*we?*"

"The girls at work," I confess. "And I'm *very* happy to report that they're all *very* excited for me right now."

Levi keeps his attention fixed on the menu, trying to subdue a smile. "Well, I'm honored to be on a date with the hot news reporter."

I know we're just flirting, but a flame shoots through my chest.

Our waitress places a basket of warm bread and a small plate of dipping oil in front of us. She looks to be about my age, and I can tell that she's startled by Levi's attractiveness. It's almost like she's blushing when she talks to him, even though I know she doesn't mean to be. Levi seems to spur this flustered reaction out of people, even though he doesn't even try. He's just *that* good-looking.

After debating whether we should split a bottle of red wine, we both ordered our own glasses. I ordered the Penne alla Vodka, and Levi asked for the Chicken Parmesan. When the waitress takes our menus away, we're left with no other choice but to stare at each other. No more distractions...*other than the bread.*

"Can I tell *you* something now?" Levi asks to mimic my previous question.

"Of course," I say, my eyes widening.

He folds his hands. "I kind of had a thing for you since the first day I saw you."

I tilt my head to the side and grab a piece of bread. "That's odd, since you only saw the back of my head. I must have really good hair."

"You do have really good hair," Levi laughs. "You'd run your hand through it, flip it over your shoulder, all kinds of things."

I narrow my eyes at him. "You must have really been bored in that courtroom."

Levi is wearing a light blue button-down shirt and a watch. The dimmed lights of *Mama Bella* make his eyes look even darker than usual. His jawline is sharp, and for the first time since I've met him, he has a little bit of stubble. I think I like it even *better* this way. His curly hair is thick and messy, just like mine tonight.

My tousled waves are falling down my shoulders, and I swiped an extra layer of my typical brown eye shadow across my lids. I'm wearing a navy blue, long-sleeved blouse and black jeans with heels. I feel *good* right now at dinner. Since I know there's nothing to lose, I somehow feel more confident than ever.

The waitress…with an apparent crush on my date…places our wine glasses in front of us. "Enjoy," she says. "Your meals will be out soon."

Levi takes a sip. "Fancy."

I smirk. "I imagined you as more of a beer guy."

"I am," he says. "I'm just trying to be fancy."

"I'm *not* very fancy," I admit. "I just like wine."

"You need it, you know, with how hard your job is."

I laugh. "You think *my* job is hard? *Your* job is hard."

Levi swirls a piece of bread in the dipping oil. "I watched your reports when you were covering that trial. I wanted to see how the news was making sense of the case, and I was impressed with how you handled it all."

I roll my eyes. "Impressed?"

"You were in that courtroom for eight hours a day," he says. "Somehow, you condensed a day's worth of information into, like, two minutes. It was easy to follow and made sense. Fair and balanced, even. I don't know how you did that."

"You were in that courtroom, too."

"But I wasn't documenting it and trying to summarize it," he says. "I was just in the background *studying* it."

"Well, thank you," I say. "I used to write down every detail. But over time, I got better at it. Now I realize what's important right away. It's easier."

Levi takes another sip of his *fancy* wine. "So, what's it like being a news reporter?"

I laugh. *It's a loaded question.* "It's like being a filmmaker."

"Noelle Spielberg?"

"In a way." I flip a pile of hair off my shoulder and feel it fall down my back. "I write, shoot, produce, and direct a small movie every day. But instead of taking years to complete it, I get it done in one day."

Levi squints in curiosity. "So, what made you want to be a movie producer?"

I look up at the dusty wall sconces beside us. "I've always loved to write," I explain. "My college journalism professor always said, *'To write is to live forever.'* When you die, your work doesn't. It lives on. That always stuck with me."

Levi raises his eyebrows. "That's deep."

"So, *hot attorney,*" I say, placing the attention on him. I can't believe I'm being so forward. *This is so unlike me, but so is going on a date when I know it can't go anywhere.* "What made you want to get into law?"

Levi tilts his head to the side, giving off the impression that he's pondering the question. "There's a lot of wrong in the world," he says. "I want to make some of it right."

"You did an exceptional job in the Kaylee Wood interview the other day," I admit, picturing him bundled up in front of that yellow caution tape. "Your love for your job really came through, you know?"

"I hope so." Levi nods. "I just know that her family is counting on me. What they're going through is terrible. I can't change what happened to her, but I can change how the family grieves with justice and closure."

"That's really nice," I say, noticing his eyes shine through the dim lighting. "It's really nice how passionate you are about it, I mean."

The waitress returns to our table with steaming hot plates of food, setting our respective dishes in front of us. "Do you both need anything else?"

Levi and I speak in unison. "Parmesan cheese—"

The waitress laughs at our synchronicity and quickness. Levi and I shoot each other a knowing look that communicates: *Did we just say the exact same thing at the exact same time?* We both burst out into laughter. (Great minds think alike, in the form of dairy preferences, apparently.)

The waitress nods. "I'll be right back with that. For both of you."

Once she heads back to the kitchen, Levi laughs. "When I was little, and they had those Parmesan cheese shakers out on the tables, my mom would let me unscrew the cap and eat a spoonful of it. Gross, I know."

My mind flashes to Delilah and me, here at *Mama Bella,* just a few tables over, when we were kids, doing the *exact* same thing. My mom would let each of us have exactly one spoonful. Sometimes, I'd save it for my pasta. But most times, Delilah and I would just put it directly into our mouths, laughing as flakes of cheese spilled out onto our lips.

"I did the *exact* same thing when I was a kid," I say. "With my sister."

The waitress comes back with two shakers full of Parmesan cheese. "Here you are."

"Thank you," we say in unison.

She leaves our table with blushing cheeks, then drops off a fresh bread basket to the couple next to us. The restaurant is starting to clear out as it gets later in the evening— younger couples taking the spots of the older ones. Levi looks at me, and then the Parmesan shakers, and then our spoons, and then back to me again. *I know just what he's thinking.*

Levi sighs. "For old time's sake?"

"For old time's sake."

We unscrew our respective Parmesan cheese shaker caps, dig our spoons into them, scoop out two heaping mounds of cheese, and sprinkle them onto our dinners. *I can't wait to tell Delilah about this.*

"This is the way to do it," Levi says, making sure he's getting an even distribution.

"I wish this were more socially acceptable," I say, doing the same.

My Penne alla Vodka is buttery and pink and cheesy, and Levi's Chicken Parmesan looks amazing. We start to dig into our meals, and since there's no pressure, I'm not consumed with my typical first date anxieties — *Do I have food on my face? Am I talking with my mouth full? Am I overstuffing my mouth?* — and instead, I feel like I'm just eating with a new friend. That's all this can amount to, anyway.

Levi takes a bite of his chicken. "Do you think you'll be at WJDN forever?"

I stab a noodle with my fork, wondering how in-depth I should go with this answer. "I actually have to make that decision pretty soon."

"A decision?"

"Here's the story." I take a heavy sip of my wine. "Back in college, I interned at The Sunrise Show in New York City."

"I might have known that," Levi says. "From some light social media stalking."

"Creeper," I tease. "Well, I want to make it back there someday. To work for real."

I can't tell if the look on Levi's face is one of surprise or disappointment, but I can tell that he *assumed* the answer to his question would be that I was planning on staying local.

"That's…big." Levi wipes a fallen curl away from the center of his forehead. "How do you make that happen?"

I tell him about climbing the rungs of the news market ladder. I tell him about how I need to jump from market 150 to market number *one.* I tell him that, in order to do that, I need to find stepping stone stations along the way. I tell him about my plans for *The Rundown* that Ruby created for me on that green place mat — that I'll be traveling to Virginia Beach, Nashville, and San Francisco in the next couple of months — and how I'll be determining if *those* towns could be my next moves up the journalism ranks. I tell him that these trips are *crucial* for mapping out my future. I tell him that ultimately, I want to get back to where I began in the Big Apple. I tell him that I could be leaving our hometown of Joyfield…*for good*…within a matter of months.

"This is a lot." Levi stares down at his plate, soaking in the information overload.

"The dinner or my plans?"

"Both."

I *don't* tell him that discussing my future plans is my subliminal way of letting him know that I don't want anything serious. That I can't *have* anything serious. That, unless I'm planning on staying in Joyfield for the rest of my life, we would be long-distance for the *rest* of our relationship. I hope he'll get the hint— we're just on a *date*, and that *dating* is as far as this is going to go. Besides, we're work acquaintances, even though I ruined that with our New Year's Eve kiss.

I direct the focus back to him. "Are *you* planning on staying in the area forever?"

"I think so," he says without conviction. "I'm not opposed to moving, but I have planned on staying here. You just never know, you know?"

I don't know what to make of his comment. Is he quietly saying that he would move for the *right person*? Could the right person potentially be *me*? I don't want to look into it too much, but he could have said he would *never* move. He seems to have a fluid future living situation, possibly depending on others. *Significant others.*

"It's overwhelming." I decide to keep it light. "I just try to focus on the here and now. Live in the moment and have as much fun as I can."

Levi looks up at me, shooting an electric bolt straight through my chest. "I think we have the same idea then."

"I think we do."

Levi's face turns to a *serious* expression. "Hey, I've been wanting to ask you something. But I don't want it to come off as inappropriate."

"Oh, jeez." I suck air in through my teeth. "Now I'm scared."

"Nothing to be scared about." Levi laughs.

I tilt my head in anticipation. "I'm ready."

"There's this fundraiser in Joyfield in the spring. A dance, or like an event, for people with special needs. It's a national organization that travels from town to town to host each one. This year, the proceeds are actually going to *Brew For You*. I think it's called—"

"The *Under The Stars* Dance?"

"Yeah," Levi says, looking surprised that I've heard of it. "I guess this is the second year they're having it in Joyfield."

"My sister wanted to go last year, but something came up." I grab another piece of bread and dip it in the oil. "I wanted to take her—"

Levi looks up at me. "I was wondering if *I could* take her this year."

My eyes widen. Out of *all* the things Levi Winters could have asked me about tonight, this was *nowhere* on my list of possibilities. I feel like I'm going to tear up as my chest swells with love and gratitude. Levi wants to take *Delilah?* I don't know if he's doing this out of the goodness of his heart or if he just wants to win *me* over. But the reason doesn't matter. It's the kindest thing anyone has ever offered.

"Are you asking my sister out on a date…while you're out on a date with *me?*"

"I might be."

"Definitely." I put my hand on my chest. "She would *love* to go. Thank you."

"It's no problem." Levi looks nonchalantly back down at his menu. "It seems like a great event, and your sister seems—"

"You're going to love her," I confirm. "She's like me but better."

"I'll have to see for myself," Levi says. "But I can't imagine that she's *better*."

Once we finish our meals — and Levi insists on paying the bill, despite my performative arguments — we take a short, chilly stroll around the block. The winter evening is on the warmer side tonight, and with the right winter jacket, it feels kind of refreshing. Our feet clomp on the sidewalk as we try to avoid patches of ice.

"I can't believe I never heard of you," Levi says. "I went to high school ten minutes away from here, and I didn't know who you were until that courtroom."

I look up at him, staring at his profile. "That's what I said." I motion to my high school, which is less than a mile up the road. "We weren't too far away from each other."

"I like this area." Levi kicks a rock across the sidewalk. "I think I'm so happy to be back because I left. It took going away for a little while to feel settled now."

"I hope to feel settled someday." I fold my arms across my chest to keep in the warmth. "I'm the opposite of settled right now. I could be out of here in June."

"I'd miss you if you moved, you know." Levi looks down at me, smiling softly.

"You would?" I smirk with skepticism. "There are other reporters who could interview you, you know."

"I won't do an interview for anyone else." Levi laughs, crow's feet lining the sides of his eyes. "I exclusively do interviews with Noelle Fenwick."

"I'll have to call our next story an *exclusive*," I say. "They'd might even make a commercial promo for that."

We reach Levi's car under a streetlight, and he turns to face me. Looking up into his eyes sends a swarm of butterflies back into my stomach. Neither of us is talking. We're just looking at each other. And before I know it, he's wrapping me up in an embrace. The warmth of his arms feels so good, and not just because it's so cold. My face is pressed up against his warm chest, and I feel his hands sliding up and down my back. I'm in a place I never imagined I'd be— in the arms of Levi Winters.

"I like you, Noelle," Levi whispers into my ear. "I like you."

I close my eyes, feeling his words rush a heat through my chest. "I like you too."

I don't know why I admitted it out loud, because I never even came to terms with it myself. I had never blatantly thought in my head: *I like Levi.* I always swallow the feelings and jitters that surface when he's around, and I never let my mind make it any more than that. But I said it out loud to Levi at the same time that *I realized it.* I do like Levi, *and now he knows.*

He releases me while keeping his arms resting behind my back. His face is closer to mine now than it was before our hug. "You're ambitious. You have dreams, goals, and plans. You don't settle. I like that about you."

"Thank you," I manage. I look away, avoiding eye contact, afraid that I'll catch more feelings if I look directly at him. I focus my gaze on a street light. "I talk a big game, but we'll see if it happens."

"Hey." He puts his finger under my chin and lifts my head up to look at him. He's *forcing* me to look at him, which is *forcing* me to come to terms with my feelings. "I believe in you."

I feel the warmth of his breath, his body. I feel like I can't breathe. My heart is pounding. My lips feel like they're shaking. I feel like my entire body is on fire. He uses his finger to pull my chin closer, and soon, we're just millimeters apart.

And that's when he kisses me for the second time.

Twenty

THE "A" BLOCK

Myra and I are about halfway through our 500-mile road trip from Ohio to Virginia for the weekend. While January isn't the most *dreamy* month to head to the coast, it's expected to be in the high sixties this weekend. From the snow, ice, and cold that we've been dealing with *all* winter long in Joyfield, this heat wave makes me feel like we're headed straight for the desert. *My seasonal depression could not be happier.*

I turn down the volume on Myra's *Summer Beach* playlist—something she's using to trick our minds into thinking it's summer vacation. Her beautiful dark curls are tied up into a floppy bun. Deep purple cat-eyed sunglasses shield her dark eyes.

"So, when are we going to talk about this?" I say.

"About what?"

"Seriously?" I shoot her a glare while simultaneously shooting my arms out at my sides. "I've been waiting for you to say something for, like, 250 miles."

She checks her GPS. "It's only been about 220—"

"Come on, Myra!" I fold my arms with force. "What is going on?"

Myra scratches her neck with one hand while keeping the other on the steering wheel. She takes a breath. "Nothing is actually...*going on.*"

I blink, waiting for more information. "Okay?"

"Okay, fine," Myra says, shifting in her seat. "Something is *kind of* going on."

"Like what?" I'm trying to monitor my volume and excitement, but it's not going well. "Are you two, like, dating?"

"Oh, no way," Myra scoffs. She nervously tucks a nonexistent piece of hair behind her ear. "We've been hooking up."

"What *kind* of hooking up?"

"Like, the kind you saw—"

I smirk. "Like the kind I saw...*which time?*"

Myra turns her head to look at me and stares a little too long before turning her attention back to the road. "What do you mean...*which time?*"

"Oh, I don't know." I flip my hair over my shoulder for effect. "I'll tell when *you* tell."

"I *am* telling," Myra shoots back. She clears her throat. "It started, like, a couple of months ago. Just casual hookups. That's seriously all there is to tell."

"And why didn't you tell *me?*" I dramatically grab my chest as if I'm offended. I mean, I kind of *am* offended. But it's not like she told everyone else *but* me. It's still top secret.

"I didn't want to tell anyone." Myra taps her palms on the steering wheel. "We're basically the only two employees at WJDN. I didn't want the word to get out. I didn't want it to get *weird* in the newsroom. I couldn't handle that."

"You could have secretly told me," I whisper. "You know I wouldn't tell anyone."

"I do trust *you*," Myra confirms. "I just didn't want any unintentional weird eyes, or weird vibes, or weird looks—"

"What makes you think I would give you weird looks?" I purposefully raise my eyebrows up and down at record speed. "I would never do such a thing."

Myra laughs. "I'm sorry for not telling you. Don't take it personally."

I shake my head, feeling bad that I'm *making* her feel bad. "I understand. It's okay."

"So when was this *other* time?" Myra asks urgently.

I smirk. "Outside of The Highball near the dumpsters last week."

"Oh," Myra groans, slapping her palm to her forehead in embarrassment. "You saw that?"

"Oh yeah." I wrap my arms around myself, sliding my hands up and down my back, shaking my torso. "A whole lot of... *this.*"

"Sorry you had to see that," Myra says. "Does anyone know about any of this?"

"Delilah," I blurt out. "I'm sorry, she's my sister. I had to—"

"She doesn't count," Myra says. "I mean specifically anyone at *work*?"

"Only...Paige and Ruby."

Myra's eyes nearly pop out of her head, and her hands fly up into the air. "Only Paige and Ruby? Are you kidding me?"

I turn in the passenger seat to face her, trying to calm her down. "I mean, they only saw your New Year's Eve *ball drop* kiss. They *didn't* catch you guys later that night, and they *didn't* see you at The Highball either—"

"Good," Myra sighs, regulating her breathing back down to normal. "They can think it was just for the ball drop. No big deal. We'll keep it that way."

I'm relieved that *both* nights are now out in the open. Well, not the *open*. But at least discussed between Myra and me. *I thought I was going to combust from keeping a secret like this for so long.*

I compose myself. "Am I going to be meeting *Ethan* on this trip?"

"Maybe," she says, looking out the window.

"You've never told us anything about him other than his name," I say.

Myra sighs, glancing out the window at the mountains in the distance. "He has red hair. Green eyes. A total ginger, totally not my type. Can be very funny, but also annoying."

"Ethan seems a lot like Nate." After saying the words out loud, and once they settle into my system, my eyes widen from the sudden realization. "Wait, is Ethan—"

"The name *Nate* spelled backwards? Close enough, at least? Yes."

"N-a-h-t-e?" I spell the letters out loud, growing more confused by the second. "*Nate*...with a mysterious *h* in the middle?"

Myra laughs. "Is the closest name I could think of," she confirms.

"So, for as long as you've been talking about Ethan—"

"I've been hooking up with Nate? Yes. Case closed."

I look back at the open road ahead of me, seeing the mountains level out into flatness the farther along we go. "Did you two talk about, like, *dating?*"

"He's asked me a million times," Myra whispers. "Don't ever tell him I told you that."

"Nate is a good guy," I admit. "But don't ever tell him I told you that."

Myra laughs, adjusting her cat-eye sunglasses on the bridge of her nose. "I've never been in a serious relationship," Myra says. "I don't know *how* to be a girlfriend. I don't even know if I *want* to be a girlfriend."

I raise my eyebrows. "It might be a good time to learn."

* * *

We're driving across a steep, metal bridge, and while the eighty-foot drop to the water below makes me a little jittery, Myra's confidence from driving over this *thousands* of times washes me with a wave of calmness. The sunset paints the sky in an ombre of orange and yellow, and the puffy pink clouds look like cotton candy. The buildings ahead make me feel wanderlust and excited. *I can't wait to try this city on and see how it fits.*

Once we're on solid ground again, I stick my arm out the window, gliding my hand up and down an imaginary roller coaster through the salty air. Old-fashioned, flashy billboards advertise everything from $5 shirts to $10 crab buckets. A few locals are riding their bikes and walking their dogs, enjoying the absence of tourists.

On the beach side to our right— hundreds of hotels, condos, and motels line the coast like a Monopoly board. On the bay side to our left— mini golf courses, diner-style restaurants, and ice cream shops stack on top of each other. A multi color ferris wheel flashes up ahead. It truly feels like summer. *I didn't realize how much I needed this moment until now.*

When we finally pull into Myra's driveway, I stare up at her adorable childhood home. It's exactly how you'd expect a beach house to look— a tiny box raised up on wooden stilts, with pale yellow shake siding and navy blue shutters. A huge decorative seashell hangs from the wooden door. *It looks like an Airbnb listing.*

Myra puts the car into park. "Here we are."

"I can't believe you grew up here." I unbuckle my seat belt and get out of the car, stepping onto the damp pavement. "This is like what you see in a Nicholas Sparks movie."

"You could say that," Myra says, shutting her car door. "Are you ready to travel back in time? Get a glimpse of my childhood?"

"Of course." I grab my nearly torn suitcase out of the backseat. "I've already learned *a lot* about Myra Cole today."

"Helloooooo!" Myra's mom sings as she squeaks open the front door, her arms reaching out wide towards us. "I'm so glad you two made it here safely."

We walk up the wooden stairs and into the kitchen, which is perfectly decorated in a Pinterest-worthy coastal beach-house theme: light blue cabinets, cream-colored walls, seashell picture frames, and a bowl of what appears to be fake fruit on the island. Myra's mom embraces us *both* in a firm hug before I even introduce myself.

"Mom, this is Noelle." Myra motions in my direction. "She basically *runs* WJDN."

"I've heard so much about you," she says. "I'm Sharon.

Sharon Cole. Welcome."

"Your house is stunning," I say. "I think I want to move here already."

Sharon's short, curly brown hair has threads of gray woven throughout, but she doesn't look a day over thirty. She's wearing a light blue and white pattered maxi dress, with a matching turquoise necklace, earrings, and bracelet jewelry set. *I like her vibes.*

"Well, Myra tells me you have an interview here tomorrow at the local news station," Sharon says with a wink and a nudge. "So…you *could* move here if you wanted."

"That I do," I admit. "It's a possibility."

When I planned to come to Virginia Beach with Myra — the "A Block" of The Rundown — I started researching the local news stations. The area's most-watched channel, WVAB, is hiring a morning reporter. While neither the starting date nor the proposed salary was listed in the job description, I decided to update my resume and apply.

I was shocked, but also grateful, when the WVAB news director, Kathleen Seasons — the Virginia Beach equivalent of Bill Calloway at WJDN — emailed me two days later, saying she'd like to interview me. I told her about my trip with Myra, and the timing all worked out perfectly. It was like pushing a ball down a hill. The application was the first push, and now it's just rolling on.

Once we put our suitcases away, Myra and I walk outside to her backyard, where her dad is setting up a fire. The sun has almost set, but strings of vintage light bulbs connect from tree to tree overhead, illuminating the entire backyard. Marshmallows, chocolate, and graham crackers sit on a wooden table, and I can feel my mouth begin to water for the sweetness. And finally, for the first time since we arrived, I can see the glistening shimmer of ocean water in the background. *It's perfect.*

"My girl!" Myra's dad rushes over to her, squeezing her so tightly that she becomes airborne for a split second. He's bald, but like a *shaved* bald. His arms are the size of tree trunks, and he is extremely tall. Now I know where Myra gets it. "I missed my girl."

"I missed you too," Myra muffles into his chest. "Dad, this is Noelle."

"I'm Johnathan Cole. Nice to meet you." He brings me in for a hug, even though I was planning on a handshake. "Any friend of my girl's is a friend of mine."

"Thank you. Your house is beautiful," I say. "How long have you lived here?"

"Since we got married," Sharon says from behind my shoulder. She's coming out to the fire with a charcuterie board in her hands. "Twenty-five years."

"First house we ever bought," Johnathan adds. "We were planning on staying here until we saved enough money to move somewhere bigger. Closer to the ocean. But we ended up loving this place so much that we just stayed here."

"The grass is greener where you water it," Sharon chimes in. "So we watered it."

The four of us sit around the fire pit, vintage lights shining overhead. We're now roasting marshmallows, and I feel like I'm back in middle school. My hands are sticky, my mouth is chocolaty, and my heart is happy. I love being someplace new, with new people, talking about new things. The sun is about to cross the threshold of the water, and I'm mesmerized by the line drawn between the ocean and sky.

"What do you guys like about living here?"

Myra blows on a marshmallow. "Here she goes, being a reporter again."

I shrug my shoulders. "I'm just a *curious* person," I defend.

"Well, our families are from here. That's a big part of it." Johnathan says. He points towards the highway. "I run a restaurant down the road. The same locals come in every weekend, and the same tourists come in every summer. They're the extended family."

"*I'm* the one who runs that restaurant," Sharon teases. "It gets wild there. But I agree. Seeing the ocean outside your window, people coming in fresh off a beach nap, and serving them their favorite foods. It's the best."

I tilt my head and look at Myra. "I didn't know you guys had a restaurant."

Johnathan and Sharon glance at each other. "She didn't tell you?"

"No." I shake my head. "She didn't."

"It's called Myra and Jane's." Sharon smiles, bumping her husband in the shoulder. "We named it after our girls."

I look at Myra, narrowing my eyes. "Girls...*plural?*"

"Myra and her sister," Johnathan confirms. "Our girls."

"I didn't know you had a sister," I say to Myra. "Where is she?"

Sharon hesitates before speaking. "Jane was Myra's younger sister." She clears her throat. "She died from cancer when she was seven. Myra was only ten. It was really hard on her, even though we *all* know she doesn't like to talk about it."

"My quiet girl," Johnathan adds.

Myra looks at me, raising her eyebrows in a way that says:

You got me. "My name is Myra Cole, and I don't like to talk about my problems," she says. "I keep them a secret."

I motion my head in her direction, but keep my eyes fixed on her parents. "She *is* good at keeping secrets."

* * *

Myra drives me to WVAB News bright and early in the morning, giving me words of encouragement for the entire ten-minute drive. The sunrise here is just as beautiful as the sunset, and I like seeing a beach town in its off-season.

"The better you do, the better chance you'll get hired, which means the better chance *I'll* get hired someday," Myra jokes. "No pressure."

My heart has not stopped beating since I woke up. This could be my next stepping stone station. The one I get hired at...*this year.* In six short months. This could be my next rung on the ladder on my way to New York City. It could all start right now.

Walking into the station lobby, I can tell the building is already nicer than WJDN's, but not as fancy as The Sunrise Show's. It seems to be somewhere in the middle. The sleek metal doors and huge silver picture frames displaying photos of their anchors and reporters give the impression that they take pride in their news station. *It even looks like their floor has been recently mopped.*

A receptionist walks me to the WVAB newsroom on the second floor. This newsroom is about *double* the size of ours — both in width *and* height — with triple the number of desks and employees. The scanners make the same beeps and squelches as the ones back home, making me feel a little *homesick*, in some strange way.

Beautiful women and handsome men sit at their desks, some typing scripts and some fixing makeup. Assignment editors talk on two phones at once. Photographers hustle to upload their footage into the editing software. Reporters in tight dresses practice reading their scripts aloud. It's similar to what I'm used to, but more full of life here— more busy, more energetic, more chaos.

"Right this way," the receptionist says, leading me inside the news director's office.

"Thanks," I say nervously. I still can't believe they even *have* a receptionist here. (WJDN just has a buzzer system.)

I turn the corner to see a gorgeous woman sitting at a large desk with a blonde, curly bob haircut. Her royal blue eyes match her royal blue blazer, which hangs over a tight black dress. She's wearing a full face of makeup, and it appears as though she has the appearance of a *former* TV news reporter.

"Nice to meet you, Noelle. I'm Kathleen Seasons, the news director here at WVAB." She stands up from her pink office chair to shake my hand. "Thanks for coming in."

"Thank you for having me." I take a seat in the chair across from her.

Her office is painted a sky blue, but I notice that she has a lot of *hot pink* accents— pointless decorations, office supplies, and picture frames with images of who I assume are her husband and kids.

She sets a pair of thick-rimmed glasses on the bridge of her nose and looks down at my resume, freshly printed and sitting on her desk. "I see that you're currently a reporter in Joyfield, Ohio." She looks back up at me. "I also watched your reel. Impressive."

"Thank you," I say, my palms anxiously sliding back and forth on my thighs.

"I see that your contract is coming up in June," Kathleen says, taking off her glasses and setting them down. "One of our reporters is leaving us around then, and we need to replace her. We have a few candidates."

"That would be good timing." My hands begin to feel clammy when I realize that I *am* one of the candidates she is referring to.

Kathleen sits back in her seat. "So, Noelle. What made you want to get into news?"

The million-dollar question. It's a loaded question, and I have 800 answers for it. *Is it appropriate to say that it's because when I grow up, I want to become Hilda Harrison?*

"I love to write," I admit. "I love to write stories and share them with thousands of people. Highlighting the good in the world, holding leaders accountable, and shining a light on pressing issues in our community. I understand that I have a unique platform as a reporter and storyteller, and I take that extremely seriously. I really want people to trust me, whether that's with the people I'm interviewing in person, or with the viewers watching at home. It's a privilege. I think what we do is really important."

I realize that my answer probably sounds to her like a well-rehearsed boilerplate, but it is truly how I feel about my job. I really do feel like if I could find a place to work that doesn't have the "if it bleeds, it leads" mentality and really values in-depth and human-interest reporting, I could produce stories that make a difference in the world. I'm determined to find a place to work where stories like that could be possible.

"Very good," she says, looking satisfied. "Do you have any

questions for me?"

I pause for a moment, *pretending* like I have to really *think* about this next question. "What is the starting salary?"

Kathleen smirks, knowing this question was bound to come up. "$35,000, which is exceptional for our market," she says. "Substantial vacation, healthcare packages, all of it."

I'm disappointed by the salary, but not surprised. "Are your reporters usually out on stories *alone*? Or do you have camera people?"

"We take reporter safety seriously here." Kathleen looks down at her desk, trying to sound convincing. She leans in closer. "Very seriously."

Since she didn't answer my question, I know her comment is just code for: *it's just more of the same here.* No camera people. *You're alone, so suck it up.*

I clear my throat. "When can I expect to have an answer?"

"Within the next couple of months," she says. "You'll know by the time your contract is up."

I think about living in Virginia Beach for a few years. I love the beach town, and I love Myra's family. I think about how this would just be the "A Block" in *The Rundown*, and that I'd have many more hills to climb after this one. I'm sure Delilah and my parents would love to come here and visit, since it is a vacation destination.

I do feel homesick for Joyfield. But if Kathleen decides to give me this job, *I would have to take it.*

Twenty-One

THE "B" BLOCK

FEBRUARY | NASHVILLE, TENNESSEE

Ruby and I are about two hours away from Nashville when we pull over to an abandoned-looking gas station on the side of the highway. I get out of the car to stretch my legs, and I feel the cool air whipping past my ears. It's about fifty degrees outside, so I'm getting away with just wearing a light cardigan. Ruby, clutching the gas pump, is wearing a worn-out sweatshirt featuring the 1930s faces of Bonnie and Clyde.

"I like your sweatshirt," I say, stretching my arms up into the air. "Looks comfy."

"This thing?" Ruby looks down at it. "Got it at one of those vintage stores in Nashville."

I watched Bonnie and Clyde for a film class in college, and I was immediately fascinated by Bonnie's character. Not for murdering thirteen people, even if she looked glamorous while doing it, but for how much she wanted to be *known*.

She thought becoming an actress would lead to lifelong fame, but when her career wasn't manifesting, she realized she could *still* achieve the *same goal* by being Clyde's accomplice. She was still getting in the newspapers. She was still becoming a household name. She was still becoming popular worldwide. Her ultimate destination was still achieved... *even if the journey to get there was different.*

I was captivated by Bonnie's overwhelming need to be remembered. She wanted her name in the history books. She wanted her face on the front page of the paper. She wanted to become a household name. She did it, and people *still* know who she is today.

But where did her desire to be known come from? Why do some people have this overwhelming need to become somebody?

Ruby flies down the highway, and we sing along to the melodies of Dolly Parton, The Chicks, Kacey Musgraves, and Willie Nelson. Ruby pounds her palm to the beat of the music on her steering wheel, and I slap my thighs pretending to be a drummer. I eventually rest my head in my hand while looking out the window at the Great Smoky Mountains, which have a hue of blue to them. I've never seen anything like it.

"There it is!" Ruby points to a billboard on the side of the road. "Welcome to Tennessee. The Volunteer State!"

"Yee-freaking-haw!" I pretend to circle a lasso in the air and whip it at her.

The road is straight and narrow compared to the steep, green mountains around us. We pass by one bar called *Boots and Bourbon* and another called *Honky Tonk Hillbilly.* I notice that following every hotel, restaurant, and bar is a pancake restaurant. *Pancake Palace. The Pancake House. Pancakes*

Galore. There are trillions of them.

"Do you guys eat anything in Tennessee other than pancakes?"

"Whiskey," Ruby says. "One place around here even has whiskey-flavored pancakes."

To reach the other end of the suburbs where Ruby's parents live, we have to pass through the heart of Nashville. It looks like a busy southern city— bar, concert venue, bar, restaurant, bar, line-dancing studio, bar, guitar shop, bar. It's like every building along this street is just *dying* to host a party. Ruby swerves in and out of traffic, trying to avoid hitting both curbs and pedestrians.

It's like I'm watching a movie out my window. One brunette, wearing a white cowboy hat and matching sparkly boots, drunkenly struts down the sidewalk wearing a *bride* sash. A group of women wearing various animal print dresses, who I assume to be her bridesmaids, chase after her with drinks in their hands. Music is blasting. People are singing. An old couple is dancing. I've never seen a town so busy in the middle of the day. *This reminds me of a southern version of New York City.*

"Is it always this lively?" I lean up in my seat to get a better view out the window.

"You haven't seen anything yet," Ruby says. "It's still daytime."

The photos of country music legends hang as banners from the telephone poles. Jimmy Buffett. Patsy Cline. Kenny Rogers. Loretta Lynn. The names and faces of country stars who made their mark on the music industry are plastered all over this place, even though many of them aren't even living anymore. They'll be in the fabric of this town for all of eternity, even after they've died.

"You know why I think Bonnie wanted to be so famous?"

Ruby blinks her eyes. "Who the hell is Bonnie?"

"Bonnie and Clyde," I laugh. "I think people just want to be remembered. Like these country singers. I don't think it's about the fame they have when they're *here*. I think it's about the remembrance they'll have when they're *gone*."

"Pretty insightful, northerner." Ruby chomps on a piece of gum. "Are you saying you want to kill people? Or be a singer?"

"Neither." I look out the window at the chaos. "I think people want their time here on Earth to *mean* something. That's why some people want to be famous."

Ruby turns down a road called *Honky Tonk Boulevard*. "Maybe we're afraid that if we aren't remembered, we didn't do anything important enough to be remembered *for*."

"And therefore, our lives didn't mean anything," I continue. "That's why some people have a need for fame. Because being famous equals being remembered, and being remembered equals having *meaning*."

"I think you just want to be rich and famous," Ruby says.

"I think I just might," I joke.

*   *   *

"Cheers to Rubyyyyy," a table of her hometown best friends sing into the humid bar air, raising their shot glasses above their heads.

"Cheers to a night of bar hoppin' on Music Row," Ruby shouts back.

Ruby's strawberry blonde curls are up in a messy bun, and

large silver hoop earrings dangle from her ears. She's wearing the same kind of *jean-jacket-cowboy-boot-combo* that the rest of us are wearing. Her friends look like they are *from* here. I'm also wearing a jean jacket, but instead of splurging on official cowboy boots for the occasion, I'm just wearing the boring brown boots that I wear to work all the time. Nobody seems to notice, and if they do, they don't say anything.

After swallowing the poison in unison, we all wince. I feel a flame shooting down my esophagus and down into my stomach, warming it up like a hot cup of tea.

"What is this?" I ask, still squinting from the pain.

"The Prairie Fire," Ruby says through her teeth, closing her eyes. "It hurts so good."

I put a hand over my chest. "What's it made of?"

"You don't wanna know, northerner."

"Tequila and hot sauce," her friend answers. "It's Ruby's favorite. We do this every year on her birthday, and have been since high school."

Ruby does a little dance on her bar stool, shimmying her shoulders from side to side. "Another year older, another Prairie Fire down the hatch."

We sit at a crowded table at *The Belt Buckle* in the heart of Nashville. The floorboards are the same dark wood color as the wall panels. A huge disco ball hangs in the center of the dance floor, surrounded by a large stage for live music. It's barely even dark outside, but the place is already filled with people. It's a stunning mixture of college kids, girls on their bachelorette trips, and local southerners.

"Welcome to The Belt Buckle!" A handsome man walks up onto the stage and makes the announcement into the microphone. The sheen of his leather jacket shimmers against the disco ball's flares. "How are y'all feeling tonight?"

The crowd cheers back, signaling that they are feeling *good*.

The man stomps around in his cowboy boots. "We're startin' with some live music from one of our favorites here in Nashville. Please welcome: *The Passion Flowers!*"

"Oh no," one of Ruby's friends says.

Ruby's eyes widen. "Is she still—"

The crowd starts to cheer again, just as the man starts shouting back into his microphone. "I'm gonna turn things over to the lead singer, the star of the show, the woman of the hour: *Whitney Tusings!* Take it away, Whit!"

"Yep, that's her," another friend confirms.

Ruby shakes her head. "I thought she played at—"

The friend rushes in to respond. "The bar down the street that we were planning on *avoiding* tonight? Yeah, us too."

A woman with straight blonde hair, whom I assume to be Whitney, grabs the microphone. She's wearing a denim mini skirt with a matching jean jacket, of course, which has silver sparkly fringes on the chest. Her light pink cowboy boots come up to her mid calf, and they're gorgeously embellished with rhinestones. She looks like she's headed straight to the Country Music Awards.

"I wanna thank you all for coming out here this evenin' for some country music," she shouts into the crowd. "One, two, three, four—"

The band starts blasting a cover of *The Way You Love Me* by Faith Hill. I look at Whitney on stage right as she makes eye contact with Ruby in the crowd, and both of them look stunned to see each other. Whitney keeps singing and dancing anyway, visibly trying to distract herself.

One of Ruby's friends points a thumb towards me. "Can

someone explain to this northerner what's going on?"

Ruby leans in my direction, still keeping her eyes glued to Whitney. "Noelle, this might come as a surprise to you. But Whitney and I used to…*date*."

"Her?" I don't mean for my shock to come off in the wrong way, but it probably does. I attempt to clarify. "I mean…I just didn't know…"

"Yeah," Ruby answers all of my questions at once. "We were together for a long time, but she cheated on me with her drummer. Who was a *guy*, by the way?"

Whitney sings into the microphone, pounding her right cowboy boot on the ground to the beat. I wanted to ask Ruby more questions, but it's so loud in here that I can barely even hear myself think. We stay at The Belt Buckle until the end of the song, and since the night was pre-destined for bar *hopping*, we *hop* over to the next bar.

I picked up my speed to walk arm in arm with Ruby. We shove our way through a sea of people. It's getting chilly outside, so I'm glad I'm wearing at least some form of a *jacket* right now. My fake boots clomp on the sidewalk.

I lowered my voice to Ruby. "I didn't know you dated—"

"Women? Surprise," she says, shooting out a jazz hand. "Whitney was my first girlfriend, and I was hers. But apparently, a *girlfriend* wasn't what she wanted, even though she seemed pretty confident to me."

We squeeze between a swarm of bachelorette party attendees walking in our direction. "If she didn't cheat, do you think you guys would have worked out?"

"Maybe," Ruby answers. "She's trying to make it big in music, wants to stay in Nashville. I don't know where I want to be. That was hard for her to comprehend."

"I understand that," I say, thinking of Levi. "This moving around stuff makes everything harder. Maybe your paths will cross again someday?"

"I don't need a woman. Or a man. I'm lovin' the single life." Ruby points back to her group of friends, who are following behind us. "Plus, look how many girlfriends I already have!"

Once we get into the next bar called the *Bourbon Saloon* and order our drinks, we dance in a circle to Dolly Parton's *Jolene*. It's my fourth tequila sunrise of the night — after I've already consumed three of Ruby's mystery birthday shots that I've never heard of — and I'm starting to feel it. I look up at the specks of dust floating in the air towards the ceiling, illuminated by the nearest spotlight. I know my life in Nashville wouldn't look like this *every* night, but I really like the vibes. It's the "B Block" of *The Rundown*, and I'm really in the thick of it now.

A deep voice speaks into a microphone, and it booms throughout the bar. "Let's welcome the birthday girl to the bull," he says. "Ruby May, come on down."

"A bull? Are they talking about me?" Ruby frantically looks around the room. "I didn't even know there was a bull in here."

"There is," one of her friends teases.

Ruby glares at all of us. "Which one of you bitches said something?"

One of her friends gently raises her hand. "Sorry, I had to. Now go, birthday girl."

We make our way over to the mechanical bull in the middle of the bar. Ruby slides off her cowboy boots, enters the arena, and bounces up and down a few times on the inflatable platform. About a dozen people are lined up on the outskirts, hooting and hollering for Ruby's upcoming performance.

"I'm going to kill you guys," she shouts.

"You got this," the friend who volunteered her says. "Just hang on tight."

Ruby jumps three times on the inflatable padding to get enough height to land on the bull's back. She plops down, puts her right hand on the handle, waves her left hand in the air, and screams, "Bring it on, *mechanical bull operator guy!*"

The bull starts moving to the left. Then to the right. Then a little bit up, and a lotta bit down. Each movement is met with collective oohs and aahs from us and everybody else watching in the crowd. We collectively applaud and yell words of encouragement.

"I knew I could do this!" Ruby screams.

But right as she expresses her confidence, the *mechanical bull operator guy* spins her around just fast enough to throw her off the bull and onto the inflatable padding. She stands up and dusts herself off, adjusting her dress back to its intended position. Her hair is hilariously disheveled, and I think her eyeliner is even smudged up a bit.

"You have got to be shittin' me," she yells to the man. "I was doin' so good."

"Next," the man says, ignoring her complaints. And then… he points to *me*.

I shake my head. "Oh, I'm not in line."

"Come on, northerner," Ruby says. Her friends chime in on the peer pressure. "This is part of your Nashville orientation. Get up there."

I feel my cheeks flush, but they're right. *When else would I ever do this in my entire life?* I slip off my non-cowboy boots and launch myself onto the bull by bouncing my way there.

Just like Ruby, I place one hand on the bull and the other in the air. *I hate knowing that all eyes are on me right now.* I guess it's now or never.

"Ready!" I give the *mechanical bull operator guy* an anxious head nod.

And there, in front of Ruby, her childhood friends, and about forty other people in the bar, I ride the back of a mechanical bull. The crowd cheers and cautions along with each movement, and eventually shrieks a simultaneous "awww" when I'm forcibly thrown off.

"You were robbed!" Ruby yells. "Blind! You were robbed blind!"

"I have to admit that was sort of fun." I bounce my way back over to the group. "But I think I like watching *other* people more."

"Welcome to Nashville," Ruby says. "Where we ride bulls and drink hot sauce."

* * *

Ruby and I drive to a little breakfast place — serving a variety of pancakes, because what else would they be serving — up the street from her house in the suburbs. There are newspapers, hanging in frames from top to bottom on the exposed brick walls, filled with printouts of good news stories from Nashville over the years.

"Here y'all are," the waitress says, placing chocolate chip pancakes in front of me and blueberry pancakes in front of Ruby. "Need anything else?"

Ruby nods slowly. "Can I get just some extra butter and syrup, please?"

"Of course," the waitress says. She's wearing a black-and-white checkered apron, her hair folded into a French twist, looking like a staple of southern hospitality.

I rub my temples. "I took two Ibuprofen an hour ago, but nothing is working." I take a sip of my coffee, which is filled with vanilla creamer. "Maybe this will do the trick."

Ruby takes a sip of her black coffee. "This stuff should do it for you," she encourages. "It's a hangover cure."

A woman in her mid-fifties walks up to a mini stage to the left of the waitress station. She's just wearing jeans and a white sweatshirt, but still looks put together. Her dark hair is pulled up into a messy bun, mirroring how my own hair looks this morning. I notice layered gold chains hanging around her neck, all looking like they have some sort of meaning.

"Do all of your restaurants and bars in this town have *stages*?" I ask.

"Pretty much." Ruby's hair is in a ponytail, still unbrushed from last night. She points her fork towards the tiny stage. "Live music at all times."

The woman starts singing a rendition of Patsy Cline's *Walkin' After Midnight*. She has the voice of an angel and the stage presence of a ballerina. She looks like she belongs on a bigger stage, somewhere that is not...*here*. Not on this little stage in this little restaurant.

"Oh my gosh," I whisper, leaning in towards Ruby. "She's really good."

"Mary. That's her name," Ruby says. "She's my mom's friend. Sings here every Sunday morning. It's how she gets her singin' fix, I guess."

I listen to Mary's angelic voice while savoring every bite of my angelic pancakes. When she starts singing *Crazy* by Patsy

Cline right after her first, my jaw drops. She is absolutely incredible. If this woman were to try out for American Idol, not only would she make it through the first round, but she would win the entire thing.

"She should be a *professional* singer," I whisper. "Why isn't she?"

"Always dreamed of it," Ruby says with a mouthful. "Always told my mom she wanted to make it big. She's a receptionist in a doctor's office now. Just sings for fun."

"She could *be* the next Patsy Cline," I say.

Once the song ends, a trickle of applause fills the restaurant.

"Thank you," Mary says softly into the microphone.

As the thumping in my head continues with every beat of Mary's next song, I can't help but take in her voice. She should *be* one of those faces hanging on a poster throughout Nashville.

If two people are equally talented, what makes one person *famous* and the other *unknown*? Is it a lack of determination? Is it all about luck? Is it just based on timing?

Maybe Mary can't afford *not* to have the stability of a normal nine-to-five job. Maybe she values the vacation and healthcare that come with her day job *more* than pursuing her passions. Maybe she's a single mom who can't risk taking a chance on something that might not work out in the end. For her, maybe it's just all about *reality*.

All I know is that this woman *could* make it. But I watch quietly as she sings on this little stage, in this little pancake restaurant, where she'll probably be singing forever.

Twenty-Two

THE "C" BLOCK

Taking off is always the worst part.

"It's okay," Paige says, squeezing my hand without an ounce of worry in hers.

"Almost done," I breathe.

I close my eyes and press my back against the squished, hard economy seat. *In, out. In, out.* I suck in air through each bounce of turbulence on the way up. It's not until the plane flattens out — flat and horizontal like it *should* be — that I feel an ounce of relief.

"We've reached 30,000 feet, our cruising altitude," the pilot says over the intercom. "It should be a smooth ride from here. It's about four hours to San Francisco. The temperature upon arrival is sixty degrees. Sit back, relax, and enjoy the ride."

"Thank God," I whisper, exhaling. "Hard part is over."

"I hate landing," Paige says. "And even then, I don't even really mind it."

"I hate taking off," I say. "I'll be fine the rest of the way."

Paige plugs her headphones into the monitor jack. "I'm going to start *High School Musical*. I'll talk to you in an hour and a half." She presses play.

I'm eye level with a cumulonimbus cloud in the center of a deep blue sky, which is casting a shadow on the land beneath it. The tall mountains below us look like little bumps from up here. I take a deep breath and try to relax, thinking about how I'm headed to the "C Block" of *The Rundown*. My travels to Virginia Beach and Nashville were exciting, but since this trip requires a *plane*, it takes my excitement to a whole new level.

I scroll through some movie options of my own. The Notebook? Too sad. Legally Blonde? Saw it too many times. La La Land? Seems perfect for the occasion. Even though I'm going to a city nearly 400 miles away from Los Angeles, it's still California, right? I press play, adjust my neck pillow, and try to get as comfortable as possible for economy.

"I love that movie," Paige whispers once she sees my selection. "Emma Stone and Ryan Gosling…a match made in heaven."

I love the full circle moment with Mia at the coffee shop. In the beginning, she's just an underpaid employee, serving coffee to famous actresses. But in the end, *she's* the famous actress, and coffee is being served to her. It makes me think of all those americanos I got for Hilda Harrison. Someday, if I'm really lucky, some little intern will be getting *me* an americano. I'll have my own full circle moment. *I'll be Mia in my own realm.*

The movie is all about being a dreamer, and that's why I've always connected to it. I like to consider myself a dreamer. I got to The Sunrise Show as an intern, right? Doesn't that mean I can get there *again* for a real job? But I realistically know that the odds aren't in my favor. Even if I end up working in San Francisco someday, there's no guarantee that I'd make it to New York City afterwards. I could take all the necessary steps to get there, and it still might not work out.

"Shit," I mumble under my breath as the plane suddenly drops. It begins to shake, as if the pilot is driving through a valley of rocks. The seat belt sign dings.

"As you can see, we are experiencing some slight turbulence," the pilot announces over the intercom. "We have turned the seat belt sign on for your safety."

"You okay?" Paige looks away from Troy Bolton and towards me. "It's all good."

"I'm fine, thanks." I continue watching La La Land, letting the bold colors and catchy songs distract me from realizing how close I am to the stratosphere.

Paige opens a small bag of white cheddar popcorn and dances in her seat to one of the *High School Musical* songs. I giggle at her excitement and joy over Troy and Gabriella.

Paige is a free spirit. Sure, she might not know what she's getting herself into when it comes to the local news industry. Yes, she seems to just want to be on the television screen. Yes, she's probably more concerned about her social media following than about her audience's trust. But her ignorance is bliss, and the more jaded I'm becoming, the more I want to be just like *her* again.

Even if she doesn't know it, Paige is still living through the magic of it all. She's bouncy with a fresh start to a new career, and all of the excitement the industry brings. She's innocent, and that's what makes her fresh. That's why it's nice to become friends with the new girl. She's constantly reminding me to *enjoy* work, even though she doesn't realize she's doing it.

* * *

The San Francisco air is a beautiful mixture of bitterly cold and refreshing. Even though it's only March, the breeze from the bay makes it somewhat chilly all year long (according to Paige). The sky is a perfect light blue color with not a cloud in sight, and everybody seems so happy here because of it. I can't believe I'm setting foot on the West Coast for the *first* time in my life, and so far, I love it.

Paige and I walk along Fisherman's Wharf, an adorable waterfront neighborhood home to souvenir shops, coastal restaurants, and unique museums. The buildings are all so cute and colorful, like everything is in some shade of pastel. The loud screeching sounds of cable cars wail in the city, somewhere among the skyscrapers home to technology giants.

I notice that there's a massive, thick layer of fog hanging over the horizon — way past the large boats and fishing rods in the distance — over the beautiful waters of the bay.

I point to it. "I don't understand how that fog is so thick when there's not even...*clouds*."

"It has a name," Paige says.

She's still eating her salted caramel gelato with the mini spoon they give you, and I just finished my peanut butter cone. Each of them was eight dollars a piece, but it was so good that I'd do it all over again. *You can't find gelato like this anywhere in Ohio.*

"You *named* your city's fog?"

"I didn't name it. The city did." Paige pulls out her phone and begins typing something into her Instagram search bar. "There's even an account. It's called *Karl the Fog.*"

"Your fog's name is...*Karl?*" I observe the profile as my eyes adjust to the screen.

"Yep. Isn't it so cute?" Paige tucks her phone in her back pocket and readjusts the colorful scarf tied around her neck. "What other city would do that?"

We walk by the Painted Ladies and rows of Victorian-style homes, all in those poppy pastel shades of traffic light green, robin egg blue, and baby girl pink. When I was little, I frequently wondered why all the buildings in Ohio were always some ugly variation of brown or gray. Why couldn't someone's house be, like, bright purple? Why couldn't an office building be, say, neon orange? I like that San Francisco *didn't* get the Midwestern memo. I like that they believe in *colorful* architecture.

"I always wanted a light pink one," Paige says, pointing to one of the homes. "With those big bay windows. Could you imagine?"

"Someday when you come back here," I say. "That's what you want, right?"

"Maybe." Paige tosses her empty gelato cup in a nearby garbage can. "I don't know where else I would want to be. San Francisco is market ten, so it's up there."

"I understand," I say. "It's really hard to figure it all out."

We walk past a cluster of precious sea otters, sunbathing on wooden planks. They are loud and stinky and squirmy, pushing each other off into the water to make more room for themselves. They bob their heads in the fastest and funniest way possible, so I take out my phone to get a video.

"They smell," Paige says, scrunching her nose. "But they're kinda cute. I used to tell my parents that I wanted one as a pet when I was little."

I laugh. "What would you name it, *Karl*?"

"Carl with a C," Paige jokes. "There's also a little neighborhood about thirty minutes away called Sausalito. I always said I wanted to name my future dog that. Its nickname would be *Sauce*. How adorable would that be?"

"Maybe you can have a *Carl* and a *Sauce* someday in your pink Victorian-style home with a big bay window." I place my hands on the wooden railing, watching the sea otters fight for more room. "Sounds like a dream."

Paige takes me to a coastal restaurant next door, famous for their sourdough bread. From the number of signs I've seen *advertising* sourdough bread bakeries on this block alone, I can assume it's a popular food item here. *I can get behind a city that supports and produces mass quantities of bread.*

Paige orders a bread bowl full of clam chowder, and I just get a *plain* sourdough bread bowl with a side of butter. Paige makes fun of me for it, but I'm still nauseous from the flight. It's a combination of being an anxious flier and having motion sickness from the turbulence. *This always happens when I fly.*

"I can't eat after a flight," I explain. "Except gelato. And plain bread, apparently."

"That sucks." Paige dips the lid of her bread bowl into the soup and takes a bite.

I savor a piece of the tangy bread. "I take it you're not a nervous flier like me?"

"Not at all," Paige says. "I don't like being in one place for too long. Most times, flying is the only way out of places, so I like the idea of it."

I hold up a piece of my flaky crust. "I like a city that likes bread."

This restaurant has an industrial feel, with exposed brick walls and silver pipes overhead. Light bulbs covered in large mason jars hang from chains, shining down onto each table. This place has *beach* vibes, but not *ocean* vibes, which I'm finding are two different things.

"How are you doing being away from home?"

"I'm fine with it." Paige taps her acrylic nails on the table. "But Joyfield isn't my *ideal* living situation. No offense."

"I get it." I take off my jacket and wrap it around the back of my metal chair. "I wouldn't want to live there if I weren't *from* there. Plus, it would be so hard being from a place like *this*…and moving to a place like *that*."

Paige takes another bite of her soup. "So, did I beat Myra and Ruby?"

I narrow my eyes at her. "What do you mean?"

"Is my hometown better than theirs?" Paige shuffles in her seat, eager for me to answer. "I want you to like it *here* the best. They save the best for last, you know."

I raise my eyebrows knowingly at her. "I like them each in their own little ways," I say. "But hopefully, I'll be living in *all* of them at one point. So I can't really choose."

"The day is still young," Paige says. "I'll win you over."

Once we're done eating our carbohydrates, we walk around to another neighborhood with a gorgeous view of the Golden Gate Bridge. The water is flowing peacefully beneath it. I look up at its giant red arches, which look ginormous compared to our tiny statures.

Paige outstretches her arms when we see it. "It's like Full House. See?"

I tilt my head to the side. "But I thought it was…*golden?*"

"It's because we're crossing the *Golden Gate Strait* of water," Paige explains, placing her hands on her hips with confidence. "See, I learned something in high school."

"That…and that the fog here is named *Karl.*"

"I learned that one from Instagram," Paige says.

* * *

If you had told me last year at this time that I'd be a wedding date for a new WJDN reporter — in a bay front city on the other side of the country — I *never* would have believed you. But somehow, here we are.

Paige and I arrive at the wedding venue, called The Fran, in an Uber. The fancy stone building sits gracefully on the edge of the water, overlooking the shimmering waters of the bay behind it. The sky is getting darker, and the stars are coming out, setting the scene for this black-tie affair. *Where I don't know a single soul except for Paige.*

I smooth out my black dress as I get out of the Uber and secure the fur shawl around my arms. I catch up with Paige, who is already a few steps ahead of me. She's wearing a bright red dress that falls to her mid-calf, and her blonde hair is tied up in a high ponytail. We're both wearing similar-looking nude high heels, but I can already tell that I'll be dancing *without* mine tonight.

"I love that I don't know anyone here," I whisper, walking alongside her into the venue.

"I *wish* I didn't know anyone here," Paige says. "It's like a high school reunion for me."

"Is that why you watched *High School Musical* on the plane?"

"*Subconsciously*, maybe yes." Paige says. "You should be a psychiatrist."

We walk into the wedding, which, upon first glance, seems to have cost at least $100,000. The floors are a deep, red carpeting with navy swirls. The ambient, soft lighting makes me squint to see clearly. The cream-colored, soft drapes hang at every imaginable corner. This place is fancy. Like, *fancy* fancy.

We spot our names written in silver marker on a giant mirror, revealing that we're seated at table number eleven. Paige puts a card filled with money in the designated *card box*, and we get two glasses of red wine from the bar. There must be *fifty* tables spread throughout the large space — which looks big enough to host a ballroom dance competition — so we go on a scavenger hunt to find *said* table number eleven.

"Not there, not there," Paige says.

"Wait, maybe over there," I add.

"The numbers are starting to go backwards."

"Let's try this way," I say.

We look like we're heading through a corn maze to reach our destination. I try to avoid staring intently at everyone as I pass by— between the handsome men in expensive tuxedos and the beautiful women in designer cocktail dresses that reach the floor. *I suddenly feel underdressed.*

"Found it!" Paige points to her name tag. "Finally."

"This is so high-end." I pull out my chair, which is covered in a cream silk bow.

"Welcome to weddings in an expensive city." She motions

to the nine-tiered wedding cake in the corner of the ballroom. "Maybe I'll have to get married in Joyfield someday just so I can *afford* it."

I slide my hand along the champagne colored cloth napkin and take in the oversized ballroom around me. It looks like a scene out of Bridgerton. Chandeliers dangle from the ceiling. The dance floor sparkles with hints of gold. The ceilings must be thirty feet high. I definitely *do not* belong here, which makes me *want* to be here even more. Our table seats eight people, but Paige and I are the first ones to arrive.

"I hope people from my high school aren't seated *with* us," Paige says, flicking her ponytail over her shoulder. "I'd die."

"That's how you know the bride, right?" I unprofessionally rest my elbows on the table, leaning in to hear the background details of this evening. "From high school?"

"Yes, but I didn't even really know her that well." Paige fixes a strap on her red dress. "But here we are."

I'm taking a sip of my wine when the remaining six people — three young couples — fill up the empty seats at our table. Paige shoots me a glance, confirming that, yes, these people *are* from her high school. She performs the fake greeting and small talking ritual, but luckily doesn't have to for long before the reception begins.

"May I have your attention, please?" A woman, whom I assume to be the wedding coordinator, rapidly clinks a fork against a glass. "It's time for us to introduce the bridal party."

The ten-piece band starts playing loud, upbeat music. The bridal party enters the reception couple by couple — the groomsmen's sage green ties matching the bridesmaids' sage green dresses — as they perform short dances, dramatically chug their drinks, or use a prop to get the audience's applause.

Then, last but not least, the bride and groom are welcomed into the venue with a standing ovation.

"Introducing the new Mr. and Mrs. Stephen and Brianna Paisley!"

The bride's gown is dramatic and voluminous, like something Cinderella would wear. She's holding white lilies, encased in leafy greenery, secured with a sage-green bow. The groom is wearing a *white* tie to differentiate himself from the groomsmen, of course. The couple dances and spins their way to the center of the ballroom floor, where they share their first dance to Elvis Presley's *Can't Help Falling In Love*. A smoke machine kicks on, spreading a white cloud at the couple's feet.

"Is that supposed to symbolize Karl the Fog?" I whisper to Paige.

"I hope it has *some* kind of meaning," Paige says, tightening her ponytail. "Or else it would be a *huge* waste of money."

As my eyes remain glued on the beautiful bride and groom, I see Paige's head on a swivel to identify the guests sitting in their seats. Her head suddenly freezes on one table across the dance floor, and I see her eyes widen. She looks like she just saw a ghost.

"See that guy with the dark hair at table three?" She subtly points. "That's the one who dumped me. I had no idea he was invited here on his *own*. I thought he was *my* plus one."

"That sucks," I whisper back. "Is the girl sitting beside him—"

"His girlfriend? No. It's his sister," she laughs. "Thank God."

After Paige confiscates enough Cosmopolitans to quench Carrie Bradshaw for the entire duration of Sex and the City, we begin to feel loose enough to start dancing in front of 400 strangers, so we head out onto the shiny dance floor. Early 1990s and 2000s beats pulse through the crowd, but it's still too early for people to be overly confident in their movements. We bounce from side to side, drinks sloshing around in our hands.

The songs begin to transition from fast to slow. We start heading back to table number eleven when *Unchained Melody* starts to play, and all of the couples who were previously sitting down take our places. *I start to wonder if people think Paige and I are a couple.* I'm walking next to a woozy Paige until someone stops her from behind.

"Hey."

It's the ex-boyfriend. He's a young guy with recently trimmed dark hair and light brown eyes. He's just a little bit taller than Paige, and his black tuxedo looks like it's one size too big. He's cute, though. Looks nervous, and maybe even a tad guilty.

Paige looks at him before turning back around to keep walking.

"Can we talk?" The man tries again, reaching for her arm.

Paige turns around and snaps. "What?"

"I want to talk." The guy clears his throat, looks into her eyes, and reaches out a hand. "Can we talk on the dance floor?"

She looks down at his hand and then back up at him. "I don't want—"

"Please?"

I feel like I'm not supposed to be witnessing this interaction, so I'm relieved when Paige accepts his invitation to dance (even if it takes ten awkward, silent seconds). I walk back to our table alone, happy to be excused from their tension.

I sit down in my overly expensive seat, watching Paige and her ex-boyfriend slow dance on the ballroom floor. They don't look like they're fighting, but they're definitely in the process of...*conversing.* She's not getting too close to him, but after a few minutes of talking, a sweet smile appears on her face. And then a few moments later, *a laugh.* I wish I could hear their conversation, but we have a four-hour plane ride home tomorrow, with plenty of time for me to catch up.

Watching them sway back and forth underneath the giant chandelier — along with all of the other dozens of couples out on the dance floor — makes me think of Levi. I want him here, dancing with me. I want him to spin me around and hold me close. I want his hazel eyes to look into mine.

I'm getting too emotionally invested, and I can't blow it off any longer. Whatever concerns about professionalism and ethics (and my *what-if-I'm-moving-to-another-city-soon* anxieties) are being washed out of me. I don't care about any of that stuff in this moment, here across the country, looking out at all the couples slow dancing. *I just want him.*

Twenty-Three

THE FOLLOW UP

APRIL | JOYFIELD, OHIO

David hums to himself as he enters the newsroom in a tune that sounds like it's coming straight from the Beatles themselves.

"No guitar today?" I ask.

"Left her at home."

David grabs the empty chair behind my desk and swirls it around to sit beside me. He's wearing a zip-up gray sweatshirt with some kind of skull-and-crossbones design screen-printed on the front. He rests his feet, encapsulated in black motorcycle riding boots, on the filing cabinet beside me, causing some dirt to fall onto my desk.

"Seriously?" I say, pointing at it.

"It's fine, man. Just chill out." He rests his hands behind his gray-haired head. "So, how's the world traveler doing over here?"

"I'm happy to be home," I admit. "It was fun, though. I felt like I was on tour all over America. I must take after you."

"You're more like the Fenwick triplets than you think," David says. "But it's always nice to sleep in your own bed."

"How many states have you been to?" I let my shoulders relax for the first time all day. *David has this calming effect on people.*

"All of them. Well, except for Alaska. That one is still on my bucket list." He stares up at the dirty popcorn WJDN ceiling. "Went to lots of countries, too."

"Out of all the places you've gone, which one was your favorite?" I put my feet on the filing cabinet alongside his, taking a break from the script I'm writing.

"Here," David says. "There's no place like home, as they say."

I cross my arms over my chest. "I don't believe that for one second."

David laughs. "How did your interview go? Where was it, Virginia?"

"Virginia Beach," I answer. "It was good, I think. They're looking to hire someone in June, which would be perfect timing for me. But I *still* haven't heard if I got the job."

"You're going to get it, no doubt," David says. "Even though I'd be pissed that you'd be leaving me here."

"I'm more like the Fenwick triplets than I think, remember?"

"I know, I know. It's in your blood." David admits.

"I went to three cities in three months," I remind him. "Plus, I'm going to New York City next month for my birthday. I have been bitten by the *travel bug*, as they say."

I look at David, who is now looking out the window. For the first time in months, there's finally no more snow on the tree branches visible from our second-story newsroom. You can actually see…*green.* The sky is blue instead of its typical dingy gray. The grass is bright green instead of its common beige. The bushes and shrubs are leafy instead of ice-capped. Spring has arrived in Joyfield, and since we only get nice weather about six months out of the year, there's a happiness in the air that we haven't felt in a while. It's like the seasonal depression is slowly but surely lifting.

I rest my chin in my hand. "Why did you come back *here* after being *there?*"

"Besides the band breaking up, I missed my bed." He folds his hands in his lap and twiddles his thumbs in circles. "I missed my family and friends and everybody here."

"But didn't you love New York?"

"Of course, I loved it," David shrugs. "But I was only *there* because of the band. So, when the band went away, what else did I have there?"

"Couldn't you have found a *new* band to perform with?"

"Nah. That part of my life was over," David says. "I felt like my time there was up."

I observe his wrinkles. "Do you ever feel sad? You know, about giving up?"

David looks down at the stained carpeting. "I didn't…*give up,*" he says, rolling up the sleeves of his sweatshirt. "My dream was to play the guitar, and I still do it every single day. But instead of playing on a stage, I play in my living room. Instead of performing in front of thousands of people, I just perform for you guys. Instead of playing in big cities, I'm playing in my hometown. I'm still *living* my dream of being a guitar player, but I just play for a different audience. It was never about the *people* who were listening. It was always about my love for the *instrument*."

I sit with his words for a moment. My mind flashes to writing. I love to write stories. It shouldn't matter *who* I'm writing those stories for. The realization gives me a mental sigh of relief. Whether I'm in Joyfield, Virginia Beach, Nashville, San Francisco, or New York City, I'll be a writer. And the thought of that brings me a tremendous amount of happiness. No matter where I make it, I'll still be doing what I love. *Writing stories.*

"That's a good way to look at it," I finally say.

"Think about your dad," David continues. "He didn't technically *give up* on his photography dreams. Even though he doesn't work for National Geographic, he still practices photography every day. It's like me and the guitar. It was always just about his love of the *camera*, not about *who* was looking at his photos. Maybe it was never about the big job for him. Maybe it was just about his love of the art. Same passion, different audience. We're alike in that way, he and I."

"Maybe you should have been a career counselor," I tease.

The blinking cursor on my computer monitor seems to be screaming: *Finish this script! Get back to work! The clock is ticking!* But I ignore it. Talking to David is the best part of my day, and his wisdom is exactly what I need right now.

"It's hot as balls in here." David unzips his gray sweatshirt and drapes it over the back of his chair. "Anyway, what was I saying?"

I laugh. For David, it's always as hot as balls, or even sometimes, as *cold* as balls. I don't know what temperature they're supposed to be. "We were talking about dreams."

"Oh yeah." David takes a sip of his coffee, which sits in a mini Styrofoam cup from the break room. "Sometimes it's not that you're necessarily *giving up* on a dream. Dreams can change. They shape shift. Manifest themselves differently. If you don't end up doing *exactly* what you said you were gonna do, it doesn't mean you failed. It just means your dreams changed, and that's okay. Just as long as you don't give up on the *passion* itself."

"So, if you stopped playing the guitar entirely, and my dad quit taking pictures all together, *that* would be the true crime?"

"The crime of the century." David tightens the laces of his left motorcycle boot. "We're still doing what we love. Just in a different way."

My eyes glance at the photo of Daniel in the tiny wooden frame leaning up against my speaker. "Do you think he would have come to the same realization?"

"Maybe, maybe not." David takes in the image of his college-aged brother, frozen in time. "Maybe he would have ended up coming back to Joyfield and acting in plays for the local community theater. Maybe he would have become an adjunct professor and started teaching theater classes. Or, maybe he *would* have made it big on Broadway, starring in movies and TV shows. Who knows. But either way, as long as he was still *acting*, he would have succeeded no matter which path he took."

I sit back in my seat, crossing my arms over my chest. "We should have recorded this conversation. David Fenwick is the *Dalai Lama* over here."

"Maybe I'll start a podcast," he teases. "*Dreams 101 with David.*"

"I'd listen to it," I say. "How else would I know what to do with my life?"

"Listen, kid. Sometimes you *leave* a place with different dreams than you originally *went* there with. Plans change, mindsets change, dreams change. Just keep the thing you love in your life somehow, and you can never go wrong."

I glance at the photo of Daniel on my desk, with a ponytail and a college diploma staring me in the face. "He sticks in my mind a lot. Even though I didn't know him."

"Me too, kid." David stands up out of his chair, stomping his dirty motorcycle boots back on the ground. *I feel like he's hiding a tear drop.* "Me too."

Once David turns around and starts talking to Nate, I see an email notification pop up on my phone. It's from Kathleen Seasons from WVAB News in Virginia Beach— a name I've been waiting to see for weeks.

My heart starts to race. My palms begin to sweat. *Will this email contain my answer?* I open the email as fast as my fingers allow me to. It reads:

Dear Noelle,

Thank you so much for interviewing with WVAB and for considering us as your next professional destination. We are pleased to offer you a reporting position with us starting in June. I was impressed with your interview and reporting credentials. Please respond to me with your answer. We would be thrilled and honored to have you working at our station.

Sincerely,
Kathleen Seasons
News Director, WVAB

I stare at the words, rereading them over and over and over again. Are my eyes deceiving me? *Did I really get the job?*

I remember Kathleen saying that there were a *few* candidates up for the position. *Was I the candidate she chose?*

I stare out the window, watching the green branches flutter in the wind. I feel my heart swell, like I'm finally turning a new leaf. All of these months of questioning and pondering… *solved.*

This can be my *next step* — my next step towards the long journey back to The Sunrise Show — and a sign from the universe that I'm headed in the right direction. I'm on track to get to my dream destination. This email feels like a sign that I'm doing the *right* thing with my life.

I want to jump up and down and scream the news across the newsroom, but I can't. I can't tell anybody here. I turn to face my computer monitor, staring blankly at my blinking cursor. *I got the job.*

I look at the picture of Daniel on my desk, smiling back at me. I've always had this feeling that he would have made it to Broadway. He would have made it into the movies and TV shows. He would have made it big. And looking at him… looking back into my eyes right now…*I think he's thinking the same thing about me.*

Twenty-Four

THE CONTRACT

I told my parents and Delilah about my job offer at WVAB last night. While their words were filled with excitement and pride, I could tell that behind their eyes were secret feelings of worry and sadness. Especially Delilah's.

Even though they seemed to be nothing but happy for me — even Delilah giving me a giant hug with tears in her eyes — there was a sadness like a dark storm cloud over our living room. Not one of their sentences made me feel intentionally bad. But it was the hugs and tears and *meaning* of it all that shot an arrow right through my heart.

I don't necessarily feel guilty, but I do feel like my heart was breaking in some strange way. The email itself is so exhilarating, but thinking about what it all means is scary. Moving out of my childhood home. Not living with my parents anymore. And worst of all, it would be the *start* of a lifelong move away from Delilah.

I told them I had to email her back soon with a decision, and they let me know they would support me no matter what I decided. This is a choice that weighs so heavily on my heart that it feels like an elephant is sitting on my chest.

When I get into my car this morning to begin driving to work — my two human interest story pitches floating around in my head that I know Bill will decline — I call Levi. I've found that we leave for work at the same time each morning, and over the last couple of weeks, it's become our morning ritual to call each other.

"Are you ready for tomorrow?" I say, observing the bright green grass in front of my childhood home, which is alleviating the remainder of my seasonal depression.

"I guess you could say that," Levi says through his car's Bluetooth system.

"You are going to be amazing," I confirm. "You have nothing to worry about."

"Only the mental health of Kaylee Wood's family members for the rest of their lives. But other than that, yeah. It should be a breeze."

The trial begins tomorrow in the same courthouse where I met Levi. It's going to be a long stretch of days and hours — something that I won't be getting paid overtime to cover — but it's for the justice of this young girl. I am privileged and honored to be the one covering her story. Her message needs to be shared with the community, if not the *world*. National news outlets will definitely be picking up this story. But it all starts with *my* reporting, here in tiny market 150.

Aside from my usual *reporting on a murder trial* jitters, I'm extra anxious for this case to begin because I get to see Levi in action. I get to see him in front of the courtroom, presenting his opening arguments, fighting for the justice of this young woman. I get to see him fighting with the attorneys on the other side of the aisle, fighting for what he knows is right. I get to see him present the evidence of his very first trial ever, especially because it's such an important one. *I can't wait to see him doing what he loves.*

"I will be there the whole time," I say.

"Which makes me more nervous," Levi says.

I scoff. "You can't possibly be telling me that I make you nervous. *It's just me.*"

"Yeah, knowing that the hot news reporter will be watching me from the stands, eight hours a day, for like a week straight? Makes me totally calm."

"I can't imagine making somebody nervous." I laugh. "Hey, can I tell you something?"

"Of course," Levi says.

I clear my throat. "I got that job. The one in Virginia Beach."

Levi hesitates for a beat. "That's great, Noelle. I'm so proud of you."

"Thank you." I press on the brakes as I approach a stop sign. "I don't know if I'm going to take it or not, though. I feel like I have to—"

"You definitely have to," Levi says. "This is the first jump up towards your dreams of working in New York City. You've got to—"

"But I could stay here for a couple more years," I say. "I don't have to go now—"

"Yes, you do," Levi says calmly. "This is a great opportunity for you."

Staring out at the streets of Joyfield, fresh off a months-long snowfall and starting to bloom into spring, I feel my eyes become damp. I pass the community library, and then my high school, and then *Brew For You.* I think about my parents, Delilah, Levi, and my friends at work. I do really love my life here, and I've always known that I'd be leaving eventually. But now that the opportunity is presenting itself, I don't know if I want to leave.

"We'll see," I say. "We'll see."

* * *

"Noelle, will you come into my office?"

As soon as the words leave Bill Calloway's mouth, muffled by the thin walls of his office, I simultaneously take a deep breath and close my eyes. It's the worst sentence you can hear from a boss. It feels like you're being called to the principal's office when you're not sure what you did wrong.

I push my hands against my desk to release my swivel chair from its regular position and take the ten dreaded steps to Bill's office. Myra and Nate give me the smirky side eye as if they're telepathically confirming: *Haha! You're being called to the principal's office!*

I could have texted them about the WVAB job yesterday, but I don't want to tell anybody besides my family and Levi until I know for sure what decision I'll be making. I don't want to start rumors or scare anybody over something that might not even happen.

"Hi," I say. My eyes meet Bill's eyes, and it makes me nervous.

"Have a seat," Bill says. He's wearing a soft smile, which is weird to me. *I never see him wearing any kind of pleasant facial expression unless he's mentally connecting the dots between a murder and a robbery.*

"How's your day going?" I awkwardly sit down in the mid-century modern style metal chair adjacent to Bill's desk.

"Fine." He's tapping all five fingertips together, as if he is creating a triangular tent formation with his hands. "Listen, I wanted to talk to you about your contract."

"Okay." I notice that my right leg is bouncing against the deep blue carpeting.

"June, is it?"

"Yep," I confirm. "Coming up soon. I can't believe how fast—"

"That would make a full *two* years here at WJDN." Bill leans back in his chair, resting a hand behind his head.

"Hard to believe," I say.

"Well, I'd like to make it *four*." Bill slides a stapled set of papers across his desk and in my direction. "I'd like you to sign on for another contract. We don't want to lose you, Noelle. You've been an incredible asset to the team. Since you're a hometown girl, we could see you rising up to be Ed Sterling once he retires."

I take the stack of papers into my hands. It's lots of fine print written in black ink, like I'd need an attorney to look it over. *Hey, this could be a job for the hot attorney.*

The timing of this conversation is impeccable. I'm still riding the high of getting a huge job offer, and now Bill is giving me even *more* things to think about. But I'm actually *glad* this discussion is happening now. I'd like to be presented with all my options first so I can make an *informed* decision. While my brain feels like it's going to explode, this is the best chat for the current moment.

"Interesting," I say, my eyes glued on the tiny words. "This would be signing on for another two-year contract? Then we'd just see what happens after that?"

"Yes." Bill motions to the bottom of the first page. "The first step is signing that dotted line."

I *never* thought of becoming the next Ed Sterling. I only ever dreamed of becoming the next Hilda Harrison. I visualize it in my mind: sitting behind the WJDN anchor desk, reading off the teleprompter, sitting back in my chair, switching to look at camera two, repeat. *I was bored.* But if I were being honest with myself, the odds of *that* happening are *much* higher than they ever would be at The Sunrise Show. *My future could be here.*

"Interesting," I repeat, genuinely considering his offer.

"We can get you filling in anchoring as much as possible these next two years," Bill says confidently. "Get you lots of practice behind that anchor chair."

Just as quickly as I can see my future flashing before my eyes, I think of the most important thing for this conversation. *Money.* How much *more* would he offer me to stay?

Bill is dangling a shiny object in front of me, and he can probably see in my eyes that it's working. He has me thinking about my life, my dreams, and my future. But I've been doing this long enough to know that he's using these images to *avoid* having a contract negotiation conversation. The conversation that needs to be held right here, right now. I won't be distracted away from it.

"This would come with a raise, though, right?"

Bill's expression falls to one displaying: *shit, she remembered.*

"Flip onto the next page," he says, the brightness in his eyes dimming.

I feel a small wave of relief crash through me after asking

the question, and I'm suddenly *excited* to see his offer. But when my eyes fall to a list of small numbers, my hope deflates like a popped balloon.

Year One: $27,000.

Year Two: $27,500.

Year Three: $28,000.

Year Four: $28,500.

I look up at Bill, reminding myself to temper my words. "I'd be starting year three with the same salary the *new* reporters are getting?"

I immediately feel bad when the words leave my mouth. I feel like I'm throwing Paige under the bus, and I don't mean to. That's not my goal. But this concerns *salary transparency.* If Bill knows that *I know* what other people here are getting, he should feel more inclined to give me what I deserve. *He should, anyway.*

"New reporters are starting at what *you* started at," Bill lies.

"Actually—"

I stop myself. This isn't the fight that I'm trying to fight right now. I don't want to fight about Paige's salary. I want to fight about *mine.* Regardless of the pure *absence* of a monetary incentive to sign another contract at WJDN, my eyes flash to the last three digits of each of those numbers. Are they seriously only giving a $500 raise *per year?* It's almost insulting. Especially knowing what Ed Sterling makes, and what I can only assume Bill Calloway makes, I feel my blood boiling.

I clear my throat, regaining my composure. "Can this be negotiated?"

"Probably not." Bill cocks his head to the side, drawing air in through his teeth. "This is pretty standard. The numbers all come from people even higher up than me."

I feel myself slipping under the words of Bill. His demeanor makes me feel like I'm dumb for even bringing this up— like even bringing up the possibility of a negotiation is just a waste of breath. He has an authoritative way of making you feel like his words are golden, written in stone, and cannot change under any circumstances. But I know that it's all an act. It's all an act to keep me down. It's all an act to keep *all* local television news reporters down. But I see through it.

I remind myself that Bill is coming to *me* with this proposal. In a way, he needs me. He *wants* me to renew my contract. He *wants* me to become the next Ed Sterling of Joyfield. He *wants* me to stay here forever. That's a big ask, and because of that, the ball is in *my* court. The power is in *my* hands. *I* hold the power here.

"I'm thinking more like $40,000."

The words spew out of me like lava. Just as confidently and quickly as I brought up the dreaded *money* question, I shout out this number.

Bill's mouth explodes in laughter. "They'll never go for that."

"Especially if I'm going to be filling in anchoring too—"

"Filling in anchoring is an opportunity," Bill says. "It's a learning experience. You should be *thankful* for the chance to do it. You kids these days are so ungrateful—"

"I *am* extremely grateful for the chance to anchor," I clarify. "I just want to be paid for the job I'm doing. I want to make the anchor wage *when* I'm anchoring."

I *am* grateful for the chance to anchor. I understand how lucky I am. I am aware that people would *kill* for that opportunity. But Ed Sterling is making tens of thousands *more* than I per year. So, when I'm filling in to do *his* job, shouldn't I be making the same rate?

This doesn't even include the fact that I should be making *at least* double for being a reporter. Since we are doing the jobs of five people, even taking anchoring out of the equation, I *still* should be making more. I can't believe they can get away with paying us what they're paying us.

"Make it $30,000," Bill blurts out. "Plus one extra personal day per year. Happy?"

Bill makes it seem like I'm being a bitch for putting up a fight. He tries to make me feel like I'm being needy, annoying, and privileged. But I know that it's all an act. We should *all* be making more. If I can squeeze a couple thousand extra bucks off of this dude, I'm going to do it.

I exhale with force. "Just to add to this conversation, I do want to let you know that I got another job offer yesterday at another station. They're offering me $45,000. I just want you to take that into consideration."

I know it's a lie, and I feel immediately bad for increasing the salary. (Increased by a lot, I might add.) But I know that he's never going to offer me that much. I just want Bill to know that, apparently, I'm a hot commodity. *Not really, but he's allowed to think that.* If he wants me, he's going to have to fight for me.

"I'll see what I can do," Bill says, shocked. *He looks surprised that I even had the guts to apply for another job outside of WJDN.* "Just think about it."

"I'll think about it." Then I perform the most *girl boss* move of all time: I take the papers, stand up, and walk out of his office.

On my way back to my desk, Myra and Nate give me the

same smirky side eye, but this time, asking: *Why were you sent to the principal's office?* I flash my papers at them and sit down without any further explanation.

I sit at my desk with a full feeling in my chest. Bill knows where I stand on the salary that I *would* want for my third year, even if I don't decide to take the job in the end. I feel like I not only stuck up for myself, but also for *every* young female television news reporter. Did I actually do anything? Not really. But I put up a good fight. When I could have just said yes to his first offer, I didn't. Bill now knows that if he wants me, he'll have to fight a hell of a lot harder to keep me.

I decide to walk downstairs into the studio and talk to Ruby (but pretend like I'm just going to the bathroom). I know that she'd appreciate this conversation more than anyone. She's had her share of salary negotiation conversations— many of which have ended in tears and an unsatisfactory outcome.

Ruby is sitting at her desk in the weather center, just beside the green screen. She looks up at me, and I can't identify the look on her face, but it's a mixture of shock and frustration. Her eyes look red, and she's not her typical happy-go-lucky self.

"I still can't believe this," she says, staring at her computer monitor with one hand in her hair. "I've been wanting to talk to you. I'm just trying to process—"

"What's wrong?" I walk closer to her desk, my boots squeaking against the floor.

Ruby turns her computer around to face me once I'm close enough to see it. It's a lengthy email from Bill, sent earlier that morning.

I try to scan the text as quickly as I can, but before I can make sense of the information, Ruby says, "I can't work at

The Highball anymore."

"Why?" I continue scanning Bill's message. "Why not?"

Ruby answers my question by reading the email out loud. She clears her throat.

"Dear Ruby, it has come to our attention that, in addition to your role as Chief Meteorologist at WJDN, you have also been working as a bartender at The Highball in Joyfield on nights and weekends. After much consideration, WJDN management has decided that this does not align with our image or values as a community television station. We do not want one of our main faces of WJDN serving alcohol to potential viewers. We also do not want to give off the impression that our employees need to work a second job. We are asking you to quit your position as a bartender. Failure to comply with this command could result in the termination of your contract. Feel free to contact me if you have any questions. Sincerely, Bill Calloway."

"Are you kidding me?" My jaw drops. "How can they—"

"I just, I can't—" I can see Ruby searching for the words. Her eyes are still glued to the monitor. "I haven't been able to look away from this. I don't know what to do."

I rub Ruby's back as soon as I hear sniffles and see tears running down her cheeks. "I'm so sorry," I manage. I press my cheek to the top of her head. "It's gonna be okay."

"How am I going to afford—" Ruby sniffles back more tears. "My student loan payments aren't even halfway gone."

I embrace her in a squeeze as she cries through each sentence. "It's okay," I repeat. "You're going to be okay. We can figure something out."

Ruby's sadness turns into anger as she rereads a portion of Bill's email, the light from the computer screen illuminating her face. "They don't want to give the impression that their employees need to work a second job? Well, most of us *do* have to work a second job."

I pull up a chair and sit down beside her. "Translation," I say. "They don't want the community to *know* that they don't pay their employees enough money, so that they *need* to work a second job."

Ruby pulls the sleeve of her blue sweater over her hands, using them to wipe away her tears. A strawberry blonde curl falls over her shoulders. "I mean hell, it's not like I was lyin' on the bar lettin' people take body shots out of my belly button."

I laugh. "Are you sure about that?"

Ruby manages to laugh through the streams of water running down her face. "I actually love it there. I'll miss it. But I'll miss the tips more. I never thought that I *wasn't* allowed to work there. Maybe I should have asked permission—"

"It's better to ask forgiveness than permission," I reassure. "If you had asked permission, then you would have never even worked one shift there."

Ruby stares at the email, highlighting different sentences with her cursor. "This does not align with our image or values as a community television station," she reads aloud. "It's just about how it makes them look. Maybe if they would pay me a livable wage, I wouldn't have ever even thought about workin' there."

It does not align with their image or values. That's right, it doesn't.

It doesn't align with their reporters spending a majority of their time feeling unsafe. It doesn't align with making reporters work ten-day stretches without extra pay. It doesn't align with paying their news professionals a fair salary.

They don't care if we live or die. They don't care about our mental health. They don't care if we can pay our bills.

We're disposable. If I decide not to renew my contract, they'll just get another journalism major fresh out of college to take my place. *We're replaceable.* If Ruby chooses to stay at The Highball, they'll simply find a new meteorologist in no time. *We're temporary.* They know reporters will try to move up the news ladder, so they don't have to take care of them during the short time they're here.

They have it figured out. We're just a cog in the machine. They don't care about us as humans, as compassionate storytellers, or as people who love the community they report on. We're content creators. *And we only cost them less than thirty grand.*

Twenty-Five

THE JURY TRIAL

I'm wearing gray plaid pants and a black sweater, and I have my hair secured up into a messy French twist. The courtroom is chilly, so I'm crossing my arms to keep the heat in close to my chest. My legs are crossed, which makes me notice just how badly my black, high-heeled boots need cleaning after the long winter we just had. An old-fashioned reporter's notebook sits in my lap with a pen tucked into its binding, patiently *waiting* to be used for the next few days straight.

Cell phones are not permitted inside a courtroom. That means my usual way of taking notes for a story — via the *notes app* on my phone — is not allowed. I have no other choice but to go *old school*, making me feel like Barbara Walters in the 1960s. It's actually nice to be forced into *not* having my phone for once, knowing that it's tucked away in my bag. All I can do is sit down, look around, and observe.

The courthouse is absolutely breathtaking— from the

classic exterior to the vintage interior. The dark wooden walls of the courtroom match the dark wooden gallery benches. The chandelier, covered in diffused, white light bulbs, illuminates the witness stands. The oversized, regal ceiling tiles must be twenty feet above my head. Huge windows display beautiful views of Downtown Joyfield. You could hear a pin drop in here. It's not a bad place to spend several working days. I'm not obsessed with covering criminal trials, but having *this* type of setting be my office for the day never gets old.

I'm anxious for Levi. Not only can I not wait to see him today...for obvious reasons...but I can't wait to see him present his arguments. I can't wait to see him in action as the hot attorney. I can't wait to see him as a lawyer *live* and in person. I'm honored to have a front-row seat to watch his first professional case.

A row of teary-eyed people sits two rows behind me, and I notice that they're all wearing matching blue t-shirts reading: *Justice for Kaylee Wood.* The thought of what they're going through makes my heart ache. I can't imagine having to lose somebody in such a brutal way, especially knowing that you'll have to listen to the *alleged killer* try to talk their way out of it. This is going to be a long week for this family.

I turn my head, glancing at them with kind eyes. They know I'm here to report on this case. While some of her family members make eye contact with me, they don't smile back, and I respect their privacy enough to turn back around. It's not that they're *mad* at me for being here — I'm sure they would want Kaylee Wood's story shared with the world — they just probably don't know what my intentions are. *Am I just here to exploit her murder for content? Am I here to sensationalize what happened? Am I going to present this case fairly?*

I wish they knew that I want justice for Kaylee just as much as they do. I wish they knew that I'm on *their* side. I wish they knew that I'm shedding light on her story to prevent it from happening to someone else. Maybe if I get the chance to talk to them, they'll find out that I only have *good* intentions. But in the meantime, to them, I'm just the shady reporter sitting in the corner.

My daydreams are interrupted when a long line of important people walks into the room, one by one. My eyes immediately start searching for Levi. Attorney, court reporter, attorney, clerk, security officer…*hot attorney*. There he is.

Levi looks nervous and intense in a way that I've never seen him before. He's wearing a dark navy suit with a white button-down shirt underneath. His thick, curly brown hair is combed into place, and all of his stubble is gone. He looks utterly adorable, and while there's no sign of a *smile* coming from him anytime soon, I know that those dimples are in there somewhere. I have butterflies in my stomach due to the mere sight of him, and I love knowing that I can *stare* at him for the next week straight.

Levi takes a seat at the counsel table, opens up his laptop, and gets out his notebook. Shuffles of paper, screeches of chairs, and whispers of observers fill the previously silent courtroom. I watch as Levi's hazel eyes scan the room, taking mental inventory of *who* is sitting in the gallery. When he spots me, he doesn't outwardly make it obvious, but his face transforms from one of worry to one of calmness. It's like he's telepathically communicating with me, and it fills me with electric pulses.

"All rise," a court bailiff demands. "Court is now in session. The honorable Judge Benjamin Novah is presiding."

We stand as the judge enters the courtroom, and he takes a seat at his bench. It looks like the most comfortable and coveted seat in the house. The judge spends the first few minutes checking off housekeeping items — going over the day's schedule, confirming attendance of the important people, discussing procedural rules — and then it's *go time*.

"Bring in the jury," he says.

"All rise for the jury," the bailiff demands.

The doors open, and the jurors walk in a single file line to their new home for the next several days: *the jury box*. They range in age, race, and gender. Some look like they're dressed for a corporate job, while others appear like they just rolled out of bed. Some seem like they're going to take this seriously, while others look like they're just here because they *have* to be. Some seem like they just took a shot of espresso, while others look like they're ready to take a nap. *It's an extreme range.*

"You may be seated," the judge says.

The judge reminds the jury of their oath: not to discuss the case with anyone, to remain impartial and unbiased, and to avoid any questions that come from journalists. They have a big job. The fate of Kaylee Wood's alleged killer is in *their* hands.

The anxiety in my chest starts to build. For the young woman we're here to support. For Levi and his first prosecuting case. For the story I need to complete on a short deadline. The courtroom is now full, everybody is in their seats, and the trial is *starting*.

"We will begin with opening statements." The judge clears his throat. "Prosecution side, you're up first."

Levi pushes out his chair and stands up, carrying nothing in his hands but the weight of the day he is about to have. My heart pounds for him. He walks over to the jury box and plants his feet firmly in front of the twelve individuals he must spend the next week persuading. He takes a shallow breath before speaking.

"It was a cold night in December when the defendant, Brandon Smith, made a decision: a decision to *kill*. Over the next several days, you will hear how Brandon Smith *chose* to step foot onto the Joyfield Running Trail, where he did not intend to run; he intended to *murder*. It is our claim that he did *not* know *who* he was going to murder that night. That he was out on the prowl for his next victim. That he was going to stumble upon an innocent young woman. That innocent young woman turned out to be Kaylee Wood, who you will learn was in town for the weekend to visit a friend. Kaylee went for an innocent run — one she expected to return home from — but she *did not* return home. The keyword here is innocent, which makes our defendant, Brandon Smith, *guilty*. We will spend the next few days proving to you that it was *him*."

Levi walks up and down the jury box as he speaks — bouncing between the left side and the right side — making eye contact with each juror one by one. His arms move away from the center of his body, then back in front of his long torso. He's authentic and honest, not fake or dramatic. You can tell that he *knows* the truth, which only makes his argument that much more believable. He *believes* each word he is conveying. His eyes display passion and truth, and his body speaks intensity and demand.

"You will hear how Brandon Smith grabbed the ponytail of Kaylee Wood. You will hear how he violently pulled it in his direction. You will hear how this young woman fought back in self-defense. You will hear how brutal the physical altercation became. You will hear how this man wanted to take her life away from her. You will hear how our defendant ultimately left her to *die.*"

I hear sniffles from the group of people sitting behind me. It makes me close my eyes and suck in a breath because I feel so *terrible* for them. Hearing the gruesome details of Levi's opening statements is bad enough, but I know it will only get worse as the week goes on. They'll have to hear about each *brutal* detail.

"You will see the photos from the crime scene. You will hear, first hand, from a witness who was there that night. You will watch a video from the security cameras. You will hear from the police and medical examiners who were on the scene. You will hear about how the defendant fled the scene after *knowing* what he had done. You will hear all of the *facts* leading up to the death of Kaylee Wood."

My eyes are glued to Levi, not just because I *like* him, but because his words are absolutely captivating. Every person in this courtroom has to be thinking the same thing, no matter what side they're on. He's great at communicating, and not only that, but persuading. It's intoxicating to watch him present his arguments, and you can tell that he got into the right profession.

Levi has the same level of passion for being an attorney that I do for being a reporter. We *both* want to work our way to the top. We *both* want to help other people through our work.

We *both* want to do well. How we choose to spend *forty hours* of our week *matters* to us, and this mutual understanding has brought us closer together.

"After all of this evidence is presented to you, it will paint a very consistent picture for you. One that you cannot deny. Brandon Smith violently attacked and killed Kaylee Wood. I will ask you, the jurors, for a verdict that reflects what happened to Kaylee: that Brandon Smith is *guilty* of first-degree murder. That Brandon Smith is *guilty* of aggravated assault. That Brandon Smith is *guilty* of fleeing the scene to avoid apprehension. The next few days will prove to you why *all* of this is true. Thank you."

Levi walks calmly, but confidently, back to the counsel table. He seems to be relieved that his opening arguments are over, but the intensity in his expression remains. It's like he's still riled up inside from the adrenaline rush that swept through him with every sentence he spoke. Something like that isn't just going to go away in an instant. His heart will probably still be pounding for the next ten minutes following that intense presentation of evidence.

Once Levi takes a seat and pushes in his chair, he glances over at me, giving off that telepathic look. *He sees me.* I know that he's happy I'm here watching him, sitting in the first row with a pen and paper like Nancy Drew. A flame lights up in my chest. I'm beginning to have feelings of *love* towards Levi Winters, and knowing that I'll have to stare at him in this courtroom for the next several days is *not* going to help my case.

I crouch down and grab my phone out of my bag, so that I can secretly and quickly check the time. I'm expecting to see that an hour has passed, but what I don't expect is a missed

call and a text from my mom.
It reads: "Delilah is in the hospital."

Twenty-Six

THE STANDBY

The fluorescent lights on the ceiling of the hospital hallway pour onto me like lava. I feel it weighing down my shoulders, chest, and brain— like I have no choice but to try and kick my way through the thick substance. I sprint down the hallway and frantically search for room 111, where I know all the answers to my question lie.

I'm one step away from the room, but my feet won't move me any further. I lean my upper body forward and peek into the doorway, where my mom's eyes meet mine.

"Hey," she whispers, standing up from her chair.

She walks towards me with a look of concern, which gives me enough energy to pick up my feet and start walking again. When we get close enough to hug, she squeezes me and sobs into my chest. It's so hard that she isn't even making a noise. I can tell that she's been holding these tears back, and now is the time for the dam to break. I want to ask her a million questions, but I just hold her instead.

"Is she going to be okay?" I whisper.

My mom sniffles. "We think so."

We think so? What does she mean she *thinks* so? My heart starts to race. I feel like I'm in the beginning stages of the most severe panic attack of my life. I want to jump out of the nearest window and sprint as far away from this hospital as possible. There was never a question in my mind that Delilah *wouldn't* be okay. She *has* to be okay.

"It *will* be okay," I tell my mom, shoving my feelings of shock down deep inside my chest. "She will be fine."

We slowly walk back into room 111 together, hand in hand. My dad is sitting in an uncomfortable chair next to Delilah, who is lying with her eyes closed in the hospital bed. She just looks like she's sleeping, resting, and relaxing. Aside from her hair being a little messy, she looks completely normal.

I shake my head at him. "What even happened?"

"She was diagnosed with a Ventricular Septal Defect. They've been calling it a VSD," my dad whispers. He stands up and joins us in the corner. "It's common for people with Down Syndrome, I guess. We didn't know she had it. We never even heard of it. She was making breakfast in the kitchen and just…passed out."

"*Passed out?*" I basically scream to ask the question.

"She was born with it, but we didn't discover it until now," my dad says. "It could have been missed on scans when she was younger. It must have been."

"She might have to have surgery," my mom adds. "Open heart surgery."

An ache wraps around my heart and wrings it out like a wet dishrag. *Not Delilah.* She doesn't deserve this. Nobody deserves this. My heart pounds as I try to wrap my brain around it all. *How are we just finding out about this now?*

I look over at her. The ends of her brown hair barely hit the top of her hospital gown. I watch her chest rise up and fall down in slow motion. Images of us together as children flash before my eyes— all of the inside jokes, the laugh attacks, watching our favorite TV shows with mint chocolate chip ice cream, growing up having her as my best friend, the endless memories. I can't *not* have more memories with her. *It can't end this way.*

"But we don't know yet," my dad reassures. "We don't know."

We hear a sharp inhale come from Delilah's chest, and it startles us all. But she looks nonchalant— like she's just waking up for the day, no big deal. Like she's *not* in a hospital room in a hospital gown. Her eyes open briefly, then fall heavy, then open up again. She's trying to focus on the three of us, but it's taking extra effort.

"Hey there, Delilah," I whisper, walking over to her bedside. "We're all here."

"Hi," Delilah says.

The softest expression of a smile causes the apples of her cheeks to puff up, just slightly. I can tell that she's internally happy and relieved we're all together. I take a seat in the uncomfortable chair that my dad was sitting in, and hold Delilah's hand in mine.

"How are you feeling?"

Delilah falls back to sleep, and I'm reassured when I see the rise and fall of her chest. I'm *relieved* by our split-second conversation, but I'm desperate for more. I need to talk to her. I need to hear her voice. I need to go back to how things were.

We hear a knock on the door, and a middle-aged man in a long, white coat follows. "Hello," he says quietly, walking in closer towards us. "How are we doing?"

"Any news?" My mom looks pained and worried. "Anything at all?"

The doctor is holding a chart full of papers. "She will probably need that open heart surgery we mentioned. Test results showed that it's needed to make the necessary repair."

My dad holds the back of his hand to his forehead. "Open heart—"

"I don't want to say that it's *not* serious, but I can assure you, these procedures are far more advanced than they used to be. She will be in the best hands," the doctor says.

"When?" I tuck my hair behind my ears. "When would she have it?"

"We'll get something scheduled." The doctor looks at his clipboard. "I'll be right back in a little bit, and we'll talk about our options."

My mom, dad, and I stare at each other— all in the presence of a sleeping Delilah. I keep mentally reminding myself that she is *alive*. She looked at me. She talked to me. The doctors have the diagnosis, and they already have the solution. She is going to be okay. But looking back at my parents, I know how difficult this entire process is going to be emotionally. *There is going to be a long road ahead, I can already tell.*

"I'll be right back," I tell them, walking out of room 111 and into the hallway.

I rest my back against the cold wall, sinking down until I'm sitting on the floor. Nurses and doctors are far enough away that they don't notice me, and I'm thankful for that. I need privacy right now.

I hold my head in my hands and cry, sob, wail. I can't picture my little sister with any of this— a heart defect, a possible open heart surgery, an illness of any kind. It makes me *scared* to think about what her future will look like. It makes me terrified for our entire family.

I check my phone to find a response from Levi. I texted him on my way out of the courtroom to let him know what was going on…and *why* I was leaving so urgently. This was *not* the day of work I wanted to miss, but when it comes to my family, I have no choice. What was I going to do, stay there?

The text reads: "Is everything okay? I worried about you."

"It's all good," I type out. "I can't wait to hear about your day. Kick ass in there."

I put my phone back in my pocket. I stare at the clock on the wall and realize— any minute *not* spent with my parents and Delilah is a minute wasted. I stand up on my wobbly legs, wipe away my tears, and head back into the room.

For the first time since I got here, my parents don't look like they're in pain. There's a glimmer of hope in their eyes. When I look at Delilah, I realize it's because *she is awake.* Her eyes are open, causing a wave of relief to wash over me.

"Hey there, Delilah," I say, walking over to her.

"Hi," she says. It's like *deja vu* from earlier, but this time, she's more alert.

We hear another knock on the door, and my chest tightens up in anticipation of the doctor's arrival. I don't know how much more news I can handle right now. But I want to speed up this entire nightmare, and if talking to the doctor is the way to do that, I'm willing to listen.

But it's not the doctor. It's a young man with thick glasses. Upon further inspection, I realize that it's Anthony from *Brew For You.*

"Anthony?" Delilah whispers in shock. Her eyes widen.

He's holding a bouquet of flowers in his hands — with a bulk of the stems being leafy greens, bright eucalyptus, and long ferns — making the entire arrangement green-themed. He walks over to her hospital bed and hands them to her. Delilah accepts the bouquet like a Miss America winner.

"Thank you," she says in disbelief.

"They didn't have green flowers," Anthony tells her. "So I got *greens* instead."

"My favorite," she says.

"I know you like green," Anthony reiterates.

Delilah glances over at my dad, who is smiling knowingly at the interaction. She's probably embarrassed that not only my mom and I are watching this exchange, but my dad. This makes me laugh, and even though I try to hide it, I can't. It's too cute.

"This is Anthony," Delilah tells my parents.

"Hi, Anthony," my mom and dad say in unison.

My mom stands up to give him a hug, and my dad shakes his hand. He's wearing a bright green *Brew For You* sweatshirt and baseball hat, appearing as though he just made a stop at the flower shop after the early morning shift at work. Delilah sleepily smiles at their shared meet and greet — and while any other day this would totally humiliate her — today she is *happy* about it.

"Is she going to be okay?" Anthony's big, brown eyes look towards my parents.

My dad clears his throat to prevent crying. "She's going to

be just fine."

"I'm sure she'll be back to work soon," my mom says.

My parents told me that Delilah was scheduled to work at *Brew For You* this morning, so when they called Manager Mike from the hospital to let him know what happened, the news traveled fast. Anthony told us how devastated he was to hear that his *favorite coworker* was sick, so he knew that he had to come visit her.

"I'm sleepy," Delilah says in the middle of our conversation.

My mom kisses her on the forehead. "Sleep."

"I will go back to work," Anthony says, realizing his cue to leave. "Bye, Delilah."

"Bye, Anthony," she whispers, shutting her eyes.

I walk over to Delilah's bedside. "Get good sleep, okay?"

"Promise," she says.

I wink. "Promise Thomas?"

She hints at a grin. "Promise Thomas."

It was only a matter of a few hours, but from when I first woke up this morning to *now*, my entire mindset has changed. This morning, the only thing on my mind was *work*. Covering the Kaylee Wood trial. Seeing Levi in the courtroom all week. What I'm going to be telling WVAB about my job offer.

But in this hospital room, the only thing I care about is Delilah. And my parents. Their health and happiness are the things I would ditch everything else in my life for. *This* is the only thing that matters. That *really* matters. Being here. *With them.*

Twenty-Seven

THE ONE (WO)MAN BAND

I spent another eight hours covering day *two* of the Kaylee Wood murder trial. I was relieved to know that Delilah was at home resting with my parents. I *couldn't* have gone to work today if she were *still* in the hospital— my conscience wouldn't have allowed for it. Knowing she was home made me feel at peace. (Well, as peaceful as I *could* feel, knowing in the back of my mind that she'll be undergoing an open heart surgery in the near future.)

We found out that Delilah's open-heart surgery is scheduled for about two weeks from now. The doctor has been extremely reassuring, but it doesn't make matters any easier. I don't care how advanced the technology is. I don't care how skilled the doctors are. I don't care how good the facility is. (Well, actually, I care *deeply* about all of those things.) But it doesn't make Delilah's pain any easier. It doesn't alleviate a majority of my worries, which are growing by the minute lately.

Levi did another unbelievable job today prosecuting the case, and I enjoyed listening to him fight with the defense. It's one thing to watch him present evidence, but it's another thing to watch him fight the opposition. I don't usually think that being abrasive and angry is sexy. But when it's being done by Levi Winters — and he's sticking up for what's right and just — *it definitely is.*

I wrote my story on the day's events and presented it live on the evening news, right in front of the courthouse where I first met Levi. It was *finally* time for me to go home, but due to a sudden turn of events and a frantic call from the newsroom, my day *still* isn't over. I'm now going to the scene of a water main break. *Yay for me.*

"Have fun, girlfriend," Paige texted me. "Go get 'em."

"I'll try," I replied.

Paige is the new girl, so *she* should be the one sent to cover breaking news like this. Bill somehow thinks that sending *me* is the way to go. Sure, I'm the veteran reporter. Sure, I'll get it done. Sure, he can trust me. But Paige *should* be the one who gets sent there. That's the purpose of seniority, right? Don't you get it a little easier after a while? It's nothing against her, though. *It's everything against Bill.*

I drive down the streets of Joyfield, thinking about what it would actually be like to leave this place. The flowers are blooming in the window boxes of nearby houses, and the street is covered in water from last night's rainstorm. I drive past the beige structure that is my alma mater, Joyfield Area High School, and then the small brick building that is the Joyfield Community Library. *This is the only home I've ever known.*

I have to decide whether to accept the job offer at WVAB very soon, and it's been weighing on me. Looking out at the cracked sidewalks where Delilah and I used to ride our bikes, and seeing the ice cream shop we'd go to in the summertime, it all makes me so sentimental. When I left this town for The Sunrise Show, I knew I'd be returning back here *four* short months later. But this time around, it would be *forever*.

Once I get to the scene of the water main break, I park my news car in an empty parking lot. It's across the street from the Joyfield Post Office — but there's not a *street* there anymore — it's now a *river*. About five inches of dirty water rush downstream. If I wanted to get to the post office, I'd have to *swim* there. A couple of blocks down the road, I can see water spraying up out of the ground like a geyser. This section of Joyfield has been turned into a temporary water park. *What a mess.*

I start writing a script on my phone, but an incoming call from Levi distracts me. I answer it, letting his deep voice infiltrate my Bluetooth system.

"How's Delilah?" His voice sounds concerned. *I love that this is his first question.*

"She's good," I say. "Just waiting for the inevitable."

"As long as she's feeling good right now, that's all that matters," Levi says.

I watch the water rush before me. "Thanks for asking," I say.

"She might be my favorite Fenwick, you know."

"She's *everybody's* favorite Fenwick." I roll my eyes at myself. "Great job again today, by the way. I'm sure Kaylee's family was proud."

Levi is in the middle of talking through his main prosecution points when I notice a man staring at me from a block down the road. He's on the same side of the "river" as me, so he would not have to *swim* to get over here. *I wish the water were dividing us.* He's wearing a white t-shirt and jeans, puffing on a cigarette. His striking eyes are peering straight into my news car.

It's understandable, though. When I see a news car, I *also* try to see which on-air talent is sitting inside. Not in a creepy way, just in a *curious* way. But this man is making me feel uncomfortable. I feel like he can *see* me staring back at him. There's something about that stare, like he *wants* something from me. It almost looks like he wants to talk to me. I wish he'd look away. Walk away. *Go away.*

"And that's how I think I'm going to win them over," Levi says.

"I think you have a really good case," I admit after not fully listening.

The man is slowly inching closer to my car, moving about a foot in my direction every minute. Even if I try *not* to focus on him, I can see him in my peripheral vision. There aren't any first responders out here to "protect" me. The man kicks a rock, looks up at the sky, takes a puff of his cigarette, and does everything he can to convince me that he's *not* staring. But I know he is. He's moving closer, showing *no* signs of leaving.

"I have to go. Have a great rest of your shift," Levi says.

I fake a cheerful tone. "Thanks for checking in."

I continue trying to write my script, but this man is just sitting in the corner of my eye. I hate knowing that there's someone around me who *isn't* a first responder. He's now just about eight feet away from my news car, leaning his back against a red brick building. Even though I've made sure that my doors were locked at least *six* times since I parked here, I lock them *again*.

The sun is setting, but the pink and yellow highlights in the sky allow for some final beams of light to shine down on me. I eventually have to do what I've been *dreading* to do all night long: getting out of the news car for my live shot. With my shoulders and chest tightly wound, I slowly get out of the car and begin unloading my items from the trunk. The day is almost over. *I can do this.*

I set up my camera so that the rushing water and spraying geyser are in the background of my shot, and I stand in front of the lens. I can't see the man from the direction I'm facing, but I assume he's somewhere behind me. I plug in my microphone and earpiece, anxious to hear Myra's voice on the other line. I feel like I'm in the presence of a ghost: tense and worried, but nothing I can do about it.

"Hey," Myra says once I'm connected.

"Hey," I whisper. "Do you see a guy behind me?"

Myra pauses. "Don't see anyone. Just water. Lots and lots of water."

"If you see anyone in the background, let me know." I check over my shoulder. "There's been some creepy dude out here tonight."

"No, I was thinking I'd just let it go," Myra teases. "Of course I'd tell you."

I soon hear the fanfare introduction welcoming viewers to WJDN. I'm supposed to be thinking about how I'm going to *convey* my story — how I'll move to the side to show the water rushing behind me, how I'll step behind the camera and zoom into the geyser, how I'll annunciate each sentence

— but I can't stop thinking about *that guy.*

I hear Ed Sterling's voice ringing in my earpiece. "A large water main break in the heart of Joyfield has resulted in many road shutdowns and flooding throughout the city. Our Noelle Fenwick is live there with the latest on this developing story. Noelle?"

"Good evening, Ed." I stare into the lens, trying to concentrate. "City officials tell me that a fourteen-inch water line burst earlier today, shutting down the road here in front of the Joyfield Post Office behind me."

I keep reading my script, but my mind is elsewhere. I feel like I'm a little girl running up my stairs at night, thinking there is someone chasing after me. Like I'm walking through a haunted house, *knowing* there is a monster somewhere coming to get me. The sun in the sky is setting lower and lower by the second, and suddenly I'm thankful that we're moving closer to summer so that it stays *lighter* outside for longer.

I try to refocus. "Drivers are being asked to avoid the area. Local water crews say that the roads will be treated, and residents can expect the scene to be cleared soon."

I stare into the camera lens, the sky darkening into night, and I feel my heart pounding. I want to get out of here. *I want to go home.* There are only a few seconds between now and my shift being over, and they can't pass fast enough.

"You're clear," Myra says after a beat.

I don't even say goodbye. I waste no time, unplugging every cord in sight and tearing down all of my camera and lighting equipment. If there were a contest for how fast someone could pack up their news stuff and leave a scene, *I would win.* I turn my head over my shoulder. I'm almost done. The saying *'having eyes in the back of your head'* would be really great to have right now.

I rush to put my things back into the trunk, without a single ounce of organization. The man is about four feet away from me now, just kicking rocks. I sprint into the driver's seat, shut the door, and start driving away. Adrenaline is pumping through me.

On my drive home, I start to feel angry. I think about Kaylee Wood— what happened to *her* could happen to *anyone*. I think about the young, female news reporters out there like me. We are *one-man bands,* doing everything with no extra set of eyes. Multimedia journalists who do it all. MMJ for short. We don't have 360 degree vision. We can't be fully aware of our surroundings. We can't focus on our jobs and our safety at the same time. The thought of it makes me sick to my stomach.

How can news stations even allow this for their employees?

Twenty-Eight

THE B-ROLL VIDEO

"Are you excited?" I ask, putting a chunk of Delilah's hair into my curling iron.

"Nervous." Her eyes meet mine in the mirror. "But excited."

"With Levi as your date, you have nothing to worry about." I release the clamp and watch as a spiral curl falls down her back. "Plus, you'll have me there too."

"I'm going to steal your man." She stretches a black ponytail holder between her fingers and pretends to shoot it at me through the mirror.

I smirk back at her reflection. "Just for tonight."

It's been a few months since Levi asked to take Delilah to the *Under The Stars* dance, and I haven't been able to stop thinking about his kindness ever since. Delilah was absolutely *thrilled* when I told her about going, and we were dress shopping at our local mall a mere twelve hours later. She's been so excited for this day, and I'm so glad that her VSD diagnosis isn't stopping her from attending.

Once every strand of hair is curled to perfection, I twist some pieces near her temples and pin them back with sparkly bobby pins. I set her half-up, half-down hairstyle in place with some strong-hold hairspray, which makes Delilah cough dramatically.

"No, thank you." She fans the air in front of her nose. "Are you trying to kill me?"

I point to the bottle. "This is the *good* shit. Your hair won't be moving."

"I'm telling mom."

I fold my arms across my chest. "About what?"

"You said *shit*."

"*You* can say shit *too*, you know."

"*Shit*," she whispers back to me.

We're getting ready in Delilah's room. While her walls are painted white, everything Delilah could choose a color for is some variation of green— lime green, emerald green, sage green. Her bed is decorated with a green quilt and matching green pillowcases. Even her lampshades are green. This would usually be considered *too much* of one color, but for Delilah, it somehow works.

"Makeup time," I say, grabbing a stick of liquid eyeliner.

"Not a lot," she says.

"You mean you *don't* want a smoky eye?"

She rolls her eyes. "Not like last time."

Delilah has always been like my little doll— always letting me style her, do her makeup, and try different hairstyles. Even though it's because she's my little sister, it's also *deeper* than that. I've always wanted her to be seen like the *rest* of the girls in her class. I've always wanted the world to know that she's their *equal*. I've always wanted her to send a message that even though she may be different, she is *just* as powerful.

I swipe a light brown eye shadow across her eyelids and press some gold sparkle into the corners. I tap some light pink powder onto the apples of her cheeks, followed by the tiniest wisp of highlighter on her cheekbones. I apply a sophisticated, mauve-colored gloss to her lips. *Voila. Here she is.*

"Now, go like this." I press my lips together, moving them around.

"Like this?" She mimics the motion through a smile.

Delilah was instructed to "take it easy" tonight, and if it wasn't for her recent hospital stay, there's no way she'd *listen*. Delilah is always a ball of energy, and no doctor's orders can change that. But knowing that she's scheduled to have open-heart surgery, things have seemed *different* in the Fenwick household. Not in a way that I can put my finger on, because nobody has been blatantly acting weird. But there's just something in the air: a worry, a panic, a *dread*.

I lift her long, evergreen-colored gown off the closet door. "It's time."

"Finally."

I help her slide the velvety fabric up her body and guide her arms into the dramatic, whimsical sleeves. It's a modern gown that prom magazines would consider to be *stylish*. That was important to me when helping her decide— I guided her toward something elegant and grown-up. *Nothing childish.* I wanted her to look like the grown-up woman that she is. I wanted her to be the best-dressed attendee of this dance. I wanted her to show the world that she's a beautiful, adult woman. Here she is now, standing right in front of me. I zip her up, spin her around to face me, and beam with pride.

"You look amazing," I say.

Delilah looks at herself in the mirror. "I know."

We hear the doorbell ring from downstairs. I get butterflies in my stomach as if Levi is picking *me* up for a date. But he's technically picking up *both* of us.

I gasp. "He's here!"

I can hear Levi's deep voice near the front door talking to my parents, and it sends my brain into an anxious spiral. This is the first time he's meeting them. This is the first time he's meeting Delilah. This is the first time he's meeting the entire *family*.

Delilah and I stand at the top of the stairs. "Ready?" I shout down to them.

"We're ready," they shout back in unison.

Delilah walks down as I trail closely behind her, making sure she doesn't trip on the floor-length fabric. I watch my parents and Levi watching Delilah, and I flash some jazz hands in her direction. Given everything that she's gone through recently — and is about to go through soon — my parents look like they're about to cry.

Levi is standing in a black suit, holding a bouquet of cool-colored flowers. He has a green tie wrapped around his neck (he got the memo) and a green pocket square. Looking at him looking at my sister, I feel like my heart could burst right open.

"Here I am," Delilah announces. She places one hand on her hip and the other behind her head. She struts off the last step and into the foyer.

Levi hands her the flowers. "You look beautiful."

"Thank you," she blushes.

Levi gives me an awkward side hug. "And so do you."

I'm wearing a simple black dress with a low bun, intending to blend into the background for the entire evening. I want to look as camouflaged as possible, letting the light shine on my sister.

My parents perform their oohs and ahhs as Delilah gives yet another twirl in the foyer. My little sister looks like a true grown-up now. We put on our fancy jackets, say goodbye to our parents, and walk arm in arm with Levi, as he walks the Fenwick sisters out the front door.

* * *

We walk along the sidewalk into the Joyfield Community Center, where a giant banner reading *Welcome to a night Under The Stars* hangs from the entrance. Like a true gentleman, Levi opens the door for us, escorting us inside.

The hall is decorated from floor to ceiling in springy, flowery decorations— hot pink streamers, orange carnations, mini disco balls, and yellow sunshines. The vibes: *happy*. One side of the room is lined with tables of colorful drinks and snacks, and the other is home to the DJ booth and dance floor. Dozens of couples are already out there dancing, and I feel like we're late to the game, even though we're five minutes early.

A woman in a blue, sparkly gown grabs the microphone. "Good evening, everyone. Welcome to the *Under The Stars* dance— you all look very lovely this evening."

The crowd applauds when I notice two familiar faces walking through the entrance: Manager Mike and Anthony from *Brew For You*. They're both wearing dark suits and matching navy blue ties, and I'm just now realizing how much they look like father and son. I watch as they scan the crowd, desperately trying to find someone they know. They finally make eye contact with us and wave.

Once Delilah sees them, I watch the expression on her face change from one of *coolness* to one of *blushing.* She hesitantly waves back to Anthony from across the community center, and I feel butterflies in my stomach on her behalf. But like the awesome big sister I am, I *pretend* not to notice. (I secretly smile to myself anyway, though.)

The woman with the microphone continues speaking. "Tonight we're raising money for a very important mission right here in Joyfield. Half of the proceeds from tonight's dance will be going to the *Brew For You* coffee shop in town, which I've heard has been quite successful. Let's give that organization a round of applause, shall we?"

"Looks like Anthony will be partying with us tonight," I whisper to Delilah through the loud claps of the audience members.

"Shut up," she not-so-quietly whispers back to me.

When *The Twist* starts playing, everybody on the dance floor starts, of course, *twisting.* I grab Delilah's hands and spin her around, causing her green dress to flutter in the air. One side of her perfectly pinned-up hair has fallen, but it looks cute in a messy sort of way. Levi spins himself around using Delilah's hand, and she squeals with laughter.

I've seen Levi Winters present opening arguments to a jury. I've seen him at The Highball after he's had too many drinks. I've seen him fresh off a shift at the courthouse. I've seen him giving an interview at a crime scene, tears in his eyes. I've seen *a lot* of Levi Winters—but seeing him dance with my sister is totally new. I love seeing him let loose, even if it is only *a little bit.* I love seeing him dance. I love seeing him with *Delilah.*

When a slow Frank Sinatra ballad starts to play, all of the couples begin to link up. But before Levi even has the *chance* to ask Delilah to dance, an unexpected visitor swoops in before him.

"May I have this dance?" Anthony asks Delilah.

She takes his hand. "Sure."

They walk to the center of the dance floor and begin to sway back and forth to the music. For a while, they're just smiling at each other. But as each second passes, their comfort level rises. They seem calm and happy, like this is how they've always *wanted* to be. *I wonder how long Anthony has been planning for this to happen.*

Levi looks at me to repeat his original question. "May I have this dance?"

I laugh, grabbing his hand. "Even though I was your *second* option? Sure."

I reach my hands around his neck, and he spreads his hands across my lower back. After a few seconds of looking into his eyes, I press my head into his chest and close my eyes. It feels so safe and warm, like our first date at *Mama Bella*, before we get into the car. As if I couldn't love being in Levi's arms any more, he kisses my forehead.

I look out at Delilah and Anthony dancing, and I smile at them. Just two Fenwick sisters dancing with the loves of their lives. I'm happy my sister is getting this precious moment. I'm happy she's getting to experience these grown-up emotions. I'm happy that she's currently happy and healthy. I dread what the future holds for her, but I'm so grateful to witness this moment *right now.*

Once the song ends, Anthony releases Delilah and practically sprints back towards Manager Mike. The sight of his sudden departure causes Levi and me to laugh hysterically. Delilah makes her way back over to us, trying to hide the fact that she is both blushing *and* smiling. Again, like the wonderful sister I am, I don't make a fuss.

"I can't believe you blew me off for Anthony," Levi teases. "I thought I was your date."

"You still are," Delilah reassures. "Promise Thomas."

The next song starts to play from the DJ booth, but I can't tell what it is right away. It's not until I hear those strums of the guitar that I realize it's *Hey There Delilah.* I feel my chest swell up in an instant. A lump fills the back of my throat.

Levi holds out his hand to Delilah. "Can I have...*this* dance...*this* time?"

"Sure," Delilah laughs.

Levi and Delilah make their way out onto the sparkly dance floor, and they begin moving to the chord progressions. String lights hang down from the ceiling and illuminate the tops of their heads. I watch as Levi's green tie moves with Delilah's green sleeves. They're doing more talking and smiling than *dancing*, but I'm thrilled watching their connection. *This is all I've ever wanted to see.*

I'm left here to stare at them, my back leaning up against the wall. I smile in their direction at the sweet moment. I take a video of them on my phone, because I want to remember this moment forever. If I were to produce a feature about Delilah, this would be my "b-roll video" because it describes her so perfectly.

These lyrics that I've heard a million times send an ache right through my chest. It's something about this moment that makes the words hit harder than ever before. With these sights and sounds before me, I start to cry.

Suddenly, I know how I'm going to respond to Kathleen Seasons at WVAB.

Twenty-Nine

THE DEADLINE

"Kathleen?" I say into my phone, which I am currently white-knuckling. "It's Noelle Fenwick. From WJDN in Joyfield?"

"Hi Noelle," Kathleen recalls. "I've been looking forward to hearing from you."

I just got home from another long day of work covering the Kaylee Wood murder trial — and it ended up finally being the *last* day — because hot attorney Levi Winters *won* the case. The jury found Brandon Smith *guilty* of first-degree murder, aggravated assault, and fleeing the scene to avoid apprehension. As for a motive? We still don't know. But Kaylee Wood's friends and family can now rest *somewhat* easier knowing that her killer will spend the rest of his life behind bars.

"Yeah," I say, staring at myself in the mirror. I just changed out of my tight, royal blue dress for some workout clothes, even though I'm probably *not* going to work out.

"Have you made your decision?"

"Yes, actually, I have."

I think about The Sunrise Show, and images of Hilda Harrison sitting at that glass anchor desk scroll across my mind like a montage. I think about getting her americanos. I think about jumping over camera cables with Eliza. I think about being in that studio. It's not that it's *not* going to happen…it just might happen even *later*.

"I actually decided *not* to take the position."

There's a pause on the other end of the line. "Oh?"

"Yeah," I repeat. "Thank you so much for the opportunity and for bringing me in for an interview. I appreciate it more than you know."

"Thank you for letting me know." Kathleen's voice seems stunned, like she was *not* expecting this to be my answer. "Best of luck to you, Noelle."

"Thank you," I say, relieved that she didn't ask any further questions.

I end the call and hold my phone close to my chest. I feel like a giant weight has been lifted off my shoulders. I feel as light as a feather— like I could just rise up towards my ceiling like a helium balloon. I made a decision, and it's *finalized*.

My decision to renew my contract at WJDN was entirely my own. My parents didn't push me into it. Delilah didn't push me into it. Levi didn't push me into it. Sure, they're influences. But this decision was mine, and I'm proud of it. What's two more years, you know? In the grand scheme of things, that's like *two more seconds*.

I don't think I'm ready to move out of my parents' house just yet. I don't want to be away from Delilah in the wake of her open-heart surgery. I don't want to be away from Levi since we have been forming this incredible friendship. It's not that I'm *planning* on staying in Joyfield forever. It's not that I won't *eventually* be moving up the corporate news ladder. It's not that I'm *erasing* The Sunrise Show from my end goal. *I just need more time.*

I'm holding back from taking the first leap. I know I'll jump someday. My dreams are still the same. But right now, I want to be with my parents. I want to be with Delilah. I want to be with Levi. I'm also thrilled to spend more time with Myra, Ruby, and Paige— but not *Bill*. He's somebody I still need to figure out how to deal with.

I look at the Polaroid picture of Delilah and me on Christmas morning. She has her arm over my shoulder in a way that says: *this is my sister, but also my friend.* Our matching holiday pajamas *and* matching hair colors are uncanny. I pick up the film, smiling down at the little square. *This is what I'm choosing.*

I walk over to my vanity and look at my little *Acceptance Speech* taped to my mirror. I think about all the mornings I spent reading this aloud in New York City, pretending to accept an award that I *still* don't know the origin of. The handwritten ink is like a memory, frozen in time, that made it to this moment. It's not that I'm *giving up* on this dream. I'm just postponing it, kicking the rock a little further down the road.

I'm in the middle of picturing my vanity at Westerfield Apartments when I notice that I'm getting an incoming call from none other than Eliza Swickley. *Perfect timing.* I need a reminder that my dreams aren't lost.

"Hello?" I answer, trying to sound cheerful.

"Hi," Eliza says. "Ready for New York City?"

"*More* than ready. After the week I've had."

"Same. I need a vacation," Eliza says. "Doing the job of five people is getting old quickly."

"I know." I smile. "Plus, I finally get to hear your secret."

"Yeah, *finally*." Eliza laughs. "I've been dying to tell you."

I put my phone on speaker so that I can tie my messy hair into a loose, low bun. "I don't understand why you can't just tell me over the phone."

"You'll see," Eliza says. "You just have to see it for yourself. I promise it will be better in person. You'll be happy you waited."

I laugh and sit on my bed. "This *better* be good."

Thirty

THE "D" BLOCK

MAY | NEW YORK CITY, NEW YORK

A waitress wearing a black apron arrives at my table, holding two humongous pieces of Oreo cake. She sets one down on the crinkled place mat in front of me, and the other at the empty place setting across the table.

"Thank you," I tell her, already holding my fork in my hand.

I smile at the thick cubes of chocolate, taking in their decadent sights and smells. I take a huge chunk out of its edge, with all of that thick icing, and shove the entire bite into my mouth. It's *oily* and *sugary* in the best way possible. I close my eyes and chew, with my mouth watering even though the cake is already inside of it. I have literally dreamed about eating this cake again. *This is one of the best moments of my entire life.*

This is the first time I've been back to New York City since my internship, which means this is my first piece of cake from the Starshine Diner in years. The Uber ride here from the airport made me feel like I was traveling back in time— the traffic, chaos, and noise taking me back to those four short-lived yet sensational months in college. Part of me feels like I was living here yesterday. But another, more realistic part feels like it was a million years ago.

While *The Rundown* that Ruby created didn't include New York City as an actual stop — since it's my ultimate destination and end goal — I'm still mentally referring to this trip as the "D Block" of my travels. It's the perfect bookend to a year of traveling to new cities across the country.

"Psssst," I hear from behind me.

I know that sound could only be from one person. "Could that be…Eliza Swickley?"

I turn around and see her parading through the 1950s-themed diner with two huge, black suitcases. A navy sweatshirt is draped over her shoulders, and she's wearing thick sweatpants to match. Her hair is longer and blonder than ever, and somehow she looks even younger than she did in college. Looking at her for the first time in person — this many years later — makes me feel like I'm looking into a time capsule. She squeezes me into an embrace, and we dramatically sway back and forth for a few moments.

"It's been so long," she says, rolling her luggage beside mine.

"Way too long," I agree.

Eliza takes a seat across from me and shivers, holding each of her arms with the other. "I forgot how freezing New York is."

"That's because you live in Florida." I'm wearing a white t-shirt and jeans, and my sweatshirt is packed away in my suitcase. "To me, it feels like summer."

Eliza motions towards the Oreo cake sitting in front of her. "You didn't."

"I did." I set my hand on my stomach. "I'm going to have a *food baby*."

"At least it's not a *real* baby." Eliza grabs her fork and takes the first bite of her cake. "This is the best day of my life," she says with a mouthful.

"Think of it as our *birthday* cake," I say, holding up a fork full of it. "Cheers."

Even though my birthday isn't until next week, and Eliza's isn't until the week after that, this is our *birthday trip*. Since we both have May birthdays and have been craving a trip back to the city, this is the best place and time for the occasion. I can't think of a better way to celebrate my birthday, to be honest.

Eliza sets her fork down. "I can't do this anymore," she says, leaning back in her seat. "I'm going to throw up."

"Only a few bites in?" I eat a glob of frosting. "What happened to you?"

Even though we've only known each other for a short period of time, it feels like we've been friends for decades. I think it's because our internship experience was so unique. Those four months joined our hearts together so closely in a way that nobody else could ever understand. Because of that, nothing has changed years later. The city and The Sunrise Show have tied us together for life.

Eliza looks around the restaurant. "Remember that one time I chugged a milkshake in here so fast that I was sick for *two* days?"

I motioned to a booth on the other side of the diner, beneath a green *I Heart NY* neon sign. "Remember when we sat over there, soaking wet, since we walked here in the pouring rain without umbrellas?"

Eliza laughs. "It feels like another lifetime. It *was* another lifetime."

Once we pay the bill and gather our suitcases into our arms, we walk out onto the sidewalk and take in the musty-smelling air. One whiff smells like hot garbage. The next smells like steam from a nearby hot-dog stand. Another smells like a luxury perfume from a passing businesswoman. Taxis and Ubers zoom past us. Horns and sirens blare into our eardrums. Businessmen and tourists battle each other for sidewalk space. We're here. *We're home.*

Directly across the street from the diner, Westerfield Apartments towers over us. It appears to stare down at us, whispering, "Hello again."

I think about the first time I ever saw this red brick building — scared and alone with so much unknown ahead of me — when my parents moved me in. I once stared at this building through tears of *fear*. Now I'm staring at it through teary eyes from *achievement*.

"There she is," I say, looking up at its exterior.

Eliza does the same. "You know what we should do?"

I smile. "Ask if we can go inside?"

Eliza looks over at me. "It's like you were reading my mind."

I squint my eyes. "I wonder if they'll let us in *just* to see a room, though."

"Let's do it," Eliza says, starting to walk. "The worst thing they can say is *no*."

* * *

The traffic light signals for pedestrians to cross, and we begin brushing elbows with people using the crosswalk alongside us— a polarizing mix of visitors and locals. One man, wearing a long overcoat and wireless earbuds, makes no apology to the man he just collided with. Two young girls wearing heels and sparkly blouses walk towards a night out on the town. An older couple wearing supportive shoes walks extra slowly to point out the Empire State Building down the road. We squeeze our way through the foot traffic, dodging the idle cars awaiting green lights, with our rolling suitcases following closely behind us. *We're back, baby.*

There's something about New York City that makes you feel so small and unimportant. Since I'm like a big fish in a small pond back home, I *need* this feeling of humbleness. It's like gazing up at a giant mountain range, looking out over a vast ocean, or looking up at a skyscraper— it feels *nice* to be small. In the grand scheme of the entire world, I'm insignificant, and that fact takes pressure off of myself. *Nothing really matters.*

Once we make it to the Westerfield Apartments lobby, we traipse inside onto that cranberry-colored carpeting, where the geometric-patterned rug is still spread out under those vintage leather chairs. The old, rickety elevator dings near the staircase. The old-fashioned brass chandeliers still hang from the ceiling. The vibes still haven't made it past the 1950s. It feels like we're just returning from a long day at The Sunrise Show.

"Can I help you, ladies?" A receptionist asks from her desk, looking at us with a confused expression. "Are you residents here?"

"No," Eliza says. "This is going to sound weird, but we lived here a few years ago."

"We just wondered if we could take a look around?" I add.

The receptionist looks skeptical, so I immediately feel like her answer will be *no*. But instead, she surprises me by saying, "Do you have a place to stay?"

Eliza looks at me. "We were going to get a room at the hotel down the street," she says. "We didn't make any reservations yet."

"We have a lot of vacancies right now because of the spring season of internships ending." The receptionist stands up from her desk and walks towards us, revealing that she's wearing a tailored black suit. "We're renting out rooms. It's $100 per night. You could stay here while you visit, if you'd like."

Eliza and I look at each other simultaneously, eyebrows raised in mutual agreement: *absolutely*. Staying at Westerfield Apartments? I never thought I'd be able to see my *shoe box* of a room ever again, let alone *sleep* in it. I thought its image would only live in my memory, so I'd love the chance to *relive* that memory.

"Yes," I say. "We would love that."

The woman walks back to her desk and takes out two keys. "These will take you to your rooms. You can pay on the way out. Have a nice stay."

"Thank you," Eliza says, taking the keys from her. "We are so excited to be back."

We hold back *verbal* shrieks of excitement — but display them proudly on our faces — on the short walk over to the elevator. It doesn't open until a solid thirty seconds after pressing the button, but once it does, I'm transported right back to those early mornings and late nights. *The slow-moving ascensions.*

"What floor are we on?" I ask once we get inside.

Eliza presses floor *four* once the doors close. "Yours."

"No way!" I hit her in the arm. "This is so nostalgic."

"I always liked your floor better," Eliza says. "Better view."

"My view was of a church and a liquor store," I say. "At least you looked out into the courtyard with the picnic tables."

"I didn't want to be able to see *grass* when I came to New York," Eliza says, leaning against the metal elevator wall. "I came to the city to see a *city*."

The doors open to floor *four*, and Eliza and I roll our suitcases onto the carpeting. I follow Eliza down the hallway as we race to find our rooms — passing *my* old room on the way there — until we find rooms 411 and 412 around the corner from the communal bathrooms. We unlock our respective doors and walk inside, realizing that *all* the rooms in this place look exactly the same. *It feels like we just opened the doors to the past.*

"This is *insane*," I hear Eliza's voice shout through our shared wall.

"I know," I shout back, setting my bags on the ground. "It's the same as we left it."

I notice the radiator under the tiny window, with white paint chipping off of it, just like mine was back in the day. An identical vanity to the one I set my *Acceptance Speech* on years ago sits to the left of the small sink. The chase in the corner of the room, the pathetic amount of square footage, the light blue quilt on the twin bed— it's the same. It looks even *smaller* than I remember it. *I can't believe I lived in a room this size for four months.*

I spin around and land on what would be my bed for the

night. "I could not be happier," I yell to Eliza through our paper-thin wall. I close my eyes and rest my hands behind my head. "Could not be happier."

"Same," I hear her yell back. Her voice sounds calmer than it has all day, and by the lack of sound coming from her room, I can tell that she's also lying down. "Dude, same."

"When do I get to find out what your secret is?"

"Tomorrow," Eliza says. "You'll know in 24 hours."

"Fine," I groan. "I've waited long enough."

I walk over to the window and look up at the skyscrapers. The sun is setting over the city, casting a golden glow on the buildings. Even though it's not directly in front of me like before, I see the Byzantine Catholic Church. I see Sip City Wine and Spirits. I see the Italian restaurant that was once called Rocky's, but is now a bodega. I hear the sounds of city buses, ambulances, and taxis. I close my eyes and take a deep breath. *Goodnight, New York.*

* * *

After being woken up to the sound of jackhammering, Eliza and I had a long, city-themed day of getting in our 20,000 steps. We went to see a Broadway show, got our favorite vodka sauce pasta in Little Italy, and even went to the top of 30 Rockefeller Center. We stopped by our favorite bars and coffee shops, and last but not least, reveled at the sight of The Sunrise Show. While we did not see Hilda Harrison in the flesh, we did see her on a giant television monitor plastered to the exterior of the building.

We went back to Westerfield Apartments to shower and change into our *glam*: dresses, heels, makeup, and hair. I'm wearing a sleeveless black sparkly dress. Eliza is wearing a tight, silky royal blue dress. We look like we're going *out*…to a much-needed destination. We are headed to our favorite comedy club with a three-drink minimum and half-priced appetizers, and I truly couldn't be any happier.

The Uber ride to the club fills my heart with what feels like glitter and sequins. The neon lights from the nearby bars and stores infiltrate the windows of our Uber like colorful reflections off a disco ball. It's so dark outside that you can see the full moon and constellations of stars above the skyscrapers. It's a Saturday night in New York City, and being driven to this club makes me feel like I'm a celebrity being driven to the Hollywood red carpet.

The entrance to the comedy club is so dark that I feel like I need to pull out the flashlight on my cell phone. We make our way through the admission line and get our first (of many) drinks, finding a small two-person table near the center stage. I always like being as close to the action as possible.

When going to the movies, most people *don't* like to be in the first or second row. *Not me.* I want to feel like I'm *inside* that movie. The same goes for comedy clubs, too, I guess. The closer the better. Eliza and I could stick out our arms and touch the stage, and the spotlights for the upcoming comedians are shining onto us, too.

We used to come to this comedy club all the time to see the lineups of comedians— from writers on late night television shows to people with large social media followings trying to make it big. Tonight, however, there was nothing on the calendar besides an *open mic* night. While it's not our preferred method of entertainment, we'll take whatever laughs this evening that we can get.

A young waitress arrives at our table, wearing black from head to toe. I tell her that I want the spinach artichoke dip appetizer, and Eliza tells her that she wants the mini charcuterie board. I hold a glass of sparkling rosé in my hand, and Eliza sips on a dirty martini. I try to soak in my surroundings— we're enjoying each other's company during our birthday month at our favorite comedy club, with loud music playing, in our beloved major city, feeling just the right amount of tipsy. *Life can't get any better than this.*

When the lights flicker on and off three quick times, we know the show is about to begin. A man who I assume is the host for this evening's *open mic* night walks sheepishly onto the stage, grabbing the shiny microphone to introduce the first comedian in tonight's lineup. He tries to warm everyone up with some bad jokes, feeding off the audience's forced and pre-drunk excitement.

"Oof," Eliza sighs to me.

"It can only go up from here," I whisper.

The host swaps places with the first comedian in the group: a young, scrawny guy wearing a black T-shirt and jeans. He steps up nervously onto the small platform and smiles when the audience politely greets him with whistles and applause. For a split second, I feel nervous on this stranger's behalf. It has to be tough to be the *first* one to go up there. *I really hope he doesn't bomb.*

"How's everybody feeling tonight?" The comedian asks nobody in particular.

Each comedian has fifteen minutes to perform. I think about how long fifteen minutes sitting at the anchor desk feels, but I don't know if the time would go faster or slower in this environment. If you're doing great, it probably feels fast. But if your set is tanking, it's probably the *longest* time of your life. I cringe at the thought of embarrassment, let alone *second-hand* embarrassment, and because of that, I genuinely hope that all of these comedians experience the *first* case scenario.

The man spends *his* fifteen minutes talking about politics, and then transitions that into impressions of famous people. I have always been a *sucker* for impersonations. No matter how good or how bad they might be, people pretending that they're other people *always* make me laugh. When the comedian's fifteen minutes are up, the host comes back onto the stage to relieve him.

"Give it up for Jeremy!" He screams into the mic. "That was hilarious, thank you."

"He was pretty good," I whisper.

Eliza throws the last of her drink back into her throat. "He was okay," she says.

The host clears his throat. "It's time to introduce our next comedian."

The waiter arrives with our spinach artichoke dip appetizer and mini charcuterie board. I'm picking up my first chip and dipping it into the cheesy mixture when my heart stops at the next sentence I hear.

"Next up, Eliza Swickley!"

I cough, holding the back of my hand to my mouth to refrain from full-out choking. "Is this a joke?" I look over at her in pure shock.

"Surprise," she whispers excitedly to me.

I watch as Eliza gets up out of her seat and walks up onto the stage, grabbing the microphone from the host. I take a sip of my drink to wash down the chip that I'm still choking on. *I can't believe my eyes.*

Eliza…is *up there?* Doing comedy? Did I fall asleep and now I'm just *dreaming?* This can't be real. But somehow, seeing her silk blue dress shine up on that stage, I know that it's really happening.

"Hello, New York!" She yells into the mic. "How are we doing tonight?"

The crowd cheers for her. I'm still blinking and shaking my head in disbelief. There's nothing left for me to do besides sit here and watch what's about to happen before my eyes. This was her surprise all along? But why? *How did she even get to this point?*

"See my friend right here in the front row?" Eliza points to me. "She didn't know I was even coming up here to perform tonight. She thought we were coming here to make fun of *other* comedians."

The audience erupts into laughter, and I find myself turning and waving to everyone sitting behind me. I see hundreds of eyeballs staring back at me. My cheeks flush with pinkness, and I feel my face getting hot over the attention.

For the next fifteen minutes, Eliza talks about our time living in New York City. She makes fun of the garbage on the streets and how the locals here aren't exactly friendly towards tourists. She tells stories that, even if I didn't know Eliza, I would still be laughing hysterically at. Her timing, cadence, and mannerisms are everything, and for a moment, I find myself forgetting that *she's my friend* up there.

While she doesn't explicitly name The Sunrise Show, she talks about what it was like to work for the number one morning news broadcast in the entire country as a measly little intern. She talked about getting coffee orders wrong and printing scripts out backwards: just little intern-in-a-big-city things. But the way she talks about living in the Big Apple as an outsider is hilarious, not just to me, but to everyone here.

"Thank you, guys. Good night."

The audience roars with applause and whistles. Eliza hands the microphone back to the host, then sits back down at our table. We're sitting so close that she's basically seated within seconds of performing. She nonchalantly pairs a piece of cheese with a cracker and takes a bite as if *nothing* happened.

She turns towards me. "So, where were we?"

I blink rapidly at her. "*That* was your surprise?"

"Yes," she says with a mouthful. "I've been taking up stand-up comedy."

"I have to give it to you, this was the most *perfect* way you could have told me." I watch as our waitress places two more rounds of drinks in front of us. "Well done."

"There's one more thing," Eliza says.

"Don't tell me you're going to go up there again," I say.

"I quit my reporting job."

"You…what?"

Eliza turns to face me, taking a sip of her fresh drink before speaking. "I quit reporting and got a boring *nine-to-five* job instead. Working in insurance. It completely sucked the life out of me. But it was *triple* the pay and *half* the hours. Too good to pass up, you know?"

I tilt my head. "Okay?"

She clears her throat. "I was feeling pretty depressed about it after a while. But our local Florida bar started hosting these open mic nights. I was always *kind of* interested in stand-up comedy, so I gave it a try. Turns out, *I love it.* I love it so much,

Noelle, you have no idea."

"So, you traded one job for *two*?"

"Kind of." Eliza smiles, pairing a piece of meat with a cracker. "I have a boring little day job to give me a *paycheck*, and this exciting little comedy gig to give me a *purpose*. I have more *money* than before, and I'm actually more *passionate* than before, too. With reporting, I was always trying to mesh those things into *one*."

"Yeah?"

"But here's the thing," she says. "I never fully achieved either."

I smile in awe at her, sitting across from me like she just figured out the secret to life. Here is this woman, whom I met as a young college girl, who has been secretly going through the same thoughts and questions *I have*. And all of these long years later, she seems to have figured it out. She has a new system and a new lifestyle that gives her both *passions* and *paychecks*.

I like where she's going with this.

"You were incredible," I say, shaking my head. "Sorry for all the questions, I'm just trying to process everything—"

"I think I figured it out, Noelle." She crosses her legs. "You need a stable job. You need to support yourself. You need to be independent. Then pursue your passions on the *side*. You know, until that *side* gig can become your *main* gig someday. You can have the best of both worlds until then."

"Are you saying you want to be the next Amy Schumer?"

"That's the new plan." Eliza smiles. "But until then, I have my *nine-to-five*."

Thirty-One

THE FIELD

JUNE | JOYFIELD, OHIO

Over the years, I've fallen in love with my news car. My box of tissues is always on the floor of the passenger seat. The wrappers encapsulating my lunchtime granola bars are always shoved into the cup holder. My coffee-scented air freshener is always hanging from the rear-view mirror. Even though it's not *my* car, I've driven it more than my own car. But today, since I have to visit the Joyfield Auto Body Shop, I have to take a different one.

It's as unsettling as being told that I'd have to sleep in a different bed.

I dreadfully get into the driver's seat. I spot no box of tissues on the passenger seat floor, somebody else's candy bar wrappers in the cup holder, and not an air freshener in sight. I also realize that this car doesn't have Bluetooth or an auxiliary cord to plug my phone into. I groan, knowing that I have no other choice for today's travels— I have to listen to public *radio*.

I drive down the streets of Joyfield to the scene of a train derailment on the other end of town. Even given my shitty car situation — and shitty story for today's broadcast — I can't help but be overwhelmingly happy. *Delilah's open-heart surgery is over. It was successful. She made it out on the other side.* The doctors said she did better than expected, and she's to follow up with them in six months. For those reasons, no matter what today looks like, there is absolutely nothing that can bring me down. It's all been put into perspective for me. *My sister is okay, and that's all that matters.*

Summer has arrived in Joyfield once and for all. The snow has melted, the flowers have started to bloom, and the sky is actually clear for once. The sun is setting, casting pink and orange hues over the streets. The seasonal depression has lifted off my mind, and the weight of Delilah's surgery has been lifted off my chest. I feel as light as a feather, like I could just float around with ease.

It's officially summertime. My travels are over. Levi and I have been doing amazing together. The Kaylee Wood trial is over, and Levi *won* it for them. I'm almost afraid to say it, *but everything is perfect.*

I turn on our local oldies radio station. *Day Tripper* by the Beatles starts to play, and I tap my hands on my steering wheel to the beat. I sing along and dance in my seat, turning the volume as loud as possible. Since I probably wouldn't have thought to put this song on my *regular* listening rotation, I'm thankful for the radio in this moment. I haven't heard these lyrics since I was little, dancing to them with my dad in the living room.

I had just given my live report for the 5:00 news and was packing up to go home when Bill called me to cover this train derailment. I just wanted to go home and see Delilah. I just wanted to call Levi. I just wanted to eat some dinner. But *someone* needs to cover this story for the nighttime news, and even though I won't get any overtime pay for it, I'm the only person for the job.

"Couldn't Paige do it?" I had asked Bill over the phone.

"I had her covering the early morning shift today," Bill explained to me. "She's probably sleeping right now. You're it, Noelle."

I'm exhausted, but because of my internal good mood, I don't even feel like I need an energy drink or caffeinated coffee to get me through the night. *I'm happy.* Thinking about what Delilah has gone through, and the scare she put us *all* through, I'm beyond relieved. I think the feeling of *relief* might be the best possible feeling a human can experience, and I'm on a high from feeling it now. Light. Airy. Free.

Once another round of cheesy radio commercials finishes up, I hear the strumming of a guitar from a song that I immediately recognize. It's *Hey There Delilah.* The radio has blessed me with yet another sentimental song that I have no choice but to listen to. Staring out at the sunset, tears started to fall. *Happy tears.* I smile, even though I can start to see the outline of a disheveled train up the road.

Once I reach the scene, the sun has officially set. The stars begin to emerge overhead. There's not a person in sight. I park in a convenience store parking lot a few steps away from the chaos. *This is better than the side of the road.* Parking lots are like gold for reporters. I've never been so thankful to come across pavement as when I started this job. Out of grass, mud, and gravel…*pavement* is obviously my favorite thing to park on.

I put my car in park, make sure my doors are locked, and observe the scene in front of me. The train is *completely* derailed, with the line of boxcars twisting and turning until the last one lies horizontally on the ground. Houses line the streets surrounding the tracks, and I think about how close the train came to crashing into some of these structures. It must have been a miracle. A big, messy miracle.

I start writing a script on my phone, using the press release sent out by local police and describing the setting in front of me. I keep making sure that my doors are locked every five minutes…*as if they could mysteriously unlock themselves.* It's a nervous tic I have when I'm waiting for a live shot. It must stem from my internal anxiety about the absence of people around me. I'm, once again, completely alone in the dark. *Lock. Lock. Lock.*

"How's it going?" A text from Levi pops up on my phone.

"Oh, you know," I respond. I take a picture of the train and send it to him.

"Wow," he says. "You there by yourself?"

"I'm here with my team of hair and makeup people," I jokingly reply.

"Be safe," Levi says, ignoring my joke. "Should I come out and sit with you?"

"I didn't know you were hired by WJDN as my security guard," I say.

"I'm serious," Levi says. "I want you to be safe."

"It's my company's job to make sure I'm safe," I say. "They apparently think I'm fine."

I know my message is a total lie, but I don't want to worry Levi. Bill and the newsroom *never* think about whether or not we're actually fine out here. They just want the *story*, even though they don't consider how it's retrieved. They don't think about logistics, setting, time of day, or anything like that. They're safe and warm in the WJDN building, and we're left to figure out the outside world for ourselves.

I notice a man staggering in the distance. I can't make out his age, but he's wearing a sweatshirt and jeans. He looks to be some kind of intoxicated. I hold my breath, hoping he doesn't make it towards the convenience store. *But where else would we be going? To see the train?* I breathe out a sigh of relief when he turns down an alleyway.

I don't know if it's a sudden burst of confidence or an overall realization about the *insanity* of this situation, but I decide to text Bill. I still haven't told him whether or not I'll be renewing my contract with WJDN, so the ball is technically still in my court.

"It's dark here, no sign of life. Creepy dudes walking around me." *Send.*

I don't give him a call to action. I don't explicitly state that I want to leave. I don't tell him what I want to do. I want to see what call *he* will make. I'm subconsciously testing him. I want to see if he truly cares about my safety, my concerns, my well-being. Do I want to get out of here right now? Definitely. But I want the decision to come from a higher power...*just like it should.*

Three dots appear, signaling that Bill is texting back, but they quickly disappear. *Nothing.* I stare at my phone screen, the blue light electrifying my eyeballs. The dots appear again, stay for a few seconds, and once again: *nothing.* A few minutes pass. I'm still staring at the blue light, waiting for those little dots to reemerge. *Nothing.* No response is ever sent. I'm left feeling a little empty and defeated, but also a little bit...*happy.*

I'm proud of myself for sending that initial text. It pushed Bill to at least *think* about a response. Even if he ultimately retracted it, he typed one out. I made him picture this situation. I made him put himself in my shoes. I made him consider safety. Even if I didn't get anywhere, it's the thought that counts. *That's one small step forward for me, but one giant leap for all reporters out there.*

It's almost time for my live shot in front of the derailed train— a backdrop that I'm not even sure will *show up* on camera. I look up at the sky through my windshield. It's cloudy. You can't even see the stars or the moon. It's a pitch-black sky, blanketing the rows of houses and train tracks beneath it. There's no reason for me to actually be here, because on a television screen, it will probably look like I'm standing in front of a *black cloth.*

I know I should get out and set up my camera, but I close my eyes and bang my head against the headrest a few times instead. *I don't want to do this.* I just want to go home. But like the wonderful journalist I am, I slink out of my car anyway, shutting my door quietly behind me. I walk back around to my trunk and open it to see my camera bag, tripod case, and lighting equipment staring back at me. *I can do this. My day is almost over.*

As with my usual camera setup, I keep everything extremely close to my driver's-side door. I extend my tripod legs, click my camera into place, and raise my LED light to the desired height. I plug in my microphone and adjust the camera settings. Throughout this process, I try to look over my shoulder as much as possible to "be aware of my surroundings." But as I set up my live shot and put my earpiece in, I find it hard to focus on all of these things at once. *I'm trying my best, dammit.*

Everything is in place. *Lights. Camera. Action.* But I still have a few minutes, so I decide to go back into my car and resume a seated position for a little while longer. It's just freshly June, so once this time of night hits in Joyfield, it's chilly. I feel like I could be wearing a coat, but, of course, I never do. I get back in the driver's seat and lock my doors once again, closing my eyes in anticipation of my upcoming live shot.

I take a deep breath in and out. I think about Delilah, my job, my parents, and my life. Everything is as *good* as it could be right now. I'm trying to channel peace. I'm trying to channel lightness. I breathe in and out. Calmly. Quietly. *Peacefully.* I'm so tired— I worry this meditation might turn into a nap. The next time I plan on opening my eyes is to check the time, but I open my eyes to a strange noise instead. *It's my car handle jiggling.*

"Hey, I have a story I want to tell you about."

My heart stops when I hear the muffled voice through my driver's side window. It's the man who was walking on the sidewalk earlier. I lock my doors again. If it wasn't for this pane of glass, he would be just inches away from my face. His eyes are so glossy that he's not even really making eye contact with me, even though he's talking directly *at* me. He's standing so close to my camera— I'm afraid he could stumble as a result of his drugged and/or drunken stupor and knock it all down.

"I need to tell you about this story," he says.

As I previously noticed from his earlier sidewalk stroll, this man *is* wearing a sweatshirt and jeans, and he *is* staggering from some form of intoxication. But upon further inspection, I can assume he's in his 30s or 40s. His wobbly cadence makes him look like a zombie, making *me* feel like I'm in the beginning scenes of a horror movie. He jiggles my door handle again…and again…before *pulling* on it more violently. *He's trying to get in here.* Back and forth, back and forth. My heart *pounds* from the sound of it.

He starts back up again. "I need to tell you about—"

"Go away!" I yell without looking at him. "I'm going to call the police."

He backs away from my window and catches sight of my live shot set up for the first time. He trips into my camera, poking the side of it like he's poking a bear. It makes my tripod wobble on its legs, sending a shock wave of *anger* through my center. *Is this guy going to touch my stuff?* He drunkenly giggles at the movement. I feel like steam is about to spray out from my ears and nostrils. I want this guy *gone*.

My shoulders are tense, but I keep looking at my dashboard. I figure the less attention I give him, the better. Maybe he'll think he's just dreaming, eventually. The tension in my chest starts to ease once I see that he's slowly staggering away towards the convenience store. It's like he doesn't even know about our recent interaction— like he's already forgotten about it. Before I know it, he's gone. *I need to get out of here.*

Even though my live shot is now just minutes away, I text Bill. "I'm leaving. Someone tried to get into my car. Not safe here." In a panic, I press *send*.

I look behind me and see that the man is far enough away that I can get out of my car, grab all my equipment, throw it into the back seat, and drive away. I do it all within a matter of seconds, to the point where my camera is still connected to my tripod. It bounces around in the back of the car with every bump I hit. *I really hope none of this stuff breaks.*

Before I know it, the scene of the train derailment is getting smaller and smaller in the rear-view mirror behind me. Tears well up in my eyes. I didn't even want to work a double shift tonight, let alone one that ended up like *this*. I just want to go home, get under the covers, and fall asleep instantly. I want to pretend this day never happened and that this man never existed.

My mind shifts from the scene…to my *manager*. I texted Bill to let him know I felt unsafe, but he didn't do anything. Of course, *I could* have done something. I could have left. I could have been in control. But the point is, he didn't care. He wanted me to get the story. He didn't care about my safety. This is something I've suspected all along, and it's now confirmed. *I need to fend for myself.*

Part of me feels guilty for thinking this way. *Am I being dramatic?* I think about social workers who have to show up at random people's homes at all hours of the night to protect children. I think about nurses in overcrowded emergency rooms who are getting physically assaulted by patients. I think about teachers who are underpaid and overworked with thirty kids in a classroom. Other professions out there have it *way worse* than I do. Nobody is going to die if I don't go to work. But I still feel unsafe. Is this a societal issue? Are we *all* screwed if our titles are 'employee' rather than 'manager'?

Images of Kaylee Wood pop into my mind as I drive through the streets of Joyfield. I think about how scared she must have been. I think about the physical battle she fought. I think about her last moments. Tears slide down my cheeks just thinking about it. While I don't mean to compare what just happened to *me* with what happened to *her,* I realize that you just can't predict the outcome. You never know who you're up against. Kaylee could have lived. I could have died. *You just never know.*

All young, female news reporters — out in the field, alone, in the darkness, without an extra set of eyes — could turn into Kaylee Wood. What happened to *her* could happen to *any* one of us. I certainly don't want to end up like her, and I don't want anybody *else* to end up in her shoes. It's not preventable, but it could be lessened. I don't want this to continue in our industry, which I'm slowly learning is the norm across local news.

What is the fix here? Even if we *were* given camera operators, the extra set of eyes doesn't necessarily guarantee safety. We can't just *not* do live shots at night when there's breaking news to be covered. The mase in my glove compartment is no match for a man who comes up behind me when I'm reading from a script. I don't know what the solution is here. But *something* needs to be done.

Once I pull into the driveway of my childhood home, I open up my work email on my phone. My blood is pumping through my veins. My heart is pounding with anger. I type out a new message for Bill, one that should have been sent a long time ago.

After typing and retyping for longer than I'd care to admit, I'm finally content with my final version.

Bill,

I was placed in a situation tonight that not only threatened my safety, but also potentially my life. I am requesting a meeting in your office tomorrow morning. Something needs to change.
NF

Thirty-Two

THE STATION

I feel the blood pumping through my neck as I take each step up to the newsroom. I didn't sleep last night. I was too awake— tossing and turning, planning what I'm going to say, thinking about my career in news. But most of all, I spent it wondering how Bill would react.

I walk over to my desk, drop my bags on the filing cabinet, and march back over to Bill's office. I'm trying to maintain my composure on the outside, even though my head is thumping with anxiety. Nate and Myra shoot me a confused look that asks: *you're voluntarily going to the principal's office?* Yes, I am.

That's because Bill never responded to my email last night, just like he never responded to my text before that. I'm going to talk to him whether he wants to or not. This conversation is long overdue.

"Come in," Bill says once I'm inside his office. He seems extra cheerful in his tone, proving a point that nothing is wrong in his eyes. "How was that train derailment?"

I don't respond. I just sit down in the chair across from him. "About last night," I say, both calm and stern. "I need to talk to you about it."

"I emailed you back," Bill says, eyes locked on his computer screen. "A few minutes ago."

"Oh. I didn't see it." I shake my head in surprise. "What did it say?"

Bill turns his computer screen around to face me, and I mentally read the words as he summarizes them aloud. "I just said that you have to be more aware of your surroundings, next time," he says. "Which is something I always say, by the way."

I shake my head. "But that's not the problem—"

"Reporters need to be on high alert at all times. Watch their backs." Bill's voice is turning angry, and his cheeks are flushing with redness. "I don't understand what's so difficult about that. Assess the scene, Noelle. You're a reporter. You should be good at that—"

"Trust me, I did. We *all* do." I feel my head swell to the size of a balloon that could burst at any moment. "This is about *where* and *when* we're being sent—"

"I don't know what else to tell you." Bill throws his arms in the air before turning his computer screen back in his direction. "This is what you signed up for."

I try to maintain my composure, knowing that anger would get me nowhere. "The reason I'm bringing this up is for *safety* to be made a priority when assigning story and live shot locations. Thinking about the scene, the time of day, whether the reporter would be *alone* in a desolate area in the dark somewhere, like last night—"

"Safety is our first priority," Bill interjects. "But *you're* responsible—"

"I really think we need to implement the buddy system." I take a deep breath to continue calmly. "It would be a huge help to have an *extra* set of eyes on the scene—"

"This station can't afford that. We can't afford to have *two* people going to *one* story. We divide and conquer."

"I'm just saying to consider the reporter's environment," I say with force. "I could have gone live in the studio last night, for example. The anchor could *read* stories when a scene is unsafe for the reporter. Maybe no more *solo* live shots—"

"There will always be solo live shots," Bill shoots back. "End of story—"

"But I thought *safety* was your first priority?"

"Let me explain this to you," Bill says in a childish tone. "Bigger news stations have bigger budgets. Bigger budgets mean bigger staff. A larger staff means more people to go on a news story. We don't have that luxury. *Solo* always."

"Then maybe *nobody* should go to the story." I shake my head. "If safety is your first priority, that is. If a scene isn't safe, then nobody should go to it."

"The train derailment had already happened," Bill says, waving his hands in the air. "The scene was cleared. It wasn't like the train was going to run into you—"

"I'm not talking about the *train*," I clarify. "I'm talking about the scene *around* the train. The darkness, the nobody being around, the feeling unsafe."

Bill pauses for a moment, not knowing what to say next. "You caused mayhem at the start of last night's show," he says. "If you didn't think you could go live at this, quote on quote, *scary* scene, then you should have made that decision earlier."

"I tried!" I throw my arms up into the air. "I texted you. You didn't respond."

Bill forms a confused expression that could win him an Academy Award. "I didn't know that you—"

"Yes, you did!" I shout. "I saw the text bubbles!"

"The text bubbles?"

"Nevermind," I sigh, not wanting to spend a bulk of this conversation explaining what a text bubble is to Bill.

Bill narrows his eyes at me in disapproval. "Even if you had another person with you, that man could have *still* come up to you last night."

"I know that." I take a breath, trying to regain my composure. "I'm just calling for *something*. Not *just* the buddy system, but a more conversational approach to reporter live shots. The time and place. Will it be dark? Is the area desolate? Just more *awareness* from management's perspective."

Bill huffs. "Again, this is what you signed up for."

"But it wasn't always this way," I say. "Reporters used to have an extra set of eyes back in the day. But I *don't* have eyes in the back of my head. When I'm setting up my camera, checking audio levels, setting up my shot, adjusting my lighting and focus, and listening to voices in my earpiece— I can't pay attention to a 360-degree view of everything going on behind me, or *who* is behind me. Or even if a car is coming. That happened to me once, too, you know. I got splashed—"

Bill cuts me off. "I can't get into this right now."

"Especially in light of this whole Kaylee Wood thing."

Bill's voice turns angry and defensive. "*Please* tell me you aren't comparing what happened to you last night to Kaylee Wood."

With that, I choose stay silent. I am not comparing myself

to Kaylee Wood. I'm comparing what happened to Kaylee Wood…with what *could* happen to me. Or Paige. Or any other reporter in local news. We are putting ourselves in those kinds of dangerous situations, and I don't want to be the subject of another crime scene.

I calmly and slowly stand up from the chair, heading for the door. I can't have one more back-and-forth with this man. I'm not asking for a 24/7 security guard. I'm not asking for a freaking *handgun.* I'm asking for a little more concern. A little more awareness. A little more conversation. That is *not* too much to ask.

Before I grab the door handle, I leave Bill with one final thought. I feel warm tears welling up in my eyes, but I ignore them. "Just so you know, I'm not bringing this up for *me.* I'm bringing this up for all of the young, female news reporters who are too scared to bring this up for *themselves.*" With that, I shut the door.

By the time I reach my desk, I see that Bill has sent out an email to everyone in the newsroom. I can't tell whether he wrote it while I was on my way from his office to my desk or had it drafted earlier this morning. It reads:

Dear team,

We want to remind the folks in the newsroom that safety is our first priority when out in the field. However, we still need to uphold our values of bringing our viewers the news they need to hear, no matter what time of day. This is a reminder to be extra cautious, especially at night. Stay vigilant. Please don't hesitate to contact me if you have any questions.

Sincerely,

Bill Calloway

I sit silently and motionless, staring at the black text on my computer screen. I hold my breath while reading the email from beginning to end, still in disbelief of Bill's lack of regard for our safety concerns.

His message places the blame back on *us*. It's not taking responsibility for the action, or in this case, the *inaction*, of the news organization. Rather, it's making the reporters feel like we're the ones at fault. For not having eyes in the backs of our heads. For not making *being aware of our surroundings* a priority when we're speaking on live television. For not having one eye on the sidewalks and one eye on our scripts. This message points fingers at the wrong group of people.

I feel like quitting. Quitting out of frustration. Quitting out of resentment. Quitting from not being able to change the status quo. I don't know where to go from here. Is this a fight that I'm willing to put up with? Would I ever be able to win this argument? Would management even address my concerns? Something tells me that the answer to each of these questions would be *no*.

I want to cry for those of us who just want to grow up and become Hilda Harrison someday, because I'm afraid this will become the one obstacle preventing me from getting there.

Thirty-Three

THE VOICE OVER

"I don't think I've ever been so frustrated about something in my entire life."

I say the words to Levi, who is walking alongside me at the Joyfield Community Park. A canopy of fully-greened trees hangs over our heads as we look out towards a long line of pavement ahead. The road we're walking along circles the park, which contains a swing set and volleyball courts. It feels like a beautiful summer day, with a light breeze, hopefully removing any sweat smell from me.

"It's just not right," Levi says, kicking a rock across the pavement. "There's not a union you could join there?"

"There is no union," I say.

Levi tilts his head. "Could *you* start one?"

I sigh. "There was a reporter who left WJDN the month I started," I explain. "She tried to start one, but none of the unions wanted to work with her. They wouldn't return her calls or emails. She found out later that a union had been burned by our company before, so they just avoided us altogether."

"Interesting." The legal cogs in Levi's mind are spinning around an invisible wheel. "Most unions have a list of companies that are *hostile to labor.* Maybe WJDN is on that list? Unions can choose *who* they want to represent."

"They probably don't want to touch the news industry with a nine-foot pole." I roll my eyes, adjusting my fallen bra strap. "I don't know what else to do. I don't even want this change for *myself.* I want it for the people who come after me."

Levi looks at me with his deep hazel eyes, which are now sparkling in the sunlight. "You could try another union? Call a few others and inquire again?"

"Bill found out about that reporter contacting the union, and he was *not* happy. He almost fired her for it, but her contract was up soon, so he knew she'd be leaving soon anyway." I groan in agony. "Plus, I don't want to risk getting in trouble, and then not being able to do *anything* at all, you know?"

Levi's bicep muscle flexes as he pushes his hair out of his face. "And you're sure that *all* local news stations operate this way?"

"I really don't know," I admit. "I know the station in Virginia Beach was similar. The news director there didn't really answer my question. More news stations isolate their reporters to save money. Not sure if it's all of them, though."

Levi shakes his head. "I'm just trying to figure out what other options you have."

"Lawsuit?" I stretch my arms above my head and bend side to side, trying to loosen up my tight lower back. "Come on, hot attorney. You *have* to have the answer to this."

Levi leans his head, visibly weighing the options. "Negligence, emotional distress…there are some routes you could take. But a lot of times, you have to *prove* that your company intentionally tried to cause harm."

"I don't mean to be pessimistic," I say, looking up at a giant cumulonimbus cloud in the sky. "But I feel like they'd still win. They'd *make* me lose. I can't go up against a company."

Levi looks like he's about to drop a truth bomb. "Noelle, I hear everything you're saying. I've read case study after case study of situations just like this. I hate to tell you this, but the company *usually* always wins. They keep fighting until they've drained you mentally *and* financially. I just feel like you'd be fighting a battle that is ultimately a systemic issue."

"So, no union and no lawsuit." I drop my head in frustration. "Then what *can* I do?"

Levi looks at my side profile. "You really wanna know?"

"Yes, please," I say. "I'll take any advice I can get."

"Leave."

I shake my head in uncertainty. "Leave?"

"Leave WJDN," Levi says. "That's the real way out."

I can't help but laugh. "You want me to…*quit?*"

"I don't *want* you to quit," Levi reassures. "But it's the best way to make an impact."

"But then I really wouldn't be helping *anyone*."

Levi exhales sharply. "What would WJDN do once they're down to *zero* employees? They'd *have* to implement some safety rules. They'd *have* to raise their wages. They'd *have* to start listening to what employees want. Or else they'd have nobody."

I hop over a small puddle. "Our staff is already down to

nothing."

Levi cracks his knuckles and twists his torso. "That's how change usually happens within companies. From the inside out," he says. "If they keep that revolving door swinging to the point of losing everyone, they'll be forced to make a change. Or else, they won't be able to continue. You'd be contributing to that internal change."

"But it's my *dream*." While walking, I hold my eyes closed for a solid two seconds before opening them again. "I would be giving up on my dream. Over *this*?"

"It all depends on what you're willing to put up with," Levi says. "You have a choice, Noelle. You can choose to put up with this bullshit until you reach The Sunrise Show, or you can leave and change the industry from the inside out."

I've never thought about *not* chasing my dream. Not working in the news. Not making it to The Sunrise Show. Not living in a New York City brownstone apartment. Not interviewing celebrities. Not being known and remembered across America. Not shedding light on the stories that actually matter in the world. It seems like a lot to give up. It was all I had ever pictured for myself…so to *leave it all behind*? I can't even fathom it.

"I don't even know what else I would do," I say.

"I'm not talking you into leaving," Levi says, shooting his arms out. "I think you're amazing at what you do, and I think it would be awesome if you worked for The Sunrise Show someday. I don't want you to give up on your goals. That's the last thing I want. You just have a problem right now, and I'm trying to help you solve it by going over your options. It's what I do for work, you know?"

I fidget with the ring on my finger, which is now too tight

due to swelling from walking in the June heat. "This might just be something I have to put up with," I admit.

"Okay, let's say you take that route." Levi and I round the corner of the road, positioning ourselves towards the volleyball courts. "Do you think I *wanted* to take my Civil Procedure and Federal Courts classes in law school? Absolutely not. But I had to *suffer* through those classes because they were part of my overall course curriculum. I *had* to take them to become a lawyer, which was my end goal. I *had* to put up with the bullshit classes on the way there. They're unavoidable."

"So you're saying to treat each news station like your...*Civil Courts* class?"

"Civil Procedure. Federal Courts. Two separate classes," Levi laughs, his famous line dimples making an appearance. "But pretty much, yeah. Every job, every hardship, every frustration— they're all just courses in your curriculum that you *have* to get through. They're mandatory to get to the top. It just depends on how many courses you're *willing* to suffer through. It's all a prerequisite."

"When you put it that way, I don't know *how* many of these mandatory classes I'm willing to take." I notice a patch of purple flowers on the side of the road. "It seems like the entire path forward is these mandatory classes that I *don't* want to take."

"Then you might need to change your curriculum," Levi says.

Suddenly, I feel like crying. If I *do* decide to leave, it wouldn't *just* be because of this safety issue. It's working nights and weekends. It's working double shifts with no overtime pay. It's working every Christmas and holiday. It's the low wages. It's doing the job of five people. It's the inability to write the stories I *want* to write. It's the hard news. It's the sexism. It's dealing with Bill. It's working for a corporation. It's the time spent away from my current family and the time I will spend away from my future family. *It's a combination of everything.*

"I don't know how much of this job I like anymore," I admit, teary-eyed.

"It's okay." Levi rubs my upper back. "You have time."

"I don't have time." I shake my head. "I need to tell Bill whether or not I'm renewing my contract this month."

"You'll know what to do. I believe in you, remember?"

A tear escapes from my eye and streams down my cheek. "Thank you," I say the words kindly and softly, and I mean them. I feel lucky to have a man in my life who cares about *my* career and goals.

Life is always good with Levi. He's constantly uplifting, optimistic, and upbeat. He's somebody whom I *want* to be around, and not just because I enjoy staring at his cute face. He's becoming one of the *best* parts of my life, and while nothing is official between us, I don't ever want us to be apart from him. *I want him to be in my life.* He wants what's best for me, not only personally, but professionally. That is so important to me in a partner.

All the things I used to say about dating a work acquaintance and not wanting to make things awkward have been thrown out the window over the past couple of months. I feel like my initial reservations about dating Levi aren't even a figment of my imagination anymore. He's no longer the hot attorney. He's no longer the lawyer in the courtroom. He's just...*Levi.* A guy I like spending time with.

Once we get into his car, I stare at his side profile —

observing how his line dimples are more defined from my passenger vantage point — and watch as he puts his car into drive. The blue lights shining from the buttons on his radio display illuminate his face in colorful hues as we pull away from our parking spot.

"Hey," I say, looking over at him.

"Yeah?"

"If I *did* leave the news, what would you make of it?"

Levi tilts his head to the side in thought. "I'd be indifferent," he says. "Just want what's best for *you*, no matter what that might be."

I look up at the moon. "Would you like me any less?"

Levi laughs. "Why would I like you *less*?"

"Well, you wouldn't be able to see me in courtrooms anymore."

Levi raises his eyebrows. "Guess I'd have to find another reporter to stare at."

"Seriously, though." I rest my elbow on the ledge of the passenger side window and stare out at the passing trees. "You like me because of my job. You like me because of my dreams, goals, and plans. You like that I want to make it big. If that all went away, then—"

"I never liked you *because* you were a news reporter," Levi explains.

"You didn't?"

"No." Levi shakes his head, driving onto the main road. "I like you because you're ambitious. I like you because you want something *big* out of life. I like you because you have aspirations and goals. I don't care *what* they are."

"Really?" For whatever reason, I feel a tiny paperweight lift off my chest. "But what happens if I *don't* have a dream to follow anymore? Nothing to aspire to?"

"You'd find a new dream." Levi reaches his hand across the center console and places it on my thigh. "I know you by now. You'd *never* stop looking."

I internally beam with excitement, knowing that Levi actually *does* know me this closely. "Thanks," I say. "This has been really helpful. I've been really lost—"

"Hey," Levi whispers, looking over at me. "You're going to be fine."

I look out the window, watching the streets of Joyfield pass by me like a video montage. "I hope so," I say. "I really hope so."

"Just decide what you're willing to deal with," Levi says. "If there are a few classes you can push through, just push through them. But if you hate every single class—"

"Change the curriculum," I say with a wink. "I get your analogy...*hot attorney*."

Thirty-Four

THE SWEEPS PIECE

"Come on in."

Amy Wood, the mother of Kaylee Wood, waves me onto her front porch. She's wearing a sleek, black dress to blatantly symbolize mourning. When she pulls me in for a hug, I let my camera bag and tripod case slide off my arms and drop onto the concrete step. Her blonde hair smells like citrus, but her perfume smells like coconut. I squeeze her back. I sigh in her warmth and sadness.

When she releases me, I see that her eyes are filled with tears. The death of her daughter wasn't even *six* months ago, and she's forcing herself to talk about it. I know she doesn't want to, but she wants her daughter's story out there— and she's trusting *me* to share it. Based on our most recent phone call, she's not speaking with any other reporters about this. I have the exclusive, and I'm packaging it into a *sweeps piece* for July.

In television news, the quarterly "sweeps months" — every February, May, July, and November — are also known as *all hands on deck* months. You're not allowed to take a day off, your stories are double in length, and intense reporting is required. That's because it's when TV ratings are paid the closest attention to. It's a competition. *All of the channels are doing it, so you can't be left behind.*

The screen door squeaks behind her, letting a cool breeze of her home's air conditioning wash over me. It's a hot summer day— I'm just wearing a light blue sundress and sandals. I walk into the foyer and kick off my shoes, setting my equipment in her hallway. The door shuts behind me, and I'm relieved to be in *cold* air for the first time all day.

That's the thing about being a reporter. You're not just *in* people's homes by way of their television screen or cell phone. You're actually *in* people's homes. There's a strange level of comfort and trust that comes with this— literally walking around barefoot in a stranger's home as they allow you to follow them around with a camera. It's an immediate and intense bond. A bond that requires gentleness and *trust*.

"You have a beautiful home," I say, looking up at Amy's cathedral ceilings. "This looks like something out of Architectural Digest."

Through her sadness, Amy laughs. "I don't know about that," she says. "But thank you. My husband built this house twenty years ago."

I notice a large family photo on the wall from when Kaylee was little. She's seated on her mother's lap, and I assume that's her father and brother sitting beside them. They're all smiling in matching red-and-green holiday sweaters. The happy family of four has turned into a sad family of three.

"Will anyone else be joining you for the interview?" I ask gently.

"No," Amy says directly. "My son has been keeping busy, spending lots of time with his friends. My husband hasn't really been getting out of bed much. He's in there now."

I follow her lead into the living room. "That's no problem," I say. "Just wondering."

The room smells like a vanilla candle. The carpeting is soft and beige, matching the walls and furniture. Everything in here is some variation of white, cream, or brown. Exposed wooden beams lie flush against the ceiling, and there's a brown-bricked fireplace in the corner. As warm and inviting as this place looks, it feels *empty* inside.

"I was thinking I could sit here," Amy says, motioning to the couch. "Can I pull up a chair for you?"

"I think that's perfect," I say, putting my hands on my hips to assess the location. "I'll just pull up this foot rest right here, if that's okay?"

"Are you sure you don't want something more comfortable than a foot rest?"

I laugh. "I've interviewed people standing in three feet of snow." I motion to the beige footrest. "This right here is like a throne."

Amy takes a seat on her cream-colored couch. She nervously tucks a blonde strand of hair behind her ear as she watches me set up my equipment. I intentionally perform some much-needed small talk — about the gorgeous decor of her home, the family photos on the walls, and the hot summer temperatures outside — to distract her from the intimidation of the camera setup. She's probably in her 50s, but looks to be in her 30s. She's a *beautiful* woman with an *ugly* situation.

I have her snake the microphone wire up underneath her dress, clipping it to her black collar. I plug the other end into my camera and make sure all the settings are correct for our indoor environment: white balance, focus mode, audio levels, and frame rate. It's all ready to go. *I'm* all ready to go.

I sit on the footrest across from her and take a deep breath. "Before we start, I just want to *thank you* for trusting *me* to do this story."

Tears already start to well up in her eyes. "You're the only one I'd do this with," she says.

"Thank you," I say, smiling softly. I motion to the camera beside me. "See all of this? It looks super intimidating. I don't want you to look at it. I want you to look at *me*. You're just talking to me, okay? And I'm not scary."

Amy smiles. "You're not scary," she repeats. "Okay, I'll just look at you."

"Great," I say. "Can I make you laugh for a second?"

Amy wipes her eyes with a tissue. "I'll take all the laughs I can get."

"This isn't live," I say. "So I like to tell people…you could accidentally say *shit* during the interview, and it doesn't matter. It can be edited out. Okay?"

Amy laughs through her tears. "Okay," she says. "*Shit.* How's that?"

"I didn't even start rolling yet, so it's perfect." I lean over and press the record button. "*Now* we're rolling."

Amy's expression levels out into one of seriousness, but I keep the look on my face soft and gentle. It's just a conversation between the two of us, and I want her to feel comfortable knowing that. Sure, this will be broadcast out to thousands of people in the Joyfield area and beyond— *Kaylee*

Wood's mother speaks exclusively with WJDN News about her daughter's murder. But this is more than the sensational stuff. *It's about her daughter.*

"Tell me about your daughter," I begin. "Just tell me what she was like."

"Wow," Amy says with a sniffle. "How can I sum up Kaylee. Well, she was kind. She was giving. She always did everything she could to help me. When she was little, she surprised me by running the dishwasher. But I didn't realize until *later*...that she actually filled it with laundry detergent instead of dishwashing liquid. She was just a kid. It was hilarious. But she was always looking to help out."

"I have to ask you," I begin. "Can you tell me about the moment...when you *found out* about what happened?"

"Disbelief." Amy presses a tissue to both eyes.

She tells me about the heartbreaking phone call she received from the police. How she traveled the 45 minutes to Joyfield to meet with investigators. How she had to identify her beloved daughter in the hospital. She tells me the tragic details with sadness, but with dignity. She knows she *needs* to tell the world about what happened. She knows she *needs* to get through this for her daughter.

"And we still don't know of any *possible* connection to Brandon Smith?"

"I can't *legally* call him a serial killer." She holds up two fingers and quickly pulses them. "But he's been *linked* to two other homicides in the past decade."

"Seriously?" I say.

"But he was never *convicted* of anything before. Which means they couldn't even bring up those previous allegations in court, which frustrates me. Even though the jury found him guilty on *all* counts, I still wish they had known about his history. They have to treat each case separately, I guess. But Brandon Smith has a past. A past that they won't tell you about. A past that *just* caught up with him now."

"That's terrible." I shake my head.

"Nobody knows how many evil people like him are...*out there.* Waiting, watching. For no good reason. I don't know what the deal with Brandon Smith is. I don't know whether he seeks these women out in advance. Nobody knows about the inter-workings of his mind. But people *do* this stuff, and *we're* the ones who have to be on high alert because of it."

I picture that man trying to get into my car, pulling and yanking on the door handle. I feel guilty comparing my situation to this, but who knows what *could* have happened that night. Amy is right. Evil people do evil things, and you don't know *when* or *where* or *why* they're going to strike. Because of it, we just have to watch our backs at all times.

"How do you feel about the sentencing?"

Amy shakes her head. "A lifetime behind bars isn't long enough for what he did to my daughter." Amy sobs into her hands. "He could be in prison for the rest of eternity, and it still wouldn't be long enough."

I reach out and touch the top of her knee. "It's okay," I whisper. "Take your time."

Amy sobs for another minute, which causes a tear to stream down my face. I feel its warmth before I taste its saltiness. I can't imagine the pain this woman is going through, along with her husband and son. But all I can do is listen to her and give her daughter justice with a *remarkable,* thorough story.

"What's your message to other young women out there?"

Amy sighs and blows her nose. "I don't know what the

answer is. I can't say *never* leave your house again. I can't say *never* be alone in public. I don't know what to say to young women. But I guess just limit your exposure to these threats. Don't be alone in barren areas if you don't have to be. Don't walk home alone at night. Those basic things, I guess. Just don't make yourself a target— *which isn't even fair to say, by the way.* I really don't have the answer. Women shouldn't have to think about this stuff, but sadly, we do. So, restrict your risks, I guess."

For a moment, I think about playing this entire interview for Bill when I get back to the newsroom. He should see firsthand what *could* happen to his reporters. He'd probably just think I was being dramatic, or that I was comparing apples and oranges unnecessarily. But it's about *minimizing* your chances of something happening to you, even when you can't completely guarantee your safety.

"Amy, I just want you to know something." I put my hand back on her knee. "I am so sorry this happened to you, first off. But I am so proud of you for speaking up on your daughter's behalf. A lot of people wouldn't do this, but you *did*. You're brave and strong, and I know Kaylee would be so proud of you. I certainly am proud of you. Even if this story could help just one person—"

"Then I did my job," Amy completes my sentence. "Even if it helps one person."

It could be a young woman trying to avoid becoming the next Kaylee Wood. It could be a set of parents who lost their child a few years ago. It could be a young person grieving the loss of a loved one who was killed. It could be a criminal seeing what consequences their future could potentially hold if they make the wrong choice.

This story will help at least *one* person out there. And that one person…*might be me.*

Thirty-Five

THE CUTAWAY

"Happy birthday!" Everyone shouts in unison towards my dad and David — who were *forced* into wearing matching party hats — as they blow out their birthday candles.

We're in my dining room with about a dozen people crowded around our kitchen table. The cake in front of them is coated with light blue buttercream frosting and reads: "Happy 55th Birthday Dominic, David, and Daniel." Even after the death of Daniel over two decades ago, the *duo* still celebrates their birthday as if they were still a *trio*.

Talking about the "missing triplet" has never been an issue in my family. Nobody refrains from using his name, or even bats an eye when an old memory is brought up. Even though Daniel died the year before I was born, I still refer to him as my *Uncle Daniel.* I say the name with as much confidence as if he were standing right here next to me. I feel his presence, and I can only attribute it to my family's years of communication about him. No walking on eggshells. *He existed once, so he will exist forever.*

"Pose for a picture!" Delilah tells them, pointing her Polaroid camera at them. "Ready? One, two, three…smile!"

The flash reflects off their identical-looking faces. I only think of my dad as *my dad*, and I only think of David as *my Uncle David* (or just David, the WJDN master control operator at my workplace). Because of that, when I see their faces positioned together like this — with the same cheeks and hair and teeth — it makes me laugh. They're clones of each other, and I can't help but wonder what Daniel would look like standing here, too.

"I see you're taking after your dad," David says to Delilah.

"My dad uses fancy cameras," she corrects. "I just like the Polaroids."

"Everybody, grab a plate," my mom interrupts.

She begins cutting the cake and scooping ice cream from cartons— chocolate chip cookie dough, regular vanilla bean, and mint chocolate chip. *This is my idea of a perfect meal.*

I give her a side hug. "I love you, Mom."

Since her hands are full, she kisses me on the cheek instead. "I'm so happy you had off today and could be here. Our house is complete."

As I eat my cake and ice cream mixture, I stare at a photo of the triplets from a college party that was strategically placed near the cake. They look so alike, but not only that, *they look so happy.* Little did they know that, just a couple of months later, their lives would change forever. They'd never be able to recreate a photo like that again.

"Whatcha looking at?" My dad bumps his shoulder to mine.

I snap out of my daze. "Just looking at the three of you," I say with a mouthful of dairy and frosting. "You guys were so young."

"Definitely *not* 55 in that picture." He takes a bite of his cake. "Twenty-something."

I rest my elbow on the island. "Do you think he would have made it?"

"Made it to what…*55?*"

"No." I laugh and spoon some ice cream into my mouth. "To New York City."

"I think so." My dad points to the photo of the three of them. "He was more motivated than David, and I ever was."

I sigh. "It sucks that you can never find out, you know?"

My dad adjusts his party hat. "Sure does."

This is a conversation that I'd be *afraid* to bring up to anyone else in the world who lost a loved one, but not my dad. Not anyone in my family. Talking about Daniel is a way for them to connect with him. I *love* hearing stories about their long-lost brother. I *love* listening to them talk about him as if he were still around. I *love* being connected to a close family member whom I'll never have the pleasure of meeting.

"Hey dad," I say, munching on some blue buttercream. "I'm thinking about leaving news."

"It's about time," my dad says in a sarcastic tone.

I hit him in the arm. "What do you mean…*it's about time?*"

He shrugs his scrawny shoulders. "You're amazing at what you do, sweetie. You really are. I love watching you on TV because you're a natural. But the shit you put up with—"

I laugh. "You think it's *bad?*"

My dad tilts his head. "They put you through the wringer."

I shoot my arms out. "How come you haven't discussed this with *me?*"

"I want you to be happy." He takes his party hat off and sets it on the kitchen table. "If you're happy working in news, then I'm happy. But I want you to be treated well and paid fairly, which I don't think you are."

"Wow," I say, picking up his party hat and placing it on my head. "Thanks for telling me."

"I just did," he says.

David walks over to us, pretending he's a boxer by punching the air close to our torsos, but never *actually* hitting us. "What's going on over here?"

My dad lightly punches him back in the shoulder. "Noelle wants to quit her job."

"Dad!" I smack him in the arm.

"There's only room for *one* Fenwick at WJDN," David says, puffing out his chest. "I always knew I'd be the last one standing."

I roll my eyes. "Okay, fine. I don't know what to do. I feel like leaving news."

"Why do you want to leave?" David asks, leaning his back against the table.

"A variety of things," I say.

"Thanks for being specific." David takes a bite of his cake. "Why *don't* you want to leave?"

I glance over at the photo of the Fenwick triplets in college, filled with happiness. "I don't know," I say, eyes locked on it. "I just feel like I'd be giving up on a dream."

My dad brushes a cake crumb off his shirt. "As long as you're doing what you love, in *some* capacity, then there's no problem. Who cares about the actual *job*?"

David crosses his arms. "What *do* you love? Writing?"

"Yes, writing."

I wasn't expecting a family counseling session today.

"Then find another *way* to write," David says with an obvious tone.

I point to the photo of the three of them, near the cake that is now halfway gone. "But what would *Daniel* think? Would he *yell* at me for giving up?"

"He wouldn't *yell* at you," my dad says with a chuckle. "There's something you might not know about Daniel. He never put up with any *shit* from anyone."

"No, he did not," David says, motioning towards my dad. "Do you remember how he was *obsessed* with getting that waiting job at *Mama Bella* back in high school?"

"That's where you'd make the best tips in town," my dad tells me. "Everybody and their brother wanted that job. They only took two kids per summer. Had to fight over it."

David laughs in remembrance. "He beat out the competition and *finally* got it. He was so pumped. But once the boss started being a dick to him — after only working there for like *two* shifts — he quit. Threw in his apron and walked out. Never went back."

My dad laughs along with him. "Then he started working at the ice cream shop, making *half* of what he could've earned as a waiter. But he loved the owners and the people there, so he stayed for the next *five* summers."

"I didn't know that," I say. "Was he a hot head?"

"Not necessarily," my dad clarifies. "He just didn't like it when someone didn't treat him right. He didn't take any bullshit, and if someone was giving it to him, he'd let them know about it. He demanded respect, even at a young age."

I never knew this trait about Daniel. While my Uncle David is definitely the most *chill* person in my entire family, my dad is pretty calm, too. I never thought of either one of them as *tough*. Maybe Daniel is the triplet who got the *tough* gene. Maybe he's the one who would have stuck up for the rest of the group. Maybe he's the sibling who would have beaten up every bully at their school on behalf of the underdog. Nobody ever described him as loud or obnoxious, so I don't think he was. Maybe he was just *confident*.

I set my empty plate on the kitchen counter. "What do you think he would've done if he were acting somewhere, but the people around him were awful?"

"He probably would've just gone somewhere else." My dad crosses one foot over the other. "A different agency. A different production. A different setting."

"He wouldn't have *dropped* acting altogether," David clarifies. "But he would've found a place where he was *respected*. He wouldn't have settled for anything less."

"I agree," my dad says.

David rests his hands behind his head, even though he's standing. "He never surrounded himself with *negative* people. He wouldn't tolerate being bullied around. If someone else was being pushed and shoved, he'd call it out. He'd stick up for others."

My dad begins to empty the overflowing trashcan. "He would drop people like a hot potato," he yells over to us. "Then he'd move to a place where he was *valued*. Once he found it, he'd probably stay."

"What did I tell you before, Noelle?" David puts an arm around me. "Sometimes you *leave* a place with different dreams than you originally *went* there with."

Thirty-Six

THE SIGN OFF

"Bill?" I say quietly while knocking on his office door.

"Come in," he yells.

"Can I talk to you?" I take a seat in the infamous chair across from his desk— the same one that I recently sat on during our safety conversation, which went *nowhere fast.*

His bifocals balance on the bridge of his nose. "What can I do for you?"

I take a breath. "I made a decision about my contract."

"And?" He isn't breaking eye contact with his computer monitor.

"And…I am *not* going to renew it."

Bill's eyes widen before he swivels his chair to face mine. "You're…*not?*"

By the expression on his face, I can tell that this was *not* the answer he was expecting. From the intensity and seriousness in his stare, it feels like the *first* time Bill has ever really looked at me. It took *this exact moment* for him to really *see* me. In his mind, there was no doubt that I'd be staying at WJDN forever. He assumed I'd renew my contract. He assumed I'd accept his first offer. He assumed I'd become the next Ed Sterling.

"No." I shake my head. "I'm sorry."

Bill leans back in his chair. "Did you get that *other* job?"

"It was offered to me," I tell him honestly. "But I said no."

Bill blinks dramatically, as if that will try to make him understand what I'm telling him. "So…you're *not* staying here with us, but you *don't* have another job lined up?"

"That is correct." *It sounds worse out loud.*

Bill looks like he just saw a ghost. "I'm disappointed in you, Noelle."

I smile so lightly that it's *barely* even a smile. "I don't think this is for me anymore."

"I gave you anchoring opportunities," Bill says. "You didn't like it?"

I slide my palms along my thighs. "Just not what I thought it would be."

Bill lets out a small chuckle— one that sends the message: *good luck out there trying to find a job.* But instead, he just says, "Okay then."

There's nothing left to say, so I start walking towards the door. My chest feels heavy, but my stomach feels empty. It's not that I'm nostalgic about saying goodbye to Bill— it's that I'll be saying goodbye to *all* of WJDN soon after this. The newsroom. The community. The stories. Nate, Myra, Ruby, Paige. The thought of leaving them makes my heart feel like it's twisting in on itself.

"Thank you," I say with one hand on the doorknob. "For everything."

Bill fixes his eyes on his computer monitor. "Good luck to you."

I close Bill's wooden office door and walk past Nate at the assignment desk with tears in my eyes, trying to shield my head away from him. Myra sits at her computer, wondering what the hell I was doing in Bill's office *again.* I take a seat at my desk and make accidental eye contact with Paige, who can see that I'm crying.

"What's wrong?" She whispers.

I wipe a tear away from my eye, not looking at her. "I'll tell you tonight."

I start typing one of my final scripts on my computer, looking at the words on my screen through a blanket of water. With all of the sadness and uncertainty swirling around in my brain and chest, I still feel a tiny bit of *relief.* I know that I need to do something else with my life — and even if I don't know *what* exactly that is just yet — I'm one step closer to figuring it all out.

* * *

"Woah woah woah." Nate slams his hands on the table. "You're...*leaving?*"

"You're...*what?*" Paige leans in with a vodka cranberry in her hand.

Myra takes a sip of her drink. "I saw this one coming," she says.

"I wasn't expectin' this," Ruby admits. "When did this happen?"

Since Ruby is no longer a bartender at The Highball — even after having multiple heated meetings with WJDN management — she's now just a regular patron here like the rest of us. I like that she has a permanent seat at our table instead of behind the bar. Even though she's bringing in *half* the amount of income that she was earning before, I'm secretly glad she's getting this small break. *She deserves it.*

"It's true," I agree. "But nothing is going to change."

"We're never gonna see you again, let's just be honest," Nate says, taking a sip of his beer. "Just lose my number."

Paige shakes her head. "But didn't Bill want you to be the next Ed Sterling?"

Nate scoffs. "I think *everybody* in Joyfield thought she was going to be the next Ed Sterling. Even my grandma thinks so."

"But she *wanted* to be the next Hilda Harrison," Myra corrects. "*Not* Ed Sterling."

Ruby squints. "But you *did* get the job in Virginia Beach, right?"

"Everybody is just so obsessed with me." I take a sip of my tequila sunrise with my pinky finger in the air. "I feel like I'm being attacked by the local news paparazzi, and to be honest with you, I kinda like it."

Paige rests her chin in her hand. "So, what are you going to do?"

"I don't know yet." I shrug. "For the first time ever, I don't know."

"She lives with her parents, so she doesn't even need a job," Myra teases, taking a sip of what appears to be a vodka soda with lime.

Nate scoffs with sarcasm. "Plus, she has a rich lawyer boyfriend. She doesn't even *need* to do anything. Isn't that right?"

"Do you people know me *at all?* I need to work, or I'd lose my mind." I shoot back at them. "If you must know, I've been *applying* to jobs on LinkedIn."

"What kind of jobs?" Ruby asks.

I look down at the sticky table. "Some marketing. Some sales. Some communications. You'd actually be surprised by how many jobs there are in Joyfield."

I used to spend the final hours of my day scrolling through Instagram. But lately, I've been swiping through jobs on LinkedIn. It's surprisingly fun and addictive. Am I *directly* qualified for a majority of the jobs I've applied for? *No.* But being a news reporter gives you *so* many transferable skills that can be used in other industries. I haven't heard back from any hiring managers yet, but it's still been a fun little game.

Ever since I got back from New York City with Eliza, I haven't been able to stop thinking about her recent revelation— a *nine-to-five* "main job" with a *passion project* "side gig." It feels adult. It feels balanced. It feels *best of both worlds.* I feel like I'll end up heading in that direction, even though my future *main job* and my future *side gig* are still completely unknown to me.

"Enough about me," I say, throwing back the rest of my tequila sunrise. "What's new with *you* all? I'm craving information that revolves around someone else."

Paige sighs. "My ex and I got back together."

"Really?" I say, grabbing her hand. "That's great? *Is that great?*"

"I don't know," Paige says. "Seeing each other at the wedding made us...*rekindle*, I guess."

"Rekindle?" Ruby says. "That's a fun little word, isn't it?"

"We're going to try long distance," Paige explains. "We'll see what happens."

"Well, I'm still as single as a Pringle," Ruby says with exaggerated twang. "Same old."

I look at her strawberry blonde curls, wondering what everybody else here knows about her past love life. "Enjoy it," I tell her honestly. "Being single is fun."

"You're not single," Myra says.

"I *am* technically single," I clarify. "Talking to Levi? Yes. Dating? Maybe. Boyfriend? No."

"It's all the same," Paige adds. "You guys are pretty much *together*."

"I said I didn't want to talk any more about me," I say, pushing my palms out in front of me. "Somebody else talk about themselves, I'm begging you."

Myra clears her throat and shoves her shoulder into Nate's.

"Ouch," he says. "What was that for?"

Myra looks forcefully from him to the rest of us, nonverbally saying, "Tell them!"

"Okay, okay." Nate shuffles in his seat. "We have something to tell you."

I smirk deviously because I can already predict what they're going to tell us. Myra and Nate will *finally* clear the air about those drunken kisses. They'll officially announce that they're hooking up (or possibly even dating). Since it's been a months-long investigation — with *so* many secrets — I can't wait for the *entire* cat to be out of the bag.

Myra knows that *I know* about that night at The Highball behind the dumpsters *and* their kissing sessions on New Year's Eve. She knows that Ruby and Paige are *aware* of their midnight kiss, but that they don't suspect anything else. As for Nate, I don't know what *all* he knows. He's probably oblivious to all of it. There are a lot of missing details at this table, and it's finally time to reveal the truth to everyone.

Myra looks nervous. "Here we go," she says. "We—"

Nate coughs. "So, Myra and I—"

"We're having a baby."

Blank stares. Dead stares. Vacant stares from everyone at the table. My jaw drops. Paige's eyes widen. Ruby appears to stop breathing. Silence. You could hear a pin drop, and the sudden decrease of our table's decibel level is probably noticeable to the rest of the bar.

My stomach drops. "You're—"

"Pregnant, yes." Myra tucks a curl behind her ear. "To this guy."

"Yeah," Nate says. "Oh, and by the way, we've been hooking up."

"Apparently!" Paige screams.

"Whoooohoooo!" Ruby stands up and flutters her arms in the air. "Congratulations!"

I shake my head in disbelief. "I wasn't expecting—"

"It's gonna be so cute!" Paige rapidly claps her hands. "Do you have girl names? Boy names? I have a list in my phone—"

"I can't think about any of that right now," Myra says. "It's early."

"Did y'all tell your families yet?" Ruby asks. "They're gonna be thrilled."

"Not yet," Myra scoffs. "I don't know how they'll react—"

"It's not like we're teenagers," Nate says, shooting his arms out at his sides. "This isn't a teen pregnancy. We're in our twenties. We both have *jobs*. It could be a lot worse."

"I guess you could say that," Myra says. "I'm trying to be happy about it."

"Hey," I say, still in awe over this news. "Be happy. This is *amazing*. We're so happy for you."

We all stand up and hug each other, jumping up and down with excitement, joy, shock, and surprise. Everyone at the bar stares at us with puzzled expressions, and even some laughs emerge from some of the bar goers. All the emotions flood our hearts at once. I look at the glowing, I guess, *couple*. This was not the news I was expecting them to drop tonight. This is the news of the century. *Myra and Nate are having a baby.*

Thirty-Seven

THE FAST FORWARD

DECEMBER | JOYFIELD, OHIO
SIX MONTHS LATER

The first flakes of snow are just beginning to fall in Joyfield. Each year, like clockwork — when I see that first mini cotton ball hit my windshield — my mind is immediately transported back to my internship at The Sunrise Show.

I think about the snowflakes falling in the background of Hilda Harrison's anchor desk, with the powdered sugar dusting coating the surrounding buildings. I think about walking through the streets of New York City when the holiday decorations are freshly out, being held up by tourists looking at the window displays. I think about looking up at the multicolored Rockefeller Christmas tree lights, with the metal star so high that it looks like it's touching the moon. For me, snow will always be synonymous with NYC, and it'll always be ingrained in my brain that way.

But at this point in my life, I'm not anywhere closer to moving back to New York— *I'm still in Joyfield.* Not only am I *not* working at WJDN anymore, but I'm also not even working in *news.* It's been six months since I left the station, and I feel like I've been like a fish floundering on dry land ever since. I feel lost and wanderlust at the same time. I took Eliza's advice: I got a boring *nine-to-five* job selling advertising spots on the sides of local highways. Yes, I'm now working for a local billboard company. *So glamorous.*

I no longer have to work early mornings, nights, weekends, or holidays. It's a normal day job with normal expectations. While I'm out alone in my car driving from business to business all day, I'm *never* out alone for solo live shots late at night. Other than making sure I'm *driving* safely, there are *no* other safety concerns in this job. It's stable, steady, and secure. I'm happy, but I'm also a little...*bored.*

It's not just selling billboards. I'm also selling social media and public relations packages. When I sit down with local business owners, it's a lot like being a reporter: asking them questions, defining their story, and helping them reach the masses. But the difference? I have to *sell* these packages to them. They have to *buy* the campaigns I create for them. So, over the last six months, I've technically become a salesperson. Or as I like to say, a writer *posing* as a salesperson. *Who do I think I am?*

I found the *main gig.* Now, according to Eliza's philosophy, I need to find a *side gig.* And at the moment, I have *no* idea what that will be. She's working at an insurance agency during the day and delivering jokes at comedy clubs at night. She has the best of *both* worlds right now, and I'm determined to figure out what *my* other world is.

"Hello?" I answer Levi's call as I drive to another business.

"How's it going?" His deep voice booms in my car. "Still on for Mama Bella?"

"Craving it already," I say. "I'm paying this time, you know."

"It's about time," Levi jokes. "Since you have the money now."

I've made more money in the last six months at this advertising job than I earned in *one full year* working at WJDN. I make enough money to afford my *own* apartment now.

Yes, I live down the street from my childhood home in a small rental property. It's a tiny, pale yellow, one-bedroom house, and I love every inch of it. I absolutely *love* having my own space. To my surprise, Delilah loves it too. *She already has a pile of her stuff in my room.*

My new company covers most of my healthcare costs. My student loans are almost paid off. I bought everyone a *bigger* Christmas present this year. For the first time in my life, I don't need to rely on my parents. *I'm off their payroll.* The feeling of financial independence has lifted a weight off my shoulders that I didn't even know was there. I'm even saving some money in my bank account. I love everything this job is providing for me, but I still feel like a stranger when I go into the office.

When I think about the newsroom, a deep feeling of homesickness pulls in my chest. It's like picturing a house that I once lived in, but can never return to. There was an odd level of comfort at WJDN. It wasn't uncommon for people to be screaming profanities at each other across the newsroom. It was loud and chaotic. Sometimes, I'd kick off my snowy shoes and just run around the place in my socks. It felt like *home*. But at my current job, if I'd accidentally slip an f-bomb, the place would probably burn to the ground. The people are night and day from what I'm used to. *I guess I was just introduced to professionalism.*

"Where are you at for work today? The courthouse?"

"Today? The law office. Right now? Hiding in the bathroom so I can talk to you," Levi says in a near whisper.

"I'm honored," I say. "Go ahead. I don't want to get the *hot attorney* fired."

"Okay," he says. "Have a good day. Get that money."

"I'll try my best," I say. "Go get those bad guys."

"I'll try my best," Levi repeats.

The phone call disconnects, and I refocus my attention on the snowy road. After turning it on and off throughout my drive, I turn the defrost back on, hoping to clear my icy, dirty windshield. The evergreen trees lining this highway are covered with a dusting of flurries. I pass by my alma mater, the library, and the ice cream shop. The sudden realization hits me: *I gave up.* I'll never be Hilda Harrison. I won't ever sit behind that anchor desk. I'll never work on The Sunrise Show. *I broke the promise I made to myself all those years ago.* The thought of it makes me sick to my stomach, but I know that I made the right choice.

Up until this month, I never understood why people *wouldn't* follow their dreams. I couldn't even fathom it. Why would you ever give up on that one, magical thing you've always wanted to do? But this year made me realize *how much* thought actually goes into it. I used to think that being able to pay your bills, being safe in the workplace, and having a work life balance ranked *second.* That passion was in *first place.* But all of those "monotonous" things can become the *most* important, because they're the reason we go to work, right? You can't pour from an empty cup.

In high school, I remember learning about Maslow's Hierarchy of Needs. It's all about what it means to become the best version of yourself. *Self-actualization,* to put it in fancy terminology. We *all* want to make it to that place— where you reach your potential, experience deep meaning, and become self-fulfilled. But before you can get there, you *first* have to meet your basic needs. Physiological (food, shelter, clothing) and safety (health, protection from danger, financial stability). These boxes must be checked...*before* you can move up the hierarchy. Before you can make it to the top. Before you can achieve self-actualization. To sum it all up, you *can't* have creativity, achievement, and purpose *without* food, shelter, and clothing. You have to work from the bottom up. At WJDN, how could I *ever* achieve self-actualization when the job wasn't providing me with the *basics?* Maybe it does come down to pay. Maybe it does come down to healthcare. Maybe it does come down to basics. *All this time, had I been working backwards? From the top down?*

"Hey, honey." My mom's voice pours through my car speaker. "How are you?"

"Hi, Mom." I press on the brakes as I approach a stop sign. "How's your day going?"

"Just took Delilah to her doctor's appointment."

"Hi Noelleeee," I hear her sing from the passenger seat.

"Hi, DD." I tap my cold fingers on the steering wheel. "I'll stop by to see you both later, okay? Before I go to dinner with Levi tonight—"

"Your boyfriend," Delilah announces.

"Yes, he's my boyfriend." I can't *not* laugh. "Levi is mine, Anthony is yours. Old news."

"*You're* old news," Delilah says.

That's another *new* thing that happened in the past six months: Levi and I are officially dating. I was against it from the beginning— constantly listing all the reasons we *shouldn't* date. But since I'm staying in Joyfield for the time being, and I don't work for the news station anymore, all of my old reasons flew right out the window. Aside from the fact that I'm head-over-heels in love with Levi, the removal of those barriers helped speed up the process.

"We'll see you later, honey," my mom says. "We love you."

"Love you guys too," I say. "DD, I'll be at *Brew For You* tomorrow morning for a business meeting. I'm bringing a client there."

"Thanks for your business," Delilah says.

I've been spending three, four, and sometimes *five* hours a day driving in my car from business to business…from meeting to meeting. In addition to consuming copious amounts of music and podcasts along the way, I spend most of my days talking on the phone with everyone in my life. Sometimes it's Myra giving me updates on her baby. Other times, it's David calling to tell me about a crazy story in the newscast. Most times, it's Levi calling me from the bathroom.

Until I figure out what the "side gig" to my new "main gig" will be, I'll just drive around, make the best of my new job, talk to my loved ones, listen to my favorite songs, and enjoy my higher pay. For the first time in my life, I'm going to stop searching for the *next* thing and just focus on enjoying the *current* thing. What more is there to do? The pressure is off. *A new dream will find me at some point.*

Thirty-Eight

THE FEATURE STORY

My phone leans up against my mirror next to a tube of mascara, with Eliza's blonde hair shining through its screen. Since our New York City reunion earlier this year, we've texted here and there — sending videos to each other on Instagram as long-distance friends do — but haven't talked over the phone in a while. But since she *just* texted me the words, "life update," *urgency* was the catalyst for this much-needed call.

"Yessssss?" I answer, running a brush through my tangled hair.

Eliza looks straight into the camera. "I got a *permanent* gig."

"You already told me," I say. "At the insurance place."

"No," she scoffs. "At the comedy club in Florida. Where I've been doing the occasional *open mic* night, remember?"

I blink dramatically into the camera, eyes widened. "Like a *residency?*"

"I'm not Adele in Las Vegas or Harry Styles at Madison Square Garden," Eliza corrects. "But kind of like that, yes."

"That's such great news. I'm so proud of you." I set my hairbrush on the vanity. "I'm going to have to fly to Florida to watch you."

"Every Thursday night for one hour," she says. "But by the time you make the trip, maybe *New York* will have picked me up by then."

"When the *side* gig turns into the *main* gig," I say, remembering our conversation during our reunion trip. "When you're the next Amy Schumer."

"Exactly." Eliza slides a blazer over her shoulders and points to her collar. "Because if I have to do *this* every day for the rest of my life, I might die of boredom."

"Is working in insurance *that* bad?"

"Imagine, like, cleaning tombstones for a living. Or fixing copy machines." Eliza smudges her deep pink lipstick with her ring finger. "That's what this job feels like. But my paychecks? Payday feels like getting...*high*."

"My new day job isn't *that* boring." I pierce a silver earring through my ear. "I wouldn't compare it to fixing office supplies."

"Is it your dream job? When you're eighty years old, will you look back on this time and feel sentimental with nostalgia?"

"Yeah...*no*." I impale my other earlobe with the matching earring. "It's just a job."

"You got the *main* gig down," Eliza says. "What's the *side* gig?"

"Still trying to find one." I sigh as I slide on a bracelet. "Just got the main one."

"You'll find one." She clasps a necklace around her neck. "You will. By the time I'm a famous comedian, you'll be a famous...*something*."

"What if fame isn't the goal anymore?"

"Then you'll be a *happy* something."

Even though I haven't figured it out yet, I know Eliza is right. A real job would give me a paycheck, and a side project would give me a purpose— but I don't even know *what* I'd do. Should I take up pottery and start selling bowls on Etsy? Should I start a book club at the local coffee shop? Should I get involved with a pyramid scheme with a girl from high school? I need to get my spark back, but I just don't know where to find it.

"Do you remember working in news—"

"It wasn't that long ago, Eliza," I remind her.

"I'm going somewhere with this," she scoffs. "The boss was always focused on the *lead* story. *The lead story.* What would be the *lead* story for the day?"

"Oh yeah," I say. "If it bleeds, it *leads*."

"Well, people always tune in to watch the *lead* story." Eliza runs a comb through her hair. "But they *really* just wanna watch the story after the first commercial break. The fluff piece. The human interest. The feature. The one about...*dogs* or something."

I find a light scarf that matches my maroon sweater and drape it around my neck, leaving it hanging open. "You mean the stories that *I've* always fought to do?"

"You had it right all along." Eliza pushes her flyaways down with a burst of hairspray. "Everyone is so focused on the *lead* story. But people just wanna watch the *feature* story. That's all they truly care about."

I laugh. "Can you call up my old boss Bill Calloway and tell him that for me?"

Eliza nods with approval. "They watch the lead stories because they *have* to. They watch the feature stories because they *want* to."

"That's your new life analogy," I clarify. "You work your insurance job because you *have* to. You work your comedy gig because you *want* to."

"That's it, girlfriend." Eliza stands up from her get-ready area and takes her phone with her. "The best case scenario? When the lead story *is* the feature story. When they're one and the same. But that hardly happens. You have to be extra intentional to *make* that happen."

"You're right," I say. "Two birds with one stone."

"Well, that's *my* new goal," Eliza says, walking towards her bedroom door. "I'm working until my comedy gig takes the place of my insurance job. When my source of passions and paychecks collide— *that's* when I'll be truly happy."

I pick my hairbrush up in my hand, lift it above my shoulder, and let it fall to the floor dramatically. "Boom," I say. "Now *that* is a mic drop."

"I gotta go," Eliza says, turning off the lights in her room. "Call me when you need some more life advice."

"You know I will," I say.

After I hang up the call, I open up my rickety closet doors to decide on a pair of dreaded work pants. I'm professional from the waist up, but from the waist down, I'm still wearing my favorite pair of hot pink sweat pants. (I've been sleeping in them since high school.) I can't part with them, despite the widening holes in the inner thighs.

Pushing news dress after news dress along the skinny, white

pole — from the pink one I wore to cover the opening of a new restaurant, to the blue one I wore on Election night, to the purple one I wore to cover a gun safety protest — I realize that I need to buy some *non*-news clothes. Things that aren't skin tight. Things that aren't in loud colors. It's time for a wardrobe change, but in this moment, I have no choice but to make a selection from what I already own.

They catch my eye in the back of my closet: my favorite black slacks with the stretchy waistband, deep pockets, and tiny white polka dots running up and down the legs. I beam at them in remembrance of my internship days. *How have I forgotten about my favorite stretchy pants?* I wore these every single day at The Sunrise Show.

I slide them over my legs and hike them past my butt. I look at myself in the long mirror fastened to the back of my closet door. These pants are tighter than they once were, but they're more comfortable than ever. Not too shabby. *I'm suddenly craving Oreo cake.*

Once I crawl into my icebox of a car, I think about how lucky I've been to grow up with a *garage* my entire life. At my new apartment, I have to park along the side of the road like a *normal* person. I turn on the heat and rub my hands together, blowing warm air through them. Snowflakes turn into ice flakes as they hit my windshield, and I suddenly wish I were wearing gloves. The cold air makes my nose run like an elementary school child on the playground. *I need a tissue.*

I reach down to grab my tissue box from the passenger side and slide my hand into its plastic barrier. And…no tissues left. *Dammit.* I need a napkin or something. *Do I have something in my pocket?* I reach into the pocket of my stretchy polka dot pants, and I feel something. It's a tiny piece of paper crumpled into a little ball. *It's probably just an old business card from a source at WJDN.*

I slowly unravel its contents on my lap, and with freezing cold hands, I flatten out the crinkled paper. When I see the black words staring back at me in Times New Roman font, it's like I'm transported back in time. *Book Writing Club. Westerfield Apartments. Tuesdays from 5:30 to 6:30 in the dining hall. Come write a book with us!*

I stare at the text. It's not about *what* it says— it's the fact that I have a little piece of New York City with me, in my hands, right now. It's a physical memory from the *best* time of my life. It's been here in Joyfield with me this entire time. I slide my thumb across its wrinkles, and my heart feels like it's smiling. I set the crinkly souvenir in my cup holder, put my car into reverse, and head off to my new workplace.

I've been overdoing it with the music, podcasts, and phone calls lately, so I turn on the narration of an *audiobook* I recently purchased. It's a twenty-minute drive to the office, and just a few minutes into the trek, the narrator's voice sends me into a trance. A long stretch of snowy Joyfield highway spreads out in front of me as cotton ball-sized snowflakes smack against my windshield. I'm completely immersed in the sights and sounds from the comfort of my little car, but when I reach for my water bottle and notice the little paper in my cup holder, I smile at it.

Book Writing Club. That's not even something I would have imagined myself to be interested in. If I had seen the flier for the club at Westerfield Apartments earlier in my internship, would I have joined? Would I have attempted to write a book?

There's one word in common with the contents of this little paper and what I'm currently immersing myself in. A book.

Hmm. *A book.* My eyebrows raise as if I were asking the Joyfield highway in front of me a question. *Could I write a book?*

The serious part of my brain takes over the driving, while the creative part spirals out of control. *Could I write a book?* Is this what the universe — and the entire state of New York — is trying to tell me right now? It was never the *news* that I loved. It was writing. *It was always about the writing.*

I've never written anything besides newspaper articles, broadcast stories, and journalistic pieces. I was always a *serious* writer and a *nonfiction* storyteller. I don't know how to write anything else. Besides all the uninformed and ignorant individuals calling my stories fake news, I never even considered writing anything fake.

Ever since that eighth-grade English class, the only way I ever imagined writing for a *living* was by becoming a news reporter. It was the only logical and achievable route: writing about what was happening in the world. A singer needs something to sing about. A writer needs something to write about. What else is there to write about besides current events? But instead of writing other people's stories...*could I write my own?*

I eventually pull into my designated parking spot at the office, watching snowflakes hit my windshield. I hesitate before getting out. I feel like I'm onto something. I feel like I'm going to head down a road that I've never traveled before. I can't get the thought out of my head. Could this be my new "passion project" that Eliza says I need? Could this be my *feature story* that eventually turns into *the lead story?*

Thirty-Nine

THE WRAP

"How is it that we live in the same town, but we barely see each other?"

I slam my car door shut, balancing my phone between my ear and shoulder. "Because you're the *hot attorney* who works seventy-hour weeks," I say in a childish tone. "And I just got a *big girl* job, remember?"

"I know," Levi laughs on the other line. "I just miss you. I feel like I saw you more when you worked at WJDN."

"The back of my head, that is." I walk the icy steps up to my apartment entrance, careful to avoid the invisible patches of black ice. "Do you miss staring at me in courtrooms?"

"Oh, absolutely," Levi says. "Do you miss staring at *me* in courtrooms?"

"Like you wouldn't believe." I fumble with my keys, trying to locate the one with Sharpie markings indicating *my* apartment. "Why else do you think my stories were *extra* well written on the days *you* were presenting?"

Levi sucks in a burst of air as if he's *thinking* about his response. "Maybe it was just my well-executed, magnificent opening arguments."

I open my rusty front door, and the smell of cinnamon and vanilla hits my nostrils. "I think it was the magnificent way your shirt sleeves hugged your bicep muscles," I admit. "That's where *my* attention was, anyway."

"I could never take my eyes off of you," Levi says. "Even when my eyes *should* have been focused on the twelve jury members in front of me."

I kick off my shoes and place them on the little waterproof mat beside my door. "Do you think the *honorable judge* Benjamin Novah knew we had a thing for each other?"

"He had to have known," Levi says. "People could probably spot our tension from a mile away. I'm sure everyone could feel it."

I throw my purse on my rickety kitchen table. "Like they were watching the beginning stages of a romance movie?"

"Just like the ones you force me to watch, yes."

"I don't *force* you to watch rom coms," I clarify, assuming a horizontal position on my comfortable brown couch. "You end up loving them."

"Well, I mean, they aren't my *first* choice. But once they're on—"

"You love them," I say. "Which is the point that I'm trying to make."

Levi hesitates for a moment. "I love *you*," he finally says. "So that means I'll watch whatever cheesy movies you want to watch, just to make you happy."

It's been about three months since Levi told me that he

loved me for the first time. We were at my apartment after yet another dinner date at Mama Bella, and it just flew out of him like a bird out of a cage. There was no special buildup or anything romantic— he just said it as plain as day, like he was just stating a simple fact.

We've shared "the L word" plenty of times since then, but hearing him say it now *still* sends a ping right through the center of my stomach. It never gets old.

I look up at my popcorn ceiling, noticing the yellow water-stain marks. "Those movies aren't *cheesy*," I clarify. "But I love you too."

"By the way, I'm driving to a dinner meeting with my team," Levi says through his Bluetooth car speaker. "Then I'll be over afterwards. How was your day?"

"Oh, you know." I prop an extra pillow under my head. "Got my advertising campaign for a funeral home rejected, but then a doctor's office signed my contract for a series of billboard spots. You win some, you lose some."

"I understand that concept pretty well," Levi says.

"You usually *win* more than you *lose*," I reassure. "I'm constantly losing."

"You *win* more than you *lose*," Levi repeats from my earlier statement. "It's probably hard for businesses around here to find extra money to advertise. So when you get them, that's a big deal. You should be proud of *all* wins."

"Thanks for staying with me through all of this," I say, bouncing my foot resting on my crossed leg. "It's been a hard couple of months."

"Even though you're not my *hot news reporter* anymore, you're still my *ambitious* girlfriend. You'll find something you love. That's what I love about you." Levi's engine shuts off.

"I'm here. I'll see you soon, okay?"

"Have fun," I say. "Get some vodka sauce for me."

Once I hang up the phone, instead of doomscrolling on social media, I look out the window from my couch. The snow looks like glitter descending to the ground, and its calmness gives my brain time to think. My mind flashes to this whole *book* ordeal. Earlier today, I transferred that little *Book Writing Club* paper back into my pocket— so I take it out and stare at the black text. *Writing a book?* Where would I even begin?

I was never an avid *reader*. Throughout high school, we were required to read *two* books per month outside of our regular English classes. We not only had to write book reports on the novels we chose, but also take *tests* on them. It was another thing I had to check off my academic list. It was another educational chore. It was another form of homework. Being forced to read made me *not* want to do it. I'd always pick the shortest book possible, scanning the library shelves to find the book with the thinnest spine. Because of this, the thought of *reading* has always left me with a sour taste in my mouth: *dread, work, burden.* Once I graduated, I never picked up a book again.

It wasn't until I recently started listening to audiobooks in the car that I thought to myself, hey, I actually like this long-*form storytelling.*

My mind flashes to Bill at WJDN, always telling me to "tighten up my scripts." I always wanted to include one more line, one more piece of information, one more sound bite. *Two minutes* was never enough time for me to tell a story. I always wanted the *entire* show. Because of this, Bill would always say, "It's not a *book*, Noelle. Shorten your script." I was always heavy with the pen, lengthy on the keyboard. I've always had a lot to say, I guess. *Maybe Bill's criticism was really telling me to be an author all along.*

I slink off the couch and stand up a little too quickly, causing a rush of lightheadedness and little black dots appearing in my visual field. I storm past my kitchen and into my bedroom, opening up the drawer of my vanity to search for a piece of paper. Among the collection of gel pens, sticky notes, and paper clips: my *Acceptance Speech.* It stops me right in my tracks.

I slide my thumb up and down the page. This used to serve as my north star, my moral compass, my future plan. The edges of the white notebook page are crinkled and nearly ripped. The navy blue ink has faded along with my dreams of working in news. My handwriting is a snapshot straight from my college years. *I had completely forgotten about this thing, which was once so special to me.*

This unidentified speech has followed me through every stage of life— reading it aloud in New York City during my internship days, flipping past this page during WJDN morning meetings, staring at it taped to my childhood bedroom mirror. But here I am on the *other side* of this manifestation when I've *left* news and when I've *changed* my plans. This is the first time seeing this paper after I've given up on The Sunrise Show, and the thought of it makes my eyes feel heavy.

It's in this exact moment that I decide something life-changing: I am not going to *mourn* over this. I am not going to *cry* over this. I am not going to be *depressed* over this. I flip over my *Acceptance Speech*, laying it on my vanity. The blank page faces the ceiling. It's like a fresh Microsoft Word document, with an imaginary blinking cursor just *trying* to intimidate me. For some reason, my heart is pounding. I grab a pen and begin filling the white space with words.

"I can't believe I'm here with you today talking about my new book," I scribble down on the crinkled white paper. "Writing this book has been the highlight of my life, and I'm so honored to be able to share it with you all today."

I stare at the words. Similar to how I don't know what *award* I was accepting before, I don't know what *book* I'm referring to. I don't know *who* I'm delivering these words to. I don't know *what* exactly I'm describing. But I can't think too much about it. I'm just going to innocently write this down with no pressure. See how it *looks*, hear how it *reads*, explore how it *feels*.

"I've learned a lot about myself while writing this book. It's really a love letter to figuring out *what* you want to do with your life. You don't have to be afraid of *changing* your dreams, as long as you always work to find a *new* one. Someone I love once told me, 'You can have a boring *nine-to-five* that gives you a paycheck, and a side *passion project* that gives you a purpose.' You can work until those things become one and the same."

I sit back in my chair, glancing at a photo of David playing his guitar in the WJDN newsroom. I snapped the picture from my last shift, right before I was about to go home. In the absence of Bill, he was singing and strumming along to *Time of Your Life* by Green Day. He's wearing his infamous zip-up gray sweatshirt with a skull and crossbones on the front. Even though we're related, I think *fate* brought us together.

"Someone important to me always says, 'Sometimes you

leave a place with different dreams than you originally *went* there with.' Dreams change, and that's okay. Just as long as you're still doing what you love, regardless of what *audience* is watching."

I look around my new bedroom. While Delilah isn't next door anymore, and my parents aren't down the hall, I know that all of them are just right down the road. It feels good to have my own place, and I know this wouldn't have been possible — or at least financially responsible — without my career change. My walls are light blue, and while the beige carpeting is stained, it's soft and clean. I'm happy here, and for the first time, I can admit that I'm also happy with my choices.

I look at the graduation picture of my Uncle Daniel in that tiny wooden picture frame, which is now leaning on my nightstand. This photo has been with me everywhere. His smile, which obviously mimics my dad's, shines as he proudly holds his college diploma. His long, dark hair slicked back into that low ponytail reminds me of how mine looks right now.

"No matter if you stick with your original plan or not, *either way*, you'll always end up in the place you were *meant* to be all along," I write.

I pick up my new handwritten manifestation and tape it to the wall beside my vanity, then put my hands on my hips to assess the placement. I decide that it needs something else: that tiny *Book Writing Club* paper to accompany it. I tape the crinkled item to the bottom of the page, filling the remaining open space. *Perfect.*

I don't know what any of this means, but I have to start working towards *something*. I have to at least try. A "side gig" that could become a "main gig." A *feature* story that could become the *lead* story. A passion project that could become a permanent career.

And if writing a book doesn't become the thing I'm *destined* to do with my life, I'll just move on to the next. Because, like Eliza with her insurance job — if I have to sell billboard spots and advertising packages for the rest of my life — *I might just want to die.*

I return to my comfortable brown couch and set my laptop right where it belongs: in my lap. I pull up a blank Microsoft Word document, and as expected, the blinking cursor intimidates the hell out of me. I'm just going to see what pours out of my brain. And after pondering it for a few minutes, I start to type:

> *"I can't believe I'm standing in front of you all tonight accepting this award," I whisper into my bright purple hairbrush. Its rubber handle is clenched in the grasp of my left hand, and I look down to notice strands of curly brown hair tangled throughout its bristles.* I should probably clean this thing.
>
> *I stare back at my reflection in the mirror, positioning my fictitious microphone back into place below my chin. My black pajamas are a sparkly ball gown. The messy bun on top of my head is an elegant topknot. My fuzzy pink slippers are a pair of rose gold pumps. Last night's mascara smudge is a smoldering smoky eye. My apartment is an auditorium. My vanity is a podium. The horns and sirens reverberating through my window pane are just hoots and hollers from audience members.*
>
> *I clear my throat and continue reading. "I have been*

dreaming of accepting this award for Best Morning Show Host for years."

Forty

EPILOGUE

DECEMBER | NEW YORK CITY, NEW YORK
   TWO YEARS LATER

Looking out at the New York City skyline — through the window of this *extra-large* Uber to accommodate our luggage — I feel a lot less intimidated than I used to.

When I first moved here for my internship at The Sunrise Show, I was in a completely different headspace. *Anxiety* from the unknowns of not knowing anybody in the city. *Uncertainty* stemming from working at the largest news platforms in the world. *Confusion* about what life after graduation would bring. But now, instead of looking out at this skyline with feelings of *pure fear*, I'm looking at it through a lens of *pure joy.* I'm feeling nothing but calmness and contentment. There isn't a weight sitting on my lungs. For the first time, *I can finally breathe.*

"You okay?" Levi asks, running his finger over the shiny diamond on my left ring finger.

"Yes," I say honestly. "I've never been better."

His deep hazel eyes fall onto me. "You'll be great tomorrow."

I exhale with an audible sigh. "I hope so."

Levi and I got engaged last New Year's Eve to symbolize the night of our first kiss (or so he says). It was at Nate's annual party. Instead of kissing me when the ball dropped, he got down on one knee instead. Everybody there apparently *knew* what was going to happen, so they watched for it— squealing and shouting and hooting and hollering when the moment surfaced. Ever since, my pear-shaped diamond has flashed on my left hand. And in true symbolic fashion, we're planning on getting married *next* New Year's Eve.

My chin rests heavily in my hand as I watch the snow flurries create a powdered sugar dusting on the New York City skyline, casting a reflection on the shiny Hudson River. I know Westerfield Apartments is inside that concrete cluster somewhere, and the thought of it makes me smile. I think about sprinting through those streets at midnight with Eliza. I think about riding the subway, feeling like a true city girl. I think about getting the chance to work at my dream company. *It feels like another lifetime.*

Looking at the city from the outside in fills me with nostalgia. But it's not just from thinking about the *past* memories I've made here— it's from thinking about the memories that I'm going to be making *tomorrow*. I originally came here without knowing the true purpose of my life. But today, I'm going back because I've figured it out.

"Here we go," I say, watching the skyline get swallowed by the Lincoln Tunnel.

"Wonder how long it takes to get through here," Levi wonders out loud.

"Fourteen minutes," I blurt knowingly. "Unless there's traffic."

"Has to be longer than that," Levi questions. "Isn't it over a mile long?"

I pull out my phone and open the timer app, pressing *start*. "We'll see."

"What do you want to bet?" Levi asks.

I flash my engagement ring towards him, watching it cast a mirage of sparkly rainbow dots on the seat in front of me. "If I win, I'll sell this thing and pocket the cash."

"Deal," Levi agrees.

After the first major twists and turns of the underwater tunnel, I finally spot the light at the end of it. It shines a little brighter than I remember. It makes me think about the *dozens* of times I've traveled through here, each time with a *different* concern or worry. Will I mess up Hilda's coffee order tomorrow? What if my alarm doesn't go off in the morning for some reason? How many years will it take for me to get back here? But now— I'm totally calm.

When we're out on the other side, I stop my timer. "Seventeen minutes," I say.

Levi flashes his dimples at me. "Guess you have to keep the ring."

I hold it out in front of me, shaking my head. "Fine," I say. "I guess I will."

My pupils adjust from the tunnel's darkness to the city's brightness— watching tourists, professionals, and students walk along the dirty sidewalks. Before I know it, we're driving past Westerfield Apartments. I admire the red brick building, thinking about all the precious memories I've made inside of it.

"That was where I stayed." I point towards the fourth floor. "I had a room right there."

"Looks like a prison." Levi's warm hand rests on top of mine. "My city girl."

We begin to cruise through the craziness of Times Square—the Macy's window displays are holiday themed, the electronic billboards blink through advertisements for merchandise, and yellow taxis line every inch of the streets. The honking of horns and blaring of sirens fill up my eardrums. My home away from home. *I made it back.*

I answer a call from Eliza. "Helloooo?"

"Hey girl," she says. "Still on to get dinner tonight? I just got to the hotel."

"Of course. We're almost there, too," I say. "Oreo cake?"

"It's all I've ever wanted," she says. "I can hardly wait."

"I can hardly wait for *tomorrow*," I tell her.

"This is *such* a big deal," Eliza shouts into the phone. "Not to scare you or anything. But I wouldn't have flown the entire way from Florida to New York if this wasn't huge."

I laugh. "Thank you. For making the trip, and for being here to support me."

"I wouldn't miss this for the world," she says. "See you guys soon."

Once we pull in front of our hotel, my eyes immediately fixate on the old-Hollywood lights framing its marquee: *The New Yorker.* This is much fancier than staying at Westerfield Apartments. It feels very New York City, which makes me feel like *I've made it.* We step out onto the chilly sidewalk as our driver walks around to his trunk to retrieve our luggage.

"What brings you into the city?" *This is the first time he's spoken on our entire trip.*

The air smells like hot dogs and pollution. "Something exciting is happening tomorrow morning," I say, grabbing my bag from him. "Thank you so much."

"You're welcome," he says, slamming his trunk shut. "Good luck with whatever it is you're here for."

* * *

The studio looks exactly as I remember it: vast, passionate, and magical. I stare out into the sea of monitors and microphones. Floor directors and camera operators leap over cords and dodge between cameras. It's busy and chaotic, but full of life. Butterflies are flying around in my stomach over the sight of it all, and my mind is running nonstop. It's where I once was, it's where I wanted to return, and somehow...*it's where I ended up after all.*

"Two minutes," a producer shouts.

"You can head on over," another producer says to me.

I breathe out a shaky sigh. "Okay," I whisper.

My heels click across the sparkly floor until I reach the white couch that Hilda Harrison sits on in the entertainment center. She's shuffling through a pile of scripts on her lap when she looks up at me. I take a seat across from her, noticing the *cold brew americano with a double shot of espresso* in her hand.

She sets it on the coffee table between us. "How are you feeling?"

"Nervous." I slide my hands back and forth on my lap. "But I'm ready."

"Thirty seconds," the director shouts to us.

Hilda is wearing a red blazer over a fitted black dress, and her *red* heels and *red* lipstick complete the color-coordinated ensemble. I'm wearing a deep purple dress with nude heels, and my dark hair is swept over my shoulder. The thin, silver necklace of the New York City skyline that my parents got me a few Christmases ago lies flat on my chest. A hairstylist sprays down the last of Hilda's blonde flyaways, and a makeup artist sweeps some translucent powder down her nose. And for the first time in my life…*they even do the same for me.*

"You're not a stranger here," Hilda reassures. "You have me right here with you."

The director points to the camera. "In five, four, three, two—"

Upbeat intro music begins to *blare* throughout the studio, causing my heart to pound so violently that I'm afraid I'll need a medical professional. The cameras swivel to the couch we're positioned on, which sends a shock wave of nerves through my center. I see a "two-shot" of us appear on the nearest monitor. *This is really happening.* It all feels like a fever dream, especially as Hilda says—

"Welcome back to The Sunrise Show. I'm Hilda Harrison, here in the entertainment center with Noelle Fenwick."

"Thank you so much for having me," I say politely.

I feel my body slip into that same television news reporter mode I used to feel when cameras were on me, but in a different way this time. I remember that I'm *not* here to interview someone else…someone else is here to interview me. *(But that person just so happens to be Hilda freaking Harrison.)* I think about *why* I'm here, and the confidence from that thought begins to slow my heart rate back down to normalcy.

"Before we get into your debut novel, I want to let the audience know something: Noelle was an intern here at The Sunrise Show back when she was in college. Talk about a full circle moment."

Hearing her say the term *debut novel* on national television — and knowing she's associating those words with *me* — causes me to shake my head in disbelief. I can't believe that I wrote and published a book, let alone that I've made it onto The Sunrise Show to *promote* it. The world works in mysterious ways, doesn't it?

"That's right." I glance around at the floor-to-ceiling windows. "It was the best time of my life, and it feels just like yesterday."

"I feel like it was just yesterday, too." Hilda flashes a fake smile at the camera before looking back down at her stack of scripts. "As you all know, our viewers *love* to read. That's why *we* love using our platform here at The Sunrise Show to highlight new authors and recently released titles. That brings me to you, Noelle. Tell us all about your book."

Where do I even begin?

"Well, it's called The Lead Story," I explain. "I can't believe I'm here with you today talking about my new book. Writing this book has been the highlight of my life, and I'm so honored to be able to share it with you all today."

In my peripheral vision, I see my book cover graphic flash on the monitor. I know this means viewers at home are seeing that image on their television screens — instead of seeing *me* talk — so it makes me feel a little more comfortable to go on. *I suddenly wish this were a podcast interview instead.*

"I've learned a lot about myself while writing this book. It's really a love letter to figuring out *what* you want to do with your life. You don't have to be afraid of *changing* your dreams, as long as you always work to find a *new* one."

I'm finally speaking the words that I wrote down two years ago — on the back of that *Acceptance Speech* notebook paper — that has been hanging in my apartment ever since the day I decided I wanted to become an author. I never knew *when* or *where* I'd need to deliver these messages, but as Hilda asks me these interview questions, it's all coming back to me. Without my knowledge, *this* is the moment I've been preparing for all along. This is the moment I wrote those words for. Here I am speaking them aloud, not even practicing, but *for real.*

"Did anyone inspire you to write this book?"

"Lots of people," I answer honestly.

My eyes glance over to my personal *fan club* in the back corner of the studio: my mom, my dad, Levi, Delilah, and my Uncle David, along with Myra, Ruby, Paige, Nate, and even Eliza all the way from Florida. They're all crowded together, looking excited and proud and nervous all at the same time. The sight of everybody I love in one place stings my eyes with salty tears.

"How so?"

I look into Eliza's eyes from across the room. "Someone I love once said, 'You can have a boring *nine-to-five* that gives you a paycheck, and a side *passion project* that gives you a purpose.' You can work until those things become one and the same. That's the kind of thing that this book explores: how to get the best of both worlds in your career."

"Seems relatable for people at any age," Hilda says, narrowing her eyes. "What do you want people to take away from this book?"

I turn my attention to David, who, even in this fancy news studio, is still wearing that same *damn* gray sweatshirt. "Someone else important to me always says, 'Sometimes you *leave* a place with different dreams than you originally *went* there with.' Dreams change, and that's okay. Just as long as you're still doing what you love, regardless of what *audience* is watching. That's what my main character goes through."

Hilda leans in towards me. "This is a *fiction* novel, right? It sounds like a bit of a *personal* experience."

"Yes, it's a *fictional* novel with *fictional* characters, which is a lot different than writing news stories," I explain. "But the underlying theme matches what I've been exploring. No matter if you stick with your original plan or not, *either way*, you'll always end up in the place you were *meant* to be all along."

Hilda shoots me a knowing look. "A lot of this book is about working in news, which I can relate to," she says. "What do you want people to take away from that part?"

I exhale, tapping my foot with nervous energy. "This book is *not* an attack on news reporters, journalists, the press, or the media. *It's the total opposite.* This book shifts the conversation when it comes to local news *organizations*. The corporations. The industry. The conglomerate. *That* is where the problem lies."

"I see," Hilda whispers.

I refocus on my posture. "Local news reporters are taken advantage of by their companies of employment, and many of them *leave* the industry because of it. We can't *afford* that loss as a democracy. Journalists are the reason we *have* democracy, so we need to keep fighting for their rights, their respect, and their prosperity in the workplace. We're nothing without information, so we're nothing without them."

"I agree." Hilda nods, careful not to say too much about this topic.

Even though Hilda is currently making millions at The Sunrise Show — and is getting the royal treatment nowadays — I know she understands where I'm coming from. She's been through the local news trenches. Even though it might have been different back in the day, she was once a small market journalist. Everybody has to start somewhere, and while she may have had more *respect* when she was working her way up through the ranks, I'm sure she faced *many* of the same challenges that we do today.

Hilda eyes up the ring on my finger. "Before we tell our audience *where* they can buy your book, I notice that you have a sparkly new ring on your finger."

"Yes." I giggle embarrassingly towards Levi, not thinking she'd ask this question. "I'm engaged to a man named Levi Winters."

"Congratulations, my dear." Hilda looks to the director, who signals that our time is nearly over. "You can find the link to purchase The Lead Story on our website. We'll have more coming up after the break on The Sunrise Show."

"We're clear," a producer says shortly after.

I let out the biggest sigh of relief. *I did it.* The butterflies fly out of my stomach, and the racing thoughts fly out of my brain.

Once the first commercial airs, my friends and family rush over to the entertainment center. One by one, Hilda graciously hugs everybody. But once she spots Delilah, her red heels click over to her.

"There she is," Hilda says, giving Delilah a hug. "I watched your *Brew For You* feature in the control room, and it's fantastic. I'm told that it will air *tomorrow* morning."

"Thank you," Delilah says, beaming with pride. "I'm excited to see it."

A few months ago, when I was contacted to promote my book, I decided to name-drop *Brew For You.* It couldn't hurt, right? Well, one thing led to another, and they flew an *entire* production team to tiny Joyfield, Ohio. They interviewed Manager Mike, Delilah, Anthony, and the whole crew. Even though WJDN never covered it, the coffee shop will now get *national* attention and probably donations. *Whatever, Bill.*

My mom joins in the conversation. "Thank you for doing *both* stories with my girls. I couldn't ever repay you for this."

Hilda winks. "*Two* Fenwick girls, *two* days in a row, on The Sunrise Show? You should be one proud mama."

As I watch my friends and family…and now *fiancé*…talk to my forever role model, I couldn't possibly be filled with any more gratitude. Everything worked out. I still made it back to The Sunrise Show, but in a different way. In a better way. *And I couldn't have planned it any better myself.*

* * *

We're shuffled into the green room, where we eat leftover bagels and drink cold coffee. I was their *last* guest of the day, so they didn't need the room for their typical A-list celebrities.

"Is this where famous people hang out?" My mom whispers to me.

"Yes. See that over there?" I point to a desk with a swivel chair and a computer. "That's where I used to sit as an intern."

"Dominic," my mom shouts over to my dad, repeatedly

pointing at the desk. "Noelle used to sit over there."

"But this is where they house the famous people, right?" He shouts back, unbothered by my previous role in green room operations.

I laugh. "Yes, the famous people get ready here."

"Like Ryan Gosling?" Delilah asks.

"Yes, and remember when he told me to tell you...*hi?*" Delilah folds her arms. "You were lying!"

"Promise Thomas, I wasn't lying!" *Even though I was.*

"Promise Thomas you *were,*" she says.

I look around the room. "Hey, Delilah, this place is called the *green* room. It's meant for you. It's your dream. It's literally a *green* room."

This tiny place — once filled with celebrities and producers during my internship — is now filled with my friends and family. The fact that they're all getting to see where I interned is even more special to me than anything involving my book. *For the first time, I really feel like I've made it.*

"Good job today, girl," Myra says.

"Did you *pay* these people to let you come back here?" Nate teases.

I embrace them in a three-way hug. "Love you guys. Even you, Nate."

Myra and Nate are now officially parents and *officially dating.* They're still working at WJDN and rent a tiny house together near the station. Myra's parents are constantly traveling up to Joyfield to help take care of the baby, who is sweetly named *Jane* after her late sister. Her mom cried when she heard about the namesake, knowing that *Myra and Jane's* Restaurant in Virginia Beach suddenly had a whole new meaning.

"What about me?" Ruby says, clomping over to us wearing...*cowgirl boots*. Only she could pull them off in a northern metropolitan city.

I suffocate her strawberry blonde curls with a hug. "It's been too long since I've heard that southern accent."

Ruby finally secured a meteorologist position in Nashville, and her salary is decent enough that she doesn't have to risk getting a bartending job on the side. She's living in an apartment atop a small pancake breakfast place, of course. She started secretly dating her weekend weather producer, and they've been pretty serious for a few months now.

Paige walks up to me next, giving me a tight squeeze. "You were amazing," she says. "I can't believe the person who *trained* me on reporting 101 was on The Sunrise Show today."

"Thank you, new girl." I rub her back. "Thank you for being here."

Paige moved back to San Francisco last year and landed a job at her hometown news station as an entertainment producer. Even though she knew she'd be giving up her *on-air* dreams for a while, it was too good an opportunity to pass up. She got back together with her ex, and they live happily ever after in a Victorian-style home. (And yes, it's light pink with huge bay windows.)

I'm beginning to form a headache from a lack of caffeine and the shakes from a lack of carbohydrates, so I pour myself a cup of coffee and spread jelly on a bagel. I stare into the sea of family and friends, feeling like I'm in a dream, when David walks up to me.

"Great job today, sweetie," he says, reaching an arm around me. "Proud of you."

"Couldn't have done it without you," I say. "Thanks for

coming all this way."

"I'd *never* miss a chance to come back to New York City," he says.

Levi, with his thick, curly hair, walks over to us. After all this time, I still feel like my heart is going to beat out of my chest when I see him. He will always still be the *hot attorney* to me, and to all the girls at WJDN, for that matter. But he's so much more than that to me now. He's the person who got me through this *entire* journey, and I know he would have supported me no matter which path I chose. He never guided me with *his own* interests in mind. Whether he was staying in Joyfield or moving across the country, he always wanted what was best for *me*.

"I'm so proud of you." He whispers the words into my ear as he wraps me up in a warm embrace. "I can't wait to marry you."

"I can't wait to marry you, too." I muffle the words into his chest, even though I'm standing on my tiptoes. "Thank you for helping me get here."

"I didn't do anything," Levi says, releasing me. "You did it."

Once Levi starts talking to Delilah across the room about who knows what, I spend a few moments alone before Eliza comes and stands right next to me. We're shoulder to shoulder, looking out at the green room just like we used to— the same beautiful view of Manhattan sprawls across the huge windows, the bright yellow makeup chairs line the walls, and the same basket of hard candies and cough drops rests on the end table. It's been years since we've stood in this spot, and while it feels like decades have passed, it still somehow feels just like yesterday.

"Here we are again," Eliza says with a breath once she's next to me.

I shake my head. "Do you know how many coffees we brought into this room?"

"Millions," she says. "Nothing short of a million."

I laugh, pointing to a spot right in front of a small orange couch. "Remember when I spilled Hilda's americano right about there?"

"I helped you clean it up," Eliza says. "Stained my favorite Zara khakis."

"And I'll never live it down."

Eliza sighs. "You made it back," she says. "You did it."

"So did you," I remind her. "*You're* headlining a New York City comedy club tomorrow night. The one we *used* to go to, I might add."

Eliza nudges my shoulder with hers. "Look at us."

We turn to face each other in the midst of our realization: we've made it back to New York City. Not in the same way we originally intended, but even *better.* While we both gave up on the *dream* of becoming Hilda Harrison, we never gave up on the idea of having a *dream.* We could have fallen back on our boring nine-to-five jobs. We could have settled and stopped looking for something else. We could have accepted our traditional lives. *But we didn't.* We continued dreaming. We discovered new ideas. We found other desires.

They started out as our side gigs, but they eventually became our *main gigs.* They started out as our secondary quests, but they ultimately evolved into our *primary pursuits.* They started out as our fluff pieces, but they finally transformed into our *lead stories.* Our source of purpose and paychecks have collided, and it all led to this moment.

Looking back, I don't think either of us would have been

as happy if our initial plans had worked out. I don't know if being Hilda Harrison would've made Eliza happier than being a *comedian*, or would've made me happier than being an *author*. Maybe being a comedian and an author were what we were supposed to be all along, but it just took a short detour (through the news industry) to get there. Standing here together right now, I can't imagine our lives panning out any other way.

A young woman wearing an *intern* badge hesitantly walks into the green room, desperately looking for someone to help her. "Excuse me," she says softly.

"Hi," I say, motioning for her to come inside. "Come and join the party."

She's holding two hot coffees in her hands. "I somehow accidentally ordered *three* cold brew americanos for Hilda Harrison instead of just *one*. Must have been a mistake on the app. Does anybody want these other two?"

Eliza and I look at each other, smiles beginning to grow on our faces.

I nod. "We'll take them."

About the Author

Nicole Marie is an author, journalist, and storyteller. She resides in Pennsylvania with her husband and the rest of her family just around the corner.